ROSES
FOR
MAMA

An Italian-American Saga

Joseph A. Criscuolo

JOSEPH A. CRISCUOLO

Roses for Mama
An Italian-American Saga
Copyright © 2001
Joseph A. Criscuolo

ISBN: 0-9709175-0-3
Library of Congress Control Number: 2001129105

Printed in the United States by:
Morris Publishing
3212 East Highway 30
Kearney, NE 68847
1-800-650-7888

Chapter One

Giuseppe Alanga raised the wicker-encased flask to his lips and sucked in a long, gurgling swallow of his own wine—not the Lacrima Cristi, but good just the same. From the corners of his mouth, some of it ran down in two purple trickles that dampened the ends of a drooping mustache still heavy and deeply black without a single strand of gray. With the flask still to his mouth, his head upturned, his glance caught sight of the mountain.

On this early morning of April, in 1906, a gentle breeze blew softly against his cheeks, and he watched as the same breeze distorted the plume of thick, white smoke spurting straight up from the cone of the mountain, breaking up the massive column into fleecy, detached clumps of wool. Still studying Vesuvius and the mass of smoke, he hung the flask on a branch of a lemon tree. The waxy, green leaves were still wet with morning dew.

"The smoke; it's still white. That's good," he thought. But yet his mind was not at ease. All the last week of March the animals had been acting strangely. The cows lowed forlornly, horses and mules were skittish. The townspeople along the banks of the Sarno told of fish thrashing and churning up the water in frenzied schools. And just yesterday, three wells in the neighborhood had suddenly lost their water.

"Bad, bad." The words escaped from his mouth almost inaudibly, and Giuseppe's uneasiness grew. These signs were known to him. His thoughts went back to the time when he was just a young boy of twelve, in 1872. The animals and the fish, then, too, had been disturbed in the same manner. Many wells suddenly had gone dry then, too, and the smoke from the mountain puffed out white clouds for a time. Then the smoke turned gray, a dark, leaden gray. And with the gray had come the eruption. Involuntarily Alanga shuddered, and to reassure himself that the smoke was still white, he broke his reverie and focused his gaze again upon the mountain. His brown, callused hands cupped his chin as he stood staring at the summit of the mountain.

Again, his mind drifted back to that day in his youth when he first came to know the ashy taste of terror; when he discovered that there was something even stronger than his brawny blacksmith father. And he remembered how, as a wide-eyed little boy, he used to delight in watching his father hammer red-hot metal into bars, horseshoes, tools, and utensils for all the townspeople and peasant farmholders, who lived in and around the tiny village of Boscotrecase.

How his eyes used to fill with pride and amazement to see his father working at the forge, amid steam, heat and flame. Only once did the boy ever notice anything that brought a flicker of alarm to his father's eyes.

That was the day long ago when Vesuvius had unleashed its furious rage. The horror of that day, when it seemed to young Giuseppe that the end of the world had come, flashed vividly before his eyes. He heard again the thunderous roar of the mountain as it belched out flame and ash and stone. He felt again the shaking of the earth under his feet as the mountain convulsed that day, and its womb contracted, sending tremors and shock waves in horizontal surges that toppled houses, trees, animals and people. The great stone bridge that spanned the Sarno split as if made of wood, and then plunked into the tortured waters of the river.

The day of the eruption, he remembered, as he remained eyeing the smoking cone, had been the very day that his new-born brother, Matteo, was to have been baptized by Padre Andrea in the village church. In the early morning hours of that day when his brother was to have become a little Christian, the mountain exploded into life. A thousand times more fiery and noisy than the fireworks shot off in the piazza on San Gennaro's feast day, the thunderous roar of the eruption woke everyone alive at that moment even as far away as Naples and Castellammare.

The screams of his bawling sisters, the prayers of his mother, the curses of his father, came again to his ears. As if it had happened yesterday, he could see his mother collecting her brood about her and tying towels across the children's faces and pillows on their heads to protect them from ash and fumes.

After the first angry shout of the mountain and its accompanying shake of the earth, it had become quiet. But from human throats, prayers, curses and cries of lamentation pierced the pre-dawn darkness; donkeys brayed and hens cackled to add to the awful din. People began to come out of their houses, and in the piazza of Boscotrecase, the flickering light from scores of lanterns looked like so many fireflies clustered together in small swarms.

In all the towns at the base of the mountain—Ottaviano, San Sebastiano, Terzigno, Pompei, and in the cities of Naples and Castellammare as well, hasty preparations were underway to carry the image of San Gennaro in procession. And in Boscotrecase, it had been no different. With Padre Andrea in the lead, swinging the censer, reciting the litany imploring San Gennaro's aid in their hour of peril, men and women, young and old, raised their voices in a chorus of supplication. After the circuit around the piazza, the procession progressed from the town square and out along the main thoroughfare of the village. Slowly it inched its way, arriving at the limits of the town proper, and at the beginning of the countryside. The first farmstead the throng of marchers reached was Alanga's, the blacksmith. A long, stony alley, bordered by Lombardy poplars extended from the roadway in a straight path to the front door of the red-tiled, massive, stone farmhouse.

Giuseppe could still hear the sound of Father Andrea's voice as he called a halt to the march. And he could picture again how willingly the carriers had unburdened themselves of the heavy baroque platform on which sat the gilded and jewelled bust of the saint, whose hand was upraised in benediction.

Then the natural light of the sun at last broke wanly above the crowd. Maria Alanga, Giuseppe's mother, made her way down the path from the house with baby Matteo in her arms. Giuseppe and his sisters came running behind her with arms full of bread, and Papa with wine. Maria kissed the priest's hand in reverence and then kissed the statue, while Papa passed out the bread and wine to the weary porters. All along the roadway, men and women had gathered together in knots of four or five, waiting for the signal from Father Andrea to resume marching.

Then in one great, thunderous spasm, with rocks and pebbles thrown upwards from the mountain's mouth, the volcano split the rim of its crater. A shower of black lapilli began raining down in a pelting drive that stunned and bruised whatever was hit. Large boulders, too, dislodged from the edge of the crater, began cascading down the slopes. Clouds of steam snarled furiously from the ruddy maw of the mountain; and where there had a moment before been light, now there was a pall of darkness that stretched over the landscape for miles around. A blanket of heavy, moist, sticky volcanic ash, mixed with lighter, gas-pocketed pumice blotted out the feeble rays of the sun. Adding to the horror of the awful outburst, were the sudden darts of lightning that rent the darkness in zig-zag bolts of blinding light. Grumblings from deep within the mountain struck the ears like the muffled roaring of so many beasts chained deep in the bowels of a subterranean cavern.

Even as he stood now beneath the same mountain, recalling that awful day long ago, Giuseppe remembered how panic spread among the people as the violence of the elements increased. How amid shrieks and screams, the crowds blindly began to retrace their steps back towards the village and their homes. He could see them jostling each other wildly, stumbling over each other, and stepping on each other's heels in the hazy half-light, coughing and choking. Everywhere, terror-stricken voices pierced the obscurity of the unnatural light:

"Mamma mia, I can't see!"

"Giannino, where are you?"

"Holy Mother of God, it's the end of the world!"

And Giuseppe remembered how his mother turned on her heels and herded her children before her along the path to the house and away from the fear-maddened throngs. Close behind, followed her husband and Don Andrea, still clasping the censer in one hand and the flask of wine in the other.

"Hurry, shut the doors. Keep out the ash, or we'll all choke," the blacksmith shouted to the priest. And to his son, he commanded: "Giuseppe, light the lamps again so we can see." All the while he was busy pulling shut the heavy wooden shutters of the windows.

Father Andrea struggled to swing together the ponderous front doors as the boy succeeded in getting the kerosene lamp on the table to emit a feeble light that softly bathed the occupants of the room. The priest had just accomplished his task, when the portals were rudely pushed open. He had almost been knocked to the floor. He stumbled backwards but managed to keep his balance. The four carriers entered the room, bearing the image of the saint on their shoulders. The golden shine of the image was gone, dulled by a layer of black dust. San Gennaro, it seemed, was seeking refuge in the house of Alanga, the blacksmith.

Exhausted and spitting out flecks of ash and dust, the four men lowered the image to the floor. Straightening up, one of them said, "We couldn't leave him out there," adding in a tone of playful irreverence, "this old *faccia gialliata*"—Old Yellow Face. The manner in which Giacomino addressed the saint shocked no one. Even the saints get a scolding from Neapolitans.

Outside the house, only faint cries were discernible in the distance; and closer, the sound of shattering roof tiles breaking and falling under bombardment of pebbles and large stones that were descending from the skies like hail. Ash and volcanic debris, in places drifting up to a depth of a foot, swirled in a black snowfall. Gusts of demonic winds that blew from every direction at the same time propelled the ash into cyclones of fury that gyrated crazily over the landscape. Tremors of the earth and stabs of lightning increased in frequency and intensity, adding greatly to the terror of man and beast.

"We are safe from the stones and ash within these walls," Giuseppe remembered his father saying. His father's words had brought reassurance to all of them, and for a moment the words allayed doubts and fears. No one said anything, and Alanga continued. "My own grandfather helped to build this house with his own hands for Don Alfonso, the *padrone* of all this land. He built it like a fortress from top to bottom."

Although the house might withstand the weight of ash and stone, there was no chance it would survive the new danger soon after unleashed. A tremendous gurgling and bubbling sound, like soup when it boiled over in the black cauldron over the fire in the *focolare*, dominated all other noises. Someone in the house flung open a shutter. Spilling over the rim of the crater, a huge mass of black-crusted, red-speckled ooze had begun its slow descent down the slopes. A solid, smothering wall of creeping death, gaining momentum and height, slithered downward in mammoth tongues of fiery slime. Pushed onward and onward by the mass behind it, the flow reached a crest of eight feet in height.

The main thrust of the lava flow was concentrated in two streams, one lumbering westward towards the towns of Torre del Greco, Torre Annunziata and Resina on the coast of the bay; the other stream headed straight south toward Boscotrecase, Scafati and Pompei. The avalanche of hot mud and molten rock, creeping on its relentless downward journey, crushed, pulverized and swallowed everything animate and inanimate in its path. Looking at the advance of this juggernaut of death and destruction, those in the house realized the imminence of eternity—that it lay but a distance of three hundreds yards away. For a minute, the men stood mesmerized, staring in morbid fascination at the monstrous excrescence which threatened to annihilate them all.

With a start, Giacomino broke away from the group and ran to the door. "Good God, let's get out of here. Not even our bones will they find," his arm pointing to the window, "if that catches us. Hurry, move, move!"

Giacomino's three companions stepped across the room to his side. Maria, too, made ready to herd the children towards the door, until her husband's restraining hand touched her shoulder.

"You won't last ten minutes out there. There is no air to breathe, just hot ash and sulfur to burn your lungs."

In the few moments he'd had to think, the decision whether to remain in the house or to flee, had to be made; and he chose to remain.

"Signor Alanga is right. One can only strangle and suffocate within minutes out there," agreed Padre Andrea. "Let us resign ourselves to what God has destined for us." Raising his hand in blessing, he uttered in a strong voice, the ancient formula of absolution: *Ego te absolvo...*" and made the sign of the cross over the heads of all those in the house. The four men waited only for the priest to finish the rite. They murmured a hurried "Amen" and then tied handkerchiefs over their mouths.

"Close the door behind them, Giuseppe," ordered the boy's father. The boy did, just as the last man stepped into the black and red whirlwind. For a moment, he peered after their hunched-over shapes resolutely negotiating the way down the tree-flanked alley to the road, before he closed the door again.

"Only a miracle can save them," whispered Padre Andrea, more to himself than to anyone.

"And us," added the somber blacksmith, who had heard him.

Already the shed that had served as the blacksmith shop had tumbled before the onslaught and was no more. It had stood fifty yards from the rear of the house on a slight rise overlooking a stand of lemon trees. The once lush foliage was gone now, seared by hot blasts, so that only stark, skeletal remains shot up from the ground like a bed of coral from the ocean floor. Within minutes of the obliteration of the smithy, the first trees along the bottom of the rise, spontaneously burst into flame because of the intense heat generated by the molten lava, and were consumed.

In one last desperate measure to do something, anything, to protect his family, Giuseppe remembered, his papa had erected a makeshift barricade of household furniture. With Padre Andrea's help, Papa had piled up the furniture in a front corner of the room, and roofed it over with the massive table and heavy bedding. Into this cubicle, he had placed his wife and children, entering last, after the priest.

No sooner had they entered, when a rumbling, grinding sound reverberated throughout the building, and the rear corner of the house shuddered.

"This is the end." The same thought coursed through everyone's mind. Mama pressed baby Matteo closer, while Papa arched himself over his little girls to form a human shield. The boy slammed his forearm over his eyes. His head bowed, his eyes closed, the priest in a breathless whisper prayed: "Into Thy hands I commend the spirits of Thy servants, Oh Lord." His voice trailed off. He did not expect to finish his prayers before the debacle broke loose upon them.

Even now, after all the years that had gone by, Giuseppe had not forgotten the fear that had gripped his heart at that time when he expected to die in moments. His own heart kept thumping madly, in rhythm it had seemed, with the sobbing and wailing of his sisters.

Huddled together in the semi-darkness, for the lamp had now burned low, they all waited for that awful moment when the house would come crashing down over their heads. Minutes went by; the bubbling and the gurgling of the lava flow could be distinctly heard outside the house, and yet nothing happened. No walls came crashing in, the roof did not fall. Neither did the ground open under their feet to swallow them alive. Minute after anxious minute continued to mark the passing of time, and still the expected upheaval did not occur.

New sounds battered the ears of the terrified occupants of the ramshackle shelter that Papa Alanga had thrown together. Unmistakably, trees were crashing down, buildings elsewhere were collapsing. The forces of destruction had reached the town. The frightening din of falling stone and splintering wood intermingled with the muted shouts of human voices crying out in agony and panic. In the house, they heard the mad symphony of dissonance, orchestrated to the constant, heavy roll of the lava flow in the background. At first, the sounds heightened to a discordant crescendo, and then gradually died away like the rolling of muffled kettle drums.

When finally, a day later, the occupants of the house opened the door, they looked upon a strange and deserted world. And as their eyes roved from point to point, it seemed as if they had awakened from a long slumber, during which, by magic, they had been transported to some primordial world, a place filled with grotesque, truncated shapes. Where once the village of Boscotrecase had stood, with its balconied *palazzoni* centered around the palm tree lined piazza, only mounds of rubble were to be seen.

Here and there a lone wall, supporting nothing, stood jaggedly against the horizon. In some places the facades of buildings had been sliced away, so that the furnishings within were exposed for all to see; a bedstead dangling over a tilted floor; a pile of broken chairs, tables and cupboards smashed together into a heap of kindling; a picture of the Madonna still hanging on a wall, its glass unbroken.

The nave of Bosco's church was gone, yet, surprisingly the campanile, the tallest structure in the village, had suffered little damage. Some of the tower's roof had fallen in, and a long, jagged crack extended upwards from the lintel of the doorway. But the bells still hung and would once more ring out to toll the knell for the death of Boscotrecase.

Horror-stricken, Father Andrea and Papa and Mama scrutinized in amazement the devastation all around them. How is it, they wondered, not a house stood whole in Bosco, and yet theirs remained untouched?

When Padre Andrea and Alanga walked to the back of the house, their eyes opened wide in disbelief. Plainly, in some mysterious way, the lava flow had veered away, had been deflected by some force, away from the house. The two men studied the landscape. It was clear to them that the lava flow had rolled over the rise, destroyed and buried the grove of lemon trees directly behind the house, and then, some five yards away from the rear wall of the dwelling, had suddenly changed course. The flow had swerved eastward to completely bypass the building. The smoldering crust of the lava bed, flattened out now to some six feet in thickness, spread out as far as the eye could see.

"An underground shock, a collapsing fault," mused the blacksmith, "must have caused the flow to shift away from the house. What great fortune for us, eh, Padre Andrea? A timely movement under the surface must have had enough force to alter the path of this," and he threw out his arm weakly to indicate the mass of molten mud stretching before them.

Father Andrea took hold of Alanga's arm. With a nod of his head in the direction of the town, he said sadly, "There, they were not so fortunate. Our Boscotrecase is a ruin, my friend." Papa Alanga turned slightly, about to say something to the priest, but instead addressed his wife whom he spied coming towards them.

"See, wife, how we were saved. The ground moved just in time to turn away the stream of lava from the house. Nature unleashes, and Nature leashes."

"It was the hand of San Gennaro that saved us, husband." A tinge of color came to Maria's cheeks as she continued to speak. Her eyes took on a sparkle that betrayed the emotion surging in her breast. She hesitated a minute and then went on. She placed her hand on Father Andrea's arm. "In the house just now, I saw my little Teresina do a strange thing. I saw her go to the statue of San Gennaro, where they left him on the floor. She began to pull on the fingers of the statue.

"But what are you doing, child? I asked. This is only a statue. It cannot move its hand."

" 'Mama,' she answered me, 'the saint won't open his hand now. I saw him do it before, and now he won't hold my hand.' What are you saying, my little child? This is only a statue. It cannot move its hand. She insisted: 'But Mama, yesterday, when we were all together in the little house that Papa made in the corner, and Mariuccia was hugging me tight, and Giuseppina was crying, and Concettina was hurting my leg, I peeked out from under Papa's big arm, and I saw good San Gennaro go like this with his hand.' " And the mother imitated the little girl's gesture. She lifted her hand straight up from the wrist, the open palm of the hand with fingers stretched out to signify Stop!

"Is it a miracle, Padre Andrea? Did San Gennaro perform a wonder to thank us who gave him shelter?"

"Teresina is a child, Maria. She is only a little girl of four years. What she saw were the shadows flashing on the golden head. That's all it was." It was the voice of her husband speaking, before the priest could open his mouth. And he went on: "The child thought she saw something move, but her eyes were playing tricks on her."

"Perhaps, Michele, but such miracles have been known to happen." And before the priest could say more, Alanga laughed and turned away and started walking back to the house.

Later, in the house, more than once, Maria's eyes caught her husband staring fixedly on the two upraised fingers of San Gennaro, stiff and immovable in benediction.

Time and again through the years, his mother never tired telling the story, and Giuseppe knew that his mother went to her grave believing in her heart that a miracle had taken place. Teresina's eyes had not played tricks on her.

And when San Gennaro had been restored to his niche in the new church of Boscotrecase, each time Maria Alanga entered the church, she never failed to lovingly kiss his upraised fingers.

Chapter Two

Engrossed in his memories, Giuseppe had not heard the footsteps approach him. Suddenly he was aware of the touch of a hand on his shoulder, and he was brought back to the present by the smiling face of his youngest son, twelve year-old Francesco. The panorama of the long-ago time that had been unfolding before his eyes dissipated in a flash as he turned to see the smiling face and sparkling green eyes looking at him intently.

"Papa, I called you three times. You did not answer me. Were you thinking of tomorrow, when we leave for America?" A thrill of excitement was evident in the boy's rush of words. Without a pause, he went on: "I, too, can hardly wait to go, Papa, for this day to pass. You, and me, and Alfredo, and Michele, going to America, across the ocean. Mamma mia!" The deep green of the boy's eyes took on a liquid brightness that made them shimmer with light, and the face framed by a mass of coal-black wavy hair, broke out into a broad smile again as he looked up at his father. The eagerness and joy of his son brought a happy grin to the father's face, and rekindled in him his own feelings of excitement—and anxiety—that had caused him in the first place to go alone into the garden that morning. He understood the lad's emotion; his own breast had heaved, his breathing had come in short puffs as he lay in bed in the early hours of this day, thinking of the great change about to come into his life, and the lives of his family.

"What a day that will be for us, eh, Francì? For you and your brothers? America, America!" The father gave a loving tap to the chin of his son with his fist. Then the father's face grew serious. "But I was thinking of something else," and a glance, unobserved by the excited boy at his side, darted toward the mountain.

The two of them began their walk back to the house. The scent of the new spring growth emerging in the garden, perfumed the warm, April air. Their steps quickened as the aroma of fresh coffee and home-made bread wafted through the open door of the big, stone farmhouse.

"Ah, you two, at last. With so much to do this day, must I lose time chasing after you, husband? Come and eat now so the girls and I can get about our business for the celebration tonight. All of Boscotrecase will be here to wish you safe journey across the sea." Tears welled up in the woman's eyes for just a moment. She turned away from her husband and son as they entered. With nervous energy she carried the steaming coffee pot from the sideboard and placed it on the massive, wooden table in the center of the room. When she faced them, she was smiling and went about putting food on the table.

Sunlight streamed through all the windows, opened wide to let in the warmth and brightness of the Italian sun. "I was up earlier than you, Rosa," Giuseppe addressed his wife. "I, too, must see to many things. But you are right. We all have a busy day ahead of us. Everything will get done, don't worry about it. Come, come, everyone to the table. We cannot do all we must do without our bellies good and full."

Two girls stopped making beds; another put aside her broom; one more tied the finishing knot on a muslin-wrapped bundle in her lap, and they all trooped to the table. "Francesco," his mother commanded, "call your brothers at the pump. Tell them Papa's here, and we are ready to eat now. Filumena, bring over the lemon for your father's water." As Mama finished speaking, the boys came in with heads still wet from their washing at the pump. Francesco's two older brothers jostled their way to the table, and the family circle was complete around the board. In front of each one was a bowl filled half with coffee and half with milk, into which they all began dropping chunks of brown, crusty bread torn off from the several fresh loaves baked yesterday.

When he had finished his coffee and bread, Papa Alanga sliced a lemon in half, and with his big hand, squeezed the juice into his water. He raised his glass slowly and drank the tonic, while his eyes drank in the images of his seven children around the table. All of them were blood of his blood, and the pride of his life. From the oldest to the youngest, they were good and beautiful and robust. His heart swelled with joy in the contemplation of his three stalwart sons and four dutiful daughters.

The boys were of medium stature but rugged and solidly built like their father. Their teeth shone pearl-white against the skin of their faces, bronzed to a healthy hue by the flaming sun of the Campanian sky. The muscles of the arms and legs of the two older boys bulged hard and veined, toned by hard labor in field and forge. Neither could anyone call Francesco puny. With the onset of adolescence, and by working alongside his brothers in the fields he had lost all traces of baby fat. His muscles had thickened and his chest had broadened almost to the size of his brothers'. He was no longer a little boy; fuzz was beginning to show on his upper lip. More than once his brothers had caught him running his index finger over the silky hair above the lip, and they laughed as they teased him: "Tell me, little man, and is your little fish so covered?" Then laughing uproariously, they dodged the clumps of sod he flung at their heads.

In his father's eyes, Michele, his first-born, at twenty-five was *un uomo fatto*, that is to say, a man, in every sense of the word. Giuseppe had named this son after his own father, the blacksmith. Like his grandfather, the boy was strong and rugged. In the fields no one could match his stamina or endurance. And like his grandfather, he was a man of few words. His thoughts and opinions he generally kept to himself. Not that he was moody or morose; he could joke around and be playful with his brothers, his sisters sometimes, but with his father and others, he carried himself with reserve. He was practical and sensible, as it befitted a man to be; and his father was pleased. In looks, he resembled his father—thin lips, square jaw and a finely chiseled nose. Unlike his brothers with their green eyes that they had inherited from Mama, his were dark brown like Giuseppe's, and like Giuseppe's his hair was thick and curly.

His brother Alfredo, on the other hand, seven years his junior, was a dreamer. His was a world of ideas, words, concepts. Although he was no shirker when it came to physical work, his father sensed that this boy was destined someday to do something other than hard manual labor. He was pleased to think that this son's strength lay more in his mind than in his hands. Alfredo's brothers and sisters teasingly referred to him as the "gentleman" for the polish of his tastes and manners, for the "big words" he loved to use, the beauty of his script, and for his love of reading.

The "gentleman" never wolfed down food, no matter how ravenous he was when he returned from the fields at the end of a day's work. He held his fork or spoon with almost a finicky delicateness. His brothers snickered to see him in his Sunday best, with his cravat placed just so, the clothes without a wrinkle, and every hair of his head in place. They joked about their brother's aversion to bad smells and his distaste for soiling his hands. At times they jibed him: "Hey, Don Alfredo, brother dear, put on your white gloves and help me spread this cow shit, will you?"

Or: "Oh, Signore, do my smelly armpits offend your delicate nose? So sorry, milord." Alfredo was not a dandy—just too much the "gentleman" to respond in kind. Instead of condescending to acknowledge their crudeness with a spoken expletive, his usual response to their taunts was merely to smile broadly and flick his thumb from under his chin in their direction, much to the amusement, if not the chagrin, of his tormentors.

Although Alfredo was younger than Michele, he was slightly taller by a couple of inches than his older brother. His features were softer, not so angular and sharp like Michele's and his father's. The lips were fuller, in the shape of a bow, like his mother's, and his eyes were the color of sea waves like hers. A mass of silky, brown hair crowned his head so that he had to pomade it heavily to keep it in place.

In build, the taller Alfredo was less solid and broad-chested than Michele; but it was Francesco who promised to be the tallest of the brothers. Even at twelve, he was already approaching Alfredo's height. It was clear that he would outstrip his brothers in the future.

Francesco was a whirling dervish, an imp full of piss and vinegar, always ready for a lark, a gamble, a risk. The boy's spirit of independence, his disregard for consequences, was beginning to give his father some concern. But, Giuseppe reasoned, the strangeness, the unfamiliarity of new surroundings in America would soon cut him down to size.

It was in the company of these two grown sons—men—and the boy, that Giuseppe planned to embark on the great adventure of their lives on the morrow. There, they would make their fortunes, in America, father and sons combining their strength and brawn, fulfill their dreams. Then, in a year or two at the most, they would be able to bring over the women of the family, to be all together once more. And so all of them would partake of the fabled providence of the new world.

As the father continued to look upon his sons, he thought: "With three such stalwart sons by my side, what must I fear, how can I fail?" The moment of silent reflection passed from Giuseppe's mind in a flash. As his eyes lost their far-away look, he put down his glass and said, "Listen, Francì. As soon as you've finished eating, go to Salvatore *'o carrettiere*. Remind him to be here first thing tomorrow with his cart. We want to be sure to get to Naples in plenty of time. He will not be here tonight for the *festa*, or I would tell him myself."

Smoothing his dark mustache, he continued: "Rosa, dear wife, make sure that the girls finish packing the boys' things, and mine. And see to it that nothing is forgotten."

"Papa, won't you be afraid to go on the big boat to America, so far away? And without Mama? Will the boat get lost on the big sea? And how will we do without you and Michele and Alfredo and Francesco? Don't go, Papa. Stay home with us. Write a letter to Zio Matteo in America and tell him that you don't want to go anymore."

It was little Gilda, the baby of the family, who had put into words the very thoughts that Mama and her daughters had been suppressing in their hearts. Filumena, sitting next to Gilda, drew her close, and gently began stroking her little sister's neatly parted brown hair, pulled back into one thick braid.

When his little five year-old child began to cry, Giuseppe gently swept her into his arms and tickled her chin until she began to giggle. How could he explain to his little one, to any of them, to whom a trip to Naples twelve miles distant seemed like a journey to land's end, that he felt the same misgivings? To leave the land of his fathers, to break away from all that was familiar and dear to him had not been an easy decision to make. But the die was cast.

Letter after letter had come from his younger brother, extolling the opportunities for a better life in America. And so at last he had succumbed to the dream of better things for his children that Matteo had promised were sure to be theirs in the new, rich land that was America.

"If you have a strong back and willing hands," the younger brother had written, "there is work a-plenty, and good money for it. And with money, everything is possible here. One can hope to live the life of a *signore* here in America. Come, Giuseppe, leave the stagnation and poverty of Italy. Come to America with your sons. Come, build a new life. I will pay the passage for you and your sons."

And so it was that one day, Giuseppe Alanga had surrendered to his brother's urgings, lured by the promise of better things to come for them in America. The separation from his wife and daughters would be hard, he knew. But, he rationalized, it would not be long before they could be united again as a family. The rewards for all of them would be worth the pain of a temporary separation. Besides, was it not true that thousands of paesani were quitting the old country to pursue this self-same dream of freedom from want and the desire for an easier life for themselves and their children? How much easier it would be for him because he would have a brother's arms to greet him in a strange new world and show him its ways.

Giving little Gilda a kiss on her forehead, Giuseppe said to her and to all of them: "Be not afraid, little one. The big boat is strong, and it will take your papa and your brothers to America. Then, with the help of God, we will all be together again a little later. I will send for all of you. My girls will have pretty clothes and earrings of gold. Everyone will say: 'How beautiful are the daughters of Giuseppe Alanga.' So, while we are away, dream of these things that your papa has told you. And one fine day, not too far away, you will find them to come true."

He put the child down. "Come now, finish your food. We have much to do today, and you must help Mama get ready. Tonight there will be in the house of Giuseppe Alanga a *festa*, the like of which has never been seen in Boscotrecase." A wide smile illuminated his face; and whether because of his tonic of lemon water, or because of the anticipation of dreams to be fulfilled, his whole being radiated a new joy, a renewed hope that affected all of them.

The mood in the room changed; everyone began to chatter. The boys attacked breakfast with new vigor, and the girls giggled with reanimation. Mama, too, caught up in the spontaneous joyfulness of the moment, felt her spirits revive. She began to bark out orders.

"Filumena, you and Carolina help me make the tagliatelle. Eleonora, roast the coffee beans and grind them. We will need lots of coffee tonight. Gilda, be a good child and wash all the bowls and cups and keep feeding the fire until the oven outside is good and hot, so that I can bake some more bread and some biscotti. Boys, you set up more tables and benches under the arbor. When you finish, draw off enough wine and set the jugs in the cistern to cool. *Dio*, we will have to work like mules today."

Chapter Three

The males left the house on their separate tasks. Francesco made his way to the house of the cart driver, Salvatore. Alfredo and Michele soon had three more long, wooden tables set out under the arbored patio alongside the house. Then the both of them made off to feed and look after the animals.

Their father, meanwhile, walked off slowly to the forge. In the dimness of the darkened shed, now silent and without its usual brightness and heat, the blacksmith tread reverently within, as if on holy ground. Carefully he picked up one tool after another of his trade and caressed it. His rough, callused hand stroked each one gently. His were the hands of a craftsman, an artisan, with the talent to mold and shape iron into useful objects, and sometimes, things of beauty. Did they have blacksmiths in America, he wondered?

Many of these very tools had been his father's, the only intimate and personal inheritance left to him by that old man. What would he leave to his sons?

He laid the hammer down brusquely, spun sharply on his heels and turned his back on the forge, forever. The legacy he hoped to leave his sons would be more than a handful of tools. It would be America, and a future full of dreams and hopes, there, in that land to be fulfilled.

Giuseppe left the shop. The shop, he knew, was now a part of the past. He quickened his steps toward the house and toward the future.

Now the sun was shining golden in the glory of a blue, April sky. Both boys, Michele and Alfredo, were busy unpenning the animals and leading them to pasture. Across the grassland, borne on a sweet-scented breeze, came the sounds of treble voices of young girls singing as they worked in the neighboring fields.

"Listen, brother mine. Finish this work without me. I see Adelina by the mulberry trees. Tonight, you know, I won't have much of a chance to be alone with her, with everyone around." Michele's voice had a note of urgency in it, and Alfredo did not miss the light blush on his brother's face. He smiled to Michele and waved him off.

The older brother darted off, crouching low along the hedgerow in order not to be seen by any of the girls in the fields. Alfredo stood watching as his brother steadily advanced like a wolf upon its prey.

"So, Bettinella, soon my brother's hands will be caressing his *innamorata*, and here am I, petting a smelly goat." He laughed out loud as he ran his hand along the goat's back.

When Michele reached the end of the hedgerow, he stopped and gave a low, tremulous whistle. It was barely discernable above the merry singing a short distance away. The girl plaiting a panier under the mulberry tree a stone's throw away, jerked her head upwards and sidewards in his direction, her fingers still deftly weaving the strands of reeds. She knew the whistle well. A smile broke out on her beautiful, small face. Two deep, brown eyes opened wide and gleamed happily at Michele. Bending down as if to pick up more reeds, she ambled casually to his side behind the hedgerow.

Michele reached up, took her hand and pulled her down beside him, so that both of them were well hidden from prying eyes by the thick growth of bushes. They were alone together, a rare happening for them. Although it was understood that they would someday marry, and they had the blessings of both families to do so, the strict code of chaperonage traditionally maintained by the peasants of the Italian countryside, forbade lovers to be left alone by themselves.

The code dictated that a third party always be present. Mother, father, aunt, sister, grandmother stood by to see that intimacy never went beyond a formal handshake between boy and girl. A surreptitious kiss, a fondling hand on breast or buttocks, or a mere caress of face or hand could sometimes be managed. But that, only in an unguarded moment when the chaperone turned away or was diverted by ruse or chance. Unhappily for lovers, such moments were rare. More often than not they had to content themselves in expressing their feelings and their passions with their eyes. Both Michele and Adelina had become adept at speaking the language of the eyes, those eyes that mirrored their love, their longing, their pain.

But now, by good fortune, the two of them were together and alone. Soon they were in each other's arms. His passions, so long pent up, Michele enfolded her in his embrace. He kissed her long and hard. When at last his mouth broke away from hers, he murmured: "How long, oh how long I have yearned to hold you so, *piccina*."

He kissed her again, gently, never letting go her waist.

"How can I leave you, Adelina mia? How can I go to America and not see your face for a year, for two, for who knows how long? How can I wait so long to have you?" His head fell in despair. He groaned.

With the softness of a butterfly's wing, Adelina touched his face with the tips of her fingers, running them along the contours of his eyebrows, his nose, his mouth, his chin, as if she were blind. She took his head in both her hands and drew him close to her breast.

"I love you, my Michele, and I will wait eternity for you. You will come back with the riches of America in your pockets, and I will be here, still yours, and only yours."

His heart was pounding; the softness of her body excited him, and his own blood began to race madly so that he tingled with anticipation of greater closeness. The weight of his body gradually pushed her down so that she was lying on the grass, and he was over her. She sighed out his name, enfolding her arms around his neck. He kissed her on the neck, then the lips, then the breasts. His hand ran down her thigh, then pushed up her skirt and touched her inner softness.

In the distance the singing voices continued. Overhead birds warbled and chirped as they flitted about in the warm April sunshine. But the two lovers, basking in the warmth of their love, in the heat of their passion, now awakened to its fullest expression, heard nothing but the rhythms of their own heartbeats. When they were done with their love-making, only then did they become aware of the world about them. They both lay on their back, hand in hand, gazing at the sky. A sweet feeling of tranquillity and peace enveloped them. They just lay there, together on the soft grass.

Then silently the girl, as her exhilaration subsided, began to button her blouse and pull down her skirt. She sat up and tidied her hair while Michele, his back turned to her and in a kneeling position, buttoned the opening of his trousers. When he finished, he turned to look at her. They both sat side by side; then Michele began to speak.

"Adelina, forgive..."

Swiftly she put a finger to his lips. "Say nothing. What we have done, we did out of love for each other. Now I am yours always, for I have given you the only thing that is completely yours, and that can never be given again to anyone—my virginity. Take that as my gift to you, and when you are far away in America, and are lonely, remember my gift to you, and let the thought of it spur you on to hurry back to me."

Tears welled in her brown eyes and spilled over the lids. The sight of those eyes bathed as they were in the shimmering crystals of her tears, brought a pang of pain and remorse to Michele. Suddenly he burst out, almost in rage: "I will not go, Adelina. I will tell my father that I will not go, that my happiness lies here in Boscotrecase with you by my side as my wife." He turned on his heels, but the girl reached out and caught his sleeve.

"That you must not do. No, Michele mio. In America, you will do great things, I know it. I have seen too often the glow of your eyes these past months whenever the talk was of America. I know the dream that lies in your heart, and I know too, that I am part of that dream, that you go to America not just for yourself, but for both of us. Go, Michele. Make the dream come true, for yourself, for me, for our children yet unborn."

Suddenly a piercing, staccato whistle split the air. It was the signal used by the brothers since their childhood days to warn of danger, or to summon each other.

"That's Alfredo calling me," blurted Michele. "Someone must be approaching. I must go. Tonight, *amore mio*, at the *festa*, I will see you again. But go now, Adelina. No one must see us here together. "

The girl picked up her basket, peeked above the hedgerow and seeing the workers far off in the fields, quickly gained her position again under the mulberry tree where she resumed her plaiting. Michele had just enough time to reach the periphery of the flock of gamboling goats where Alfredo was standing with a kid in his arms. From there, he had been able to see his father tramping across the meadow from the far end near the forge.

"Hey, boys. What's taking you so long? Are all the goats accounted for? Mama wants you back at the house," their father shouted across the distance. Coming nearer, he beckoned Alfredo to come down from the little knoll. "Where is your brother?"

In answer to his father's question, Alfredo motioned backward with his hand and yelled out: "He's back there, passing water." Catching the clue, Michele walked into sight of his father, pretending to be buttoning up his fly.

"Whew!" exploded Michele. "That felt good. Eh, Papa, what's Mama got for us to do now?" He smiled and gave his brother an appreciative wink.

"She wants you to string the lanterns along the arbors and some of the trees, boys. Let the animals feed now, and come back to the house. No doubt, she'll have a dozen more jobs for us to do before evening comes."

The three men sauntered down the pathway that led to the house. Once or twice, Michele looked back unnoticed by his father and brother, until he lost sight of the figure under the mulberry tree.

Chapter Four

The evening sun had set, but the flames from a dozen glowing lanterns, shielded against a soft, April night's breeze, by their sparkling glass chimneys, sent out myriad rays of light. The entire area of the arbored patio alongside the house was illuminated sufficiently both by the rays from the lanterns and the full moon.

Everywhere, happy throngs of people were clustered together in groups, some under the arbors, some sitting on benches or standing in the poplar-lined avenue that led to the house. Some spilled out into the semi-darkness of the back yard not lit by the lanterns but where the moon cast its pale light.

Above the voices and the laughter of adults, happy knots of shrieking, giggling children scampered and caroused. The tinkling of mandolins and the bellowing of an accordion floated above the din. Mario Lucetti and his three brothers were strumming and squeezing out one merry tune after the other. Now and then, they stopped to refresh themselves with food and wine, of which there was a mountainous abundance piled high on every inch of the tables lining one edge of the patio.

"Hey, Mario, you and the brothers, now, just a bite! We want more music. Get a tarantella going when you finish, or a quadriglia, so we can dance," shouted one of the young blades. Mario smiled and waved him off as he and the other musicians filed their way to the tables.

In a tight circle around Giuseppe, a group of his neighbors were in serious conversation with the prospective emigrant.

"And in America, they say, the people there speak a language that is incomprehensible." It was old Saverio, the mule-driver talking. "How will you make yourself understood, my friend to those *Americani* that know not the sweetness nor the meanings of this beautiful tongue of ours? Why, even my jackasses understand me when I say, '*avanti, Ravanello; chiano, chiano, Ceccillo.*'"

Before he could go on, the town barber, who considered himself a man of erudition, interrupted the simple, old man's discourse. Because he read every word of the occasional periodical that reached the shop, he felt himself able to pontificate knowingly on matters of politics, religion, music and every other subject worth talking about.

"And what! old mule-driver. Do you think your flea-bitten, flop-eared old jackasses are more intelligent than man who is created in the image of God, as is an American?"

"Learned friend," retorted the wizened old soul, "I know that God in His wisdom, created me like unto Him, but of some others I am not so sure. In my long life, I have come across plenty of men, who not only brayed like jackasses, but looked like them, too, and were not half so intelligent as my Ravanello."

The circle of men exploded into laughter, and some shouted, "Bravo, Saverio, *ben fatto*." The air crackled with the sound of thighs being slapped again and again in frenzied exuberance. Realizing that he had been bested by the unschooled mule-driver, the barber flushed scarlet. He began to squirm uncomfortably at the sound of the raucous guffaws echoing about his ears. To regain his composure he puffed out his cheeks and waved his hand as if to signify the old man's comments not worthy of response.

In another area of the yard, a group of somber, black-clad matrons, their heads covered in shawls, were commiserating with Rosa Alanga.

"Ah, to be without your man, for God knows how long," one of them sighed dolefully.

"So far away, this America! A land of strangers and strange ways," another voice piped in.

And yet another: "But there are paesani there and they have come to know the ways of these *Americani*. Giuseppe and his sons will surely find comfort and aid in their midst."

Then Mama Alanga spoke, her voice strong and calm. She was sitting on a bench, her hands folded in her lap. "I fear not for my husband and my sons. Giuseppe has a brother's hand to welcome him and take him to his heart. In a land of strangers he will find refuge under a brother's roof. The cry of the blood is strong and attracts its kind to itself, brother to brother. But even if this were not so, my husband and my sons are men. The strength of their own hands and the goodness that lies in their hearts will give them the courage they need. And surely, my prayers to the good Jesus and the Madonna to protect them, will not go unanswered."

The-wisdom of her words, expressing as they did, the timeless belief in the blood-tie, the goodness of God, and the strength of a man's arm, brought nods and sighs from all the women. These beliefs, so basic a part of the nature and creed of the southern Italian peasants, had always done much to sustain them; and for countless centuries they had been able to survive injustice, poverty, oppression, and the coming and going of new social orders.

"And know, then," Mama continued, "that my Giuseppe will not let an eternity lapse before he sends for us. He will not do like some who have gone, and their women pine and languish in loneliness for years and years. He and my sons will work hard, and the drops of their sweat will turn into gold, which they will put in an iron box. And when the box is full with American gold, my Giuseppe will call for us to come."

"God willing," sighed Carlotta.

"Would to God, my sister," sighed Aunt Amelia.

"By the souls in Purgatory," others exclaimed.

Then old, toothless Lisetta, as wrinkled as a prune, and as dark, twittered in a nervous giggle. Pointing a long, almost fleshless finger in the direction of the arbor, she croaked: "See Michele, how he pines for love of Adelina. He will sweat for her, Rosa, twice as much as he will for his mama."

Her shrill laughter pierced the noise-laden air, and some of the women joined in. But Mama Alanga had no need to glance to the corner of the arbor where Michele and Adelina stood a little way off from the crowd. From time to time her eyes had come to rest upon them, and even in the half-light, she had noticed the strained, painful look on their faces.

They were seen to be whispering to each other: sad words of promised, unbroken love, no doubt, thought those who were watching. Ah, young lovers! The hot blood of youth resents such a separation, the onlookers reasoned. But what will be, will be. Love often brings pain as well as joy.

To Michele and Adelina, the reality of such love pains lay in the hearts of both of them, now that the truth of a long separation from each other was upon them. But more than that, Michele was brooding. He could not persuade Adelina of his resolve to remain in Bosco, to marry her right away. She would not hear of, nor be convinced of any of the arguments he offered. He must go to America tomorrow with his father. She insisted.

In the place of the thrill and ecstasy he had experienced during the flushed moments of his passion earlier in the day, now a sense of guilt and shame permeated Michele's soul. He had had his way with her. And now he was going to leave her—alone. Gnawing at his heart was a fear he dare not put into words. If there should be a consequence of their act of love, if she should become with child. He shuddered and could not cast out the image from his mind, of Adelina alone in Bosco without him, to face the shame and ridicule such unfortunate girls had to suffer. Everyone would label her *puttana*, and the child, "whoreson." Such was the fate of the poor girls caught in so unlucky a circumstance in the small villages and towns of Campania, Basilicata, Calabria, and Apuglia, the provinces of southern Italy.

At one point in his reflections, he was so overwhelmed by the horror of that image, he broke away from her and started to go towards his father. Adelina knew that he was about to tell his father to go to America without him, that he was going to remain in Bosco and marry her. She ran after him and grabbed his hand. Just at that moment the wild strains of the tarantella sounded. She pulled him into the center of the patio where other couples were beginning the gyrations and weavings of the dance to the accompaniment of tinkling tambourines and snapping castanets.

If the legend were true, the tarantella was a cure for the bite of the tarantula; certainly it was a cure for melancholy. Caught up in the whirl and gaiety of the six-eighths tempo, the two lovers were soon flashing smiles at each other, and their eyes became bright and vivid in the excitement of the dance. Their abandonment to the dance was a signal to the other dancers to leave off. Soon they were alone in the middle of a ring of admirers calling out a chorus of "vivas" and "bravos."

As if on cue, the musicians speeded up the tempo, and the two dancers became whirling splashes of color as they spun and twirled faster and faster. The shouts and cries of the onlookers almost reached an hysterical pitch when the last twang of the guitar and the plink of the mandolin brought the frenzy to an end. The circle of spectators converged on the couple, kissing and embracing them.

Seeing Adelina seemingly carefree, happy, smiling, Michele cast off his somber thoughts. With Adelina at his side he joined in the festivities as the hours sped by. The two of them danced, sang, ate, drank, and went from friend to friend. They readily joined in conversation, story-telling and laughter. The merriment continued far into the night. Time was forgotten in the midst of feasting and joviality.

As in all the small villages of the region, the memorable events of life, from birth to death, were occasions to be shared in a spirit of joy, or in a mood of sorrow. It was almost as if privacy was alien to the effusive nature of the southern peasant. Life was a spectacle. Or sad, or happy, it was to be shared; a spectacle without an audience was not a spectacle.

The night rushed on inexorably, and strength began to flag. Eyes became heavy, shoulders drooped and conversation slowed. Mothers were rocking sleeping toddlers across their knees, and the old folks succumbed to weariness. Some dozed where they sat.

The finale to the evening was imminent. And then it came as the musicians began playing the opening bars of the beautiful, nostalgic song of emigrants, *Santa Lucia Luntana*. A hush fell upon the crowd as Mario's clear tenor voice began to penetrate the stillness. The stars, like votive lights in a cathedral, illuminated the vault of the open skies.

The pathos of the words, expressing as they did, the pain of departing from one's homeland to seek fortune on unknown shores, pierced every heart. Tears fell on the cheeks of young and old, men and women alike.

Chapter Five

A gloriously warm sun early lit the skies on the day of destiny for the Alanga men—April 3, 1906.

Long before first light, Giuseppe and his eager sons, had gotten themselves ready in the pre-dawn silence and darkness. During those silent hours, the girls slept serenely, unaware of the quiet bustle of father, mother, and brothers. Rosa, wife and mother to the emigrants, ministered to their every need, anticipating their every want. Her eyes strayed now to this one, now to that one of her men. Diligently she imprinted on the collodion plate of her mind their every feature, the very lineaments of their faces, so that in the empty months ahead she would always have the image of those loved ones before her eyes.

A rush of sadness flooded her heart at the thought of their absence; then a rush of pride and hope at the thought of their aspirations and dreams and the fulfillment of them. She would not dampen their enthusiasm as they set off on this great venture of their lives, so full of prospects to be achieved. A fortuitous future, God grant! Lastly, her being was imbued with a wave of joy as she pictured the happy reunion they would one day know in golden America.

Even in the early dark hours of the morning, a hopeful Francesco darted like a hare along the tree-lined avenue from house to road. His ears strained to hear the clop-clop of Salvatore's cart. And then, just as the sun's first rays brought a feeble light to the dark-mantled landscape, the boy's exuberant shout: "Here he comes!" heralded the awaited moment. As if by magic, all reticence, all restraint was abandoned to the wind. Shouts and excited cries broke out. The girls, awakened and aware now, added a chorus of high-pitched female shrieks and chattering.

The old cart-driver had hardly a chance to rein his donkey to a stop, before he was besieged by anxious hands grabbing reins, bridle and cart.

"Ah, Salvatore, you're here at last. You're here, thank the good Lord. Into the cart the boys began flinging the baggage they were taking to the new world. In went stoutly corded knapsacks and muslin bundles, clothes mostly, but food, too: loaves of Mama's good bread, hard salamis, home-made cheeses, dried olives, dried figs, and rock-hard *taralli*, those dough rings with pepper in them that had to be soaked in water or wine before they could be bitten.

As Giuseppe and Rosa slowly approached the cart, somber and serious of mien, all levity departed. A hush, pregnant with sadness engulfed them all. To each of them came the realization now like a blow to the heart, of the meaning of what was soon to happen. To the mother, the loss of husband and sons; to the boys, the loss of mother and sisters; to the girls, the loss of father and brothers. The moment of separation had come. How long a separation, oh Lord! The hour that would mean, future loneliness, anxiety, fear, was upon them all. The moment of destiny.

With tears and caresses, the boys took leave of their mother and sisters. They mounted the cart and waited for their father to make his goodbyes. To each of his daughters, the touch of his rough hand on a wet cheek told them of his love more than any words. Finally, he turned to his wife and took her folded hands in his.

"Rosa, time passes like the flight of birds from here to there. One day we shall all be together again, a family entire once more. Take heart. Manage the place with the help of our daughters. We will write. I will send you money. No tears."

"Hey, now, let us be on our way, or the ship will leave without you," broke in the husky voice of the impatient cart driver. "Naples is not a spit away, you know. My Pulicinello will fall asleep in the shafts, and then we will need the hand of God to awaken him."

Like a young man of twenty-five, Giuseppe bounded onto the cart and took his place next to the driver. "Hee, yah! Pulicinello. Move on, my little sweetheart." The reins snapped, the driver's tongue uttered a sharp click. The donkey began to pull, and the wheels of the cart began to roll. Cries of "God go with you," from a chorus of female voices were answered by huskier male voices in response, "And God be with you. Goodbye Mama, goodbye, goodbye." Arms waved from one group to the other, but the road soon curved and they were cut off from the sight of each other.

No sooner had the turn in the road been made, when out of the hedgerow along its side, the figure of a girl appeared. It was Adelina. She stepped into the middle of the road, her hand upraised. In her arm she cradled a round, cloth bundle the size of a pumpkin. Michele recognized her at once. He jumped to his feet, calling on Salvatore to stop the cart. With creaks and squeals, the cart came to a halt. The girl approached. A new white shawl fringed in tassels of gold, draped her head and shoulders like a halo.

"*Buon giorno, Signor Alanga.* Hello, boys. I have made you some almond cookies. God knows when you will have the like again." She stretched up to hand the bundle to Michele's extended arm. The shawl fell from her head, and the sun's rays caught the gold globes in her ears, shooting out dazzling sparkles of light.

Michele passed the bundle to his father, who sniffing the sweet fragrance of its contents, sang out in praise, "Thank you, my good girl. They will not serve the likes of this to us in steerage. Take a whiff of these, boys," and he handed the cloth bag to Francesco. The perfume of the almond macaroons scented the air around them.

"Michele mio," the girl said quietly as the rest of them oohed and aahed over the sweets, "take this for yourself, a remembrance of me." She gave him a stiff, cardboard-backed photo of herself. The sepia colored portrait showed her standing straight and primly posed by an ornate urn on a marble pedestal. A beautiful, delicate smile curved the corners of the girl's mouth.

As she gave Michele the card, her fingers touched his, and she whispered, "You are my only love. Do not forget me in faraway America. I live only for your call to come to you. Go with God, *mio caro Michele.*" She stepped back a few paces away from the cart. And in a louder voice, quivering with tearful emotion, she wished them all a good voyage under the protection of God. The air rang with good-byes as the cart resumed its way along the road to Naples. Adelina stood smiling after them, her eyes focused on the standing figure of Michele, until he faded from sight.

All along the way through the environs of Boscotrecase, good neighbors and friends halted the wagon. Many were the well-wishes extended to the emigrants, along with gifts—now a cheese, now a loaf of bread, now some fruit. But at length the road led far beyond Bosco, and they were able to proceed uninterrupted to Torre Annunziata. After that came Torre del Greco and the other small villages along the shore of the bay. Then the Neapolitan metropolis loomed in sight. The bells of the noon-time Angelus from a dozen of the city's campaniles were ringing out as the cart began to jerk over the cobblestones of the city's outskirts.

The occupants of the cart had never before seen anything like the panorama of confusion that began spreading before their eyes. Nor had they ever heard such a medley of sounds that battered their eardrums. Salvatore guided his cart saucily through the mass of traffic crowding the Via Caracciolo, that long, wide avenue that hemmed the curvature of the bayside. In all directions they heard laughter, cries, shouts, oaths, mingling with the music of the street singers. Rising above the racket, the strains of the almost Arabic-sounding chanting of the street vendors out-voiced all the other sounds. Here, a vendor was bellowing out the glories of his eggplants and squashes; another was singing the praises of the fresh fish on his cart. Every conceivable foodstuff a human could eat, was being glorified and praised in the songs of the vendors.

All the sounds blended together to form a concert of dissonant, yet pleasing strains to the ear. The Via Caracciolo had become the setting of an opera where the bassos were the vendors; the sopranos, the screeching women; the altos the wary pedestrians; and the tenors, the teen-agers who hurled their obscenities at the drivers as they darted among carts, wagons and even some autos, in their precarious efforts to cross the street.

At last Salvatore's cart came to a stop in the dock area of Santa Lucia. Here, if it could be imagined, the activity was more frenetic, the sounds more piercing. The emigrants were massed together like swarms of bees buzzing unceasingly toward the opening of the hive. Every type of pack, sack, bag and bundle was being dragged, carried and shouldered amidst a sea of humanity. Men, women, children of all ages, even babes in arms thronged the docks. Voices babbled in every dialect of Southern Italy. Voices that were shouting out good-byes, prayers, words of encouragement in Neapolitan, Calabrian, Barese and in a multitude of regional patterns of speech from a hundred individual villages filled the air.

Staring in wonderment at the mob of people before them, Alfredo asked his father: "But what! Is all of Italy emigrating? We surely will not lack the company of paesani in the new land."

"Let us stay together, my sons. There are all kinds of villains in this mob. They will steal the very eyes out of your head." Giuseppe shifted the bag on his shoulder and adroitly prodded on his youngest son with his elbow. The father was not wrong in his surmise; a host of sharpers and low characters abounded, ready to fleece any gullible peasant. Indeed, some of the ticket agents and ships' crews were all too ready to take advantage of the more ignorant, simple emigrants.

Like birds of prey, these unscrupulous officials usually managed to victimize the more unworldly-wise peasants by imposing "surcharges" or "state taxes" on the tickets or documents where they found "irregularities." And all too often these leeches succeeded in squeezing a few more lire out of some unlettered, unsuspecting peasant, too frightened to protest.

But Papa Alanga was not one of these. He was sure of himself, sure that their tickets and their papers had been duly processed. Each paper had its proper stamp or seal. In gratitude, Giuseppe had made a present of a dozen eggs and a liter of wine to Don Romolo, the town clerk and notary in Boscotrecase. In appreciation, he had also slipped ten lire to old Massini, who been back and forth to America twice, and who had advised him well on what to do and what not to do, and what to be wary of.

Gradually, a semblance of order took hold at the docks. Out of the chaos, tickets were checked and lines were formed. People began mounting gangplanks. On deck, the greater mass of emigrants, separated from first and second-class passengers, were herded down to the hold of the ship by wildly gesticulating stewards. The loading of the human cargo and freight took hours, but by five o'clock, all was aboard.

Following their guide, Giuseppe and the boys made their way through a maze of stairways and narrow passageways. Down and down they trudged—a mob of bewildered innocents, following the leader until they finally reached an evil-smelling cavern over the screws of the ship. Tiers of wooden bunk beds filled the space. There was barely enough room for a full-grown child to pass, let alone a full-grown man. Everywhere, the passengers were pushing and shoving each other as they attempted to find a bed and stow away their possessions. The airless abyss was already getting hotter and more stinking. Poor Alfredo, his gorge rising, cast wide eyes about him.

Chapter Six

It took but a day or so for life aboard ship to settle into a routine. With the adaptable resilience of their peasant fatalism, the voyagers soon accepted the conditions of their present existence. The stinking water-closet reeking of urine, feces and vomit became less offensive with time. Nor did their palates disdain the monotonous menu of pasta covered by a watery tomato sauce, or the rancid beans, or bitter coffee. Those who had the stomach, continued to congregate around the huge black cauldrons of pasta or beans set up in the galley. There, like pigs around a trough, as Alfredo bitterly observed, the steerage passengers received their daily dole in dented and scratched tin bowls.

As often as possible, in order to escape the fetid air of their quarters in the hold, as many as were able, made their way to the decks to breathe in the salty smell of fresh ocean air. Many unfortunates, though, gripped by seasickness, lay prostrate in their cots, unable to make their way to the decks. Weak, pale, and without the energy to escape their prison in the hold, they spent the days lying inert and moaning. The rocking of the ship, the eternal up and down motion of the vessel played havoc with their stomachs. Some of these poor souls were barely able to keep themselves alive. The smell of vomit was everywhere in the hold. Especially at night, in the heavy darkness below decks, one was particularly conscious of the retching noises, the splat of effluvia hitting the floor. Not infrequently some innocent in a lower bunk found himself splattered from what came raining down from above. And adding to the general misery, were the belches and farting that echoed from one end of the cavernous hold to the other.

Giuseppe and his sons fared well enough. In a short while they had gained their sea-legs. The father, Michele and Francesco dutifully accepted and ate their portions of the ship's pasta; it was food after all, and to waste food was a sin. Their digestive system after a couple of days, adjusted readily enough to the insipid fare. They ate little of what they had brought with them from home so that Alfredo could survive. Even Francesco, the youngest, realized that his brother was suffering, and did not begrudge Alfredo a larger chunk of Mama's good bread, the extra olives, the bigger piece of goat's cheese. For, after his first taste of the pasta and the beans of the first meal aboard ship, Alfredo never touched a morsel of ship's food. And although Alfredo's color paled and his eyes lost some of their luster, he was able to retain his strength and his spirits, thanks to the generosity of his brothers.

Nothing bothered Francesco; like one of the goats he herded back in his father's fields, he gamboled all over the ship. He explored every nook and niche. He became friends with Feliciano, a crewhand who had spent most of his life on the sea. Even in his fifties, the old tar had the muscular strength and agility of a younger man.

In the succeeding days aboard ship, Francesco sought out the sailor's company. Whenever he could spare the time, the old man enjoyed the boy's company and the rapt attention the lad gave him. He filled the youngster's ear with stories of his life on the sea, and the lore of the mariner. For the first time in his life, the young listener became aware of the configurations of the constellations, the position of the North Star, the flow of the currents of the ocean. Francesco had never met anyone like Feliciano back in the confined, land-locked world of Boscotrecase.

It was soon apparent to Francesco what good fortune it was to have Feliciano for a friend, not only for the wonders the old man shared with him, but also for his kindness. Most of the ship's officers were explicitly disdainful of their human cargo, and the deckhands, generally too busy or uncivil to bother with the people from below decks.

A week out of Naples, in mid ocean, the ship encountered its first storm. Late in the afternoon, billows of black clouds obscured the sky as far as the eye could see. The wind from the north angrily whipped itself into a gale that lifted the waves to mountainous heights. The churning waters smashed against the sides of the ship, sending resounding claps of thunder throughout the hold. With each smack, human shrieks added to the roar.

As the vessel pitched and rolled in the heavy seas, terror overcame the women and children huddled together in Gordian knots. Men steadied themselves as best they could by clinging to bunk posts and railings. Their eyes bespoke their own fear.

For most of them, whose lives had been spent in the land-locked villages of their birth, the sea and its ways were as foreign to them as living in a palace. The land they knew, and how to tame it. But the sea was not their element. They feared it now in its fury, such as they had never feared the quake, the landslide, the flood. From those fits of malevolent Nature, one could run.

The rough seas rose higher as the storm progressed. The winds howled more keenly. In the steerage compartment, trunks and baggage began to slide across the floor. Bundles fell, people fell. Men, women and children doubled over in pain. Their agonized retching pierced through their stomach to reach their very backbone.

One particularly violent pitch of the ship sent a score of women reeling crazily into each other. A young peasant woman dressed in the costume of Sorrento was sent hurling with her infant backwards into Giuseppe with such force that the child fell from the mother's arms. Luckily Michele, standing by his father, was there to catch the baby. But the impetus of the woman's fall knocked Giuseppe savagely against a post. The blow knocked him senseless, and he slumped to the floor. Hurriedly Michele placed the infant back in his mother's arms to tend to his father.

"Francesco, help me get Papa up. Alfredo, get up, get up and help us." But poor Alfredo was propped up against his bunk, his knees drawn up to his chin, dry-heaving in spastic jerks. He didn't even raise his head at his brother's call. He heard nothing but the rumblings of his aching, empty stomach.

Francesco, though, although absolutely green of face, was still on his feet. With all the feeble strength he was able to muster, he grabbed one of his father's arms. Together he and Michele managed to lift their unconscious father onto his cot.

The rolling of the ship grew more turbulent, and both sons were barely able to keep themselves upright. Their father's inert body rolled from side to side on the bunk as the ship bobbed up and down on the sea like an empty bottle.

"Let's tie him down, Francì. If he falls off we'll never get him up again." Clumsily and with difficulty, the two of them secured their father's legs and chest with blankets knotted to the frame of the bunk. Then, exhausted by their efforts, they slid to the floor by Alfredo, oblivious to the pandemonium and shrieks of despair echoing throughout the hold.

The next morning, day dawned bright and serene. The sea was uniformly smooth, gently rippled now and then by mild breezes cutting across its blue-green surface. Everyone who was able, ascended to the upper decks in order to escape the foul stench which pervaded the steerage quarters.

Giuseppe awoke to find the young mother who had plowed into him, applying compresses to his head. He focused his eyes with difficulty on the faces of his three sons, each in turn. He stretched his arm to his forehead to find a lump there the size of a *pallino*, the smallest ball used in the game of bocce.

"Hey, Papa! That was some mule that kicked you! Madonna, what a cabbage you've got sprouting in the middle of your forehead." The father, remembering his fall, smiled wanly and attempted to lift himself up.

"Lie still, *signore*. Do not cause the blood to rush, or the head will pound and the swelling will increase." The grateful peasant woman whose child Michele had saved from serious hurt, gently pushed the boys' father down. In her hand were several slices of raw potato. She placed them across Giuseppe's brow.

"Lie still now. Let the potato draw away the pain and the swelling." Giuseppe acquiesced. He knew the efficacy of the traditional peasant remedy for headache. He closed his eyes.

"Go, boys. I will watch over your father. My bambino is sleeping. Go up and get some fresh, good air into the lungs. See the glory of God's new day after the storm."

With a sense of relief, Francesco and Michele, supporting, or rather, carrying their brother between them, negotiated their way among the general disarray of the quarters and the slops. Ultimately they reached the top of the stairwell and stepped out onto the deck.

Here it was heaven. The sea was calm. People were sitting everywhere, chatting and smiling, glad to be alive. Many of them had thought during the storm that their last hour had come. Just as the trio of brothers gained access to the open deck, Feliciano swooped down on them and lifted the limp Alfredo out of his brothers' arms. He brought him to the railing, opened Alfredo's collar, and with one hand around the boy's waist, he forced open the boy's mouth. "Breathe in, my boy. In, out. Suck in the fresh air." Slowly Alfredo began to revive. His color returned a little. He lifted his arms and grasped the railing. He gave a weak smile to his brothers.

"Gesu," he muttered, "I thought I was going to die."

"Ah, my boy," Feliciano said. "The sea must never be taken for granted. With one hand she caresses, and with the other she whips and lashes—like a mama." He smiled and winked. Francesco began to giggle at the old man's remark. Then with a serious look on his face, the old sailor continued. "You have seen the dark side of the sea, just as you will see the dark side of this America that you and all of these hopefuls believe to be a land of milk and honey, with arms outstretched to welcome you.

"The sea looks beautiful now, does it not? But beneath these waters, there is turmoil. The big fish are eating the little fish. The shark darts out and rips apart the unwary porpoise. The waters beneath are churning and bubbling. Nothing is at peace in the depths of the sea—nor on land, nor in life. Soon your eyes will gaze upon the Statue of Liberty in *Nuova York*, and you will think, 'This blessed America embraces me and will take me to her bosom.' But I tell you this: many a paesano have I taken to these shores, coming with hope and fantasies in his heart. And many have I returned to Italy because they found not love, but hate in this America." The old man broke out in a sarcastic laugh. "Streets paved with gold. Bah! Streets not even paved is what you will find. The *Americani* will expect you to pave the streets, and will despise you for doing it. You do not know yet what a guinea, a dago is. You will soon learn."

He looked sadly at them and turned his gaze beyond them to the others on the decks. Shaking his head, he began to walk away. "I must return to my duties. The boy will be all right now. A little more of this fresh air will bring him around." And then he was lost in the mass of humanity now crowding every inch of the open decks. The boys looked after him as he disappeared into the throng. Then they looked at one another, perplexed at Feliciano's words.

When they later made their way below deck, they found Papa on his feet and no worse off for the lump on his head. Life aboard ship resumed, and the boys forgot the somber words of their old friend. As the steamer neared its destination in the coming days, an atmosphere of gaiety took hold again with each passing day that brought them closer to the golden door.

During the bright daylight hours on deck, the passengers gathered together in groups to sing and listen to the music of mandolins and accordions. The sound of laughter and chatter was everywhere. With the realization that the ordeal of the crossing was almost over, a mood of excitement and thrill, intermingled with apprehension, touched them all. The time of fulfillment was about to dawn.

At last, tomorrow they would step on the golden shore of America. The Lady with the Lamp, with her promise of liberty and opportunity would be there to greet them. Tomorrow—the nineteenth day of April in the year 1906.

Chapter Seven

The voyage was over. Fifteen days of travail, of crowding, of stench, of seasickness, of confinement were at an end at last.

That morning found the whole horde of immigrants packed tightly together on every deck, eager to glimpse the fabled statue and shores of the new world. Preceded by slow-moving tugboats, the immigrant ship finally berthed at a pier. From there, open ferry boats shuttled the human cargo to Ellis Island, for some, to be the Island of Hope, for others, the Island of Heartbreak. All the immigrants anticipated with anxiety, dread even, the process that awaited them there, before they could step foot on the gold-paved streets of their new world. They had already heard about the examinations and the questionings, that would determine their destiny. If they should not pass—oh, Lord! If they should not be deemed worthy of entry—oh, awful, too awful to think about. To have come all this way across the vast ocean, only to be turned back, caused many an immigrant's heart to pound.

Blissful in their ignorance of the hatred many Americans felt towards them, their only concern was the ordeal that lay ahead. The vast numbers of them were unknowing of the undercurrents of animosity beginning to emerge in the minds of the Americans, who looked in alarm at the ever-increasing tide of the "huddled masses" flooding their shores. More and more, Americans were referring to the new immigrants, especially the immigrants from southern and eastern Europe as "steerage slime," "disease-ridden parasites," "anarchists."

More and more, the ugly finger of prejudice and bigotry began to point derisively at these teeming thousands of newcomers beginning to throng the cities of the eastern seaboard of the United States. These new arrivals were not like the pristine Anglo-Saxon types of the previous waves of immigrants. The newspapers of Boston, Baltimore and New York were raising the alarm—beware, America!—Catholics, Jews, Slavs and dark-complexioned peoples from the Mediterranean and the Balkans with their alien ways, posed a threat to the American way of life, the papers screamed. The tide had to be turned!

So, increasing numbers of the "undesirable refuse" of Europe among the new arrivals, found themselves being detained, rejected as unfit for one reason or another, and ultimately returned to their native lands. How many such unfortunates would there be from the ship that docked on April 19, 1906? The moment of truth was soon to be upon them all.

Tagged on their lapels with numbers that matched those on the ship's manifest, Giuseppe and his sons were brought to the customs wharf. There, all the immigrants, tightly gripping their baggage, piled into the immense hall of the reception building. Other ships as well, were disgorging their human cargo, so that a babel of languages flooded the hall in a discordant symphony of alien sounds.

Iron railings divided the huge hall into compartments and sections, much like the cattle pens at the slaughter houses. In time, at the urgings of shouting officials, this mass of dazed humanity organized itself into a semblance of order. Confused and fearful, the immigrants took their places in the lines that began filing towards the stations where doctors were waiting to examine them. At the first station, the doctors gave a perfunctory and hurried glance in order to spot any obvious deformity or skin disease. Anyone suspected of having defects of skin or body was then marked with chalk on the lapel or blouse and set aside in special holding areas for later and more detailed examination.

At the second station, Giuseppe and his sons, in a line composed only of male immigrants, had to lower their trousers and expose their genitals. They watched in both amazement and embarrassment as the doctor, his hand gloved in rubber, poked and squeezed scrotums and penises. Here, the doctors marked anyone suspected of having a hernia or a venereal disease with the letter "K", and then shunted him off to another area.

Francesco had been completely bewildered by the procedure he had just undergone. In fact, the others were just as perplexed, if not embarrassed. Many, never having been to a doctor before, and never having experienced such an intimate examination of their bodies, had visibly felt a little uncomfortable. After buttoning up his pants, the young boy caught up with his older brothers and blurted out: "Why did the man touch my *cazzo* and my *coglioni*?"

"To see if they're big enough to make babies," Michele snickered. Alfredo let out a laugh, and Francesco's face turned red. His own nascent awareness of sex was already in force. He knew well enough that what hung between his legs, was not just for peeing. He had seen animal matings enough to know how babies were made, that males and females touched and joined. And so, the man-doctor's touching him, left him puzzled. But he had no more time to ponder the strange occurrence; the line he was in was proceeding sharply to the right, and he must not get lost from his brothers. Soon he found himself along with them in the presence of yet another doctor, the one most feared. It was at this station, that so many poor souls met their Waterloo, and were declared unfit to go ashore.

Before Francesco was aware of what was happening to him, a portly, bald-headed doctor had swiftly caught one of his eyelids with his dirty thumb. Brusquely lifting the whole eyelid upward, the man peered into the boy's naked eye. For a brief moment the boy felt a sting, and makings of a tear, moistened the green iris, so that it sparkled brightly. Quickly the other eye, and Francesco was pushed forward, passing female attendants, standing by with towels and chipped, white basins that held disinfectants.

The doctor had been looking for evidence of trachoma, the highly communicable eye infection that so often led to blindness. The slightest suspicion of an immigrant having it, was sufficient reason for detention. In an open enclosure to the side of the doctor, a large number of unhappy, forlorn immigrants, mostly Jewish men, sat dejectedly on benches. Several of the women among them sobbed pathetically. One of these internees, a woman holding a child on her lap, looked up just as Michele was passing by. Immediately he recognized her, and she, him. It was Signora Torloni, the woman who had nursed his father's injury after she had caused Giuseppe to fall against the bunk during the storm.

"Oh, Don Michele. Look what they say. They say my Pasqualino's eyes are diseased. But the eyes are only red and puffy from so much crying. Babies cry, babies cry. Do not American babies cry also? Will they let us enter? Oh, *Dio mio, Dio mio!*" Before Michele could utter one word of comfort, he was unceremoniously shoved forward by the crush of those in line behind him. The sharp shouts of an official in uniform goaded the others to push relentlessly ahead. Packed together as they were, they all looked like so many animals in the stockyard chutes; Michele had to move with the flow.

Overworked immigration officials, understaffed and overwhelmed by the sheer number of immigrants, inevitably began to succumb to indifference and frustration. The incomprehensible babel, the confusion, the press of seemingly endless throngs of these foreigners had all contributed toward dulling the sensibilities of many an official who often performed his inspection, or interrogation with differing degrees of callousness or harshness. After hours of waiting, after hours of being shoved and herded, the immigrants themselves were in various states of shock that often bordered on panic. By the time they were divided by nationality for questioning by officials and interpreters, many had become so confused and tongue-tied they could barely respond to questions intelligently.

Giuseppe and his sons answered well; there was no danger of their being classified as idiots or public charges. Giuseppe made it clear that they had money in their pockets, that his brother's home on Elizabeth Street would shelter them. And so it was that Giuseppe Alanga, Michele Alanga, Alfredo Alanga, and Francesco Alanga came through the labyrinthine confusion of the processing procedures and were able to walk onto the floor of the Great Hall and into the arms of Matteo. America was theirs.

Chapter Eight

Zio Matteo, ruggedly handsome in his dark navy-blue pin striped suit and black bowler kissed first his brother, then his nephews. Again and again. Their first encounter took place at the aptly named Kissing Post, where the new arrivals, after the hell they had been through, greeted for the first time, the friends and relatives that had been waiting for them so anxiously.

"Brother mine, brother mine," first Giuseppe repeated, and then Matteo. There were tears in their eyes, tears of joy that mingled on their faces. It was minutes before the brothers disengaged themselves from their embrace.

Michele and Alfredo could faintly remember their uncle, but Francesco, still a toddler when Matteo left Italy, had no recollection of him. Nevertheless, this was his uncle, whom he embraced with sincere warmth of feeling. Zio Matteo pressed each one of his nephews in turn to his chest in a crushing bear hug.

"What fine young men, these sons of yours are, my brother. But come, take up your things, and let us leave this place. My Graziella awaits us with food and drink. We have much to say to each other, Giuseppe. At home we can eat and drink and talk." Matteo took his brother's hand, but then abruptly he stopped and just looked into his brother's face. "But what is it, brother mine?" Giuseppe asked with a little tremor in his voice. "Is something wrong, is something the matter?"

"No, no, nothing. It is just that it is hard to believe that my brother is here again by my side. So many years, so many years. His emotion spent, Matteo, broke into a reassuring smile, and he began pushing his way through the crowd of people making their way to the exits. In a short while, Matteo, his brother and his nephews in tow, made their way to the ferry boat that took them to the city. Once landed, a stream of seemingly mad people engulfed them as they walked along the street. People were laughing, people were embracing, people were crying, people were jabbering, all in a medley of strange tongues.

Through his command of English, Matteo was able to engage a hack. He, his brother and the boys all climbed in, and soon the old nag's clippety-clop brought them away from the Battery and along the streets towards Canal Street and the Lower East Side of Manhattan.

Nothing in their wildest imaginings had prepared the newly arrived immigrants for the sights they were seeing as they journeyed to their new home on this warm, April evening. Deeper and deeper the hack rode into the East Side, passing row after row of tenement houses. To Giuseppe and his sons the houses seemed to be stuck together, side by side. Their fronts were broken only by dirty windows hung with dingy curtains and brownstone stoops. Giuseppe marveled to think that these were the habitations of humans, even though he could see people moving about through the windows, and some entering and leaving doorways. Where were the balconies festooned with flowers, or the delicate loggias trellised and grilled? On the streets, everything seemed to be jumbled together—people, wagons, pushcarts, dogs, horses.

"Those are the Hebrews." Matteo pointed to the knots of black-coated, black-hatted merchants and their customers hovering and gesticulating in the doorways of the many store fronts. The dry-goods they were selling hung on racks and poles strung along the sidewalks. A sea of earlocks flapped and bounced whenever these people moved. Giuseppe and his sons had never in their lives seen a Jew; the only one they had ever heard of was Jesus.

Matteo laughed at the looks of wonderment he saw on the faces of the boys as they took in all these strange sights and sounds of the streets. "Don't worry, you will get used to everything in this America. There are people here from every nation and race in the world. There are even black people that look like they are covered with tar. And then there are the yellow people that look like they all have the jaundice. And sometimes all these colors mix, and only God knows what you come up with—a *fritto misto*." They burst out in laughter, one and all, and when they had finished, Matteo blurted out: "Look, we are coming in to our own kind." They had arrived in "Little Italy." Familiar sounds and smells hit them with refreshing comfort. A group of women and children were gathered together around a hurdy-gurdy player grinding out the strains of *O Sole Mio*. And the street vendors, some in the dialect of Sicily, and some in Neapolitan, were yelling out in praise of their wares.

Everywhere here, it seemed like market day back in Bosco. Women, a few of them still in old-country dress, were haggling and bargaining with the vendors. Pairs of men in animated conversation were walking arm in arm, just as the men did in the old country. Here and there a violent oath or swear word rang out above the noise of the street.

The hack stopped with a jolt. Matteo jumped down in front of a monstrous brown tenement house as indistinguishable as a pea in a pod, from all the others they had passed. "Here we are, home." Store fronts flanked a staircase that led up to a heavy door that gave entrance to the railroad-room flats on either side of long hallways. The boys and their father hoisted their bundles onto their shoulders, following Zio Matteo into a dark hallway and up the flight of stairs.

It was now the supper hour, and familiar smells of sauce and garlic and frying oil hit them deliciously as they passed apartments. From closed doors along the way, the muffled voices of gruff men, shrill women, or crying babies echoed into the halls. At last the climb came to an end on the third floor. Midway down the hallway, Matteo stopped abruptly, then pushed open a door.

Two little kids, a boy of seven and a little girl of five, rushed to him with excited cries of "Papa, Papa." Matteo, the others close behind him, scooped up the children into his arms, and kissed them. At the same time he called out to his wife: "Graziella, Graziella, come. See my brother and my nephews. They are here."

An attractive, tall woman, wiping her hands on her apron came out of the pantry off the kitchen to where the men were all standing. Smiling, she extended her arms and was soon embracing Giuseppe and his sons. "*Benvenuti, benvenuti.* What a joy to have my Matteo's brother and his sons in my house. At last!" This was the first time that Giuseppe had ever laid eyes on his sister-in-law. She was a delicately formed, pink-skinned madonna whose face was framed by long tresses of deep red hair woven into braids. She was not Neapolitan; she had come to America from a small village in the mountains of the Liri Valley southeast of Rome. In that region, many of the women were red-heads. When she spoke, her accent was Roman, but not incomprehensible to Giuseppe.

Matteo plunked his son into Giuseppe's arms. "Well, now, my little Matteo, kiss your uncle and your cousins who have come all the way from Italy to be with you. Here, you too, Marietta." After the frenzy of kissing and embracing was over, Matteo broke in, grabbed his brother and nephews and herded them to the table in the center of the kitchen. A large silver-plated tray covered with bottles of wine and sweets sat atop a brightly printed tablecloth of red and white squares. He began filling glasses. "Come. We drink to my brother and my nephews. May they have good fortune in their new land. Raise your glasses and drink." A little later, Graziella left the men to their conversation and began busying herself in the pantry with plates and cutlery.

"Uncle," It was Alfredo who spoke. "I have not emptied myself since this morning, and nature is now pressing for relief. Be so kind as to show me where I can make water. "He smiled, and everyone else grinned, too, because they all felt the same need.

"Ah, *o baccauso. Si, si.*" Although the word sounded Italian, it was a new one to Giuseppe and the boys. In reality, it was the Italianization of the word, "backhouse." It was the one of the first new words that Alfredo learned in the new land. Zio Matteo led them out of the flat, down the back stairs and into the backyard. They followed him towards a wooden shed. Within a few feet of it, their noses told the boys what this place was. Matteo pushed open the door and called them in. Although it was dark inside, enough light came through the open slots between walls and ceilings to allow them to see a long bench with three holes cut into the top plank.

"There, boys, there's where it all goes in. Those pieces of paper there, you use to wipe your asses, if that business is your need."

Matteo and his brother walked out, leaving the three boys to relieve themselves. Immediately the three of them unbuttoned their trousers and pissed into the reeking holes, almost in concert.

"Jesus, what a stink!" exclaimed Alfredo above the sound of the continuing splash echoing from the bottom of the cesspool.

"Remember, brother mine, this is not a rose garden," rejoined Michele. And a long "aaah" escaped from Francesco's lips.

At length their flowing stopped. Each one shook himself and buttoned up. They stepped out and the older men entered. In a short while Zio Matteo emerged alone. "Your father had to sit, boys. There is the pump to wash our hands," and he pointed to the fence. When everyone had done with a quick rinse of water over their hands, they made their way back up to the flat.

"Matteo, take them to the sink and let them wash their hands and faces with soap and water. Then come to eat, all of you, for supper is ready." And as she spoke, Graziella walked by them with a huge tureen of steaming pasta on her way to the big kitchen table. Behind her, trailed little Marietta, with a smile on her face, balancing a long tray with sliced bread on it.

Within a few minutes the men came to the table. They looked at the laden table, so covered with good things to eat, that it seemed to buckle under the weight of the food. The meal of banquet proportions, was a noisy, joyous affair, monopolized mainly by Matteo talking about America, about work, about his wife and children. Only rarey did he mention the old country, and this struck Giuseppe as strange.

When supper was ended, Graziella cleared the table and brought out a tray and set it down. On it was the familiar shaped Italian coffee pot, the *machinetta*, filled with the dark, bitter coffee that was drunk in little cups. Alongside stood the companion bottle of clear, licorice-tasting anisette used to flavor the coffee instead of sugar. Aunt Graziella filled each of the demi-tasse cups, while Uncle Matteo uncorked the bottle. He added some of the liqueur to his own cup and handed the anisette to his brother, who in turn passed it to the boys.

"Graziella, please, the children. Wash them and get them to their beds. I must talk now of a heavy matter to my brother and his sons." Zio Matteo's voice had a note of urgency in it that his wife understood. She shooed the children to the sink, and soon the splashing of water could be heard and the raucous outcries of little Matteo as his mother washed him. While Graziella washed the children, the men around the table continued to sip the coffee, and when the children were clean, their mother led them away. Matteo rose, and closed the door after them. Returning to the table, still standing, he said gravely, "I have some bad news to tell you."

Chapter Nine

Four puzzled faces studied Matteo, and as the men began to rise from their seats, Matteo gestured them to sit. He reached into his shirt pocket and pulled out a short, crooked cigar, the kind the Americans called "guinea stinkers." He lit it and pulled out another from his pocket and gave it to his brother. Soon both cigars were giving off wisps of blue-gray smoke and the acrid smell of strong tobacco.

Matteo walked into the pantry and came out carrying a stack of newspapers. They were copies of *La Tribuna*, dating from the last two weeks. "Giuseppe, brother mine, I know that you do not read, therefore, I give them to Alfredo. I know from the good hand that he writes, that he reads as well. A screaming headline on one of the newspapers, in thick, black print, hit the young man's gaze with the force of a lightning bolt:

LA TRIBUNA, APRIL 8, 1906 ITALY HIT BY EARTHQUAKE. VESUVIUS ERUPTS. VILLAGES OBLITERATED. HUNDREDS DEAD!

The youth's hand trembled as he read. His brother Michele lunged to his side to glimpse a picture showing the ruins of houses and rubble in the streets of Ottaviano, a town some ten miles from Bosco, on the eastern slope of the mountain. "Papa! It was virtually a scream that Alfredo hurled at his father. "By the holy blood of Christ, a catastrophe has taken place. Our region is destroyed!"

"But what are you saying?" Giuseppe's color drained from his face. He stared fixedly and piercingly at his son, as if to wrench words of explanation from the boy's mouth. For the next half hour, Alfredo scanned the papers, spitting out the headlines in clipped sentences and phrases that told the tragic story. From Alfredo's reading, they learned of the total destruction that Vesuvius had wrought for a week upon the villages lying at its base. Whole villages, Alfredo read, had been wiped out by ash and lava. Even in Naples they had felt the panic. Fourteen people were crushed to death there in the Mount Oliveto market.

But that was nothing to the destruction and deaths suffered in the villages hugging the slopes and at the foot of the volcano. In San Giuseppe Vesuviano, the cathedral had fallen in upon two hundred souls who had sought refuge within its thick walls. Ottaviano, a little beyond, also suffered heavily; four feet of ash had choked the town, and five churches and ten houses had fallen in. Some fifty people had lost their lives there.

"And of Boscotrecase, my son. What does the paper say of our village. Giuseppe asked tensely in a whisper.

"Papa, our village is no more. Boscotrecase, San Giuseppe and Ottaviano, all are leveled."

Giuseppe began to moan. "I should have known, I should have known. The smoke, the fish in the Sarno, the animals. I should have known. Blessed God! While we were on the sea, Mama and the girls, all our family, Matteo, were in the midst of it all, alone without us." The boys' father reeled a bit and covered his face with his hands. Francesco's eyes welled up with tears, and Michele gazed somberly at the wall; images of his mother, his sisters, and Adelina flashed one after another like so many stereopticon slides before his eyes.

Then Zio Matteo spoke: "I've read these papers over and over again. It says somewhere that the authorities evacuated hundreds of people out of harm's way to the south in time. To Castellammare and even farther. Remember what our dear mother, *buonanima*, used to say, Giuseppe. 'All is destiny.' Tomorrow I will not go to Job; you and I will go to the Italian consulate. Just Saturday I was there, but they had no names yet of the," and he hesitated, "of the dead. There the officials confirm only what the papers say, that some five hundred souls have perished. For now, we can do nothing but wait and hope for the best.

"This is not the welcome that I had in my heart for you. But we are Neapolitans. We live with hope. A man's luck changes from bad to good from one day to the next. The hour is late. You are all tired. Come, I will show you where you sleep."

Matteo put his arms around his brother and his nephew Michele, and began walking across the room. He led them all from the kitchen and through his own bedroom where he and his wife slept. The room was dark, but eerie shadows flickered on the walls. A votive candle was burning before a statue of Saint Anthony. They could see the form of Graziella lying in bed as they tip-toed through the room. In a minute they were in the next room in line. There, little Matteo and his sister were asleep in one bed. "Francesco, you will sleep there," and his uncle pointed to a single bed against the wall. "The kids are small, only babies yet. They can sleep together." It was obvious that little Matteo had had to relinquish his bed to his cousin from across the sea. The children's arms were locked around each other's necks; they were fast asleep.

The last of the railroad rooms, the one used for storage and for Aunt Graziella's sewing, had been converted into sleeping quarters for Giuseppe and the two older boys. A big, metal bedstead dominated the room, but left space for a cot neatly made up, and a wooden chest of drawers.

"Arrange yourselves as you wish. Rest. Sleep. One day brings sorrow, another, joy. Tomorrow the sun rises on a new day." Matteo turned away quietly and left them. *"Buona notte."*

"Buona notte, Zio Matteo."

Spurts of light from a gas jet cast elongated shadows upon the walls. The boys' father waved Michele and Alfredo to the big bed. He took off his jacket and shirt and placed them on a chair. He extinguished the gas jet, and the room darkened. Within a few minutes the two brothers were under the covers of the double bed, and their father on the cot.

"Buona notte, Papa."

"Buona notte, my sons."

A pall of silence settled on the room, only broken now and then, as first one, then another turned fitfully in bed. All of them lay awake for a long time, each one wrestling with his somber thoughts.

Chapter Ten

In the early hours of the next morning, even before the first light of day appeared, Giuseppe felt his brother's hand gently shaking his shoulder.

"I'm awake, Matteo. My thoughts did not permit sleep."

"As I knew they would not. Arise, we will eat something and I will take you Uptown. There, God willing, we may learn something new, some new information."

Through the darkness, the voice of Alfredo broke out in a whisper: "Zio Matteo, we would also go with you, Michele and I. We cannot wait here, sitting on our hands. May we not be permitted to accompany you and Papa?"

"Yes," their father answered. "These are two men, Matteo. We will all go to confront what we must, or good, or bad."

In the silence of the dark room, the three men dressed. In minutes they were in the kitchen where Aunt Graziella already had a pot of coffee brewing. When the men entered the kitchen, they found her cutting thick slices of crusty bread from a huge, round loaf. The four took places around the table as she placed small bowls in front of each one. Then she filled the bowls half with coffee and half with milk. The mound of bread soon dwindled as each one dipped his slices into his coffee and ate them.

A quick trip to the *baccauso*, a hasty washing at the sink, and a more careful combing of hair at the mirror hanging on the kitchen door, and the men were ready to leave. As they passed through the hallways on their way down the flights of stairs, they could hear the sounds of muted voices behind closed doors. They met one boy carrying out a slop pail to empty in the backhouse.

It was six o'clock now, and on the street a few vendors were already setting their carts in order. A few wagons lazily rumbled over the cobblestones. "Ah, the air feels good, eh? Fresh and clean. But, by the evening it will be full of dust and smells," Matteo said as he walked down the steps of the stoop. His companions were following behind him. They began walking down the street, passing more and more men—

some alone, some in groups of three or four. The workers were carrying pick axes or shovels over their shoulders. These were laborers on the way to Job. With all of them, Matteo exchanged a "*buon giorno.*"

"*Ue, Mattevone* (Big Matt). All dressed up? You do not go to Job today?" A big, barrel-chested man came up to them, his arm raised in greeting.

"*Ue, Turriddu.* Here, meet my brother, Giuseppe, my nephews. They are just off the boat."

Hands were extended and clasped all around.

"A pleasure."

"A pleasure." And so it went, until everyone had exchanged salutations.

"No, Turriddu. Today I do not go to Job. I take these to the consulate. Perhaps today there will be some news of the fate of our family."

"Ah, si. I feel for you, my friends. My heart is with you; I hope good tidings come your way today." As he was speaking, the Sicilian was nodding his head up and down as a sign of sympathy and commiseration. Then suddenly changing the tone of his voice, and with a smile on his face, he continued: "And when do you bring these strapping fellows to Job, Mattevone? They look like good men, the kind of "dagoes" Crowley likes, that shameless '*mbriacone* (drunkard). He spat out a vehement stream of spit into the gutter. "In your face, you bastard," directing both his spit and his curses to Crowley, as if the man were standing in front of him.

Then he turned to Matteo. "You know, Matteo, the paesani are digging deeper and deeper into the earth on Job, and he does not allow enough timber or time for proper shoring. Always, 'Faster, faster.' Would that a knife in his ribs push him faster to his grave, the boss-man, Crowley."

"I know what you are saying, Turriddu. His manner is the same with us who work with the cement. He pushes as if the hounds of hell were nipping at his heels. We get our asses kicked to move faster, to pour more footings in a day. It is the same with the work gangs on the scaffolds. 'Up, up,' he cries, and the stuff on the bottom is hardly firm yet." Matteo's voice was husky with scorn.

Shaking his head, he began walking away. "Ciao, Turriddu. Work awaits you, and the consulate, us." The two co-workers clapped each other on the back and went on their respective ways.

Chapter Eleven

As they approached the consulate, the Alangas saw crowds of people exiting the building. Some were excitedly waving sheets of white paper. "The lists-are in!" shouted Matteo. The four men broke into a run. In a minute, they were pushing their way into the crowd. All around them, they heard shouts of joy from some throats, and sobs of grief from others. One woman, tears streaming down her cheeks, let fall her paper. Alfredo scooped it up so deftly, that his arm and leg movements resembled the graceful arc of a ballerina.

His father and the others flanked him. Alfredo uncrumpled the sheet, and four pairs of eager eyes concentrated their gaze on that fateful print. Four columns of the names of the dead filled the sheet from top to bottom under the headings of the towns from which they came. Quickly Alfredo scanned the names from Boscotrecase under the letter "A." No Alangas.

"Thanks be to God. Papa, none of ours are among the dead."

Michele's eyes were riveted on the "S's," as he looked for the name Scarpa, his Adelina's family name. He breathed a sigh of relief. Then all four men drew off to the side. Now they scrutinized the lists more slowly. And as they read, they began to recognize the names of close friends and acquaintances who had perished.

"*Miseria*. Three of the Gentiles—mother, father and daughter, Virginia."

"Look here. Old Saverio, the cart-driver."

"And here. Aunt Teresina's son-in-law."

"What black luck for Bosco." The remark escaped from Alfredo's lips and was reiterated by all of the saddened men. Alfredo continued to read off more names of those they knew from Boscotrecase and the surrounding countryside.

"Let's go home now." Uncle Matteo, spoke. One of his hands he rested gently on his brother's shoulder, and the other took the death list from his nephew's grasp. "Francesco will want to know, and Graziella." Following on each other's heels, the four of them made their way out of the crowd.

"Now we must wait news from those in Italy," Alfredo said. "You will see, Papa, soon something will come from them, a letter, to let us know of their safety and their condition." His voice rang with a note of confidence and relief.

The four men turned homeward with a lively spring in their steps that reflected a sense of relief and encouragement. In their minds, they could picture now, Mama and the girls, alive. But now and again, dark images of ruined houses and dead friends jarred their happy thoughts, and joy was momentarily dispelled.

A crush of pedestrians and conveyances now filled the streets, for it was close to the noon hour. The closer the men came to home, the thicker the mass of humanity. The streets were teeming. People, horses, wagons, dogs, all making a veritable maelstrom of sound and motion. Matteo stopped at one of the pushcarts, gave the vendor a few coins, and soon he and the others were crunching hard, roasted chickpeas and fava beans from paper cones.

They walked at a leisure pace as they ground the rock-hard, salted beans between their teeth. The boys were busy taking in and commenting to each other on all the strange things they were seeing, while the two older men talked about the old country. Giuseppe brought his brother up to date on all the events that had happened to all the members of the family during Matteo's ten years absence. Who had married, who had been born, who had died. When at length, Giuseppe finished relating the happenings of the past, it was Matteo's turn to enlighten his brother and his nephews about the here and now. The past was over and done with; it was the realities of the present that would determine the future of their lives in this new, different world to which they had come.

Matteo began: "The most important thing here is Job. In America, without Job, you are nothing. In America, boys, Job is life; it is the food you eat, the clothes you wear, the house in which you live, the bed in which you sleep. So, tomorrow, I take you to Job."

The boys stopped talking and got closer to their uncle.

Zio Matteo continued. "Everything has been arranged. A week before you arrived I settled everything with the big boss of Job." Then he broke into a laugh. "He smokes a fat cigar, and when he's drunk, he's halfway human. When he is sober, he is a son of a bitch to all the greenhorns, the immigrants like you, and especially to the paesani. But he tolerates me because I speak good English and act as interpreter for him. So, now you have Job.

"Giuseppe, you will lay bricks with me. Michele, you will carry the hod on the boards. You will not be afraid of the heights, my boy? Alfredo, you will work with Turriddu digging and hauling. You are young and strong, and hard work is not a stranger to you, I know from the looks of you two. You, me, all of us, we will work like jackasses, but on payday the money in your hands will ease all the aches and pains of your backs and arms.

"On Job, we are all brothers. Neapolitans, Calabrians, Sicilians, we are all brothers. We all labor the same, and sweat the same. But in the end, it is our own bread we eat, and no man here can take it from us. Realize that if you are wise, you can fill your bellies and still be able to put money aside. And that is just what I have done. And you and your sons, Giuseppe, can do the same, and lead an easy life."

"An easy life, uncle? By working like a jackass—your very words?" A wry smile curved Alfredo's lips.

"In Italy, my boy, the jackass, at the end of his travail, receives a handful of oats. Here the jackass receives a handful of dollars. And when one does not eat all the dollars, a pile of them grows and swells like oats when wet. And like good oats planted in good ground, dollars," and here Matteo tapped his forehead for emphasis, "invested wisely will bring in a good harvest. With my hand on my heart, I swear to you that I know of what I speak. Heed well my words, and one day, you will say: Zio Matteo is a wise man, a man of vision."

Alfredo, more out of curiosity than sarcasm, asked his uncle: "And where is it that we put our dollars so that they multiply like the loaves and fishes the good Christ so wondrously increased? And what do you see in this vision of yours?"

"You put your extra dollars in a bank, my boy, a bank; and there you let your dollars sit, and the more they sit, the more you get in return. For letting the bank use your dollars to make more dollars for the bank, when it comes time that you go to the bank and say, 'I want my money now,' the bank gives you not only your original sum, but it adds to it what is called interest! That is, the money the bank pays you for the use of your money. And then you buy a piece of land, and a house that is one's own. That is the vision that I have, to have a house just for me and mine. A place with flowers and a garden where I can plant my tomatoes and peppers, a place where my children will have a place to play, off the streets, where we can all sit under our own arbor and eat and drink during the warm evenings of spring and summer. In a

51

beautiful city with trees and squares, away from the madness of this place. Such a place exists. It is called New..."

Before he could finish, little Marietta rushed into her father's arms from the sidewalk where she had been playing. "Papa, you're home! "I'm so glad." Matteo lifted up his daughter and swung her around in a circle. She screamed in delight as he twirled her faster and faster. He gave her a big hug and put her down. It was past noon now, and quite warm. The smell of food wafting through open windows reminded them of their own hunger. When the four of them entered the flat, Francesco and his aunt were just finishing their lunch of fried potatoes and eggs. Little Matteo jumped up from the table and ran to his father, and Graziella got up and rushed to set places for the men, while her husband recounted the events of the morning at the consulate.

When the lunch was over, Alfredo began penning a letter to his mother. Giuseppe dictated and the boy wrote. As soon as he had finished writing the address on the envelope, Zio Matteo took it carefully from his hands. "I will take it and mail it," he said. "And God speed it on its way. May it find your mama and sisters safe and whole."

As soon as their uncle returned from his errand, he urged his three young nephews to explore their surroundings. "It is a beautiful day, nephews. Go to the street. Become familiar with your new home, America." Willingly the three of them got up and left, to see for themselves the wonders of Elizabeth Street and its neighborhood. After the door closed behind them, Matteo beckoned his brother to follow. With a jug of wine and two glasses in his hands, he walked down the back stairs of the tenement into the backyard. A high, wooden fence with many slats missing, enclosed a small patch of barren earth. The two men took a seat on a bench under a lone skeleton of a maple tree. The tree was a rare vestige of vegetation in a forest of stone and brick. To Giuseppe, the absence of anything green, anything growing, was the most alien feature of this place.

Reading his brother's mind, Matteo said, "Not even a tomato plant, eh?"

"Just so, brother mine. You read my thoughts. It is hard for a man of the soil like me not to smell, not to feel the freshness of the good earth between my hands."

Matteo smiled at his brother and handed him a glass of wine. "The day will come, I hope, Giuseppe, when all of us will leave this barren jungle of stone. You will see that America, too, has its places of beauty, its flowers and its green places. Listen, Giuseppe, and hear me out. Then tell me whether what I say to you now, is good or bad. I was not speaking foolishly when I said that it is possible for you and your sons to shape your own destiny in this country, such as would never be possible in the old country. Here, the man with dollars in his pocket is king.

"For ten years now, I have labored here, mingling my sweat into the mortar I mix. In the heat of these past ten summers my eyes were blinded by the salt of my sweat as I lugged brick and churned mortar. In the winters, the blood of my veins froze as I cleared the streets of snow. Many times, the boss of that Job kept the horse in the stable because of the cold; but me and the other paesani, he sent out into the cold. To him, a horse was worth more than the "guinea." You do not know this word, but you will get to hear it more than once. It is only one of the words of scorn the Americans use to show their contempt for us."

Giuseppe suddenly recalled his sons telling him what old Feliciano had told them of such words that the Americans used. Then, he did not know what such words signified and could not give his sons an explanation of them; now he knew.

Matteo waved his hand. "To me, such words are of little consequence. But, what is of consequence are the dollars. Upstairs in my bedroom I have a little book, a bank book. Every extra penny I get is recorded in that book, so that some day, I will have enough dollars to take my Graziella and my children away from this place. Eighty miles from here, there is a fine, beautiful, little city. Giuseppe, I tell you it is a good place to be. Many of our fellow countrymen live there. I have been there, at the house of my friend, Angelo.

"It is called New Haven; and Angelo has his own house. In the backyard of his house he has a garden with a grape arbor in it and a fig tree! Imagine! And on the street of this house there are trees, trees that shade the walks. All the streets are lined with trees. The air is fresh, and a sea breeze blows from the sea, not far away. And do you know, there is a piazza across the way from Angelo's house. And just as in the old country, the paesani play bocce on the grass, and their wives sit and talk, and their little ones play among the flowers and the trees."

"It seems a good place to live, this New Haven, a good place to bring my Rosa and my children someday. Matteo, brother mine, what I have seen of this New York, I do not like. Too many people, too dirty, no beauty. "Giuseppe said these things almost in a whisper. He did not wish to offend the feelings of his brother in whose home he was a guest, and on whose generosity and guidance he so completely depended.

Matteo filled his brother's glass anew.

"Drink, brother mine. I know the ache in your heart. One day I will tell you of the things I have suffered, alone in this strange country when I first came to these shores. I had no one of my blood, no friend to share my fears or relieve my loneliness. There were nights I wept like an abandoned child does. In the stinking hole of a room I rented below the ground, with only rats and cockroaches for company, I could only find peace by picturing in my mind all your faces. It was Mama's face, and Papa's, and yours, and our sisters' that gave me the courage to go on.

" I only took breath again when I found Graziella. She brought me life again. *Basta, basta,* enough of this talk. The past is dead. But the future is alive for us." Matteo clapped his hand on his brother's knee and stood up. "Tomorrow I take you to Job."

Chapter Twelve

Next morning four brown paper bags translucent with the oil stains seeping from the thick eggplant sandwiches inside, sat on the boards by the sink in the kitchen. The aroma of fresh coffee filled the room, and the silence was broken only by the movements of Graziella doing her chores. Outside, it was still dark, but a single gas jet set low, gave enough light inside.

One by one, the four working men of the house came into the kitchen, doused their faces with water at the sink in between *Buon giornos*, and sat at the table. Already, the bowls were in place. Soon Graziella poured the hot coffee into each one. The men poured in some milk and began dunking chunks of hard bread. When they finished, they got up from the table. Saying their good-byes, the four men left the flat.

At the work site, men were already in their gangs. Some were digging, some were pushing wheelbarrows, others were breaking stone, and some were hammering scaffolds together. Workers with hods on their shoulders were climbing ladders, and men on the scaffolds were pushing wheelbarrows along planks high above the ground.

Matteo led his brother and nephews across the work site and into a large tar-papered shack filled with foremen and straw bosses. These were getting their orders for the day from a florid, paunchy man chewing on a cigar. When the door opened, he turned and saw Matteo. "Ah, so these are your dago friends, eh Matty-o? Well now, they look like three hearty buckos."

Matteo turned to Giuseppe and said in Italian: "The fat bastard is half pickled already, first thing in the morning."

"They speak only the Eyetalian, eh Matty-o? Just off the boat? Well, now, you make sure they know what the hell they've got to do, and make sure they understand I'll have no shirkers here; they work or they're out on their asses. Capeesh? McBride, sign up these three greenhorns on the payroll. Put one of the lads in Turriddu's gang, the other one with Skinny Sal, carrying the hod. The old "ghee" will be working with Matty-o." He turned away and stuck the cigar back in his mouth.

Matteo went up to a little squirt of a man who was sitting at a battered, old roll-top desk. Papers and ledgers were scattered all over the desk top. All the pigeon holes were stuffed to overflowing with papers and blue-prints.

"Now, Matty, me boy, would ye be spelling out slowly their Eyetalian names. It's a devil of a time I have making sense out of all this dago palaver." The little gnome's blue eyes seemed to fill the whole of the thick lenses in the wire-rimmed glasses he wore high on his ruddy nose.

Matteo gave McBride the information, and he watched as the names were inscribed in the ledger, and alongside each name, the amount of the weekly salary:

Alanga, Alfredo—pick-man (starting) $4.25
Alanga, Giuseppe—bricklayer (starting) $5.50
Alanga, Michele—hod carrier (starting) $4.25

After watching the man's transcription into the book, like a hawk, Matteo walked away satisfied. In ten years' time, Matteo's command of spoken and written English had become good enough to get him by on Job, on the street, and in the market place. This skill gave him a decided advantage in his dealings with the *Americani*. Early on, he had perceived the benefits of learning to speak and understand the language. Unlike the majority of the first immigrants who obstinately clung to Italian to the exclusion of English, Matteo had enrolled in night school soon after arriving in America, so that now he was quite proficient in the use of English.

In the yard, Matteo brought Michele to Salvatore *'o Sicco*, (Skinny Sal), the straw boss of one of the gangs of hod carriers. The man was all limbs, and the outline of his sharp cheekbones was the most prominent feature of his bronzed face. The shape of each rib showed through the sleeveless undershirt he was wearing, stained with flecks of cement and the red dust of bricks.

"Don't be fooled by this bag of loose bones. He'll out-work ten men. He has more strength than an ox. No one can carry a heavier hod than Salvatore. He's strong in bed, too. He's got eight kids." Matteo laughed and clapped the scarecrow on the back.

Salvatore's gaunt face broke into a smile that pulled the skin of his cheeks even tighter across the bones. "Nine—in another six months, Mattevone. I no more than open the door of the bedroom, and *per Bacco*, my Maria's belly begins to swell. That's what comes from always having my *cazzuola* in hand." Everyone broke out in a fit of laughter at the pun;

for *cazzuola*, the word for trowel, is very close to the word, *cazzo*, slang for the male organ. Skinny Sal went on, "Beh! when a man feels the hardness of brick all day, it's nice to touch the softness of woman, not so, boys?"

Again the men gave out with a laugh, and when they had finished, Matteo reached up and clapped his hand on *'o Sicco's* shoulder. "This is my nephew, Michele Alanga, just over from the old country. He works with your gang. Take care of him. Show him the ropes. He's a good boy."

Salvatore extended a bony hand as large as a shovel, and he and Michele shook hands. "The boy's got a good grip, Matteo. He'll do; don't have a care." The straw boss turned and walked away, motioning Michele to follow.

Zio Matteo gave his nephew a slight push and started walking away with Giuseppe and Alfredo. Soon the three of them came to a wide excavation in the earth where men were digging and hauling away dirt. Everywhere, pickaxes and shovels were flailing the earth; scores of men were pushing wheelbarrows loaded with soil and rock up the length of planks from the bottom of the pit to the surface. The site was a beehive of motion. Loaded wheelbarrows struggled to the surface; empty ones whizzed back to the depths.

When Uncle Matteo spotted Turriddu, he brought Alfredo to him. Everyone was bare-chested; brown bodies glistened with sweat even though the early morning sun was not at its full force. Approaching the Sicilian, Matteo called out: "*Ue, Turridu.* This is my nephew Alfredo; he works with you. You met him the other day, remember?" Turriddu nodded and motioned for Alfredo to descend into the pit. And as Giuseppe and his brother walked away, the father glanced back to see his son removing his shirt.

Now, then, Job was theirs; from this day on, and all the days that would follow, it would be Job that held their destiny in its grip. Job—a thing to cherish; a thing to hate; a thing that brought laughter; a thing that brought tears, as Zio Matteo was wont to say.

The sun of this late day in April, was not the sun of springtime. As the day wore on, it blazed August-hot. The heat was cursed in accents Neapolitan, Calabrian, Sicilian.

"Hey, kid. Put your goddamn shirt on, or you'll fry, so that not even a witch's icy tit will soothe your burnt-up hide."

Alfredo turned to look alongside to a parallel plank. He saw the toothy smile of a youth only a couple of years older than himself.

"You're new on Job, eh?—a greenhorn. Just off the boat? I can tell. Your chest has the whiteness of the inside of a woman's thigh." Then the fellow pushed on ahead of him. When Alfredo reached the level of the surface with his barrow of dirt, the youth was already on his way down for another load. As he passed Alfredo again, he said, "Remember, keep your shirt on, kid. You've got to ease into getting toughened up."

"I will, paesano. Thanks."

Shortly after high noon, Alfredo heard a whistle blow; men dropped their shovels, picks and wheelbarrows, and began walking off in all directions. Some were wiping their faces with bandannas, or dusting themselves off; some were pissing into the sand where they stood. Alfredo stood looking about, when the young man who had spoken to him about not taking off his shirt, came up to him. "It's lunch break; we eat now. You got something to eat?" Alfredo nodded in reply.

"My name is Paolo La Rocca." The fellow extended his hand to Alfredo.

"Alfredo Alanga," and Alfredo grasped the outstretched hand of his newfound friend.

"*Piacere.*"

"*Piacere.*"

"Come on up to the top. You've only got a half an hour. This is not Italy, where one makes a banquet eating an onion and a piece of bread."

On the ground above the excavations, the workers squatted or sprawled under whatever shade they could find. Once on top, the two boys slumped to the ground next to a group of younger men, Paolo's intimates. Dusting off their hands, Alfredo and Paolo began biting into their sandwiches. As they were eating, they listened in between everyone's chuckles and guffaws of delight, to the tale being told by Rico. He was known throughout the whole gang as the "Stud." True to form, the "Stud" was regaling his listeners with another tale of his conquests.

"And when the old whore saw what I gave her younger sister, she pulled me down to the bed and she says: 'No charge, paesano,' and I brought her to ecstasy.." He nudged Tony sitting next to him. "You know the one, old blue-eyed 'Blondie,' the one with the big ears; who looks like a cabbage. I got two for the price of one."

"That's some bargain, as long as you don't wind up with the clap," joined in pimple-faced Gaetano.

"Or worse yet, a cabbage-faced baby with blue eyes and sails for ears. Kootchie, kootchie-koo, little Rico. You look just like your daddy," Tony added in between chews on his sandwich.

Even Rico exploded into laughter. Some of the guys choked and gagged on their food. When the laughter, choking and snickering died down, Paolo took the opportunity to introduce Alfredo to his co-workers. After the amenities and a few questions about where in the old country Alfredo came from, and about his family, the fellows resumed eating and chit-chatting among themselves. Alfredo turned away to look off in the distance. "I'm looking for my father and my brother," he told Paolo.

"If they're working in other gangs, you won't see them now. The different gangs take their lunch in shifts. So don't waste your time, but eat now. Soon enough we will be back in the pit."

The day went by, and at six o'clock in the evening, the quitting-time whistle blew. The first day on Job was over, a day that was to be like all the others to follow for Alfredo, his father, and his brother.

Chapter Thirteen

The four Alangas walked off the worksite together, each pair of brothers, arm in arm. They were happy to be all together again. The three initiates to Job were satisfied with themselves. They had tasted Job and knew that they could digest it. Whatever trepidations or uncertainties they had felt in anticipation of Job, had melted away in a confidence that renewed itself in each heart. Their muscles were sore; their backs ached, and their bodies stank. But it was a good smell— the smell of manly labor, honest labor, and they were not ashamed of it.

Walking along in the now cooler evening air of this unseasonably hot day, their weariness began to leave them. They chatted, laughed and joked about their first day on Job. Michele recounted how a couple of bricks had fallen off his hod and almost brained a fellow below who let out a stream of obscenities that would have caused hair to grow on Saint Anthony's bald pate.

"He waved his trowel at me from below, and I thought he was going to send it through the air like a dagger at me. He was a Sicilian but I understood him well enough when he began his litany of curses: *'Porca miseria!* watch what the son of a bitch you're doing, you clumsy jackass,' he shouted at me. And then Gino, who had taken me under his wing—he's a fellow Neapolitan—shouted back: 'Easy, easy. He's new, and a greenhorn.'

"'Well, if he can't hold on to the hod, let him go back and practice holding on to his mother's titty. What! am I to suffer a cracked skull and shed my red blood because he's green?' Then Gino says: 'But think! When your eyes roll back in your head, and the whites of your eyes are showing, we'll have the Italian flag, red, white and green!'"

"'Yeah! I'll be a fucking patriot, a dead one. What an honor!' And when he laughed at his own joke, I knew everything was going to be okay. I offered my apologies. Later we ate lunch together, me, him, and Gino. The Sicilian's name is Gesualdo, and he turned out to be a sociable fellow."

Alfredo quipped: "You sure know how to make a good impression, brother mine." They all caught the pun and were still laughing as they reached home.

All during supper the laughter and conversation continued. Only Francesco remained subdued. Aunt Graziella had enrolled him in school, and he was not happy about it. In a lull during the conversation, he blurted out: "Papa, I don't want to go to school. They put me in a room with all little piss-pants learning to read the alphabet. The kids are only six and seven years old, Papa. Let me go on Job, too. I can work and bring in some dollars, Papa. In Italy I worked; I herded the goats. I helped with sowing and reaping. I helped in the forge. I carried stone. I cut brush with the scythe, working side by side with my brothers in all their labors. Is it not so, Michele, Alfredo? Tell Papa."

The boy's father sat silent for a few moments, collecting his thoughts before he answered his young son.

"Tell me, Francesco, my son. Do you see goats anywhere here? And where is anything growing? What brush do you see to put a scythe to? There is no place on Job for a twelve year-old boy where your brothers and I work."

"But Papa......"

Alfredo cut off his kid brother with a light tap on the back of his head. "Listen to Papa, and go to school. Learn to speak and write and read English. In the end, that knowledge will mean dollars in your hands. In fact, as soon as I can, I will go to the night school my friend on Job has told me about. In the meantime, learn, so that you can help me."

"It's to school you go, and not to work. We will not talk of this again." Papa's tone of voice sounded the knell to any further discussion. When their father's voice had that hard edge to it, the boys knew from experience to let sleeping dogs lie. Giuseppe rose from the table, and he and Matteo left the flat to smoke a cigar and sip some wine in the back yard. When they had left, Zia Graziella slipped some coins into Michele's hand.

"Go," she said. "In the street you will find a vendor of *gelati*. Buy yourselves some lemon ice. Take little Matteo with you. He will enjoy both the treat and your company."

The child jumped up from his chair. Alfredo scooped him up in his arms, and soon they were all clattering down the stairs and onto the street.

"So, you're in with all the little piss-pants, eh, Francì? Well, in a way, that's an advantage. You'll be the only one that does not wet his pants when the teacher scowls."

"I have no head for books, Alfredo. You are the one for books, not me. Look how long it took Don Pio to teach me to write a few words in Italian. Holy God! He bruised my knuckles raw before I could write my name. And besides, if we all came to America to make money, why can't I make some too?"

"And what do you need money for? To buy a pocketful of caramels?"

"Soon I will be thirteen years old, big brother mine. Old enough to do my share to help bring Mama and our sisters here. I miss them so. Am I not old enough not to want a few coins in my pocket to jingle? Back home I never had two *centesimi* to rub together in my hand."

"Ho-ho. The little man hasn't been in America two weeks, and already he has the American gold fever. Or maybe you've already got your eye on a pretty little American *biondina* and want to play the *guappo*. First grow some hair between your legs, my little man." Michele broke out in laughter, and he and Alfredo began jostling their brother between them.

"It's to school, you go, my little big shot. Or Papa will tan your hide. And that's that," Alfredo ended.

The boy dug his clenched fists deep into his pockets and muttered: "I'll go. And I will make money, too." Then as he squirmed out of reach of his brothers' arms, he blurted out: "And I've got hair down there, too!"

Three days later, it was a different Francesco, an exuberant Francesco who tore out of the house, running to meet his father and brothers. Darting between wagons and horses he crossed the street, shouting, "A letter, Papa, a letter from Italy. Zia Graziella says that it is from Mama!"

"Gesu, finally!" and in moments father and sons all burst into the flat. Zia Graziella, all smiles and with tears of joy in her eyes, put the envelope into Giuseppe's callused, cement-speckled hands. The flowery script of the professional letter-writer who had written it for a fee, clearly designated that the sender was Signora Rosa Alanga, Via dei Tabacchi #6, Boscotrecase, Italia. Giuseppe opened the envelope, touched the letter to his lips and gave it to Alfredo.

Everyone hushed as Alfredo began reading.

"My dearest husband and sons, praise be to Jesus Christ. This letter informs you of our salvation and well-being. And Michele, my son, your Adelina is safe and well also. The good Lord, in His mercy, has spared our lives from the destruction that engulfed us after your departure from us. With the first explosion of Vesuvius on the morning of the fourth, I abandoned the house and fled with the girls to the town. The piazza was filled with our friends and neighbors. When I saw the flames and rocks being hurled from the mountain, I decided then and there it would not be wise to remain. We joined others of like mind and took to the road to Castellammare. How fortunate that I so decided; for by the next evening Boscotrecase was no more. All those who thought to brave the mountain's fury, and remained there, perished. My dear Giuseppe, the Lord held us in His hand. I kiss those hands that prodded me to leave.

"So many dear friends, people with whom we have broken bread, are dead! The husband of your sister Teresina lost his father, Signor Vitelli, and the wounds suffered by the mother, I fear, will prove fatal. Both of them were found under the ruins of their house. The old man's skull was crushed, and she, poor woman, suffered many broken bones and cuts. And old Saverio died when he went back to the stable to free his beloved old mule. Young Carlo Esposito lost both his wife and his new baby, and the Crispis lost three of their young ones.

"And of the destruction and ruin, dear husband, I have not words to tell you. Not one stone stands upon another of our own house. But by some good fortune, the forge escaped with little damage; it is there that we live. We cook our food where you used to heat the iron. We sleep on piles of straw. The girls have made a table from some planks, and some old benches you had in the forge are our chairs. The government has given the people some blankets and clothing. From time to time the girls go to the distribution center and come back with food—now, beans, now, pasta, now, rice.

"All our animals are dead. Not so much as a hen remains. The girls and I will begin working the land as soon as we can. Our hands are willing and our backs are strong, and so we will manage. Dear husband, therefore think not of returning. Stay where you are; we will survive. Think, husband mine. More than ever our hope for the future lies in America, and not here. If ever you had doubts that you were not doing the right thing in going to America, cast them from your mind.

"Reply in haste. We all long to know of your safe arrival and how you fare. Embrace my sons and know that each night we all pray the Lord to keep you well.

> With affection,
> Your wife and daughters"

When Alfredo had finished reading, no one spoke for a moment. Giuseppe's mouth was hard set. Graziella, her eyes moist, sat with hands folded in her lap and whispered quietly to herself, "Poor woman, poor woman." But Alfredo had heard her sigh, and he answered, "No, Zia Graziella. Say instead, brave, dear, brave, Mama. Zia Graziella, you do not know my mama. Nothing will keep her down as long as she can lift a finger. Boys, what does Mama say when things get tough, do you remember?" He did not wait for their answer, but answered his own question: "*Solo la morte 'nserra la porta.* (Only death locks the door.) Don't you worry about Mama," he ended.

Everyone began talking at once, recalling how Mama did this, how Mama did that. Unnoticed, Zio Matteo quietly left the group and went to his bedroom. In a few minutes he returned. "Write to your mama, now, Alfredo. And put these in the envelope before you seal it." He handed the boy two, ten-dollar bills.

Chapter Fourteen

The months went by—May, June, July, August. The first hard impressions and the strangeness of their new surroundings had by now lost wonder for the new immigrants. The routine of daily life, the exigencies of Job in the new land took hold. Places, streets, and the people of the East Side neighborhood in which they found themselves took on a familiarity that now afforded Giuseppe and his sons a degree of security and ease. The sphere of their acquaintances was widening, too. Every Sunday Zio Matteo and a half-dozen of his cronies came together in the backyard to play *bocce*, and Giuseppe and the two older boys became regulars. The men played with the fervor of warriors fighting the last stand. Every pitch of the ball was done with deadly aim; with one finger, two fingers, the contestants measured to see how close their bowls had come to the little ball, the *pallino*. They checked and double-checked the measurements. And God help the man who moved a ball while doing so! Then, after a few matches, the players usually retired to their wine and cigars. They laughed and joked about each other, and the strange ways of the Americans, the strange food they ate and their own distaste for it. Sometimes they argued; mostly they talked about Job.

Three nights a week, Alfredo faithfully attended night school, where a prim, reedy old-maid condescendingly, but conscientiously attempted to clarify the complexities of the English language to the motliest, most hodge-podge group of foreigners ever assembled in one room. In the class there were three Italians, three Greeks, two Armenians, a Romanian, an Albanian, four Jews, one Pole, a German, a Swede, and a Chinaman. All of them were struggling to one degree or another in order to master this unfamiliar, new tongue-twisting language of their adopted country. The immigrants themselves were not immune from the humor arising from their own mispronunciations and misinterpretations. One memorable evening for the three Italian students of the class, was the lesson on the parts of the body. Arm, leg, hand, gave them no trouble. The word "face," however broke them up into fits of laughter on hearing the exchange that took place between Miss Collins and the immigrant, Giovanni, over this word.

Miss Collins: "This is your face."

Giovanni: "Me no *fessa*."

Miss Collins: "No! no! Not face-a. FACE, FACE. Don't you understand? Your FACE."

Giovanni (slightly perturbed): "Me no *fessa*. You fessa!"

Miss Collins (slightly perturbed): "FACE, FACE. your FACE."

Giovanni: "Mamma mia! I'ma no *fessa*! You *fessa*, and you mama, you papa, you seesta." The blood rushed to his head as he let out a string of epithets that cursed her and her family—all the generations past, present, and future. At this point, the two younger Italians, Alfredo and Liberato, choking on their suppressed chuckles, could no longer contain themselves and broke out into explosions of laughter. The infectious mirth caught on, and soon the whole class was laughing uncontrollably, although the other greenhorns didn't understand the underlying nuance of Giovanni's frustration. Poor Miss Collins was completely bewildered; she rapped the desk rapidly with her ruler, overwhelmed by such unseemly disorder in her classroom. In the commotion, Liberato took the opportunity to explain to the old man that "face" was the word for "*faccia*," and that Miss Collins was not calling him an asshole. All Giovanni could say in response was: "*Che brutta parola, questa, per faccia!*"

Within only a month's time, Alfredo had gained more and more confidence and skill in his study of English. Clearly he had become the most advanced student in the class. At home, he usually tested his new knowledge on little Matteo. The boy, now in the third grade of P.S. 21, spoke English as did any other American kid. So, he would swell with pride when his older cousin asked him to say something for him in English, or to correct his pronunciation. In return for his help, the little boy's big cousin treated him with deference and seriousness, and called Matteo "the little professor." The two of them fast became pals. A bond of real affection had grown between the two cousins, so that little Matteo came to idolize Alfredo. And Alfredo, on his part, loved the little boy as he would a brother. They studied together and they played together.

Sunday was their day. When the last morsel of the mid-day meal had been eaten, Alfredo only had to say: "Come on, little professor," and Matteo was out of his chair and at the door. Hand in hand, they walked the streets and avenues of the East Side that was their world.

"What is this called?" or, "How do you say in English," and the boy would respond with eager joy. In turn, Alfredo regaled the boy with yarns about Italy, his life there, his family there, his friends there. He imprinted on the boy's mind indelible images of blue skies, old gnarled olive trees, ploughed fields, goats scampering on the slopes of a smoldering volcano. He painted for Matteo, things the boy had never seen, colors he had never perceived and the heritage of the land where the little boy's father had been born. He peopled the boy's imagination with the faces and personalities of his own mother and sisters, the old cartdriver, the priest, Don Pio, women washing clothes by the stream, watercarriers, muleteers, gypsies—in short, all the characters that had made up Alfredo's world back in Boscotrecase, the birthplace of Matteo's father and of all the Alangas.

It made Alfredo happy to see Matteo's eyes shine in wonderment to learn that Boscotrecase had a coat of arms. Indeed! its own coat of arms! That's how grand Boscotrecase was. In detail, Alfredo described to him the blue shield that showed Vesuvius in the background with a feather of white smoke rising from its crater, and in the foreground, the three silver houses with red roofs, from which the village had taken its name, Boscotrecase, the meaning of which was, "Three houses in the woods."

The three houses, Alfredo went on to explain, were in reality, three monasteries. Santa Chiara, Santa Maria Maddalena, and Santa Maria Egiziaca. Around these three religious houses, the commune of Boscotrecase had grown over the centuries, until gradually, all the forests that once covered the region from as far away as the coast to the very slopes of Vesuvius, disappeared.

"Someday, little Matteo, when you get to be a big boy, your cousin Alfredo will take you there, so that you can see where your papa and my papa were born. Would you like that? Would you like to go with me to Bosco?"

"Oh, yes, cousin Alfredo. Will you really take me there?"

In response, Alfredo picked up the boy and gave him a big hug. "That's a promise, little professor. Now, before it gets too late, what do you say to a game of stickball?" It had been Matteo who had introduced his big cousin to the game; often on a Sunday afternoon, the two of them joined the gang of Matteo's little buddies in a rousing game on the street. The little kids enjoyed having their friend's big cousin play with them. And Alfredo soon became as good a player as any of them.

Chapter Fifteen

By mid September, the weather had begun to cool. On some days, in the dark, dawn hours at the work-site, knots of men gathered over little fires fed by scraps of broken boards. They squatted and spread their callused, rough hands over the flames. The heat felt good as it warmed their blood. It animated their spirits, thawed their minds, so that they would begin to chat and joke before the work whistle called them away to Job.

On this particular day, though, there were more curses to be heard, than jokes. The men were damning the previous night's rain that had turned the site into a sea of mud. As men walked, their boots and shoes made slurping, sloshing sounds with every step they took. The thick mud sucked at their feet in a glutinous grip.

Turriddu came up to his gang. "I've just been to the excavation. It's a moat there. The water is up to one's shins. I say to the boss that we shouldn't work today. But he says, no work, no Job." Angrily he sent a stream of spit into the fire. As it landed, its sizzle and crackle was drowned out by the screech of a whistle's blast. The men raised themselves up from their haunches and fanned out across the yard through the mud.

Before turning off to join his own work gang in the excavation, Alfredo poked his brother in the ribs. "Michele, you haven't said two words together this morning. It can't be the cold that has clamped your jaws shut. Uncle Matteo says that the real cold comes in November and December, when the snow comes and the ice, and the winds from the North."

"No, brother, it is not the cold that bothers me. Why is it that in the last two letters from Mama, she tells me nothing of Adelina? Always before, she has told me some news of her—Adelina says this, Adelina does that. Now, nothing. Could something be wrong, an accident, or an illness maybe?" His brow was creased in a deep frown, and his squinting eyes mirrored anxiety.

Alfredo threw his arm around his brother's shoulder. "Ah, don't worry. Mama is so loaded down with her problems over there, and the work, that it just slipped her mind to say anything of Adelina. She's got her hands full just looking after the place and the girls, and without us to help her. Forget it." He waved his brother off. "Go on, get to Job. Everything is all right."

Michele walked away, and as Alfredo started walking to his work, he suddenly felt a clap on his shoulder. It was Paolo, his mentor on Job. A strong bond of friendship had developed between the two. "What a rotten day to work. Better to have stayed home in bed, cuddled next to a nice, warm *innamorata*. What do you think? Do you have a girl, Alfredo?"

Alfredo chuckled: "I don't even have a dog!" Paolo burst out in laughter. "One of these days, Alfredo, I'm going to bring you home to meet my sister, Angelina." He pulled Alfredo's cheek, and added: "She's a beauty."

"And some day I'll let you meet my sisters." Alfredo pulled Paolo's cheek. "They are all beauties."

As the two young men approached the work pit, they could hear the workers sloshing through the water in the bottom of the trench. Turriddu's voice was ordering men to reinforce some of the shoring that had buckled or was giving way.

"It's useless to try to dig until we get the water out, lads. In a few days, it will filter down and dry out itself, but Boss says, no. We must bail it out. A work fit for mules!" He spat vehemently and went on: "We must bail it out." In groups of four, the men took positions along the length of the trenches, two on the bottom filling buckets, and two on top, emptying.

Three back-breaking hours passed, three hours of filling, hoisting, emptying. Over and over again. The level of the water was perceptibly lowering. "Another hour of this," thought Alfredo, "and it is done." At the far end of the foundation trench, where his young friend, Paolo was working, a huge mound of excavated dirt piled high on the rim above, suddenly broke away like a calving iceberg. Before anyone could shout out a word of warning, a slimy, oozing mass of muck mixed with stone, slid from the center peak. Four men working at the edge of the trench were engulfed and hurled into the open pit, atop their fellow workers below.

At the immediate site of the disaster, frantic screams split the gray, sullen skies. Soon men began running as best they could, slipping and falling, from every corner of the yard, to find a whole section of the eight foot trench almost filled to the rim with mud and stone. With their bare hands, two workers in the trench were trying to extricate a companion whose lower body only was free, the legs jerking in wild spasms. Joined by a dozen pairs of hands, miraculously they succeeded in freeing the man from the suffocating filth. Someone cleared the fellow's nostrils, mouth, and eyes of the sticky mud. The chest began to heave, and life-giving air coursed once more into the lungs. It was Giorgio the Abbruzzese, who was to be the sole survivor. When the trench was cleared of the cave-in, five of the gang's co-workers lay dead, buried alive by Job.

The five bodies, caked in a coating of red-brown clay looked like so many dead Indians. Their identities only became known as the layer of mud was scraped and washed away from their faces, to reveal the contorted features of men who had died in the agony of suffocation.

When Alfredo broke through the silent ring of workers encircling the dead, he looked down upon the inert form of Paolo, his friend, stretched out among the corpses. Afredo's head fell heavily to his chest as he moaned a soft, "Gesu, Gesu."

With the speed of the wind, news of the disaster reached the streets. Like a black tide, scores of shawl-covered women flooded the site. They screamed out the names of their men across the yard.

"Carlo!"

"Sandro!"

"Giovanni!"

"Peppo!"

On and on, the litany of names pierced the heavy air. A few policemen, fearing a tumult, were trying fruitlessly to hold back the surging tide. Husbands and wives found each other, embraced and wept. But the unfortunate ones, finding their dead, pierced the heavy, damp air with their shrieks of despair. As if the cries could waken their men from the sleep of death, the women wailed out their names, then fell to their knees in the mud. They caressed the mud-lined faces of their men, rocked the lifeless bodies, pressed them close to their breasts like mothers cradling their little children.

Crowley, O'Brien the construction supervisor, and a few policemen burst through the circle of men and women. Frowns wrinkled their brows. For a few moments they stood staring at the scene before them. A police captain pushed his way through the throng to stand beside O'Brien.

"And what have we here, now, Mister O'Brien? An accident, is it?"

"Ah, Officer McCarthy, is it you, captain? To be sure, to be sure."

"Well, it appears you've lost a dago, or two, by the looks of it."

"Aye. 'Tis a shame, I suppose, but accidents do happen now and again, and that's the way of it."

"But we'll have some order here now. Bring over one of your straw bosses to tell these bawling women in their own lingo that they must leave. And I'll be talking to you in a while, so that I can bring in my report."

In a while the mourning women were reluctantly and forcibly led away by the strong but gentle hands of the other workers. By tacit agreement and understanding that there would be no further working the rest of the day, the men, too, followed. The bodies of the dead were covered with sheets of rough canvas; Alfredo turned one last time to look at the five shrouded bodies before he left the yard. Off to the side, he saw Turriddu talking to the officer and O'Brien. Joined by his father, brother, and Zio, Matteo, the four men left the site.

In the crowd still surging towards the yard, Uncle Matteo spied his wife and little Marietta just arriving. He broke away from his brother and nephews and went towards his wife and child racing to meet him. His wife threw out her hands to him. His strong fingers encircled her own, and with the warmth of his living touch, her shoulders drooped in relief. Then he stopped, scooped up his child in his arms and gently brushed away a lock of hair away from her face.

"We are all fine, fine," and he pointed to show Graziella his brother and nephews making their way through the crowd towards them. "But, Graziella, the angel of death has touched five of our brother paesani—young Paolo La Rocca, Luciano Greco, Minnigone the Barese, Bastiano the Sardinian and Scarface Giacomo."

Graziella gasped and threw her hand to her mouth. "Giacomo, he with seven little ones. And Luciano Greco, father of three, and Paolo, so young." The other two men she did not know, but her eyes welled up in tears at the thought of the sadness and misery visited upon the houses of the unfortunate who had lost their men.

The tragedy brought a sense of mourning and loss to the whole of the East Side's Little Italy. The dead were all paesani, members of an extended family bound together by the same culture and hardships in the fight against poverty, prejudice and deprivation that surrounded them all.

At five houses, for the next three days, black wreaths hung on the doors of the places of mourning. Within each, in simple, inexpensive coffins, the dead lay in state. In every house it was the same; mourners coming to pay their respects had only to follow the sounds of weeping and lamentation through a hallway and into the flat of a tenement to where the dead one lay.

In the company of his father, brother and uncle, Alfredo had gone from house to house to visit the dead. But he went alone to the house where Paolo was being waked. In that house, he stood in a long line in the hallway until his turn came to walk up to Paolo's bier. The casket was flanked by two tall, burning tapers at the foot and head. Behind the coffin, a tall crucifix hung on the wall, surrounded by a cascade of flowers.

At the kneeler, Alfredo bent his knees, crossed himself and looked into the face of his friend. The pale face, framed by the silky black curls of hair, wore ever so faint a smile. Never had Alfredo seen his friend so still, so calm. He had to fight back an overpowering urge to grab Paolo's shoulders and shake him to life. He wanted to tap him on the cheek, as so often he had done in playful cameraderie, to see a familiar, boyish grin light up the handsome face.

Alfredo's forehead began to break out in beads of sweat. The smell of flowers, mixed with the perfumed scent of the burning candles, along with the closeness in the crowded room, began to suffocate him. He had an urge to weep, but so as not to, he lowered his gaze away from Paolo's face and brought his eyes down to Paolo's hands. Those strong hands that had wielded pick and shovel and iron bar, were now entwined with the delicate strand of a black rosary.

Alfredo stood up, turned away from the casket, and walked off to the side, where the boy's mourning mother and three sisters sat. The women were aligned in what seemed a mass of black drapery, their hands folded in their laps. Bending over slightly, Alfredo softly whispered his condolences to the mother, and repeated his words of sorrow to the first sister, then the second sister. A startled look crossed his face when he came to the third sister, sixteen year-old Angelina. Here was the living face of Paolo! The same curly, black hair, only longer, the same thin lips, the same finely chiseled nose, the same large eyes. Only a feminine softness in the shape of the features set the two faces apart, and instead of the brown of Paolo's eyes, the blue of the girl's. For a moment he remained transfixed. After a few seconds, he managed to whisper a hesitant, "*Mi dispiace*," and pushed his way out of the crowded room onto the street.

People filing into the house as he was leaving, called out to him in greeting. But he did not acknowledge them. All he saw was Angelina's beautiful face before his eyes. The image of her grief-stricken features, especially the azure-blue of her tear-filled eyes branded itself on his mind and heart.

And although he doubted that she had even taken note of him, he knew that he must see her again.

Chapter Sixteen

The funerals were over. Men went back to Job. Women resumed the care of their households. Children shouted and played on the streets boisterously and noisily. On the payday following the tragedy, the leaders of the work gangs passed the hat on behalf of the stricken families. To a man, every worker on Job contributed, gave what his heart told him was right. As the workers streamed off the work site, no one had to tell them why Turriddu and Matteo were standing to the left and right of the gate, holding dented, concrete-encrusted pails in their hands.

Clinking quarters and half-dollars, and an occasional crumpled dollar bill fell into the buckets. By the time the last man had left the yard, the buckets were full.

"Turriddu, these unfortunates were all men of your gang. Take the money and make the distribution to the widows and the orphans in the name of all of us."

"Matteo, my friend, I am a poor man with words. Do me the honor to come with me and speak in the name of us all. How can I find the words to say to the wife of Scarface, or to any of them, 'Take this dirty money; it is for the life of your man.' Can I say to these women, 'instead of the strength of your man's arms, the warmth of his breath, take this cold money and find your solace in it to comfort your fatherless children?' A man of eloquence is needed now to say what must be said in words that will ease the pain to hearts already suffering so much grief."

Matteo, moved to the very depths of his soul by the anguish of the man's feelings, put his hand gently on Turriddu's shoulder. At the same time, he placed his pail in Turriddu's empty hand.

"They will see in your eyes, my friend, what you would say in words. Your eyes will tell them what your heart feels for them. I will come with you, but it is you who does me the honor in asking me to accompany you. I will be at your house at eight, Don Turriddu." Matteo-uttered the title of respect in all sincerity, turned, and walked away.

At the supper table that night, Matteo recounted the incident. He ended by saying, "Turriddu may be a man ignorant of books and big words. But he speaks from the heart and not in the language of empty words by men puffed up with importance because they can read and write and spout out big words, men who love to hear themselves talk. Such men talk a lot, but the help they give, comes only from their mouths. But Turriddu is a true paesano; he speaks from the heart and gives with the hand."

"Si, si." Everyone nodded in assent. Matteo rose from the table. "It is almost eight, now. I must go to Turriddu."

His wife began clearing the table with the help of little Marietta. Giuseppe grabbed hold of his son Michele's arm. "Come, we will go down to the yard for a smoke." As they were leaving, little Matteo shouted out to his cousins, "Come, Alfredo, Francesco. Let's go down to the street and see if anyone is playing stickball." The boy's eyes were aglow in the anticipation of a game. He flew out the door, and his footsteps on the stairs resounded throughout the hallway as he raced to the street. The other two followed. Sure enough, a game was already in progress, and Alfredo could hear the kids yelling to the boy at bat: "Hit the ball, hit the ball," even before he and Francesco reached the front door.

Since Alfredo was deemed the worth of two players, he went on one team, and Matteo and Francesco took places on the other. The game was resumed after a short battle of words as to who should get Alfredo. Francesco came up to bat; he whacked the ball and sent it straight down the first base line to Gennaro, who let it slip right through his hands, so that Francesco was able to leap to first base safely.

"Weed! weed! You shithead. You stink," came the angry shouts from the boy's team mates. Whereupon, Gennaro turned to his critics and slapped his right arm across the crook of his left one and then flexed his forearm. It was the universal gesture whose meaning they all understood: "Up yours!"

When Francesco had flopped onto the base, a bunch of coins flew out of his pocket. He scrambled to retrieve them, but not before Alfredo caught sight of his little brother stuffing them back into his pants.

The game continued a little while longer, but as the light faded, windows began opening up wide. Above the din of the street, mothers' voices were heard calling out to their children to come in. "In the house now!" more than one voice echoed down to the street.

"Aw, Ma."

"In—now, this instant, or I'll send your father down," was more than one mother's response, and so the game broke up. The boys began drifting off in a noisy tumble.

Alfredo gave little Matteo a gentle pat on his "*culo*."

"Run upstairs, Matteo. Francesco and I will be right up." The boy scampered up the steps of the stoop and in a flash was out of sight.

Francesco felt his older brother grabbing him by the arm. "Wait a minute, Francì. Empty your pocket, that one." Alfredo pointed to the right side of his kid brother's pants. Francesco hesitated, but looking up to his brother's stern face, he slowly slid his hand into the pocket and pulled out a clenched fist.

"Open your hand."

The tight ball, of Francesco's curled fingers unfurled. In the palm of the boy's hand, lay three quarters, two dimes, three nickles, and some random pennies.

"Where did you get all that money? Did you steal it?"

Francesco glared at his brother. His lips remained tight, and he said nothing.

"If you don't tell me, little brother, you'll tell Papa. Now who is it you are going to tell where you got it, me or Papa?"

"Alfredo, please don't tell Papa. I, I earned this money." Abashedly Francesco lowered his eyes away from his brother's gaze.

"You earned it? How? You go to school. You don't work."

"Well, Papa won't let me work. He only wants me to go to school, to sit there with little girls and boys and say, "cat" and "rat" and "fat." So sometimes, instead, I play cards in the alley behind the pool hall, with the big boys. I'm good, Alfredo. I always win—mostly. They all say that I'm smart at cards. They show me respect because I play so good. I play *tresette* and *scopa*, and even the American poker."

Alfredo listened to all the boy was saying, with his own lips pressed tightly together. Then he puffed out some air from his mouth and shook his head in disapproval. But before he could utter a word, Francesco yelled out at his brother: "I want money, Alfredo. I want money, too. In Italy I never had two *centesimi* at one time. But here I can get money, and I don't even have to work for it. I play for it! This blessed America." The boy screamed out these last words. As he did so, he could see his brother's face contort into a scowl. He stepped back away from him, apprehensively waiting for his brother's reaction.

Alfredo's words came out hard and rasping. "You never lose. You always win, right? You little fool. Papa didn't raise you to be a card-trickster, a cheat at cards. No, he wants you to grow up to be a good man." Alfredo then clapped his hand on his brother's shoulder, but the boy drew away. Drawing himself up and squaring his shoulders, he spat back: "I wanted to go to work, Alfredo. You know that. I want to get money to give to Papa, so that he can get Mama here, and our sisters. Wasting my time in school is a sin, when I could be helping out too. I want Mama." Tears began forming in Francesco's eyes, but a swift movement of his hand brushed them away. But not before his brother noticed them in the boy's eyes.

A pang of tenderness struck Alfredo, but only for a moment. Thinking it the better course to shame Francesco, he blurted out, "Oh, so you want to play the man and make money. And yet you cry for your mama." As soon as the words were out his mouth, Alfredo wished he had never spoken them. No thirteen year-old boy likes to be called a cry baby, and he realized that he had hurt his brother. He reached out to enfold the boy in his arms, but Francesco flung off Alfredo's arm. He flew up the stoop, but not before the older brother had seen the wounded look on his brother's face. He called out after him: "Francesco, I'm sorry. Wait, Francì." But the boy was already out of earshot.

Dejectedly, Alfredo walked to the step of the stoop and sat down. He pulled out a cigarette and put it to his lips. He lit it and took a long puff. And then to himself he muttered: "I miss Mama, too." He knew that he had said the wrong thing to his kid brother, and he was filled with remorse. Remembering that his brother's thirteenth birthday was only weeks away, he felt even more downcast over the dispute that had just occurred. He resolved to cool his frustration and anger and say nothing to Papa; and he hoped that Francesco's hurt would fade when the boy saw that his brother did not mention the matter to Papa.

"I'll make it up to him," he murmured to himself. He finished his smoke, got up, and made his way up to the flat. "After all, when you're thirteen, you think you know it all, that you are becoming a man, and the snot is still running down your nose. But brother mine, there is still a lot to learn about becoming a man, and I don't want you to mess up the life ahead of you by starting off on the wrong path."

In bed that night, he found it hard to fall asleep. He was restless; sleep would not come to him as long as the images of Mama and the girls paraded before his eyes. And then in a while, no matter how strongly he tried to keep the picture of his mother's face in his mind, the vision of Angelina persisted in crowding out his mother's face. Finally, his subconscious mind surrendered, and his conscious mind sharply brought into focus the girl's every feature. The blood began to race in his veins; he grabbed the pillow, and wrapping it tightly in his arms, he pressed it to his chest.

The next three weeks passed with never a word or a conscious glance from Francesco toward his brother. The boy was clearly avoiding Alfredo. But on the evening of his birthday, in the midst of the small, family celebration, when he realized that his older brother had not snitched on him, Francesco acknowledged his brother Alfredo's smiles. There was peace once more between them.

Only a few days now remained in September. One evening, Zio Matteo called his brother and nephews to the table. "Sit," he said. "Know that when the bitter cold comes, and the snow begins to fall, then, my boys, there will be no more work for us on Job until the spring returns."

"But we are not afraid of a little cold," Alfredo chimed. His uncle laughed. "You do not understand what the winter is like here. It is not a little cold, a little snow. Here, the winds from the North freeze a man's very bones, stab deep enough so as to turn the blood to ice. The skies turn gray, the color of lead. And when the clouds drop the snow that loads them down, the snow covers the earth to a depth of two, three, four feet. Nothing can move; everything stops. Cement cannot be mixed, nor will it set. The pick strikes the dirt and the dirt rings back as when iron is struck."

"But uncle, how does one live then?" The question was Alfredo's.

"Like the bear, *caro nipote*, like the bear who hibernates and sustains himself from the fat stored up under his fur." Matteo chuckled and continued. "Your Aunt Graziella, like all the women here, store away as much as they can all the year long, jars of tomatoes, pickled eggplant, the strings of garlic and onions, the dried beans, all the preserves of fruits, everything, then, that can be safely salted and preserved. And to buy the coal and pay the rent, I do my own salting away. During the good time, I bring my dollars to the bank and take them out as the need arises.

"And I am one of the lucky ones, for even in the bad season, I have work that gives me dollars in return. And you will have such work, too. Down at the rail yards, there is coal to be loaded and unloaded to feed the stoves and furnaces of the cities. It is steady work during the winter, and although such labor does not pay as well as Job, it keeps one from starving.

"Furthermore, there are always a few extra dollars to be made. When the snow falls and chokes the streets, it must be cleared away so that the wagons and trolleys and cars may be driven. I drive one of the wagons into which the street cleaners throw the snow. Then poof! into the river it goes. It is back-breaking work, but the paesani bless every flake that falls, for it keeps the hunger from their door."

"Are you sure, uncle, that there will be work for us, that they will take us on to do this work?" asked Michele.

Zio Matteo laughed and whacked the table with the flat of his hand. "As long as the snow falls, and for all the days after that it takes to clear the streets of it, they will use the paesani. The snow is never too deep, or the cold never too biting, that they will not send us out. For the horses, ah, it may be too cold. But never for us. I remember the second winter that I was here in this country. A man's very breath froze into icicles as soon as it escaped from his mouth. To inhale meant to have daggers of ice pierce the throat and paralyze the speech. The horses, many of them, the Americani kept in the stables and put blankets on their backs to keep them warm. But the men, they sent out onto the streets. 'Guineas we can always get, but a horse is worth more than a guinea,' they said."

Zio Matteo chuckled again and slapped his knee. "But I say this, the Americano, like the horse, is worth only what comes out of his ass, but the guinea, what comes out of his head and from his hand. Who is the American Da Vinci, the American Galileo, the American Michelangelo? Bah!"

He gave an adoring glance to his little son and continued: "When we are here a generation and have learned the words and the ways of this land, then our children like my Matteo here, and his children, will no longer be the hod-carriers and the shovelers of snow. We will be the professors, the doctors, the lawyers. They call me "guinea" now, but my son and my grandsons they will call "Mister Doctor," "Mister Professor," "Mister Lawyer." He turned to Alfredo and his brothers. "You, you young ones will see that day, and you will remember my words, and you will say, 'My zio Matteo, he knew what he was talking about.'" Gently, unnoticed by anyone, Alfredo poked Francesco in the ribs and whispered, "Do you hear?"

Chapter Seventeen

The first week in October, the weather turned very cold. On Thursday a few flurries of snow fell. No one had to tell the men that the days on Job were numbered. More than one man's brow was furrowed over in worry, thinking about the days of hardship and want to come. In the early afternoon, bitterly cold winds off the river brought heavier snow, so that work was halted and the men sent home. Above the rush of the wind, voices cursed this harbinger of the bad times to come. The men trudged out of the yard, their hands dug deep into their pockets, their forms becoming more and more indistinct as the snowfall thickened.

At the stoop of their tenement, the Alanga men stamped the snow from their shoes, and where they stepped on the stairs as they climbed to the flat above, they left snowy imprints here and there along the way up. Inside the kitchen, they threw off their jackets. Graziella was at the table loaded with festoons of fresh home-made noodles. Her hands were white with flour, and she was just about to roll out some more dough with the rolling pin.

"*Tagliatelle* for supper tonight, eh, wife? Job is finished for today, and it won't be long before it is finished for good. The snow and the cold come early this year." Matteo dragged a chair close to the stove and began taking off his shoes. As the others began following suit, Graziella deftly wiped her hands on her apron and pulled a letter out of her pocket. She walked to the stove, saying, "This will warm your hearts, I'm sure. Look! a letter from Italy."

Giuseppe let the shoe he had removed fall to the floor, and with his hand outstretched, started towards his sister-in-law. Almost rudely, he pulled the letter from Graziella's hand. "Ah! it has been so long." His anxious words had the timbre of a groan. Roughly, his dirty index finger ripped open the onion-thin gray envelope. He extracted the two sheets of the letter almost reverently now, so as not to crumple the handwriting. He handed the letter to Alfredo. Once in the boy's hand, the room became quiet. No one spoke, and Alfredo began to read aloud. No one wanted to miss a single word of this blessed message from across the thousands of miles of ocean.

"Dearest husband and sons," he began. "Praise be to Jesus Christ. Every evening we kneel before the statue of the Madonna and recite the Rosary, beseeching Our Lady of Pompei to shower upon all of you, her blessings and protection in faraway America, and upon us here. All is well with us, ever more so because of the money you have sent. With some of it, I bought a pair of good breeding pigs, and the sow's belly is already bulging with the promise of a new litter of piglets. The goat gives ample milk, and the garden has done so well that we had much to bring to market. The girls are very happy since I was able to buy a whole bolt of good cloth from a passing vendor with the profit I made from selling the extra produce from the garden. I made them each a new skirt, and enough was left over so that I was able to make matching kerchiefs for their heads.

"I know well that it has been some time since I have written. I will explain to you now, why it is that I did not write sooner. It is never easy to bring sad tidings to those one loves, but at last the Madonna gives me the courage to do what I must. If I were there, I would take Michele in my arms and press him to this mother's heart. But it rests with you, husband, to hold him up in your strong arms as you tell him the sad words that I must now relate. You must tell him, that for him, Adelina is no more."

Alfredo halted his reading, astounded at what he had just read. Looks of consternation marked every face, and Michele slammed a clenched fist to his mouth, crying out, "She's dead, she's dead!" Aunt Graziella, her face a ghostly white, took him by the shoulders and lowered him into the chair out of which he had bolted up like a shot.

"No, no, she lives," shouted out Alfredo. His eyes were racing hurriedly down the page. Then gloomily he added, "But she might as well be."

"What do you mean, Alfredo? Speak clear, speak clear," Michele yelled to his brother.

Alfredo lifted the letter up to his face again and continued reading. "For some months past, it was clear to everyone that Adelina is with child. The thickened waist and the high belly have all the tongues in the village wagging. It can only be a matter of two months, three at the most, before her baby is born."

Michele's face turned red, then drained, and Aunt Graziella sucked in her breath in a long, sibilant gasp of air. The eyes of everyone in the room turned automatically to Michele. No one spoke a word as they waited for Michele's reaction. Would he admit to the paternity of the child? Would he deny paternity? Michele said nothing; instead he covered his face and bent over, leaning his elbows on his knees. Giuseppe stared hard at his son, then broke the heavy silence. "Read on, Alfredo," was all he said, and Alfredo did as he was told. "One sad day," he read, "Adelina's father rushed into our midst, dragging his poor daughter behind him. He was cursing and damning Michele as the father, accusing the boy of ruining his daughter and his name. Adelina said nothing, admitted nothing, even when he beat her in front of us; even so, she said not a word concerning the child's father. I stepped in between father and daughter. He turned on his heels and left. I have seen neither him nor the poor child since. But within the week following, it was noised about throughout the village, that Adelina's father had given her in marriage to someone who took her away to a village unknown. Her husband, they say, is a distant relative of the father, and a man who is twenty years her senior, and that he owns a vineyard. This is all I know. My son, it is good that you are in America. You can do nothing rash now. Stay, and forget. In time your sorrow will pass. You are young, and your life is all in front of you. With embraces from all of us, to all of you, Mama."

The letter weighed as heavily as a stone in Alfredo's hand. He walked over to his brother, lifted up Michele's hand and placed the letter in it. Then, at the kitchen door, Alfredo lifted his jacket off the hook, and left to go outside. He sat smoking a cigarette on the stoop, oblivious to the snow swirling around him. In a few minutes he was joined by his father and his uncle.

In the kitchen, Michele remained holding the letter in his hand. He spread open the pages and began reading the letter for himself, as if doubting what he had heard. Quietly, Zia Graziella gently pulled her little ones after her, leaving Michele alone.

The words on the pages floated indistinct and blurred before Michele's eyes. Only the words that said that Adelina, his Adelina, was the wife of another man, stood out, black and clear. They became etched into the convolutions of his brain. In vain, he tried to conjure up the image of Adelina's face, but those awful black words blotted out her features. A thousand thoughts began to race through his mind. He was tortured by guilt, and that, although Adelina had refused to name his as the child's father, it was truly he who was. That day they lay together in the field, that day, that day! His thoughts returned to the day of April past, when Adelina had given herself to him on the soft grass of the meadow. No matter how hard he had tried to bury the fear, to cast from his mind, the thought that there might be a consequence to their act of love, that Adelina might become pregnant, he had never succeeded in ridding himself of that spectre. And now that fear had become a reality.

Deep in his heart he knew why she had refused to name him, to blame him—because she would not be the instrument that destroyed his dreams in the promised land of America. Had she not told him so many times that he must make his mark in that magic, wonderful world beyond the sea? No, she would not be the cause of his surrender of that dream, that promise, and so she had sacrificed herself for him. Michele knew this; he put his head on the table and wept. The dream was meaningless now, without her. Life had lost its purpose for him. Even if he should have the means, the money to return, it would be futile now. Adelina was another man's wife; she could never be his. He took the letter and threw it into the stove. As he watched it burn and turn to ashes, so, he felt, had his own future turned to ashes.

Wisely, there were words that Mama had not dared to write, words that told of Adelina's father's continuing rage. He had kept her locked away in the house, out of sight of everyone, and that when Mama had tried again and again to see the girl, she had been turned away. Only once had she been able to catch a fleeting glimpse of the girl as she was passing by the window of her prison. Mama could not form the words to tell her son that the girl's father had struck a bargain with this relative of his. And how could she tell her son that this man, now Adelina's husband, it was rumored, was a brutal man, an ignorant peasant of the lowest type, a *cafone*. These things she could not find in her heart to tell him. She had locked them in her heart and had made her daughters swear on the head of the Madonna, that they too, would never breathe a word of them to their brother.

Late that night, deep in the early hours of the new day, Michele was still at the kitchen table, alone. The quiet of the tomb pervaded the house. Suddenly Michele heard the soft shuffling of bare feet, and then he felt the touch of a hand on his shoulder. He lifted his face to see this father standing beside him.

"You have something to tell me, my son?"

And Michele told him.

Chapter Eighteen

The winter was a hard one, and the new first months of 1907 brought much snow and ice. The bitter cold penetrated to the very marrow of the bones of the paesani who found labor clearing the streets of snow. They cursed the cold, but Michele who worked by their side either on the streets or in the coal yards, was indifferent to both the cold or the curses. Once he had been jaunty and companionable; now he was silent and introspective and kept to himself. He worked, he ate, he smoked, like an automaton, and not even Aunt Graziella's motherly ministrations or extra little attentions were able to coax him out of his dark moods. The coming of the fresh, warming breezes of early spring and the promise of approaching Job, did little to change his taciturnity. In time everyone had gotten used to his coldness and his silence and no longer tried to intrude upon his privacy.

One day toward the end of March, Zio Matteo announced that Job was in the offing. Work was to begin on the first day of April at the site. All the paesani were filled with the anticipation of working again full-time at their trades. Excitement spread throughout the neighborhood; it was as if a *festa* were nearing, so much was the exhilaration at the thought of Job. The women began patching and darning the men's old work clothes. In their mind's eye, they were picturing their menfolk going off each day again to work, and at the end of the week, coming home with the five, six, the seven dollars to be placed on the kitchen table.

The money would be a veritable manna from heaven. Gone now would be those meager paydays when the men came home after cleaning the streets, to put only three or four dollars on the table. Gone now, would be the tedious toil of women and the small children, who, in the evening gloom of winter evenings had had to busy themselves making artificial flowers and notions for ladies' hats and dresses, for the few quarters and half-dollars such work brought in.

Now, with the coming of Job, the days of having to eat coarse lupini beans, stale bread, and onions were over. The pinched, drawn faces of the children would fill out again, and the harried, haggard faces of their mothers would take on a new glow. The time of Job was here again with all its promise of prosperity. And the men, exhausted by their labors on Job, would sleep soundly again, the repose of the just, for all their aches and pains in tightening muscles.

So, with the men finally back on Job, there was once again coffee boiling on the stove and bread sizzling in the oil of the frying pan, sending delicious aromas throughout the rooms of Matteo's flat. One morning Matteo walked into the kitchen, pushing his fingers through his hair and yawning. He was dressed in pants and undershirt, and mumbling something that passed for "Good morning," he went to the sink. He rubbed his face with cold water, wiped it, and came to the table. Dutifully his wife placed a steaming cup of coffee before him, and he began to slurp the brew in noisy sips. As she set down a plate of two huge slabs of fried dough by her husband's cup, Giuseppe walked into the kitchen. After a hasty lick and a promise at the sink, he took a chair beside his brother. Graziella came over to him and set a cup of coffee and a plate of bread in front of him.

"You know, Giuseppe," and Matteo clapped a hand on his brother's shoulder, "today you and I, we go on a visit. To New Haven. Yes, and Michele, he shall make the journey with us. It will be good for him to get away, and for you, too."

Graziella interrupted him by her startled gasp of surprise. In all their married life, the farthest they had ventured from Elizabeth Street was on an occasional excursion over the years to Sheepshead Bay. Matteo shot a glance at his wife, and then turned back to Giuseppe. He smiled at his brother who wore now a puzzled look on his face. "I told you, remember, Giuseppe, about my friend Angelo in New Haven. Him it is that we shall go visit today. You shall see with your own eyes that what I have told you about the beauty of this place is true. It is there someday that I have it in my head to make my home. It is in this city of tree-lined streets, within earshot of the bells of Saint Michael's Church that I hope to bring Graziella and the children. And it is there where you will want to make a home for Rosa and your brood, too. You will see, you will see for yourself."

He rose sharply from the table, gave it a hard slap and commanded: "Come, let's get dressed in our finest, and let's be off."

Within the half-hour, he, his brother, and Michele were on the trolley taking them to Grand Central Station. For the first time in weeks, there was a little look of life in Michele's eyes, as peering through the windows of the train racing through the Connecticut countryside, he caught the sight of trees. Trees and more trees, green grass and low-lying wooden houses. The train sped on past the towns of Greenwich, Stamford, Darien, Norwalk, and on and on, and everywhere the same beautiful panorama of trees and green lawns unfolded before them. And Giuseppe, for whom this was the first train ride, marveled at the beauty of the landscape whizzing by. He had come to believe that America must be a treeless land of stone and brick and cement, full of noisy throngs of people jostling each other for breathing space along tenement-lined streets. But this, this that he was seeing now, was wonderful. This countryside, dotted with little houses among stands of trees and wayside flowers took him by surprise.

"*Che bellezza,*" he whispered half to himself. Matteo smiled to see the look of rapture on the face of his brother. "Nice, eh? It brings to mind the countryside by our old homestead on the outskirts of Bosco, does it not?" Images of that setting so far away, flashed through the minds of all of them. Giuseppe at that moment pictured Rosa and the girls in the days before the catastrophe, busy about their chores in the old stone house; he saw himself and the boys sweating at their toils in the field behind the house, and the mountain looming above them. And Matteo, too, who had left Italy when still a young man, had a moment's blurry vision of himself watching his father at the forge. And Michele, as the lush green of grassy hillsides rolled by before his gaze, saw himself lying beside Adelina, and again relived the passion of their last time together. And the memory of it caused his face to screw up in pain, and his eyes began to mist over.

"Bridgeport, Bridgeport, next stop." The raspy voice of a blue-uniformed attendant complete with blue cap, broke the reverence of their reveries. With a start, Matteo stretched his hand to touch the package wrapped in brown paper and twine beside him on the seat. It contained the cheeses and home-made sausages he intended to give as a present to Angelo. "If I am not mistaken, New Haven is the next stop." He brushed off the lapels of his jacket, although there wasn't a speck of dust on them. Michele twisted his jaw and straightened the knot of his tie. Giuseppe combed back his hair with his hands. Out of nervous anticipation, they primped themselves like actors just before going on stage.

Some twenty minutes after the halt at Bridgeport, the train pulled into New Haven's Union Station. Matteo and the others were fortunate enough to find a trolley waiting. After a few words to the conductor,

Matteo, followed by his brother and nephew, boarded the car, which started moving off in a few seconds. In no time at all, the trolley was rumbling on the tracks of upper Chapel Street. Both Michele and his father looked in wonder at the grand, old Victorian houses shaded by elms and maples. Matteo pulled the cord, and at the next corner, the car came to a stop opposite the vast square of a green park edged by a perimeter of wrought iron fencing.

It was almost noon, and bright sunlight glimmered on the white mass of the Italianate church of Saint Michael, located at the far end of the square. It was Sunday, and some little kids, being watched over by their black-clad grandmothers who were sitting and chatting on the park benches, were running and playing about in the grass-carpeted square.

"It looks like the piazza in Bosco," Giuseppe said. "Only the trees are different. They are not our palm trees."

"No," answered his brother, "but the smells are the same." His nostrils flared as he inhaled the fresh fragrances of spring grass and new-born leaves on the trees. The three men walked a short distance, and Matteo turned onto Chestnut Street, where the houses were smaller now, and closer together.

Ahead of them down the street, they heard the cries of a push-cart peddlar hawking his fruits and vegetables. Matteo saw a woman call the peddlar to a halt; he recognized her. It was Carmela, Angelo's wife. He and the others came up to her to see her fingering some greens, while the peddlar proceeded to rattle off the praises of his goods.

"*Buon giorno, Donna Carmela.*" At Matteo's words, the woman turned to the sound of his voice. Her black shawl slipped from her head, baring the graying, up-swept hair that was held in place by a shiny, mother-of-pearl comb. Immediately her dark eyes flashed in surprised recognition, and she ran over to clasp both Matteo's hands in hers. The two then began to speak at the same time. "How good to see you again, *caro Matteo*, after all these years," she gushed.

"Your good man, how is he?" Matteo cried out simultaneously. The peddlar suddenly interrupted: "Signora, please, the greens.." The woman threw up her hands at the peddlar in a gesture of impatience. She turned to Matteo and said, "Go, go, *caro Matteo*, into the house. Angelo will be so happy to see you. I will be but a minute, while I finish with this one. The sauce is all prepared, and the pasta will take but a minute, and I will fix you a nice dinner."

"Only the way you know how to prepare, Carmela," and he turned away and walked toward the house. When Angelo saw his old friend, he rushed to him, and the two of them greeted each other in flurry of cheek-kissing and embrace. Carmela had come in moments later, and Matteo proceeded to make the introductions. Then Angelo pushed his guests into the kitchen and plunked a jug of wine on the table. The men sat, talking and sipping their drinks, interrupted now and again by Carmela's fat arm placing dishes and cutlery on the table in front of their noses.

"Carmelina, run to the square and get your brothers home, those two little bandits. Tell them dinner is on the table; they can return to their play after they have eaten." Carmela was addressing her daughter, a pretty little girl of eleven or twelve years of age.

"Si, Mama." And in a second she was out the door. Ten minutes later, the boys, out of breath, disheveled and dirty-faced, burst into the kitchen.

"Look at those dirty faces. You are two little pigs!" Carmela grabbed each by an arm and led them to the sink. As they were still busy rubbing their faces with opposite ends of a towel, their father pulled the boys to his side. "This rascal is Gennarino, and that one, Gaetano." He smiled and gave each one a love tap on the back of their head.

Carmela placed a huge bowl of macaroni in the center of the table, and by it, another, of sausages and meatballs. The steam curling up from the bowls, like incense, spread a delicious smell that soon filled the small kitchen. She filled the children's plates and shooed them out to the back porch to eat there. "There's no room in here. Take your plates outside." Laughing, they all three scurried out of the hot kitchen, balancing carefully their heaped-up plates so as not to spill the sauce. They plopped themselves on the porch steps, not the least bit displeased at being evicted from the kitchen.

In between mouthfuls of pasta and sips of Angelo's home-made wine, the grown-ups talked. Everything became the subject of conversation—their families, Job, the folks back in Italy, life in New York, life in New Haven. The meal ended with a demi-tasse of pitch-black espresso coffee mixed with a good slug of anisette and a twist of lemon peel. Then, cleaning their mustaches with a swipe of the hand, the men got up from the table and left the house.

Linked arm in arm as in the old country, Zio Matteo, and his friend, with Giuseppe and Michele alongside, walked the little distance to the park, and began their promenade around Wooster Square. A warm April breeze wafted the smoke form their short, knobby Squillo cigars. (The guinea stinkers). And when they had reached the far corner of the grassy expanse, the four sat on a bench facing Saint Michael's Church. Giuseppe and his son were entranced by the beauty of the setting. The smell of the grass and the trees filled their nostrils. The magnificent elms and maples and the odd sycamore were all clothed in new leaf. Everything was so different from the ugliness and the bareness of the forest of tenements that was their home in New York. And, although, all around them in the square, were men, women and children, the din and commotion of the crowded streets of the East Side were lacking here.

"Paradise is here." The words were barely audible as they came from the mouth of Giuseppe. His brother had heard him, though. With a slight nudge of his elbow, Matteo poked Giuseppe's arm. "Is this not a fine place to bring your Rosa? What do you think of this New Haven, eh, brother mine?" But before his father could answer, Michele spoke up. "Indeed, uncle, it is a fine place. Had I a job and the means to stay, I would pursue my destiny here. Here, there is fresh air to breathe and a beauty that pleases the eye." Before Michele could go on, Angelo rose from the bench. He clapped his hand on Giuseppe's shoulder and said earnestly, "If this boy of yours wants Job here, then Job I can provide him here."

With an obvious tone of pride in his voice, he continued. "As I told you before in our talk, I have my own outfit. I'm my own boss. No straw boss over me." Ptoo—he spit a long stream of saliva out of his mouth to emphasize the distaste he felt for all those hard straw bosses under whom he had ever worked. He went on: "Another pair of willing hands, I could use. I already have one good lad, Giovanni Landino, and it happens that I need another." He looked intently at Michele. "My business increases steadily; the name of Angelo Martinelli is being carried on the winds of good fortune. The rich Americans entreat me to build them walls of stone, chimneys, terraces and balustrades, and cobbled driveways for under their porte-cocheres. And for the inside of their houses, ah, for the inside, they have me cutting and laying floors of marble. The mantels and the fireplaces of the finest marble, they contract me to construct for them, because they know that I am a master craftsman. All the city knows that my work is of the first order, and in the finest houses of the rich, they want my services. The work of Angelo Martinelli is to be seen in all the fine mansions on Prospect Hill."

Before he could go on any further, Matteo interrupted him: "Angelo, well I know that you are a *capomastro* of your trade; there is no one better in the art of stone and marble work." He was speaking more to Giuseppe and Michele on whom he fixed his gaze. Giuseppe looked toward his son, whose face for the first time in months, reflected a new vibrancy and bright coloring that a sense of hope brings to the flesh.

Angelo went on again, in a rush of enthusiasm. "This youth is well-built. Under my guidance he might well learn the fine craft of stone masonry and marble cutting, a profession that will always put bread on the table. All the tricks of the trade, all the secrets needed to turn out a work of art in stone and marble will he learn from me. I will train his eye and his hand so that he will come to know just where to hit the stone, just where to chip and slice the marble. For wages, I will start him at seven dollars the week. And his room and board will be free. I do this for you, my good friend, Matteo. I do not forget your past kindness to me. This nephew of yours, if he chooses to stay and work with me, will not undergo the miseries we two went through, in those days when we were two dumb greenhorns, new on these shores. I remember that you shared your last piece of bread with me. I do not forget, and if Michele decides to stay under my roof, he will have a decent bed in a room in the attic of my house. My Carmela's good food is hearty and plentiful, not like weedy dandelion greens we had to scrounge along the roadsides, or the half-rotten potatoes we bought for a penny. Remember those days, Matteo, my friend?"

Matteo laughed. "My stomach just took a turn in thinking how badly I treated it in those days. Beh! That was yesterday. Now we must be concerned with today." He turned to Giuseppe and Michele who were sitting together. "What do you say, brother mine, nephew mine? Can you let such an opportunity such as my good friend offers, slip from your hands? Not only will Michele reap the benefits of learning an honorable trade, but so too will you reap, Giuseppe. Dutiful son that he is, he will be able to contribute all the more in order to bring his mother and sisters to America."

Michele jumped up from the bench. With a tremor of excitement in his voice, he addressed his father. "Papa, it would mean much to me to remain here in this place. It is a fresh breath for me, this chance that Signor Angelo proffers. It will be a new beginning, the start of something good for all of us."

"It does my heart good to see you come back to life, Michele mio, to see your eyes shine again. Each man must follow his own destiny." He embraced his son. "With my blessing, and the blessing of God, follow yours, my son."

"*Bene, benissimo!*" Matteo let out a roar. "Then it is settled. Michele, you will come back with us when we leave tonight, gather your belongings and return to New Haven." Facing Angelo, he said, "Your new associate will be here first thing Monday morning, padrone. And it will give me the greatest pleasure to tell that son of a dog, Crowley, to find himself a new greenhorn on whom to vent the venom of his disdain."

Homeward bound on the train that evening, Michele remained lost in a reverie of anticipation. Matteo was thinking that now there would be one less body to crowd the flat. And Giuseppe, on his part, was composing in his mind, the letter he would have Alfredo write to Rosa. In it, he would tell her of their Michele's good fortune, and about the beauty of this New Haven that someday would be a home for all of them, God willing.

Chapter Nineteen

Again the routine of Job began anew. Each day, for six grueling days a week, Matteo, Giuseppe and Alfredo toiled like mules. At the end of each day, covered in a layer of cement dust and dirt, and stinking of sweat, they returned bone-weary to the flat. After supper, each in his turn, bathed in the huge tin tub that was brought out of the pantry and dutifully filled, bucket by bucket, by Francesco, whom they teasingly called "water-boy." The water was cold, and the soap was the coarse yellow soap Zia Graziella used for washing clothes.

With the kitchen closed off, and the tub set on the floor near the sink, first Matteo, then Giuseppe, then Alfredo, washed away the stink and grime of the day's work. One evening as Alfredo was washing himself, the image of Angelina La Rocca, the sister of his dead friend, Paolo, flashed like a bolt of lightning out of the blue before his eyes. Just the moment's vision of that beautiful face, her blue eyes, the black, curly hair, the shapely contour of her breasts, and immediately he felt a thrilling surge of ecstatic energy course through the very sinews of his loins. Mechanically he toweled his face, his arms, his chest, and his feverish thighs. Dressing himself, he again called to mind on purpose, the girl's loveliness. He let his mind's eye feast on her every feature. He knew that he loved her, and that he wanted her. He must have her.

In bed that night he tossed and turned. His frustration grew with the realization that she did not know of his feelings for her. He did not even know if she even remembered seeing him at her brother's funeral.

One warm May evening, only he and Aunt Graziella were in the kitchen. The kids were on the street playing. His father and uncle were smoking their cigars on the stoop in front of the house. Alfredo absent-mindedly fingered the spoon in his half-filled cup of coffee. Zia Graziella was wiping the supper dishes at the sink. Without turning to face him, she broke the silence. "Who is she, dear nephew, the girl that so preoccupies your thoughts?"

"What?—eh, what girl?" Alfredo stammered as the color rose to his cheeks.

"That is what I am asking you. Who is this girl that causes your cheeks to burn?" She was facing him now, and the soft smile on her lips caused him even more discomfort. Embarrassed, he lowered his eyes from her gaze. She gently took his hands in hers as she sat at the table with him.

"Five brothers I have. And when the fever caused their blood to heat and race in their veins in their longing for the *innamorata*, it was not hard to see. I got to know all the signs, my dear boy. The appetite dwindles, the eye has a far-away look that sees only the image of one face, and the head knows not what is going on around it."

Alfredo took a sip of the now cold coffee. "Zia," he said, "you remember her, you know her. Her brother was my good friend on Job, Paolo La Rocca, *buonanima*. I saw her at his wake, and from that day to this, I cannot get her out of my mind. She is the youngest one of the three sisters. She is a living Madonna, and her face is always before my eyes."

"I know who she is. It is true. She is a fine and truly beautiful young woman. Her people are Piemontesi, from North Italy. "They are a different class of people than most of what you find in this neighborhood. That family mixes very little with the rest of the paesani. The mother and the girl and her sisters stay to themselves. I do not know them to speak to, but, dear boy, I know this. If you were to go to church, to the eight o'clock Mass at Our Lady of Mount Carmel Church, you would see that pretty young lady. She, who has so captured your heart, pays homage to the good Lord every Sunday. As all good Christians should." She winked and got up from the table.

The following Sunday, as Graziella with her two children in tow, stepped onto the front stoop, they almost bumped into Alfredo. He was all spit and polish. His hair glistened under a coating of pomade. His white teeth shone through a broad smile. The children were surprised to see him, but somehow, not their mother. Little Matteo ran a few paces to put his hand in his cousin's. "You are coming to church with us, cousin Alfredo?" he asked joyfully.

"And why not?" chimed in the child's mother. "Good Christians go to God's holy church to honor the good Lord there, and His holy mother, Maria."

"Papa doesn't go. Neither does Zio Giuseppe," piped up Marietta.

"Your father and your uncle are older than Alfredo, and the good Lord understands that they work hard on Job. And so, if they lie a-bed on Sunday, it is because they must rest up for the labor they must again take up on the morrow."

"Francesco doesn't go, and he's only a kid like us," spoke up little Matteo.

"Ah, that *mascherato*," answered their mother, looking at Alfredo. "What are we to do with that little pagan?" She did not expect an answer from Alfredo, but secretly she was hoping that the boy's brother would take Francesco in hand. She was not pleased with the young boy's behavior of late, and she was wishing that her obvious concern would carry over to his brother. Alfredo full well understood the look she had given him. But he avoided saying anything, and let her remark pass over his head. He had tried to tangle once with the rascal, and he had regretted it. Let Papa handle him. Right now, all he had on his mind, was the hope of seeing Angelina in church.

As for the matter of church, church-going was better left to women and children. The women did the praying for the men; God understood, as Zia Graziella had said it, that the menfolk had to work, and that Sunday was the men's day to rest. Alfredo hadn't really thought much about church since coming to America, what with all his preoccupation with work and school. Besides, he had begun to devote more and more of his free time in reading and thinking about the social and labor issues that had such deep consequences for him and all the other new immigrants like himself. Increasingly, he had become aware of the spirit of restless dissatisfaction he saw starting to emerge even among the lowest classes of illiterate immigrants like the ones on Job. Before, the paesani back in Italy, shackled as they were by generations of unchanging traditions, plodded on indifferent to their lot in life. There, they had no power, no voice, and so they toiled on fatalistically without hope of change. Every new day that dawned, every new contact made here, though, in America, brought a change of attitude, that even the most ignorant began to sense. In the whirlwind swirling about him in this new world, no one could stand still, and even the merest peasant could not but be affected and stirred to achieve heights never dreamed of back in his little village on the other side of the ocean.

And, importantly, a core of leaders was emerging out of the churning mass of immigrants themselves. The very men, who, in the old country, would only approach the *padroni* with hat in hand and eyes lowered, were beginning to find their tongues. In America, they discovered, one could say things. Everywhere among the laboring masses, men repeated the slogan, "*L'unione fa la forza.*" (In union there is strength.) In the mills, in the foundries, on the construction sites, workers were beginning to agitate for the organization of labor unions that called for the reduction of working hours, increases in pay, safer conditions on Job. Such changes would not come about by praying, but by action.

So it was that Alfredo spent more time reading newspapers and pamphlets than his missal.

Suddenly he found himself entering the church. Automatically he blessed himself with the holy water. The congregation was made up mostly of black-clad women, and children. Alfredo walked slowly down the aisle by the side of Zia Graziella. When he spied Angelina sitting with her mother and sisters in the center section of the nave, he gently tapped his aunt's elbow. With a slight nod of his head, he indicated the pew into which they should sit. It was right across from where Angelina was sitting. So that he would have the end seat in the pew, he allowed his aunt and the children to take their places first.

On purpose, he lowered the kneeler with a loud bang, and as he had hoped, the resounding noise caused Angelina to turn her head. She gave him a startled, little glance, whether of recognition or annoyance, Alfredo could not tell. But when he saw her face spread into a soft smile, his heart skipped a beat. Their eyes met more than once throughout the Mass. Alfredo would have more than gladly lingered throughout benediction, the stations of the cross, and the litany of the saints, just to keep her in his sight.

He did not approach the altar to receive communion, but she did. He boldly turned up his face as she returned to her place in the pew. He saw her raise her lowered eyes to look at him for just a fleeting moment. That beautiful face was his communion.

At length the Mass was over. With a child by each hand, Zia Graziella walked to the exit of the church. Her nephew trailed a few steps behind, walking parallel to Angelina. Once outside he bowed his head first to the girl's mother, and then to Angelina.

On the next Sunday, at the steps of the church as Mass was getting out, Alfredo with a feeling of determination, tipped his hat and said to the mother, "Buon giorno, Signora La Rocca. I trust you remember me. I am Alfredo Alanga. I was your son's friend on Job."

"Ah. yes. Paolo often spoke of you. Thank you. Buon giorno." She proceeded to walk away, with her daughters in step behind her. Alfredo noticed Angelina turn her head slightly as she followed her mother. She was smiling.

Chapter Twenty

On each succeeding Sunday, Alfredo faithfully went to eight o'clock Mass with his aunt and the kids. After Mass, he always exchanged a pleasant "Buon giorno" with Signora La Rocca and her daughters, and then they went their separate ways. On the fifth or sixth Sunday, Alfredo could hardly believe his eyes; the girl was alone. Without the mother's presence, unafraid and unashamedly, he let his eyes feast on the girl's loveliness throughout the Mass. His heart raced every time, which was more than once, that he saw her turn her gaze in his direction.

When Mass was over, he was already waiting for her to come out. Rather unceremoniously, not even bothering to genuflect, he had hurriedly left his pew in order to reach the door before she did. Then he waited at the bottom of the steps, and when he saw her coming out the door, he raced back up the steps of the church and doffed his hat. "Buon giorno, signorina La Rocca. I notice that your family is not with you today. Is something the matter?" Then, not waiting for her to answer, he blurted out: "May I walk you home?" Alfredo knew that this was not the accepted way to approach a respectable girl if they had been back in Italy, on the street, and without the presence of a family member or older companion. But this was America where boys and girls were more independent and casual in their encounters. Besides, his ardor for the girl had made him bold.

Alfredo was an Italo-American now, adopting more and more the American way of thinking and acting. He was being molded into a different man than his father, who was too steeped in the old ways ever to change much. The challenge of Job, the street life, night school, the language, the vibrancy all around him in this new land were making Alfredo into a different breed than all his ancestors before him. Bosco was far away, and its ways were becoming more and more a thing of the past for him and his brothers.

He made bold to ask again, "Signorina Angelina, may I accompany you home?"

"Signor Alanga, I do not think it a proper thing. My mama is not here; she is not feeling well. Nor my sisters. And so.."

"Let me be your brother then," he interrupted. He started to descend the steps, hoping that she would follow. She did, and they began to walk side by side. Neither of them spoke at first. Alfredo followed her disconcerted gaze, to see a group of old, black-clad grandmothers. Both of them knew, that before the day was out, Angelina's mother would know that they had been seen together.

"Will your mama be harsh with you when they tell her we were seen together unaccompanied?" Alfredo's voice was very soft. He felt a twinge of conscience as he began to reflect that this bold act of his might cause Angelina's mother to be angry with her.

"Mama is kind, but she is Mama. Papa and my brother are dead, so we are a house of women alone. Therefore, she feels greatly the burden of watching over us girls. You understand."

"I know, I know. Don't be afraid. We live in a new world now. Things are different here. The old ways are for the old ones with their hearts still in the old country. Those old gossips," and he threw his head backward towards the knot of old crones they had just passed, "they belong rather in the alleyways of the crumbling villages we left behind, with their stench of decay. There, nothing changes, and there, all the likes of them can find to talk about, are evil things. There, they..."

"Signor Alfredo, you must not say such things. They are the grandmothers. Their gray hairs command respect. One does not change his soul because he puts on new shoes."

Alfredo cut her off. "Rather, let us talk of you—and me. Will it be all right if my Aunt Graziella should pay a visit to your mama? Perhaps then, with your mother's permission, I may call upon you. I would like that very much. Your brother often spoke of his family to me on Job. He told me that one day he would introduce his sister, you, to me. In life, he did not have that opportunity to do so. At his wake, when I saw you for the first time, it was as if he brought us together nevertheless. Your face has ever since been before my eyes."

"I knew who you were as soon as I saw you come up to the casket. Paolo had often described you to us. You are very much as he said; you are very *simpatico*." She drew her shawl closer around her face, so that he could not see the color she felt rushing to her cheeks. "I would like it very much if your aunt should pay a visit to Mama."

She gave a little cough. Hesitatingly, she continued. "You must understand that Mama, well, you see, you are a Neapolitan, from the South. And we, we are Piemontesi, from Ivrea, in the North. I know that Mama feels that we are a different people than those of you from the South." She began to turn red. "That is why she feels out of place here. That is why she has so little to do with anyone, and why she was so unhappy with Papa for bringing her here to this place. Here, there are no other Piemontesi. All are either Calabrians, Neapolitans or Sicilians. She can no more understand their dialects or their ways than she can understand the Americans. Papa's dream was to remain in the city only long enough to make enough money on Job so as to buy a piece of land in upper New York State and grow his own grapes in his own vineyards. Oh, how we used to thrill to hear him speak of how famous his wines would be. And when he died, Paolo swore that he would carry out Papa's dream. But now that dream is gone forever."

With a note of sadness in his voice, Alfredo interjected, "We have all come to this land with dreams in our hearts." He and the girl stopped a few feet from her house. Angelina quickened her step. With a slight wave of her hand, she breathlessly called back to Alfredo from the landing of the stoop, "Tell your Aunt Graziella to pay a call on Mama." Alfredo grinned broadly and said, "Tell your mama, we are all Italians, after all." He smacked his hands in exhilaration. She liked him!

Chapter Twenty-one

The first days and weeks of spring had gone by, and the early days of summer were approaching. Every day the men went off to Job, where they toiled and sweated and turned brown under the strengthening rays of a hotter sun. Michele was no longer with his father and brothers in the house on Elizabeth Street; he had left the family circle to take up his new work in New Haven.

Francesco, too, now went off to work every day. He had hated school and had often been in trouble for truancy or for fighting or disobedience. Exasperated with the boy's recalcitrant behavior, his father had finally acceded to the boy's wish to leave school and go to work. The school authorities, as they so often did, when it came to Italian kids leaving, turned the other way, and did not pursue the matter. So, with the help of Zio Matteo, the boy became apprenticed to a barber to learn the business of barbering.

"The American teachers treat Italian kids like shit," Francesco had told his father.

"Every man in his lifetime steps in shit at one time or another," Giuseppe had told him. "Very well, my son, then you will work. You wish to be a donkey, then go do as you wish." It was not the treatment that the boy had experienced in school, that had made Giuseppe acquiesce, but the realization that, of his three sons, only Alfredo had a head for books, the thirst for learning. With Francesco, he saw the futility of forcing this mule to become a horse.

Every day, then, from nine in the morning until seven in the evening, for six days a week, Francesco reported to Peppino's Tonsorial Parlor on Mulberry Street. The shop was located below ground level—a cave of mirrors. There were three barber's chairs in the shop, and three barbers. Peppino, his son Joe, and old Pietro, who had been the original owner, and who now remained more or less as a fixture in the place. Business was good at ten cents a haircut and shave, so Francesco was kept busy sweeping up piles of hair from the floor. And he washed the mirrors, cleaned the shaving mugs, folded the clean towels and made sure that the jars of pomades, brilliantines and lotions were always filled and in the right order.

His first lessons in actual barbering was learning how to hone a razor on a leather strop that hung beside each chair. Old Pietro, when business was slow, showed him how to hold the razor at just the right angle, how to flick his wrist back and forth along the strop, and then how to lather the face and draw the razor down the cheek so as not to cause the slightest knick. One night, just before quitting time, he put a razor in the boy's hand. The old man sat in a chair. "Shave me. One scratch and I'll cut off your ears."

Joe piped up: "Two scratches, and we'll cut off something else, something most important." He winked to the old Pietro in the chair, and they both started to laugh.

Francesco hoped they were joking. Nervous as a tenor on opening night at the opera, he gently tucked an apron under Pietro's chin, and then began beating the brush in the shaving mug to work up some lather. Very gently, now, the boy began applying the lather to the old man's face.

Joe yelled at him. "For Christ's sake, you're not washing a newborn's ass; twirl the brush, press on it and soften up those stiff, old bristles of his."

A bead of sweat broke out on Francesco's upper lip as he picked up the razor and gave it a few deft strokes on the strop. He placed his thumb on the old man's temple and pulled up the skin to make it taut. His own upper lip now was beaded with more droplets of sweat. He raised the razor to Pietro's face. He saw the old man wink as he bent over the face, and made the first swipe. He could hear the rasping noise the razor was making as it moved down the coarse stubble. His eyes saw a band of pink flesh appear amidst the white foam, a gorgeous swath of whole, unblemished flesh! Another swath. Whole like before. Another, and another, and another. Before he knew it, Francesco found himself toweling old Pietro's face and rubbing his own hands with the fragrant after-shave lotion, and he proceeded to massage Pietro's smooth cheeks with it.

"Well, I guess he can keep his ears," said the old man as he rubbed his face.

"And better yet, his cazzo," laughed Joe.

Regularly for several weeks after, Francesco shaved them all, Joe, Peppino and Pietro. One October afternoon, in between customers, Peppino slapped the razor into Francesco's hand. "Next customer comes in, you shave. Do a good job, who knows, he might even tip you." Before ten minutes had gone by, the door opened. Quick as lightning, Francesco jumped up from his chair, ran to the shelf, and picked up a towel and razor. He started dusting off a seat, and motioned the first man of the three who entered, to come and sit. The man walked towards the chair.

"Holy Jesus," murmured Peppino under his breath. Aloud, he said, "Ah, buon giorno, Don Luigi, buon giorno. Right this way, right this way." Peppino brushed Francesco aside as he bowed to the man. "Go sweep the floor, boy. I'll shave Don Luigi."

But Don Luigi shoved Peppino off with his arm. Facing Francesco, he asked, "You know who I am, kid?"

"Sure I know who you are. Who doesn't?"

Don Luigi laughed. "And you still want to shave me? Because if you knick this pretty mug of mine," and he laughed again, "I'll feed you to my dogs."

Francesco went to the chair and finished brushing it off with a whiskbroom. "Have a seat."

"I like a kid with guts. You're all right. What's your name?"

He sat down in the chair, and Francesco tucked a towel under the mobster's chin. There was still a smile on his ugly, swarthy face, swarthier now with a black five o'clock shadow. Two gold-capped teeth caught the light and blinked at Francesco.

"I'm Francesco, Francesco Alanga." And then the boy began covering the pock-marked face of this customer with lather. While Francesco worked on his face, Don Luigi asked questions, which the boy answered. Where was he from in the old country? How long in America? How old?

When he finished shaving him, Francesco toweled off Luigi's face, patted on some lotion, and flicked off the apron. Luigi got up from the chair, rubbed his hand along his smooth chin and leaned into the mirror to inspect his face. Then he turned to Francesco, while at the same time he pushed aside his jacket to get out his wallet from a back pocket of his pants. As he did so, Francesco spied the black holster strapped to Luigi's waist, and the amber handle of a pistol.

"Nice job, kid." He yanked out a dollar bill and slammed it into the boy's hand. "From now on, Frankie boy, only you shave Don Luigi." He turned to his two body-guards: "Come on. Let's go." They left the shop with Francesco staring in amazement at the dollar bill in his hand.

Chapter Twenty-two

The tenor of the eight or ten letters that crossed the ocean that year of 1907, was almost always the same. Rosa, as usual, inquired about the health and well-being of her husband and sons, gave them news of the well-being of herself and the girls, and finished by asking how much longer before the family would be reunited. And in answer, Giuseppe always reassured her that all was well in America, that they were all working hard to amass the money needed to bring her and the girls over. But first, he had to find a suitable home for them all, that it was out of the question that they could all crowd under Matteo's roof.

In his last letter of the year, Giuseppe informed Rosa of Michele's move to a place called New Haven. He had waited to tell her because he wanted to make sure that the boy was happy there, and that he would stay. He relayed to her Michele's own glowing words of his contentment and progress. It would be in New Haven, Giuseppe told his wife, that he intended to make a home for them all. He begged her to have patience. For, before he and perhaps Matteo, too, could make a home for their families in this new paradise, they first had to have jobs there, and money and a house in which to live. He informed her that Michele was returning to New York for the approaching Christmas holiday; perhaps at that time, some plans could be laid out.

Two days before Christmas, Michele boarded the 6:10 evening train from New Haven to New York. He had not even taken the time to eat, but immediately after work, washed himself hurriedly, put on his one and only suit, and rushed to Union Station. Underneath his jacket, a bright red tie set off the brilliant white of his shirt. The heavily starched collar he wore, cut into his neck; in spite of the hard, physical labor he did every day, working with Angelo the past seven months, he had put on weight. That was thanks to Carmela's good food and the peace he had found within himself. His face was full now, and the flesh of his body, firm. The sallow color was gone from his cheeks. Instead, a healthy glow, red-brown, shone in its place.

Not that he had forgotten Adelina or the pain he had first felt when the arrival of Mama's letter shattered the beautiful dreams of the future life he was going to make for his beloved in the new world. But he had finally come to the realization that those dreams could never be fulfilled. She was as one dead to him, and an ocean lay between them, an ocean that would always separate them now, never to be crossed by him or her. Yet, the sepia colored photograph she had given him on that last day, he always kept on top of his dresser. He went to sleep with the image of her face smiling at him from the frame.

Angelo and Carmela treated him like a son, and he was crazy about their children. He loved children. They had become his kid brothers and sister. He began to laugh again. His work he found challenging and interesting. Under Angelo's tutelage, he became ever more skillful in working with stone and marble. Angelo's praise of his work gave him satisfaction and contentment. Carmela, whom he now called "Zia Carmela," now and again used to drop the names of this girl or that girl in the hopes of arranging a match. There was her own *comare* Costanza's daughter for instance. A pretty girl, and a good cook who knew how to manage her pennies. Or, of course, there was Lidia Bertolucci, another nice girl. And, her father had money. Or, Mister Franco's three daughters were all eligible, every one of them nice girls, good girls, although the middle one had a big nose.

But Michele found no interest in women. Adelina's face alone continued to haunt him. He thought of her often, and the child that she had borne, the child that was his. At least, not for now, but some day perhaps, the broken threads of his life could be put to rights. Now, distance and circumstances were against him, and he had reconciled himself to a life of loneliness. He could not, he would not embroil himself in an attachment to another woman.

When his blood raced hot in his youthful veins with the yearnings that a man feels for the tender touch of a woman's flesh, he steeled himself against them. He fled from such thoughts. Instead, like Saint Francis, who threw himself into a bush of thorns to escape such temptation, Michele threw himself into his work, into bocce games, into smoking, into drinking wine, into companions, anything to escape the torturing thoughts.

Only once had he given in to those yearnings. Even now, when the remembrance of his attempt to satisfy the call of the flesh came to mind, he burned with shame and humiliation of that time two months ago.

After a bout of heavy drinking one Saturday night, with his workmate and now friend, Giovanni Landino, he let himself be dragged off to a bordello on Legion Avenue, a place well known to his buddy.

All the way over to the bordello, Giovanni had extolled the sexual delights with the two girls he usually used. "Ah, what a piece of ass, that Mimi is," and he kissed his fingers bunched together at his mouth. "She knows just when to squeeze her legs tight, to bring you off in a rush of joy." He laughed and slapped Michele on the back. "And the one with the big tits, Linda," he continued, "meets every thrust of yours with one of her own, and runs her hands up and down your bare ass.Whew!" and he made a grab at the half erection pulsing upwards in his pants.

Giovanni led Michele up the steps of an old stone house. He gave the door three sharp raps, and the door opened. The entry was blocked by an ugly hulk of a brute with a fat cigar protruding from two fat lips. It was George, the greeter, the bouncer, the one who made sure that the girls didn't get roughed up by a drunken, or sadistic, or dissatisfied customer expecting more than what he had paid for. The hulk had been known to knee more than one unruly patron in the groin so hard, as to render him a virtual eunuch.

Behind him a raucous voice broke out in greeting. "Hey, Johnny boy." The hulk moved aside and the flooziest dame Michele had ever set eyes on, came into view. The madam of the house, Francine, stood before them. The heavy makeup, the red, red lips, the purple eyelids did little to camouflage an aging queen. An amber cigarette holder with an unlit cigarette stuck into it, dangled from her mouth. To Michele, she looked grotesque, the kind of woman, who, if his mother should ever have seen on the street, would have crossed herself not once, but twice. But the woman's figure was that of an eighteen year-old, slender, svelte, thin waisted with firmly propped up breasts that stood out tantalizingly sharp. The hips were beautifully curved. All this, Michele saw through the sheer, body-clinging satin dress hanging from below the neck to just above the knees. A fluffy band of white feathers around the neck waved in an invisible current of air.

She looked at Michele and smiled. "Hi, sweetie. My, but ain't you a good-lookin' fella. Come with Johnny for a good time?" She turned and walked into the hallway. Johnny gave Michele a little shove, and George closed the front door. The whorehouse itself was a dump. To the right and left of the hall, were the parlors, the waiting-rooms furnished with worn-out sofas and plush chairs in which the customers sat, waiting to be serviced.

Johnny slipped two dollars into Francine's hand, one for himself, and one for Michele. The madam stuck the money into the pocket of her chemise and led them into the parlor on the left. The floor of the waiting-room was covered wall-to-wall with threadbare carpeting that had once been bright red. Now it was almost maroon in color, dulled out with splotches, stains and dirt. The nap was gone, and here and there the very threads of the tan matting underneath shone through.

The windows were covered with heavy olive-green drapes fringed 'With gold tassels. The drapes were pulled tight together, and the shades underneath were drawn down. A heavy smell of stale tobacco smoke assailed their nostrils as Johnny led Michele to a sofa. They sat down next to two young guys speaking Polish. The two smelled of beer and sweat. They flicked the ashes from the cigarettes they were smoking onto the rug, obviously telling jokes, by the uproarious laughing they did. A couple of Irishmen and another Italian occupied the other chairs. Across the hall, the right parlor was full. Now and again, a girl or two would enter the right parlor and leave, linked arm in arm with a customer. Then they would disappear up the staircase in the hall that led to the bedrooms. It was like a parade ground with people going up and down the staircase. The girls were fast workers, because one or two at a time, they began coming into the room where Johnny and Michele were waiting. After a half-hour's wait, two girls came in for Johnny and Michele.

Johnny jumped up. "Ah, Mimi, *bella mia*," he cried out. One hand slipped under her loosely-tied robe and fingered her nipples, and the other he rubbed up and down her bare buttocks as he gently bit her neck. She giggled and squeezed his crotch. Michele just stood there, lost, not knowing what to do. The effects of the alcohol were wearing off. He was beginning to feel uncomfortable and embarrassed.

The other girl bawled out to Michele: "Aw, is it your first time, dearie? You'll be all right once you're in bed with me, honey. Don't be shy," and she took him by the hand. She led him upstairs to a dimly lit room that had a sweet-sour smell to it, the smell of sex. She stood naked before him, and the sight of her black pubic hair, even though the hair of her head was blonde and the dark, brown circles around her nipples filled him with revulsion.

"Dearie, I ain't got all night." The whore came up to him and began running her hand up and down his thigh. The thought that she was still wet from the previous customer, maybe that evil-smelling Pole, choked him and caused Michele to swallow hard. He pulled away from her, opened the door and raced down the stairs. Once outside the house, he stopped and leaned against a tree. The fresh air cleared his head. He was completely sober now. He lit a cigarette and waited for Johnny. Images of Adelina, his mother, his sisters, the pretty village girls that he had known in Bosco, raced through his mind. He wanted to hide his face in shame.

Chapter Twenty-three

Getting off the train at Grand Central Station, Michele made his way to Uncle Matteo's house. A light snow was beginning to fall. He pressed the two small packages he held in his arm close to his body to keep them from getting wet. He had bought a small doll for Marietta and a bat and leather mitt for little Matteo. When he pushed open the big front door to the house, he heard the strains of bagpipe music. Someone in one of the flats was playing the traditional Neapolitan Christmas hymn on a victrola. He stopped to listen. Softly, under his breath, he began to sing the words of the *Pastorale di Natale*:

Tu scendi dalle stelle, O Re del Cielo
E vien in una grotta, dal freddo al gelo.
Mio Bambino, mio Divin,
Ah, quanto Ti costo, l'avermi amato."
(Thou descendest from the stars, O King of Heaven
And comest into a grotto out of the cold and into
the gelid.
My Christ Child, my Divine One,
How much it has cost Thee to have loved me).

Upon reaching his uncle's flat, he rapped lightly on the door. Without waiting, he opened it and walked in. Zia Graziella was at the sink washing the supper dishes. She turned and let out a cry of joy at seeing him. Wiping her soapy hands on her apron, she rushed across the kitchen to take his face in her two hands. The others came into the kitchen, and when they saw him, they ran up to him amid exclamations of greeting. Giuseppe kissed his son on both cheeks; Uncle Matteo did likewise. The two small children tugged at his coat for a kiss, too. Alfredo and Francesco shook his hand, American style.

"Sit, sit." His father dragged him to a chair and pushed him into it. His aunt already had a glass on the table into which she was pouring some wine. "See how fine he looks," she beamed.

"How's the work going? How is it working with Angelo?" broke in Uncle Matteo.

"It is so good to see you again, my son," Giuseppe said, "so good."

"Is it nice in New Haven, like Papa says?" chimed in Marietta.

"Yeah, Mike, what's it like there? How are you making out?" asked Alfredo.

"Leave the boy alone, with all your questions. There will be enough time to talk. Now let him eat." In a moment, Zia Graziella had in front of him at the table, a bowl of minestrone still warm from their own supper not long before. She cut a thick slice of bread from a round loaf and put it by his plate. Michele slipped out of his coat, draped it over the back of the chair, and began dipping his spoon into the soup.

"No one makes minestrone like you do, Zia. I'm starving." He broke off a piece of the bread, soaked it in the thick broth and gobbled it down. His aunt's eyes shone with satisfaction as she watched him eat. In between mouthfuls of the vegetable soup and bread, he began to talk. "It's so good to see you all again." He reached over and gently rubbed Marietta's cheek with his fist. "And how is everything here?" His gaze went from face to face. "Alfredo, you look like you lost weight; and Francesco, you look like you put on what he lost. And you've grown taller, too."

"Aw," Francesco replied, "he's got the love sickness. I'd never lose my appetite over a girl." He was grinning, and Alfredo's face took on a look of embarrassment. A puff of air exploded from his lips by way of ignoring his kid brother's remarks. Instead, Alfredo turned to Michele and addressed him. "So, tell us, really, how are you making out in New Haven?"

The men sat for an hour around the table over their coffee while Michele recounted his experiences—all about Job, the city, Angelo and his family, the friends he had made, his health, his contentment.

Then, with a serious look on his face, he spoke directly to his father and his brother, Alfredo. The excitement in his voice betrayed his emotion, as he blurted out: "I can get work for you Papa, and for you, too, Alfredo. In New Haven. Right now." His words began spilling out of his mouth in a torrent, and his eyes were a-light with spirit. It made everyone, especially his father, happy to see him once again as he used to be, before the time of Mama's letter. Michele continued to talk, and his voice became more animated as he went on.

"Just this past week," he continued, "we finished a job, a big job for this rich American, Mister Tyler." Michele flicked his hand up and down from the wrist to emphasize just how rich Tyler was. "We ripped out the old fireplace in the salon of his mansion. It was all of carved mahogany wood. It was covered with dragon heads, eagle heads and griffins, all highlighted in gilt. But we ripped it out because Mister Tyler desired a new one of marble. The finest Carrara marble of the purest white, broken with delicate ripples of the softest pink, is what we put in its place. A small fortune it cost him to bring it over from Italy. From floor to ceiling, we cut and fit the marble in a semi-circle, with two columns on either side of the hearth. When we finished, it looked like an altar in church. This Mister Tyler, this rich American, was delighted with our work. And truly, he had reason to be. Angelo has the hand of a master.

"His praise for Angelo, for all of us who worked on it, was something to hear. He called us Michelangelos, and that Italian artisans were the best in the world, and that even in his factory, where many Italians worked, he admired their industry. He is one of the big shots in the Sargent Company. That's a big factory on Water Street where they make all kinds of hardware. Locks and keys, door handles of brass, hinges, and all kinds of parts in metal. Well, the long and the short of it is, Papa, that I made bold to ask him, if, in his kindness, he could find places for you two in his factory. I told him of our wish to bring Mama and the girls over from Italy. I told him how much we all wanted to be together here in New Haven. He clapped me on the shoulder, as if I were an old friend of his, and said that whenever you wish to begin, he will give you work. Well? well, what do think, what do you say, Papa, Alfredo?"

Alfredo looked to his father. Giuseppe took a sip of the cold coffee in his cup. He rubbed his chin. "I know nothing of working in such a place, a factory. I have always labored outdoors. For myself, to work in such a place, I do not know if these hands of mine could do such work." He held up his hands and looked at them, studied them.

"Brother mine, you better than any of us can do such work. Did you not work in the forge at home? Did you not make some of the finest works in iron for all of Bosco? Your son has brought you a fine Christmas present!"

Chapter Twenty-four

At the kitchen table the men talked late into the night. And before they went to bed, everything had been decided. They had made their plans. The day after New Year's Day, January 2, 1908, Giuseppe and Alfredo would accompany Michele back to New Haven. There, as Angelo had promised Michele, his father and brother would be able to room and board at a modest cost, in his own home until spring. The attic was large enough for the three of them to sleep; and as for the food, well, feeding two more mouths would present no problem for Carmela. By springtime, surely, they no doubt would have found a permanent residence. If they didn't, no matter. Angelo would not put them on the street.

It was past eleven when the two older men got up from the table and went to their beds. Graziella and the children had long retired. So, only the two older brothers remained alone in the kitchen. Because of the coffee and because of the talk, and because they were once again together, Michele and Alfredo had no desire to retire.

"So, tell me, Al, what's this that Frankie let out of the bag about you and a girl?" They spoke in English, which both of them handled with ease. Alfredo dropped his head and shook it. He pushed the chair away from the table and walked to the window over the kitchen sink. For a moment, he stood staring at the falling snow blowing wildly and furiously now. Half in a whisper he said, "It's really coming down. We'll be shoveling that white shit tomorrow as sure as hell, and on the day before Christmas, yet. No matter, the dagoes'll do it. This goddamn country has no soul. No tradition in this goddamn place, nor heart for poor working sons of bitches like us. Everything is money here. And for money they suck the very blood of men, women, children, who die before their time. All the poor slobs stuck in the mines, the factories, the mills, so the big shots can make money. And the workers die before their time from consumption, the black lung, accident and exhaustion. Unless the workers unite..."

"Whoa, hold on, brother. You sound like an anarchist, like a street-corner agitator. Are you mixed up in that kind of business? Get off your soap box. I asked you about this girl that's gotten under your skin. Tell me about it, maybe I can help. Maybe I can give you some advice, maybe..."

With his teeth bared, Al shot back: "Look who wants to help. You're the one who should have taken some advice. Ho, ho, look at the mess that you got yourself into. That kid in Italy, that's your kid, isn't it? You did it in the field that day. You lay with Adelina, and you got her pregnant, while I watched out for Papa. That day in the fields, just before we left. And now Adelina is another man's wife, and you can't even claim the little bastard as your kid."

With murder in his eyes, Michele sprang up and lunged at his brother. In an instant he had Alfredo by the throat, his right hand balled up into a fist, ready to strike. Alfredo was limp in his clutch. He offered no resistance, nor did Al try to get out of the hold. In a low voice, he said, "I'm sorry, Mike. I'm sorry. I could bite my tongue. It wasn't your brother talking just now. I don't know. I'm all mixed up. Nothing's right here. Look at us. Mama and the girls are three thousand miles away. We're in a land that really doesn't want us. The golden land, the land with streets paved with gold, the land of dreams. But what dreams? Nighmares, that's what. I wish we had never left Boscotrecase, where the air is fresh with the scent of lemons and oranges, all of us together under a warm, blue sky. Do you remember that old sailor on the boat when we came over? Feliciano, I think his name was. Remember how he said that instead of gold, our people found heartbreak in this land?"

By now they were both sitting again. Mike's rage was gone as he began to realize that his brother was full of pain of his own. Not only was he caught in the throes of some personal anguish over a girl, but he was homesick, dissatisfied, disillusioned and hurt by the loss of the idealistic picture he had painted of life in America. "You think too much, you read too much. You feel too much for others, and you make yourself miserable over people and conditions you cannot change. The hell with everybody else, everything else—all those causes and workers. We'll get Mama here, and when we're all together, you'll see, things will seem a lot better. Now tell me, what's this thing about the girl?"

Al got up from his chair in which he was sitting now. "Another time, Mike. It's late. I'm tired, and for sure, tomorrow Papa and I and Uncle Matt will be out all day on the streets. shoveling." He went to the window again and looked out at the accumulating snow. "For sure," he said, and left the room.

111

For a while Mike sat alone in the peace and quiet of the empty room, looking at the dancing flame of the gas jet. Black shadows jerked and jumped on the wall. They reminded him of the marionettes that danced on the strings the puppeteers manipulated behind makeshift screens they used to set up in the piazza when they came to entertain the crowds on fair-days. What a thrill it was when he was a little boy, to watch the brave knights in armor vanquish the evil Saracens in mortal combat.

When a sudden, thin shadow shot out across the wall, it brought back to mind the brave paladin Orlando, thrusting his sword at Marsile, the leader of the treacherous Saracens. He could see himself again a little boy, wide-eyed, cheering on Charlemagne's courageous nephew slaying the hated infidels. He could almost hear again the sighs and groans of the crowd when, alas, poor Orlando and his bosom friend, Oliver, lay dying on the floor of the valley where they had been ambushed by the pagan hordes.

At last, he got up and ended his reveries by turning off the gas jet. He didn't bother to make his way to the room where his father and brothers were sleeping. Instead, he opened the door of the closed-off front room. The room had no heat, and it was as cold as a tomb. He didn't care. He wanted to be alone. In the corner, by a window, the moonlight cast silvery rays on the *presepio*, the nativity scene set up by Zio Matteo. The layout was so expansive that his uncle had had to build a special platform to hold all the figures. The plaster figures of Joseph and Mary, the three kings, the shepherds, the animals were all there. Only Bammenello, the Christ Child was missing. After all, He wasn't born yet.

But at midnight tomorrow, Christmas Eve, he knew, his uncle would gently place the figure of the Christ Child in the wooden manger between the figures of His mother and Saint Joseph. In true Neapolitan fashion, the holy family was housed in what looked like the ruins of a Roman villa with columns and friezes. The papier-mâché mountains were dotted with trees and boulders, and shiny, tin-foil waterfalls and lakes caught the rays of the moon shining through the window.

Mike stood for quite a while, studying the presepio before him, and his thoughts were flooded with the memory of Christmases past.

He looked intently at the hillsides of the nativity scene, peopled with figures of men and women, dressed in the folk costumes of an earlier century. Women bent over tiny washtubs, and there were woodsmen, charcoal burners, little children at play, hurdy-gurdy players and monks.

All were placed along the hillsides and the paths leading to the manger. On one of the hills lay a little mountain village, complete with piazza, a fountain, and a ruined castle. Little houses with miniature tiles on their roofs, clustered around a church with its tower.

Little people, and tinier animals here and there, walked the streets and byways in and around the village. A few isolated farmsteads, with animals and coops, sprinkled the hillsides. Michele's eyes began to moisten at the sight; a vision of their own farm, and Mama and the girls flashed before his eyes. He saw Adelina, too, a baby on her lap. He saw them all huddled before the *focolare*, warming themselves against the winter cold. But no, Adelina would not be there in Mama's house, in front of the fire, with their child.

He turned away from the crèche, undressed, and threw himself on the couch, covering himself with his heavy overcoat. When he awoke the next morning, it took him a moment to realize where he was. In the night, someone had piled two heavy blankets on him. He threw them off, put on his pants, socks, and shoes and went into the kitchen. The warmth there, the good smells, the brightness of the room, brought a smile to his face. He looked at the clock on the wall. It said 9:45. Only Zia Graziella was in the kitchen. Two big bowls of *struffoli*, little balls of fried dough covered with honey and candy sprinkles were on the table. They were a nuisance to make and took a lot of time, but it would not be Christmas for the children without them. It was in the kitchen that Graziella would be spending all of this day, for tonight was the Vigil of Christmas. And to mark the happiness and joy of the birth of the world's Savior on the morrow, good food, lots of it, had to be prepared for the celebration of that remarkable event.

"Ah, you're up at last. You did not even stir a muscle early this morning when I came in and put the blankets on you. The others are all gone out early—the snow. And the children are off to school. I saved some of the dough from the *struffoli* for you. Come, sit now, while I fry it, and I'll heat up the coffee."

"First, I must go to the yard."

She understood. Mike put on his coat and left for the backhouse. When he returned, a dish of four or five pieces of fried dough was on the table. While he washed his hands and face at the sink, his aunt poured his coffee. He sprinkled the dough with sugar and began to eat.

"Ah, this is good, aunt. How long have you been up, working in the kitchen? I heard nothing."

She laughed. "I've been up since four this morning, well before the men. The *struffoli* take time to make, you know. And there is so much more cooking to do for tonight's meal." She took the pot from the stove and poured more coffee into his cup. Then she filled a cup for herself and sat across from him at the table.

"I slept very little last night, thinking about all the wonderful things you told us about your work, and this New Haven where you live. Is there truly a piazza near your house there, as in the old country, with a church and a bell?"

"Zia, you would love this place." Even as he chewed on the fried dough and took sips of coffee, he talked on. "It is true, and every street is lined with trees, no matter where you go. I have walked and walked the streets to see everything. I have taken the trolley on Sundays and have ridden along the shore to smell the sea and feel its breezes. The city lies on the ocean you know, and there are two mountains on either end of the city. They are called East Rock and West Rock. From the tops, and I have been there, one can see the whole panorama of the city below. It is like a painting before your eyes. All the houses, all the churches, the streets, all so small below, and yet one can see the carriages moving and people walking. When you come, aunt, I will take you to the top of East Rock, so you can see for yourself. I promise."

"Oh, to see mountains again. I miss the mountains of my home in Italy."

"These are not like the mountains of Italy, Zia Graziella; just two sole peaks on each side of the city. But still they are mountains. It will gladden your heart to see them." His aunt finished her coffee and got up from the table. I have bread to bake and pasta to roll out, and the eels to clean. But talk on, Michele. Tell me everything."

At the counter beside the sink, she began to open jars of *la conserva*, the tomatoes she had "put up" in Mason jars the summer before. As she opened each jar, she sniffed it to make sure the tomatoes had not spoiled. Even from where he sat, Michele could smell the fragrant basil leaves that garnished each jar, and the sweet smell of the tomatoes themselves.

He pulled out a pack of cigarettes from his shirt pocket. Lately, he had started to smoke cigarettes more and more rather than cigars. They were cheaper, and he had developed the habit of lighting up more frequently over the past months. He lit one, took a long drag, and as he blew the smoke from his nose, he answered his aunt. "Zia, before I leave I will tell you everything. But we are alone now. Tell me, what is this about Alfredo and a girl?"

"Ah, Michele mio. Your poor brother! Sad, so sad. Do you remember his friend, Paolo, the poor young man that got killed on Job?" And after Michele said yes, Graziella went on to relate at length how his brother had first seen the dead boy's sister at the wake, how he had gone to church every Sunday just to get a glimpse of her, how taken with her he had become.

"He begged me to make the '*mmasciata*, to play the matchmaker. To satisfy him, I went to see the girl's mother on his behalf, to ask her permission for Alfredo to pay court to her daughter, Angelina. That's the girl's name. The mother, I found to be a rather bitter woman, full of *superbia*, the snobbishness of those from the North. The bitterness I can understand. She had found nothing but sorrow here, having lost both her husband and her only son within a short time. Alone with three daughters and no man to protect them! One would have thought that she would have welcomed so fine, so handsome a young man as your brother for her daughter.

"They are from Piemonte, you know. We found it difficult to understand each other, but we came across. Although she did not say it in so many words, I could sense her objections to Alfredo because he is a Neapolitan. At any rate, she refused. Your brother's heart was broken. Every Sunday he continued going to church with the hope of seeing Angelina again. But she was not to be seen there any more. The mother was obviously keeping the girl under lock and key. However, Alfredo did manage to meet her secretly somehow, as he told me. He pleaded then, with her to run off with him. After all, what could the mother have done if the act had been accomplished? But the girl would not go against her scruples.

"The fact is, Michele, that one fine day, Alfredo found the house where she lived, empty. They were all gone, mother and daughters. Back to Italy. So, Alfredo found out from the neighbors. This took place in October, and ever since, your poor brother is a macaroni without salt, as the saying goes. He does not speak, even to me, anymore, of this matter. In fact, he says little of anything. Only now and then, does he mutter of things I do not understand, about workers and unions and strikes. He upsets your papa when he speaks of such things. The poor boy is full of pain."

All the while she had been talking, she was working at the sink. She cut onions for the sauce, strained the tomatoes, and mixed and stirred this and that together. Then she turned to Michele. "And you, my boy, are you at peace with yourself?"

Michele knew then, that she knew, as they all must surely know, that the child born to Adelina was his. She looked at him fixedly, with her lips pursed. He raised his eyes to hers, then lowered them and said softly: "My passions and my emotions at the thought of parting from Adelina made me do a stupid thing and an impulsive, foolish act. Understand aunt, that it was the thought of losing each other for so long a time, of not seeing each other for God knows how long, that pushed us together. Before we knew what was happening to us, we lay together." He placed his head between his hands. "I prayed to God that she would not conceive, so that she should not be shamed. And who could have seen that her father would treat her so? What could I do, I here, and she, there? What have I done, what have I done?" He closed his eyes and shook his head. His aunt came over to him and gently put an arm around his shoulder.

"*Che sara, sara,*" she said quietly. "These happenings are counted in the thousands. It is what happens when the passions run high in man and woman. She now has a legitimate husband and the child, a father. Honor has been satisfied. You now, must get on with your life. You are young and must go on with the business of living it."

Michele was about to answer, when the kitchen door burst open and Graziella's two children fell into the room, laughing as they whisked off their coats. "Only half a day of school today, Mama."

"Per Bacco! look how long we have been talking, Michele. The morning is gone already." And to the children she said: "Come, I'll get you something to eat. You've been romping in the snow. You are all wet."

Rising from his chair, Michele said, "Nothing for me, aunt. I want to get some air, take a little walk." He gave a friendly tap on the cheeks of his little cousins, put on his coat and left the flat.

Chapter Twenty-five

That evening the men trooped in, weary, but in good spirits. All day long they had been anticipating the good Christmas Eve meal they knew Graziella would have ready. They washed, and laughed and talked until Graziella opened the table, put in its leaf, and placed more chairs around it so that they could all eat at the same time.

Amidst chatter and laughter, they ate. They drank wine and reveled in the food Graziella placed before them. First, a leafy antipasto of greens, slivers of cheese, rings of raw, green peppers, olives, capers and anchovies. No meat on this day of abstinence. Then, the pasta with its marinara sauce; eels fried crisp in olive oil and doused with lemon juice. Then, the squid, little rings of it and the tentacles, too, prepared both as a salad, or fried. A huge, steaming bowl of *bacala*, the codfish stew swimming in a thin broth with tomatoes and pieces of potatoes into which one dunked chunks of crusty bread. Roasted peppers, eggplant parmigiana, *patate infornite*, a recipe of roasted potatoes that Zia Graziella had brought with her from her native region in the old country—potatoes burning hot, roasted with rosemary, garlic and olive oil, and the meal was complete.

When the dishes had been cleared from the table, Graziella put a bowl of nuts on the table: roasted chestnuts, almonds, hazelnuts and walnuts. Broken shell fragments soon littered the table. And while she set up the *machinetta* in which to brew the strong, black espresso coffee, little Marietta brought out the demi-tasse cups and the bottle of anisette.

Someone brought out the lotto cards and a bowl of dried beans to use as markers, and the first game was underway. Well into the night, they played, even the children who squealed with delight every time they won. Everyone dipped into the *struffoli*, licking their fingers clean of the sticky honey coating. It was after eleven when the last game was over. When the midnight hour struck, all of them followed Zio Matteo into the front room and gathered around the *presepio* to watch him reverently place the figure of the Christ Child on the mound of straw in the manger between Mary and Joseph. It was Christmas.

Chapter Twenty-six

Even as Michele was preparing himself for bed, across the sea, in Boscotrecase, his mother was stirring from sleep. There, it was already Christmas morning, just before the break of day. In the pre-dawn darkness she slipped quietly from her bed so as not to awaken her sleeping daughters. She placed a few sticks on the embers in the *focolare*. The old forge, which now served as house, was cold. Bending over the rising flames, she warmed her hands. Without a sound, she went over to her own bed, took off the covers, and gently placed them over the sleeping forms of her four daughters, lying quietly, two in a bed.

Again she went to the fire. After she had placed some thicker logs on it, the fire began to cast a warming glow that pierced the blackness. Throwing a shawl over her night dress, she went to the table and sat, clasping her hands together on the rough planks of the table top. Pursing her lips tightly, she stared at the flames spitting higher and higher into the gloom. The wood had caught, and was burning more fiercely. Before her eyes, in the brightness of the flames, she thought she saw the faces of her husband, and then Michele's, then Alfredo's, then Francesco's. She looked harder, and the more real they seemed. She caught herself smiling to herself; then, all in a moment, the vision vanished. As the images faded away, all the loneliness, all the heartaches of separation rushed over her, and a film of tears came to her eyes.

On this greatest of feast days, she felt no joy. Her heart was gripped by a feeling of sadness, discouragement, fear. As the days had led into weeks, and the weeks into months, and the months into years, she had begun to doubt more and more the wisdom of this undertaking that had rent asunder the unity of her family. Was it not foolishness, after all, to leave the land of one's birth in search of fortune, she asked herself.

They had all been led to believe that the streets of America were paved with gold. But what gold? Giuseppe himself, as he had related in his letters, dispelled that fairy tale. Along with the few dollars that each letter brought, he had chronicled the struggles undergone to obtain them. The reality and the dream were worlds apart, even as he and she were worlds apart. Perhaps it was not God's will that one tried to change one's destiny.

Just as the leopard cannot change its spots, could an Italian become an American? As she had been born in Italy, and her father, and his father before him, and his father before him, and all generations past, was it not an unnatural presumption on their part, to turn their back on all their forefathers? But then again, she reasoned as she sat there, surely, it cannot be an evil thing to try to better one's lot in life? Her mind was in turmoil as she thought of these things. One moment found her in despair, the next, hope rising anew in her breast. "I must leave off these thoughts," she murmured to herself. "Patience, patience. I must have patience, as Giuseppe says in his every letter. One fine day, lo! he will write, 'Come,' and we will be together again." She muttered a silent prayer to the new-born Christ Child that He grant her patience.

Slivers of light began shining through the cracks of the old wooden shutters of the shed. She opened them wide and the sun's rays filled the room with light. With the brightness, her mood changed, and she rose to make some coffee. and toast some bread. The girls would be waking soon, and they had to eat. Outside, the thin film of frost that covered the stones of the walls melted away quickly. But the musty smell of dampness would take longer to disappear.

In the town, little sign of the destruction caused by the eruption in 1906 remained. What could be patched, was patched. What had to be leveled, was leveled and rebuilt. Only in the far countryside one saw ruins, of isolated farm buildings, and where once trees and orchards had grown, now the ground was covered with scrub and weeds. Many a time Rosa thanked God, that at least, there was a roof over their heads and four walls to give her and the girls shelter.

But Rosa's reflections were cut short, as one by one, the three older girls, Filumena, Carolina, and Eleonora roused themselves from their beds and came to the table. Little Gilda slept on, with the covers pulled high over her head. Gilda was the last of Rosa's and Giuseppe's children. Six years old now, and with the promise of being the prettiest of the girls. She alone of all the children, had bright blue eyes, inherited no doubt, from some Norman or Swabian soldier from long ago, who either by rape or by marriage, had added his genes to the gene pool of Rosa's ancestors. The green of the eyes of Alfredo, Carolina, Francesco, and Rosa's herself, had resulted from the blend of the blue and the brown, probably.

"*Buon Natale, Mama*," the girls said in unison. Their mother answered with her own "*Buon Natale*," and beckoned them to come to the table. They sat and sipped the hot coffee, feeling its warmth spread through their bodies. In a little while, Gilda now awake, joined them at the table, and after they had all eaten, they dressed and walked to the church in Bosco to hear Christmas Mass.

At noon they sat down to a simple meal of pasta, into which Mama had mixed several baked potatoes, skin and all, to make the dish more filling. Then, some greens fried in oil and garlic, a glass of watered-down wine, and the Christmas meal was over. They all felt the emptiness of the house, a house without males, without spirit. How lonely and desolate the house seemed on this day of days, so merry in the past with the sound of rough, hearty laughter, and the bantering of their menfolk. Now the place resembled a convent.

The afternoon came and went. A chilly twilight brought an end to the day. Solemnly they sat around the table, plying their needles by the feeble light of a kerosene lamp. Even little Gilda was sewing. They exchanged few words. Now and again, as the winter cold invaded the forge, one of them would throw some sticks on the fire.

The last few months had been difficult ones. The exceptionally cold winds blowing down from the Lattari Mountains onto the valley of Pompei, had brought early frosts which all but killed the garden. Precious little feed remained for the chickens, the goat and the remaining pigs. Without a mule and without men, Rosa had only been able to sow a small area of corn, not the hectares of corn her husband and sons had cultivated in the past. So little corn was left, that Rosa had had to slaughter one of the pigs born in the summer. The money, however, that came in the letters from America had proven a veritable godsend. Without those dollars that Giuseppe included in each letter, Rosa and the girls would have indeed gone hungry.

As they sat sewing, suddenly the flame of the lamp began to flicker and sputter. "Come, daughters, it is getting too dark to sew any longer. You will strain your eyes, and your stitches will be crooked. Put away your embroidery now." The girls obeyed and laid down their sewing. But it was too early for bed. Little Gilda ran to the *focolare*. "Mama, please come and tell us some stories, about the days when you were a little girl like me, and about your mama. And about the good Saint Francis who talked to the little birds. Your stories are even better than the ones the *cantastorie* tells when he comes to the piazza in Bosco."

Mama smiled and began walking to the fireplace. All the girls soon gathered by the light and warmth of the fire, eager to hear Mama recount again the stories and tales they had heard so many times before, never tiring of hearing them. And in the manner that legend and lore, fact and fancy, genealogy and history had been passed down from generation to generation, Mama began.

The children listened with the same wonder, the same thrill as if hearing her tales for the first time. The girls hung on to every word. They caught every nuance, every rise and fall of Mama's voice. For their mama was a wonderful storyteller, even though unsophisticated, unschooled, unlettered as she was. She punctuated her narratives now with a sigh of sadness, now with an exclamation of joy. She spoke simple truths in simple words, but with a touch of poetry, almost, that came naturally to her and without contrivance. Her tales were a reflection of all that was real and believable to her peasant mind, whether a tale about work, fate, destiny, goodness, evil, family, God. Unknowing to her, but coming naturally, she employed the art of the poet in her speech with a richness of cadence, meter and even rhyme that at all times was almost scanable.

So vivid were the images conjured up in the minds of the children in Mama's last story, that the girls shuddered and gasped aloud. It was a story she had never told before; how gypsies had once abducted her little brother, Antonio, from the piazza in Bosco during carnival time long before they were born. Their own Zio Antonio, stolen by gypsies! The girls thrilled with excitement to hear how *nonno* Giuseppe, Mama's father, their own grandfather, had caught up with the gypsy caravan on the road to Naples, and rescued from their clutches, his little son, Antonio, hidden under a featherbed in one of the wagons. With one blast of his trusty *lupara*, the musket used to kill wolves, grandfather, blew off the arm of the gypsy king who was coming at him with a drawn dagger. The evil gypsies, Mama explained, would have blinded the little boy, and then set him to begging in their wanderings through towns and villages. Thus, the girls had come to understand why Mama had such great devotion to Saint Lucy, the patroness of eyesight; now, they knew why Mama never failed to light a candle in front of the saint's statue in church. There, in painted robes of blue and red, Saint Lucy stood holding a plate with two plucked eyeballs on it, those two detached eyeballs that so frightened little Gilda, that she always covered her own eyes with her hand when she had to be with Mama praying before the statue.

Mama finished her story, leaned over and stoked the fire. "Off to bed now, and say a prayer of thanksgiving to Santa Lucia, who saved the eyes of your Zio Antonio." When little Gilda climbed into bed and snuggled next to her sister, she resolved never to turn her eyes away from the good Saint Lucy's statue.

Chapter Twenty-seven

The next morning Mama and the girls awoke to the sounds of a furious rainfall and the gusting of a wild wind that caused the heavy, wooden shutters to creak and rattle against the walls. The dark, black sky made it seem as if the night had never ended.

So they lit the lamps and fed the fire more abundantly in order to dispel the gloom and the cold.

When the rain' stopped, the sky was still a black pall overshadowing the earth. At the *focolare* Mama and the girls had just picked up their sewing, and Filumena was clearing the table of the traces of the midday meal, a watery *minestra* over chunks of stale bread. Suddenly a loud rapping at the door startled them all. When Rosa opened the door, framed against the black sky, stood the diminutive form of *comare* Serafina. In her arms, a bundle wrapped in white cloth shone out against the all-encompassing black of the woman's clothing and the darkness of the landscape.

With Rosa's steady urgings, the old lady entered. Carolina rose from the chair by the fire as the wizened form advanced into the room. Carefully placing the bundle on the table, Serafina unraveled herself from the black shawl that enshrouded her. With a sigh of weariness, as if careful not to break any of her brittle bones, she lowered herself into the chair by the heat of the fire and began rubbing her skeleton-like hands over the flames. Every joint of her fingers was grotesquely swollen and bent.

Strictly speaking, Serafina was godmother to none of Rosa's children. But, because as midwife, she had brought so many of the village babies into the world, everyone called her *comare* out of respect.

The visit was a complete surprise to Rosa, but her innate sense of hospitality came into play, and she bade the girls make some coffee and put some sugared fried dough on the table. Then she turned to Serafina and asked: "And did you walk all the way from Bosco, and on a day like this?" The old lady began cackling in response. "I'm seventy-four, heh, heh, but my legs still carry me where I want to go. But these poor hands of mine are all crippled from arthritis, so the young mothers are afraid to call me when they give birth. Many a little rosebush and bell clapper have I plucked from swollen bellies. All of yours, dear Rosa, every one of them." She clucked contentedly.

"Come to the table, *comare* Serafina. Take some hot coffee and some bread." The old lady came away from the fire and up to the table. Still smiling, she took hold of the bundle on the table and began unknotting the cloth. When the sides of the cloth fell away, a dozen fragrant pastries covered in powdered sugar, tumbled out. Little Gilda let out a shriek of delight when she saw the fluted cakes filled with rich cream, the sponge cakes soaked in rum, the crusty tubes filled with ricotta, and the clam-shaped *sfogliatelle* with their myriad, paper-thin bands of pastry dough wound round and round a stuffing of rich cream and ricotta laced with pieces of citron throughout.

"These come from the shop of my nephew over in Scafati. He and his sons are fine pastry cooks, and these are a gift to you from his son Vincenzo; she winked at Rosa and nodded her head sideways towards the girls. And then Rosa understood the purpose of this visit. Serafina was making '*mmasciata*; she had come in the role of matchmaker on behalf of the man interested in paying court to one of her daughters.

"Taste, taste. See how fine these pastries are." Then, heeding her own command, the old crone picked up a cake and bit into it with relish. "Ah, what a master baker that Vincenzo is. All of Scafati comes to his shop on the piazza to buy his sweets and *confetti*. For every wedding, every baptism, every festa, the people come to the shop to buy. I tell you, lucky the girl who marries Vincenzo Annunziata. She will have a sweet tooth, that girl."

"Girls, wrap yourselves up good and go tend to the animals," Rosa said, turning to her daughters.

"But, Mama, we already..."

"Go, go, girls. It's Christmas, and animals, too, are God's creatures, like the very ones that warmed Gesu Bambino with their warm breath in the stable at Bethlehem. Go, go, now."

Rosa picked up her cup and sipped from it as she waited for the girls to leave. As soon as they had trooped out, the matchmaker got to her task. "The fact is, dear Rosa, that my grandnephew is quite taken with your daughter, Filumena. When he was last in Bosco picking up a load of flour from Ciccone the miller, he saw the dear girl waiting for her corn to be ground. More than once, he has come to Bosco, begging me to speak to you on his behalf.

"Think, dear Rosa. You are women alone in this house, without a man to sustain you. Is it not a boon to you to know that a good man, a man with a good trade, wants to provide a good life to one of your daughters? Ah, daughters! How we mothers must be ever watchful over them to see that they come to no disgrace." Serafina paused, a trace of a malicious smile on her lips, and leaned forward a little, as if checking to see Rosa's reactions to her words. And indeed, a dart of pain raced across Rosa's face as she thought of Adelina.

"Men can be evil creatures," Serafina continued, "who think only of having their way with girls when the poor darlings are not guarded at all times. Many a poor, innocent girl has been ruined because she had no father or brother to protect her from the lust of a man. A man is like a hawk, waiting to pluck the first hapless hen he spies away from the coop. What a relief to a mother to see her daughter in a husband's care, in a marriage bed where only he has known her." She finished, and with her hands joined as if in prayer, wobbled them back and forth in front of her face.

A barrage of thoughts flooded through Rosa's brain all at the same time. For several minutes she said nothing. The face of her men, gone now for almost two years, the face of Adelina, the faces of all her daughters, reeled off one after another before her eyes. The toll of separation from her husband and sons had begun for some time to wear down her spirits. Even with the dollars that came in the letters from America, managing the farm alone with only the girls to help, was becoming more difficult. And as the months rolled by, more and more the feelings of despair and helplessness grew. At night, in the dark silence, she was assailed by a hundred fears. Not only did she come to fear for the safety and well-being of those lying beside her, but also for those loved ones across the ocean. Her Mother's heart ached at the thought of the harshness of the life the girls were undergoing, and who knew what travails her sons were suffering in America?

Perhaps this old lady's proposal was a godsend, a means to alleviate the burden of worry and care she was feeling over the girls. Could this, then, be fortune smiling on one of her daughters? She broke off her wandering thoughts and looked up straight into the old lady's face. She asked: "And tell me, *comare*, tell me about this nephew of yours. A good man, you say he is?"

"Tut, tut. Heavens," chuckled Serafina. "Vincenzo is as soft and malleable as the dough he works with. He is a gentle man, a good man. A wise woman will know how to knead him into any shape she wants." She laughed and gave Rosa a knowing wink.

"True, he is no stripling of a lad." She cleared her throat. "He is thirty years old, a sensible, a mature man, not a silly boy with his hand always in his pocket. His hair is a little thin (she couldn't bring herself to say that he had the head of a Saint Anthony), but his face is pleasant. His nose is a little long, true, but all-in-all, he is a well-made man with straight legs and a straight back."

As the woman's voice droned on and on, extolling the virtues of Vincenzo, Rosa found herself only half listening. A multitude of thoughts were crowding her mind in a jumble of confused images. In between "Vincenzo this" and "Vincenzo that," Rosa pictured herself those many years ago, cradling the new-born Filumena in her arms; the next moment she saw her daughter dressed like a little bride all in white, receiving her First Communion. Had the years gone by so fleetingly, that now that little girl was ripe enough for a man to come along and take her away? She gave her head a little shake as if to dispel the very idea. Where was her husband? She needed him now, and he was far away from her.

Could she dare make so important a decision as this, alone, without the advice of her husband? "What am I to do, Giuseppe?" she said to herself. "A man is asking for your daughter's hand, and you are so far away from me. I need your advice in this matter." She continued to converse with herself. "Things are hard for us here. Would not our daughter be better off and happy in the care of a good man? A husband to feed her and shelter her and give her children? Is this not the lot of woman, after all? Tell me, Giuseppe, what must I do, what would you have me do?" And then before her eyes, her husband's face appeared as clearly as if he were in the room with her. In his hand, he held a letter. In the blinking of an eye, the vision vanished, but Rosa knew now how she must answer Serafina.

"Dear *comare* Serafina, on such an important affair, I must first learn what my husband thinks. Give me some time to have a letter written. In the meantime, bring your nephew here so that I may see him with my own eyes. Filumena, too, must see him. When you leave, I will speak to her of this matter."

At that moment the door opened, and the girls came in. "Come, girls, have some pastry. We did not eat them all," chirped Serafina in a sweet, bird-like tweet. She rose from the table and wrapped herself in her shawl. Kissing Rosa on both cheeks, she made her way to the door. "The blessings of a good New Year on this house, and may good fortune attend you all." She smiled, winked to Filumena, and left the house.

Chapter Twenty-eight

In a few weeks after Serafina's visit to Rosa, Giuseppe received the letter from his wife in which he learned of the proposal of marriage made to his daughter by the *comare's* great-nephew. In it, Rosa described the young man's visit, his gentility, his comeliness. "He is a pastry cook," she had written, "and a man of means, with his own shop in Scafati." By letter's end, Rosa had made clear her approval of the match, and more importantly, informed him of Filumena's shy acquiescence to Vincenzo's attentions. All that was wanting now, was her father's approbation.

As he listened to Alfredo read the letter, it suddenly came to Giuseppe, that with the exception of little Gilda, his offspring were no longer little children. They had grown up now, even Francesco in a sense, and their destinies lay more in their own hands than in his. Michele was already his own man, on his own in New Haven. The other two sons, although under the same roof with him, had become more and more independent of their father as they pursued their own way in America. This new world and its attractions were taking them away from him, farther and faster than had they still been back in tiny Bosco, where change came about imperceptibly and slowly.

Had they remained in Bosco, no doubt, only a few kilometers would ever have separated any of them from each other. There, in the old country, one lived and died within sight of one's own campanile. And here, already Michele was living some eighty miles away from him, a vast distance to Giuseppe's way of thinking.

Alfredo finished reading, but Giuseppe's thoughts kept on churning in his mind, as he pictured, now Rosa, now Filumena back in Bosco. For his wife, the marriage of their daughter would mean one less mouth to feed, one less worry, one less burden. For the girl herself, if the man was to her liking, it would mean security, protection, care.

He broke off his ruminations. He said to Alfredo: "Write. Tell Mama that I give my permission and my blessing. If the man is a good man, and if Filumena consents, let it be done."

So when her husband's reply arrived a few weeks later, Rosa called her daughter to her side. "Your father has written, dear child, and he sends his blessing. If it is your wish, then, my Filumena, you may marry."

And so on a bright May morning in 1908, Filumena and Vincenzo became man and wife in the church in Boscotrecase. Afterwards, a little festa at the farm, a tearful farewell to Mama and her sisters, and Filumena rode off with her husband to a new home in Scafati and a new life. In all her twenty-one years, Filumena had never before been outside the confines of her native village, except the time when Mama had fled from the eruption in 1906, to Castellammare.

The drive along the eight or so kilometers between Bosco and Scafati seemed to go on forever. As the cart rumbled along the road taking her to a strange place, with this virtual stranger beside her, her thoughts turned to Mama and Papa, her sisters and her brothers. She began to cry at the thought that she would never see them again, once they were all in America. She turned in her seat to look at the figure of this man sitting next to her on the bench of the cart. It would be with him, that she would spend the rest of her life, and she scarcely knew him. The only instance she had ever felt his touch, was when he had held her hand to place his ring on her finger some hours ago. With a sudden movement of her hand, she clutched the clasp of her collar and with the other, she clutched the rosary in her pocket.

A little blush of embarrassment turned her pink at the thought of herself in bed with this man. Her mind wandered to the days when she was a young girl and had seen the bull atop the cow in the field, undulating in frenzied rhythm against the cow's rump. She remembered the naked body of her little brother, Francesco, and his being wiped dry after a bath, and the boy's strange private parts. And later, when she was older, hearing the married women laughing and making crass remarks about their husband's sexual prowess in bed, and details of their own wifely functions between the bedsheets.

With a flick of her head, she cast such remembrances from her mind and looked at the countryside. The cart was following a bend in the road, and ahead, not far in the distance, Filumena saw the outline of a town. "Scafati," Vincenzo said. This was the place then, where in all probability, she would pass her days as wife and mother. Perhaps, become an old woman there, and there the days of her life would no doubt unravel to its end.

"Ah, home, Filumena. We have arrived." Her husband snapped the reins sharply, and the mule came to life and speeded up its gait. Soon its four hooves resounded on the thick paving stones of Scafati's streets in a steady clip-clop. It was dusk now, and only a few people were to be seen in the near-empty piazza. One man waved to Vincenzo in recognition as the cart made its way past the line of shops across from the church which dominated the town square. The church sat on a tier of steps, ornate, like a wedding cake.

"That corner shop, that is our *pasticceria*." Filumena was able to make out some half-empty trays of pastries and a few wedding dolls through the shop windows as they neared. Then the cart passed the shop onto a narrow street that barely allowed passage for the cart. It came to a stop by the third *cortile*, an alley, really, that was flanked on either side by massively built stone row-houses. Vincenzo helped his wife off the cart. When she was down, he led her to one building, opened the door to the house, and Filumena stepped into what was now to be her home.

This night, the house was all theirs alone, for Vincenzo's parents and two unmarried brothers who lived in it too, had remained in Bosco at *comare* Serafina's. While her husband went back to the cart to bring in the bundles of Filumena's personal belongings and wedding gifts, the new bride surveyed her home.

The large room in which she stood was both kitchen and living room. The *focolare* was at the back wall of the room. In front of it, sat a ponderous table of wood with heavy chairs around it. Against the right wall there was a set of shelves that held dishes, cups, crockery. Next to that, the only decorative piece of furniture in the room, an armoire with carved claw feet and paneled doors, held the family's clothes and linens. In a corner by the window was a little table on which stood the images of saints and a votive candle, unlit and caked with drippings of hardened wax.

Only two small windows in front, facing the alley, gave any light or air to the place. Off to the left, three half-opened doors gave Filumena a glimpse of three small bedrooms, only slightly larger than monks' cells.

Vincenzo entered with bundles which he dropped to the floor. He went out again to stable the mule. Upon his return, he took Filumena's hand. "This is Mama's and Papa's room," he said, pointing to the center one. "The one on the right is where Silvio and Ernesto sleep." Gently he led his wife to the left, pushed open wide the door. "This is where we sleep." He led her into the room and closed the door.

Chapter Twenty-nine

By the time of Filumena's marriage that May day of 1908. Giuseppe and Alfredo had already been living with Michele in New Haven since mid February, working at their new jobs in the Sargent Company. Francesco, working steadily now as an apprentice barber in Peppino's barber shop, stayed behind under his uncle's roof. The boy had not been unduly sad to see his father and brother depart. Uncle Matteo and Zia Graziella were a lot easier to live with.

Mister Tyler, who had been so impressed by Michele's work, was true to his word. When Giuseppe and Alfredo arrived in New Haven, the promised jobs were waiting for them at Sargent's. It had not taken long for Alfredo and his father to fall into the routine of living in New Haven. They were with Michele now, in Angelo's home on Chestnut Street, sharing the same cold attic room. For the two dollars and fifty cents they each paid Angelo every week, they had room and board. Carmela treated them more like family than boarders.

Each evening, during the remaining cold weeks of winter, after leaving the warmth of the kitchen as late as possible, the three Alangas made their way to their beds in the attic. There, loaded with an armful of heated bricks wrapped in flannel rags, each of the men passed the bricks over the bottom sheet of his bed. Then, stripping down to their woolen *mutande*, they wrapped themselves into a cocoon of heavy blankets.

Every morning during those bitterly cold, last weeks of winter, at the crack of dawn, whether in a whirlwind of snow, or sleet, or rain, Alfredo and his father walked to their jobs the short distance away to Sargent's, and Michele left with Angelo to wherever their work was. In the factory, for ten hours each day of the six-day workweek, Giuseppe worked at a machine that removed burrs from the brass components of the locks or hinges that were made at the factory. Alfredo worked in the shipping room lifting and carting heavy boxes.

For Alfredo, the work of lifting and loading was no more strenuous than the labor he had done on the construction sites when he worked in

New York. But being confined in the warehouse taxed his patience to the breaking point. He toiled like a madman in order to throw off his pent-up adrenaline. Many of his coworkers could not keep up with him. But as the tedious weeks went by, he got better used to his surroundings, and the mental strain decreased. He was able to slow down, although he never became a slacker. And his father worked just as assiduously, happy to be working once again with metals instead of cement.

Then, on that blessed day of rest, Sunday, Giuseppe, Alfredo and Michele usually lay luxuriously in bed. Finally, arisen from sleep at mid-morning, they ate a simple breakfast of hot coffee and bread. After a bit of carefree conversation with Angelo and his wife, they left the house. Giuseppe lit his first cigar of the day, and stuffing a little bag with crusts and crumbs of stale, left-over bread, he was off to feed the birds in Wooster Square. Only a Sunday blizzard prevented his outings to the square. And, in the spring, it was only a rainy downpour that interrupted his usual routine. Then, with the advent of mild weather, all three of them, father and sons, rode the trolleys to the different neighborhoods of the city. They journeyed through them all—Uptown, The Hill, Fair Haven, Westville, the Heights, The East Shore. In this way, they soon became familiar with all the wonders and charms of the city.

The magnificence of the Green, surrounded by ponderous, black wrought-iron fencing along its whole perimeter brought to mind the grill work seen on the grounds and balconies of the estates of the *signori* back in the old country. His own father, Giuseppe told his sons, more than once, had executed such grill work in the old forge.

The elegance of the stonework of the Yale University buildings was a marvel to their eyes. Several times did Michele and his father pass a hand lovingly over the great stone blocks of the Sterling Library, or the buildings of Silliman College and the Harkness Tower. Their eyes feasted admiringly on the stone gargoyles that jutted undauntedly from tower and archway; on the lacework in stone that embellished the leaded windows; on the gateways medallioned with stone shields and crests.

"These were masters of their art, the stonemasons who built these buildings," Giuseppe often repeated, every time he saw them.

One beautiful Sunday in mid spring, Michele took his father to see the mansions of the wealthy on Prospect Hill and along Whitney Avenue. The houses were set on sweeping expanses of lawn, with port-cocheres and circular driveways in front. The houses stood majestically against the sky, their turrets rising high above the mansions' roof-tops.

Windows of leaded stain glass and exquisite gingerbread fretwork along eaves and loggias, added to the sumptuousness of the stately houses.

Pointing to one elegant Tudor house, Michele said to his father: "I have been inside that palace. It is Mister Tyler's home, where Angelo and I did our work." Giuseppe peered through the gateway of the walled estate to admire the marble statuary placed here and there throughout the grounds. "I am happy you have taken me to see such grandeur, such beauty, Michele." Then he laughed a little and added: "And now back to the real world, eh? back to our attic."

One Sunday in June, Giuseppe all by himself, took a walk along Chapel Street. He strolled leisurely, a dead cigar clamped between his teeth. The air was warm and the scent of the tree foliage and the flowers overcame even the stink of the smelly cigar stub sticking out from under his nose. Windows of the houses he was passing were open to let in sun and fresh air. He stopped to listen to a woman's voice singing the refrain of "Torna a Sorrento." He smiled, hearing again his Rosa singing as she often did at her tasks around the house or yard. The woman's singing came to an end, and he resumed his stroll.

He reached a bridge that crossed the Mill River. In the middle of it, he paused, and as if his wife were beside him in the flesh, he began pointing out the sights to her. The occasional passer-by, hearing him talk to himself, hurried past, no doubt, thinking him crazy or about to leap. "See the gulls, Rosa," he said softly; he was pointing to a flock of birds swirling noisily over the water. Then he pointed to the far shore and the mountains of oyster shells glistening white in the sun. He remained leaning over the bridge's railing for some time, watching flat cargo barges floating by, laden with scrap metal mostly. Far, far off in the distance his gaze settled on the open expanse of water.

Of course, Rosa had never seen such an expanse of water as now spread before him. He smiled to himself to think how amazed she would be to see it. But the time had come to leave off his daydreaming. He resumed his walk. A few blocks down from the bridge, he came upon a wide, tree-lined avenue to the left. A handsome church of white stone caught his eye, and when he reached it, he stopped at its front to scrutinize the stonework.

He wanted very much to enter the church; perhaps it was not a Catholic Church, and perhaps it was not permitted to go in. He was not confident enough to approach anyone passing by to ask a question in his heavily accented English, the little he knew. The people he had seen passing were not paesani, he could tell. Since many of the encounters he had had in the past with some Americans had been unfriendly, he hesitated to make contact with them. In the Little Italy of New York's East Side, or here in New Haven's in the Wooster Square area, he was at home. But away from it, he felt like the foreigner that he was.

Then, like a clap of thunder, the sound of voices speaking in Italian struck his ears. He turned to see a man and woman talking in the same Neapolitan dialect as his own. They were just about to step off the curb to cross the street. Giuseppe went up to them and asked, "Excuse me, good people, but is this a Catholic Church?" From his pronunciation, the couple knew that they were in the company of a fellow Neapolitan from their own region of the Campania. Before he knew it, Giuseppe found himself sitting under a grape arbor in the couple's backyard of their house across the street from the church. Over wine and *taralli*, they were soon conversing as if they had known each other for years. When Giuseppe told them that he was from Boscotrecase, they threw up their hands in joy. "And we are from Scafati," they cried out in surprise.

Their names were Cosimo and Anna Perrelli. In the course of the conversation throughout that warm afternoon, it came out that although the two of them had left the old country more than ten years ago, they well remembered the pastry shop on the edge of Scafati's, piazza, and the Annunziata. family that ran it. Yes, they could recall young Vincenzo Annunziata, Giuseppe's new son-in-law; it did Giuseppe's heart good to hear that they regarded all the Annunziatas as fine people. An immediate bond of friendship was formed that afternoon between Giuseppe and his new-found compatriots.

It was almost evening when Giuseppe rose to leave. In spite of the Perrellis' urgings to stay for the evening meal, Giuseppe begged off, but he promised to return soon. He said his goodbyes, and he vowed to have his son write a letter to Filumena and have her relay greetings from the Perrellis to their relatives still in Scafati.

On the walk home, he mulled over in his mind the things they had spoken about under the canopy of the leafy arbor. Cosimo's words telling of the brutally difficult experiences of his first days in America, stayed with him along his walk home. Cosimo had told him that indeed, the church across the way was a Catholic one; but he himself refused to go there ever since the Irish pastor of Saint Rose's had announced from the pulpit that Italians were not welcome in his church, that they should go to Saint Michael's to be with their own kind. In fact, ever since, Cosimo had not stepped inside a church of any kind. But Anna, his wife, ignored the priest's words, sent him to the devil, and faithfully went to daily Mass there. Every Sunday she dropped her ten cents into the collection basket along with the quarters that the Irish parishioners threw in. Any dirty looks she got for her thin dime, she ignored. The priest was too fat, anyway; she had better things to do with her money than feed his Rotundity.

Giuseppe had chuckled to himself. His Rosa would have acted likewise, and he no doubt, would have reacted as had Cosimo.

That afternoon he and the Perrellis had conversed at length about so many things. He was truly impressed with the goodness of these people, especially so, when Anna recounted how they had taken into their home *un figlio della Madonna*, an abandoned waif from the orphanage run by the Sisters of Charity. Anna was barren.

The good sisters had been only too happy to relieve themselves of another mouth to feed. When they had first shown little Antonio to her, her heart ached, Anna had said, to take him home right then and there and fatten up the little boy. With eyes beaming with love and pride, she had described her adopted son to Giuseppe. He had such big, brown eyes and lashes around them so long, that one could sit on them. And such a mop of curly hair, crowning that face that had found it so hard to smile. As Anna went on to explain to Giuseppe, he had been one of only three Italian orphans in the home. He was seven years old then, when she first saw him. The city social workers had placed the boy in the orphanage a little less than a year before the Perrellis took him as their son.

Then with feeling and many a sigh, Anna had related how the boy had come to be placed in the orphanage. Antonio's parents were a Sicilian couple, newly arrived in America. On a cold winter's day, in the six-family tenement in which they lived someone's kerosene heater exploded. Flames engulfed the wooden tinderbox that was their dwelling. The fire became an inferno, but by a miracle the little boy was one of a dozen people who had escaped the conflagration. Antonio's parents, however, had both perished in the blaze. Since the boy had no known relatives, he had become a ward of the city. And thus it was, as Anna had said, little Antonio had come into their lives, as much loved and cherished as if he were flesh of their flesh, blood of their blood.

That evening in the house on Chestnut Street, Giuseppe told all of them of the fortuitous meeting he had had with the Perrellis. "They are good paesani, good people," he said. Over the years ahead he never had cause to alter his opinion of them.

Chapter Thirty

After his father and brother left New York for their new home in New Haven back in February, Francesco remained with Zio Matteo and Zia Graziella. His job in the barber shop was by now secure, and with the money he earned there, and the money he usually won at cards, he was self-supporting. Every payday he dutifully and proudly gave his aunt two dollars for his room and board. Day by day, his sense of independence grew, and away from the eyes of his father and brothers, he felt a sense of freedom that did much to foster in him a certain self-assuredness, cockiness almost.

During the months, working in the barber shop, he had heard and learned many things about the reality of life on the streets, a life so different from what he had known on the byways and paths back in Bosco. Men of all types came into the barber shop. Most of Peppino's customers were hard-working, uneducated, simple peasant types breaking their backs on Job in order to feed their families. In the chair, they talked a lot, always about Job, their kids, the ones they had left behind in the old country.

And then there were the young Romeos, not the least bit shy about vaunting their escapades with the ladies. The tough guys came in, too, the *guappi*, who, if you stepped on their toes, would just as soon punch you out, as accept an apology. Their conversation in the chair was laced with every curse word and vile oath they knew, both in Italian and in English. In vivid language, they described all the details of the latest, bloody fight.

But no matter who it had been in the chair, each customer, whether it was the laborer, or the Romeo, or the tough guy, every one of them upon rising from the chair, went to the mirror. Without exception, he examined and smiled at his reflected image. Young or old, he spent a minute to admire his new face, passing a hand over the smooth face and pomaded hair. Then, moving the head now to this side and now to that side, so that every angle of his face was viewed, he gave a grunt of approval at the handsome face staring back at him from the mirror.

The old saying that "beauty is in the eye of the beholder," must have been first coined by an Italian. For even the ugliest, can find something to admire about himself. Deep within the Italian psyche, there lies an innate appreciation for the beautiful. It is that admiration of the beautiful that gave impetus to create beautiful objects, whether a marble statue by a Michelangelo, a painting by a Da Vinci, a mosaic by a Cosmati, and a palace by a Palladio.

Even the simplest peasant who had built a stone wall was apt to look upon the finished product as a work of art, for he had created something with his own hands for all to see and admire. The potter, the smith, the mason—ah, theirs was always a work of art to behold! But to mar a thing of beauty, that, that was a sin, an offense to the genius of man. For this reason, then, it was rare for the Italian parent to resort, no matter how provoked by his child's naughtiness, to slap the face. A whack on the culo, yes; a slap on the face, no. And should a stranger, an acquaintance compliment a child's beauty, the parent was sure to make the sign of the horns behind the back, or murmur a whispered benedica, so as to ward off the evil eye, whose attention was sure to be directed towards the child by the compliment.

Francesco was proud of his own good looks. Almost sixteen years old now, he sported a full growth above his upper lip that made him look older. Dozens of times a day, as he worked on his customers in the chair, he peeked at his own reflection in the mirrors. His looks pleased him because he was becoming interested in girls. He understood now, why the young men in the barber's chair wanted to look their best, insistent that every curl, every wave, every hair be just so.

The boy had grown taller since his arrival in America three years ago. He had filled out, too, but he was slim and well-formed. In his stocking feet he was five feet nine inches in height, and he looked even taller because he wore the first wave of his shiny black hair, high above the forehead, while the other silky waves rippled down to the back of his neck.

One hot August afternoon, when the very sidewalks baked under the merciless attack of the sun's rays, Peppino decided to close up shop.

"Boys, go home. We've had three customers all day. No one else will come. It's hotter than Dante's Inferno. Go, boys, go. I'll close up. If anyone wants a haircut today, he can go to that butcher of heads up the street." Peppino's son Joe, old Pietro, and Francesco gladly threw off the white barber's jackets they were wearing. One by one, they left the deserted shop. Outside, the heat hit Francesco's face in an all-smothering embrace. He felt as if his throat was being stuffed with a wad of cotton. Exhaling hard and long to clear his mouth of the sensation, he started to walk briskly in spite of the heat. He wanted to get home, sponge himself off with cold water and have something cold to drink, lots of it. And besides, any day now, Zia Graziella's baby was due to be born. Today was a work-day, and Zio Matteo was on Job. Only the kids, little Matteo and Marietta were home with their mother. He walked along smiling to himself to think that his uncle was to be a father again. "The old boy is still at it!" and the smile turned to laughter.

The streets were practically deserted, it was so hot. Most of the young boys, he guessed would be swimming down at the river, bare-assed and cupping their *coglioni* with their hands when they jumped into the water from half-rotted wooden piers. A few old women and little girls were sitting on the fire-escapes as he passed, fanning themselves with folded newspapers.

Just as Francesco was making ready to cross to the other side of a narrow, dank-smelling alleyway hemmed in by some dilapidated, deserted warehouse buildings, his ear caught the sound of screams and grunts of what seemed like an animal in pain. He turned to see mid-way down the alley, a gang of six youths in a circle. In the circle, he was able to make out the figure of *Beppo 'o scemmo*—Joey the idiot boy. The boy was being pushed and pulled from one boy to another. Each shove and slap the boys gave Beppo, was accompanied by shouts of: "Hey, guinea boy! Hey you stinking wop, big grease ball, your father's an organ grinder and your mother eats garlic!" The boys were laughing and Joey was crying. He flailed his arms with his eyes closed, as slobber drooled from his mouth. He could only grunt in panic and pain; his speech was limited to a few basic words, and the swear words the neighborhood kids got a big kick out of hearing him repeat. It was a game they all played with him, like teaching a dog to do tricks. And when Joey parroted the dirty words and the swear words, the boys usually rewarded him with pieces of candy.

Everybody in the neighborhood knew poor Joey. He was the lumbering, slobbering fifteen year-old giant with the brain of a two year-old. The old grandmothers on the street took delight in feeding this simple *"povera anima di Dio,"* that is, this "poor soul of God." Into his willing hands, they used to press hunks of bread stuffed with meatballs, or eggplant, or roasted peppers.

So when Francesco recognized poor Joey and realized that he was being tormented by the half-dozen Irish kids who had come from their own blocks, looking for trouble in the Italian neighborhood, he charged down the alley. In a minute his hands were on the shoulders of a red-headed bullyboy. Francesco lifted him bodily off his feet and flung him to the ground with all the strength he could muster. The red-head let out a yowl of pain when he hit the pavement.

"*Corri, Beppo, corri*—run, Joey, run," shouted Francesco. Fists were flying all over as Joey made his escape to the street, still sobbing and wiping his eyes. As Joey reached the street he almost ran into a Reo parked at the end of the alley. He kept on running, never seeing the three men sitting in the car as they watched the brawl, much as if they were watching a boxing match in the Garden.

The occupants of the car were Don Luigi and a couple of his "boys." The don had been on his way to the barber shop when he recognized Francesco darting down the alley. "Pull up by the alley," he had commanded his driver. When he saw the fight going on, he ordered the car stopped.

"We stay in the car. Let's see how the kid handles himself." Then he sat back and lit up a cigar. Through the smoke he could see a flurry of punches flying back and forth. One of the Irish kids had gotten behind Francesco and had managed to pin his arms back while one kid in his front slammed his fists repeatedly into Francesco's abdomen. With a burst of energy, Francesco kicked his assailant squarely in the groin, then flung up his arms, breaking the hold on them. Quickly, he half turned and crashed a fist into his captor's face.

"Get the fucking guinea," screamed out in pain, the one Francesco had kicked in the groin. He was doubled over, holding his crotch. The rest of the boys lunged at Francesco, backed up now against the wall of a building. But they all stopped dead in their tracks. In a flash, Francesco had yanked something from his pocket, pressed a button, and the gleam of a six-inch steel blade, flashed unmistakable in the dim light of the alley.

"Christ! He's got a fucking knife!" Francesco extended both of his arms in a broad arc in front of himself, the knife in his right hand. He tossed it to his left hand and then back to his right—left again, right again. He was crouched over, as if ready to hurl himself into their midst.

As he took in the scene, Don Luigi's eyes lit up with a gleam of pleasure, pride even. "The kid is good. The kid is good." A broad smile spread across his face. "Frankie's got guts." Then, he got out of the car, and the others, in response to the wave of his hand. The punks were running straight towards the men now, trying to make their escape out of the alley to the street. As soon as the first one reached the street, one of Luigi's "boys" tripped the fleeing tough. As the bullyboy fell, a fist crashed into the side of his head. The boy fell to the pavement with a groan. Another tough got a knee-jerk to the gut by Gino, and another, a karate chop to the back of the neck, that sent him tumbling in a heap to the ground.

By the time Francesco came to the street from the alley, all six of the Irishers were spread out on the sidewalk, writhing in agony. "Get in, Frankie." Francesco recognized Don Luigi, who turned and sent out a glob of cigar-stained spit smack on the head of the one lying closest to the car. With his foot, he rolled the prone figure aside. They all got into the car and sped off. "Drive to the club, Gino," commanded the don.

Chapter Thirty-one

On Mott Street, the car came to a stop in front of two plate glass windows on either side of the entrance to the club. Francesco saw two pink birds painted on the glass, holding a long banner between their beaks that said, "The Pelican Club." Inside, Francesco welcomed the cool breeze being sent down by the whirling ceiling fans. The walls were lined by tables stacked with chairs. As they all walked across what was obviously a dance floor, they passed a long mirror-backed bar and a bandstand with a piano and music stands on it. A couple of workers were busy sweeping and mopping the floor, getting the nightclub ready for the evening activities.

Don Luigi opened a door to the left of the stage and Francesco, trailing behind him, found himself in another world. The don walked across the room and took a seat in an over-sized leather chair behind a huge mahogany desk, embellished in carved sea shells gilded over with gold leaf. Along the walls, plaster busts, gleaming white enough to look like polished marble, sat in dark, maroon-colored niches. All the heads of Italian genius stared out with unseeing eyes from every side of the room. The bottom half of the walls were paneled in the same dark mahogany as the desk. The upper walls were covered in cloth of embossed fleur-de-lys of silver and gold against a backdrop of beige.

"Go wash yourself, Frankie." Don Luigi pointed to a door between the heads of Dante and Petrarch. "There's blood on your cheek. When you're finished, I want to talk to you."

In the bathroom, one whole wall was sheathed in mirrors from floor to ceiling. In them, the boy saw the blood below his eye, the swollen lip, the bruise on his chin. His clothes were rumpled and splotched with the dirt of the alley. He bent over the marble washbowl, turned on the gold-plated faucets and washed his face with a sweet-scented bar of soap. He wiped his face and hands on a monogrammed plush towel. Then he took out his comb and put the waves back in his hair.

He came out of the bathroom, and Don Luigi beckoned him over to the desk with a wave of his hand. "Sit down, Frankie." On the desk, on a silver tray, was a decanter of liqueur that smelled fragrantly of hazel-nut. Beside it was a plate of delicate Italian cookies smelling of rum, almond and anise. Don Luigi poured the brown, velvety liquid into two glasses and handed one to Francesco. "Here, drink this. Take some *dolci*."

He took a cookie himself, and after the first bite, the don said: "Kid, I like what I saw in that alley. I like the way you handled yourself. I've had my eye on you, in the barber shop and in the alley today. How would you like to work for me? Who knows, maybe for the organization, in time? You've got guts, Frankie, what it takes to be a man in the Honored Society. To start off, you can be my personal barber, my personal atten-dant kind of, and, depending how you follow orders, and how you carry yourself, you can go far with me—plenty of money for you, kid, a hel-luva lot more than you get for snipping hair in that fucking barber shop." Before Francesco finished swallowing his drink, Luigi fired out at him: "You like girls? You like clothes? You like money? You can have 'em all if you stick with me. Never mind this bullshit of working for peanuts in the barber shop. That kind of shit is okay for a *cafone*. But you got the makings of something better, Frankie. The only way you'll find gold in this fucking country," and he laughed, "is my way. Not the way those poor bastard paesani are doing, breaking their asses, fifty, sixty hours a week so they can put a pot of beans and escarole on the table.

"I like you, Frankie. I knew you had guts, the first time I met you in the barber shop. Remember? Remember that day, huh? Look kid, didn't I hear you say in the barber shop that you are all breaking your asses to save up enough dough to bring the rest of the family here from the old country? Your mother and some sisters, wasn't it? How many years already, and they're still there, right?"

For the first time, Francesco spoke. "A little over three years," he answered.

"How many more goddamn years before you can bring 'em over, Frankie, at the rate you guys are going? That poor bastard of my own father, working like a donkey, pushing a cart up and down these stinking streets, died before he could bring over my poor old lady and my sister. I brought 'em over, Frankie. Me, I did it, Frankie." Don Luigi stood up and slapped his chest. Then he leaned over, his face six inches from Francesco's. "And I didn't get them money by breaking my ass, either, by pushing no fucking cart up and down the street.

141

"My old man died, and my kid brother, because we was too poor to pay the doctor. He asked first for the four dollars, and when the old man said he didn't have it, the son of a bitch walked out. 'Go to the charity ward,' he says. We couldn't even lift our heads from the pillows, we was so burned up with the fever. The old man died the next night, and Rico, my brother, the next. But I pulled through. Because I was tough; and I'm tougher now. You gotta be tough, Frankie, if you want to make it here."

He stopped talking and leaned back in his chair. Everything Don Luigi had said made sense to Francesco. It was what he had tried to tell Alfredo and his father. But his brother had his head in the clouds; he read too much. And his father, all he knew how to do was to toil with his hands and his back. He had exchanged pushing a plow in Italy for pushing a shovel in America. And for what? A handful of coins instead of a handful of beans. The only difference was that at least here there were coins to be had. And Francesco meant to have them, lots of them, and fast. The opportunity was in his hands now. He couldn't pass it up.

Francesco stood up. He stretched out his hand and said, "Don Luigi, you got yourself a barber, and more, I hope." The older man smiled and grabbed the boy's outstretched hand.

"It's a deal, kid, a deal you won't regret." He dug into his pocket, took out a wad of bills and peeled off two twenties. "Gino," he yelled across the room, "take Frankie down to my tailor's. Get him some decent clothes. He's one of us."

Chapter Thirty-two

Alone, Don Luigi leaned back in his chair, cradling the back of his head with both hands. The faces of his father and brother Rico, materialized before his eyes. Something about Frankie reminded him of Rico. He had sensed it the first time he laid eyes on the boy in the barber shop. The same build, the same hair, the face so much like Rico's. He opened the top drawer of the desk and took out a framed picture of his brother. "Yeah, the resemblance is there," he said to himself. His thoughts went back to the, time his brother lay dying of typhoid, and his father, too. And himself, sick, all three of them, lying in the room of that broken-down, old tenement on Hester Street.

His thoughts went back further in time to when he, his father and brother had come over the year before from Sicily. The year the three of them landed, 1899, they came with their heads full of pipe dreams about picking gold off the streets. As Don Luigi sat musing, he laughed out loud. The only thing he and Rico picked off the streets were their teeth and the remnants of their torn clothing. All through the poorest and most rundown sections of the East Side, enclaves of different nationalities of immigrants abutted one another. Almost daily, gangs of young toughs looking for excitement and spoiling for a fight invaded one another's turf; more often than not, bloody exchanges were the result. Early on Luigi had become tough and cocky and street-wise. And early on he had come to spurn the few dollars his father earned pushing a cart, those dollars barely enough to pay for rent and food. He realized early the importance of money, real money, and he meant to have it.

It wasn't long after the deaths of his father and brother, that he found a way to stuff his pockets with more money than his father had ever seen. He joined a gang of petty waterfront thugs that pilfered from the warehouses along the docks, anything from produce to fish to clothing to machinery—anything that would fetch a price. Then the stuff was sold on the streets and under the table to stores and businesses in the neighborhoods. It was all clear profit for Luigi, and he found himself with more money in his pocket than he had ever gotten from carrying a hod.

Before long the activities of the gang came to the attention of the organized syndicate, the Honored Society, which regarded the waterfront as its own bird for plucking. One night Luigi and his buddies found themselves staring down the barrels of shotguns aimed at their heads. Luigi and his pals had been caught red-handed at the back door of one of the waterfront warehouses just as they were heisting crates of rock-hard slabs of salted cod. Being the Christmas season, Luigi was anticipating their quick and easy-disposal and a nice profit. Among the paesani, the *bacala* was one of the staples of the Christmas meal.

The *capo* of the new arrivals, sleek and nattily dressed in his pin-striped suit, lit a stogie. In a flash his "boys" began the pistol-whipping. Whacks, bangs, and thuds resounded across the backs, heads and shoulders of Luigi and his companions. With howls of pain, blood streaming in scarlet rivulets down their faces, all of them except Luigi made their escape from the blows raining down on them by jumping off the loading dock. On the ground, they picked themselves up and flew off into the darkness.

Luigi, though, had stood his ground. Blood was gushing from a gash over his right eye, and it almost blinded him. With a loud curse, he lunged at the man nearest him. He had managed to pull a stiletto out of his boot. He gave a wicked swipe that slashed the upper arm of his adversary, so that the gun fell from the man's hand. Then, a vicious kick that shoved the guy right off the loading dock. Like lightning, Luigi managed to snatch up the gun and point it straight at the head of the *capo*, all in the blinking of an eye.

"This son of a bitch is a dead man, you bastards, if you don't drop those guns." Luigi's voice rang out hoarse and with obvious determination. All this had happened so fast and unexpectedly, that the thugs halted. They looked bewilderingly at their boss, Minguccio, for a clue as what to do.

"Easy kid, easy. You—assholes—do as the kid says. Drop 'em," Minguccio commanded.

With that said, Luigi's fortunes changed. From that night on, under Minguccio's tutelage, who had taken a genuine liking to young Luigi's gutsy spirit, the boy's star rose in the Honored Society. Eventually, over the years, Luigi rose in the ranks to rule over a "family" of his own. He had become Don Luigi.

When Luigi had seen Francesco fighting the Irishers with his stiletto in the alley, he had seen a flashback of himself those many years ago on the loading dock of the fish warehouse.

And as Minguccio had taken him under is wing, so Luigi wanted to take Francesco under his.

Chapter Thirty-three

Zia Graziella's baby boy was born on the first day of September, 1909. When Zio Matteo came home from work that evening little Matteo had been the first to run up to him on the street with the news. Upstairs in the flat, the new father found women and neighbors cooking the evening meal for the family and tending his wife and new son. The beaming midwife was at the table eating biscotti with a glass of wine.

In between sips and bites, she managed to sing the praises of Matteo's new baby boy. "A fine son, Matteo, and an easy birth for Graziella. The little rascal slid right out. A son to be proud of, I say, Matteo. A good pair of lungs, and a good appetite. He is already at the breast." At that moment, Francesco walked into the flat to learn the happy news of the birth of his uncle's new son. He was wearing one of his new suits, bought a few days before, with Don Luigi's money.

For the christening, two weeks later, Francesco's father and brothers came down from New Haven on the early morning train. It was a joyous reunion punctuated with many hugs and kisses all around. Giuseppe looked with admiration on his son, Francesco, sporting a new blue suit, black bowler hat and shiny new shoes with their wing-tip design. The boy had shot up inches, and the mustache on his upper lip was full and well trimmed. Even his brothers admired his looks and knew that it would not do to call him a kid any more.

By late morning little Francis Joseph (Francesco was the new baby's godfather) was duly baptized. The rest of the day was given over to festivity. Platters of food and jugs of wine crowded every bit of available space on the table. From time to time during the late morning and early afternoon hours, friends and neighbors stopped at the flat to offer congratulations. They brought articles of food and small gifts. The afternoon advanced as people ate and drank, came and went.

By evening, the last guest had left. Only the family remained. Graziella retired to the bedroom to give her breast to the hungry baby, leaving Marietta in charge of the kitchen clean-up, and little Matteo made his escape to the street to play a rousing game of stick-ball until dark.

"Ah, now we can talk," said Zio Matteo, "without interruption and catch up on the news. I'll make a fresh pot of coffee for all of us."

"Just for you and Papa, Zio Matteo, if you don't mind. You two, talk. My brothers and I are going for a smoke and a walk on the street," Michele spoke up.

Their uncle threw up his hands and laughed as he gave Giuseppe a knowing wink. "The young rascals, they don't want to be shut up with us old men." Michele, Alfredo and Francesco were already at the door, when Matteo yelled out after them, "Go, take your *passeggiata*. But I tell you, you'll find precious few girls on the street. At this hour, they are all in the kitchen getting supper ready. Go, go," and Matteo waved them off.

"Ah, Giuseppe, good to be a young man in the prime of life, eh? Remember?" Both of them began laughing. "Marietta, child, put some coffee on for your papa and Zio Giuseppe." He sat at the table, and the two brothers began their talk; immediately the subject of conversation became the epidemic that had ravaged the homeland two months ago. The cholera. It had raged fiercely, especially throughout their own Campania and the province of Basilicata. For two weeks, the Italo-American press had described the havoc wrought by the epidemic in the crowded cities and larger towns. And although the countryside had fared more fortunate, still, deaths had been reported in almost all of the villages of the South. In their own region, in the villages along the base of Vesuvius, as Mama had written, hundreds of pilgrims from the cities had thronged the roads on their way to seek succor at the shrine of Our Lady of Montevergine in Avellino. Day and night the roadway past the farm had resounded with the refrain of the Invocation to the Madonna as pilgrims passed through Bosco. Mama's letter told of the night's darkness being pierced by the flickering lights from hundreds of candles and torches, shining like myriad stars in a gloomy sky. And in the mornings, sometimes, moribund and dead pilgrims lay along the roadsides where they had dropped.

Which pilgrim was it, stopping for a drink of water from Rosa's well, that had unwittingly brought the sickness to her door? Undoubtedly that had been the way it had happened, that she and the girls became infected. Luckily, Giuseppe told Matteo, his wife and daughters had survived, although Carolina had been seriously taken with the sickness. It was the good Father Pio, Rosa had written, who learning how sick the girl was, came by one morning. He bundled her up and drove Carolina and three other gravely ill victims of the plague from Bosco to the charity ward in the city of Pompei. There, under the care of the good nuns who labored as nurses and teachers among the orphans in the school founded by the saintly Bartolo Longo, she recovered. With loving solicitude the nuns there had tenderly nursed Carolina and the others back to health. "And now, and now, my daughter wishes to remain with the nuns in Pompei, to enter their order. Here, read for yourself, Matteo." He pulled a crumpled letter from his pants pocket and handed it to his brother across the table. Matteo began to read, moving his lips silently as he scanned the three pages of what Rosa had written to Giuseppe about the epidemic.

The news about Carolina at the end of Rosa's letter left Matteo silent and thoughtful. Then he found words to speak. "Giuseppe, my brother, they are all well, and, what an honor for you, for Rosa, to have a daughter dedicated to the service of God. He handed the letter back to his brother. He got up from the table and began filling both his and Giuseppe's cups with coffee. Giuseppe paid no attention.

As his brother filled the cups, Giuseppe stared off into space, trying to picture in his mind the face of his daughter in the somber, black habit of the nun. Then a smile came to his face, and he saw Carolina in his memory rushing to meet him as he and her brothers returned from the fields in those days long ago, her skirt bellowing about her in a whirl of red, her long brown hair blowing in the wind. He gave a wince. Was it true that nuns had their heads shorn? Matteo's voice brought him back to the present. "Imagine, a nun, in the family." To himself, he said: "How had it come about?" It was simple enough. During her stay in Pompei with the sisters, Carolina had come to love the nuns, especially for their concern for the sick children and the orphans. In the time of her convalescence, she loved nothing more than joining them in prayers, and in helping whenever she could by feeding and cleaning the little orphans.

When she was fully recovered, Carolina found it so difficult to tear herself away from the place where she had come to find so much goodness, happiness and usefulness, she tearfully begged to be allowed to remain.

To her mother and to the nuns, she explained that her staying would prove no hardship to anyone. A half-hour's walk away, was her sister Filumena's house in Scafati. And although Rosa had had misgivings at first, she realized that the girl was truly sincere in her desire to be around the little ones. In addition, the girl would be spared the hard labor and drudgery of the farm; and, she would be with her sister who was thrilled to have a member of the family, her own flesh and blood in her home.

As for the nuns, they had come to appreciate Carolina's helping hand, her gentleness, her apparent love for the orphans and were more than willing to have her devoted help. Rosa consented, arrangements were made, and Carolina began her new life.

At the start, after a simple breakfast of bread and coffee, Carolina would leave her sister's house. In the freshness of the morning air, in the dim half-light of the early sunrise, she began her walk to the orphanage. After her arrival, she spent the whole day in caring for the little ones. She fed them, cleaned them, and played games with the toddlers. Her heart went out, especially to the *trovatelli*, the abandoned infants and waifs, more often than not, the offspring of young unmarried girls who had been seduced and then deserted.

The warmth and tenderness she showed these children was not lost on the nuns. Increasingly, the sisters came to rely on her success in quieting an obstreperous and fitful baby. "Give the child to Carolina," they would say. "She will know how to soothe it."

At the noon hour, Carolina ate in the refectory among the older children who also loved to have her with them. At the end of the workday, only her promise that she would see them on the morrow brought smiles of joy to their saddened faces. Back in Scafati, over supper, she recounted to her sister the happenings at the orphanage. What this little one had done, what that little one had said, how naughty Tommassino had been, how cute Maria was, how smart, Tonio.

When it came about that two year-old Marcellino became sick with whooping cough, she could barely tear herself away when it came time to leave his side. The pitiful whimpering of the child, when he saw her preparing to leave, tore at her very heart strings. One evening when his little feverish hand clung desperately to hers, she asked permission to stay the night with him. A cot was set up for her by the side of the child's crib, and for that night, and all the nights that followed until the child was well, Carolina stayed by Marcellino's crib.

From that time on, she no longer left the orphanage, except to spend Sunday with her sister in Scafati. Instead, she occupied a little cubicle, like the cells in which the nuns slept. The furnishings of the room were simple: a little cot, a nightstand and a crucifix on the wall. As the weeks went by, the realization grew within her heart, that it was in this place, among the abandoned, unloved urchins, and working alongside the devoted women who cared for them, that she would find her happiness in life. She asked for permission to enter the order. It was granted.

Chapter Thirty-four

Giuseppe took the letter from the table where Matteo had placed it and returned it to his pants pocket. Suddenly the kitchen door opened, and Michele walked in with Alfredo behind him. "Where is Francesco?" their father asked. With a shrug of his shoulders, Michele answered, "We had no sooner finished telling him about Mama and the girls having been sick, and Carolina going into the convent, that he took off as if he were stung by a bee. He yelled back that he would return soon, and fft—he was gone."

"He hasn't seen his father in months," Giuseppe murmured with a scowl on his face, "and yet he cannot find the time to spend a half hour talking to me before I leave." He looked at the clock. "In an hour we must go to the train." He turned to Matteo. "Tell me, Matteo, how is it with him here? How is he doing? Is he behaving himself? I know he has a mind of his own. If he is not treating you with respect and does not obey you, I will grab him by the collar and take him off your hands."

Matteo walked up to his brother and placed a hand on his shoulder. "To me, Francesco is another son. In my heart, and in Graziella's heart, there is a special place for the boy. It is with love and respect that he regards us. And to the children, he is like a big brother. True, he has a mind of his own; he is *guappo*, Giuseppe, manly. He is no longer a boy, brother mine, no longer a boy. He has grown up fast here on the streets of New York. You see him as a child, but the days of his childhood are gone. He is in his manhood." A look of irritation crossed Giuseppe's face. It went unnoticed by Matteo, and he continued to talk. Just for a moment, he hesitated. "Francesco no longer works for Peppino in the barber shop. He is personal barber now to Luigi." Matteo stopped short, then sucking in his breath, he finished: "For Luigi Santuzzi, Don Luigi Santuzzi."

Anger clearly showed itself on Giuseppe's face. He shot back at his brother, "What! Francesco is in the employ of that Sicilian bandit, that gangster, that man of *mala vita*? What were you thinking, that you permitted the boy to do such a thing as to work for such a scoundrel?"

Matteo's face reddened at the tone of recrimination in his brother's voice. "It is only after the fact, that I learned of it, that Francesco told me." Before another word could be spoken by either of the brothers, the door suddenly burst open and Francesco entered the kitchen. He raced to the table and placed a fistful of ten and twenty dollar bills on it in front of his father. With a note of excitement in his voice, he fairly shouted out: "Papa, here is enough money to bring them all here. Do it right away, Papa. Bring Mama and the girls to America. You don't have to wait any longer, Here is money enough. Take it."

Instead of the joy he had expected from his father, Giuseppe grabbed Francesco's arm in an iron grip that brought a wince of pain to the boy's face. "Where did you get this money? From Don Luigi? Tell me, from Don Luigi?" Francesco said nothing, and dropped his head, like a little boy caught in a lie.

"So that's where you got it." Giuseppe picked up the bills and flung the money to the floor.

Francesco screamed back at him: "Yes, that's who gave it to me, Don Luigi. Don Luigi, who doesn't have to break his ass like a mule." The father's face turned purple, and upraising his free hand, rained three forceful slaps on his son's back. Francesco pulled himself away, ran to the kitchen door and slammed it shut after him.

Alfredo ran to the door. "Come back, Frankie. Come back. Don't run from Papa." But his brother kept on speeding down the stairs and was gone. At the moment Alfredo re-entered the kitchen alone, his father whirled around to face Matteo. "I left the boy in your care, Matteo," he shouted angrily. "And this is how you looked after him, letting him get mixed up with criminals. Why did you not send for me straightaway?"

Both Alfredo and Michele stepped in between father and uncle. It was clear that an angry exchange of words was about to take place, from the looks on Matteo's and their father's faces. Just then, Zia Graziella stepped into the room; she had heard everything. All could see that she was almost in tears. Matteo left the kitchen, slamming the door behind him as had Francesco done fifteen minutes before. Giuseppe motioned to Michele and Alfredo, as he picked up his jacket. "We must get the train back to New Haven." He went up to Graziella and grasped both her hands in his. His voice softened. "I would not have had this happen on this day of joy for you, Graziella. You have been so good to all of us, as has been Matteo. When the boy returns, tell him that I will be back to get him, to bring him under his father's roof. Tell Francesco that." He kissed her on the cheek and turned towards the door. He did not glance once at the money he was leaving behind on the floor of the kitchen. It was Michele who picked it up and put it in his pocket.

And it was Michele, who, when they returned to New Haven, made all the arrangements to finally bring his mother and two sisters, Eleonora and Gilda to America. With Francesco's money.

The very next week Giuseppe returned to his brother's house to fetch his son, to force him to come back with him to New Haven. His efforts were in vain, however. The boy had left his uncle's house, and Matteo only knew from the message he had received from Francesco, that he was with Don Luigi, and not to worry about him.

It was a sad Giuseppe who rode back without his youngest son that night to New Haven. He was estranged from his son, he was estranged from Matteo, his brother. Deep down, he felt that things would never be the same for the Alanga family. Matteo's words were still ringing in his ears, in synchronization with the clickety-click of the wheels on the track. For the entire length of the trip between New York and New Haven, his brother's words at the house that evening, reverberated in his ears. "He's a man now. He's a man now. This is America. This is America. This is America."

Giuseppe departed from his brother with the realization more than ever confirmed that now a wedge of ill-feeling existed between the two of them. And between father and son. The boy was being lost to him. All the ride home, he sat staring emptily at the landscape rolling before his eyes, his brain crowded with disturbing thoughts. Michele and Alfredo, too. Were they growing away from him? The glue that had always held them together as a family, Rosa, was missing, and without her presence, their lives had changed.

Even Alfredo and Michele, it seemed to him, were becoming strangers to him. They were fast learning the language and the ways of this new land; but he, he was an old horse that could not be taught new tricks so easily. Had it been a mistake to leave Italy to come here? In the lonely nights without Rosa, in the dark of the attic room in Angelo's house, more and more he had begun to long for the old country, the smell of the soil, the perfume of the lemon and orange trees, the odor of the animals and of the fields. He ached for the touch of his wife's warm flesh next to him in bed.

He arrived home, discouraged and weary. In the attic room that night, Michele told his father what he had done. "Papa," he said, "I have already made the papers to bring Mama and the girls to America. All I need now is your permission to send Mama the word to prepare to come and the money." He halted for just a moment. "It is Francesco's money. Shall I send it to Mama?" Both Michele and Alfredo dared hardly to breathe as they waited for their father to reply. Then, their father's voice broke through the heavy silence. "Yes. Do what you must." He said no more, closed his eyes, but did not sleep. His mind was alive with the thought that in the near future, within a matter of a few months perhaps, his family would be united. Rosa would again be in their midst to breathe life once more into what it had not been for these past years, a family whole and united. His thoughts turned to Francesco. He regretted his angry words toward the boy, his hand across the boy's back. And Matteo, his brother, who had been so good to all of them, would things ever be the same between them? With a sense of regret in his heart, he fell finally into a restless sleep.

The days and weeks to come, were anxious ones for the three Alanga men in New Haven, until at last the blessed day arrived that Mama and Eleonora and Gilda placed their feet on the shores of the new world. It was two days after Christmas, 1909. Safe in each other's embrace the Alangas were a family again.

Chapter Thirty-five

Since that day when Francesco had laid a wad of ten and twenty dollar bills in front of his father's hands on the table in Zio Matteo's house, ten years had gone by. Little Francis Joseph who had been baptized that September day, was now a boy of ten years of age. And for Rosa as she lay awake in bed on this snowy day of December, 1919, almost ten years to the day had passed since she took her first steps off Ellis Island to be reunited once again with her husband and her sons. Next to her, Giuseppe was sound asleep, and his heavy breathing was the only sound that disturbed the silence of the bedroom of her own home in New Haven.

She couldn't sleep. The throbbing in her foot had awakened her, and the pain kept her from sleep. On the wall, black shadows flickered, cast by the guttering vigil candle burning before the statue of the Madonna on a table in the corner of the room. Silently, she recited an Ave, and had just said "Amen," when a spasm of pain stabbed her big toe like a knife, and, under the covers, she grabbed her nightgown in a knot across her abdomen. In a moment the pain passed. The breath she had been holding in, she let loose in a sigh of relief.

For weeks now, the swollen, red, toe which she had snipped when trimming the nail, throbbed more and more, but she said nothing about it to anyone. She had treated the toe herself with baths of salted water and rubbings of salve. She uttered no complaints, but went on as always with the care of the house and the family. No one in the house was aware of her pain.

The pain subsided. She listened to the fierce night wind pelting the window panes of the bedroom with sleet and snow. Her mind went back to the day, ten years ago, when her husband took her from Ellis Island to Matteo's home. The dense snowfall had filled her and the girls that day with amazement. Never had they seen such a sight—everything covered in a cushion of white. And the eeriness of the sound of the horses pulling the carts they passed, muffled and barely audible, as if coming to their ears from afar, but in reality so close by.

A smile crossed her lips in the darkness, as she remembered herself drinking in the sight of her sons' faces that day as the trolley made its way to Matteo's house on Elizabeth Street. Never would she ever forget that day and that ride. Her husband, her sons, sitting there in the flesh before her eyes. She remembered how, often, through all the chatter, all the laughter, all the sighs, she had to touch the cheek of now one son, now another, as if to reassure herself that they were not phantasms of her imagination, but real flesh and bone. How they had grown, her sons, in the three years that she had not seen them! So handsome in their American suits and ties, so strong looking, so muscular. The sound of their voices and their laughter were music to her ears. All the pain of the three years without them vanished and her heart was full of joy again.

Only when little Gilda had broken out in anguished sobs, did the happy mood and laughter cease, Rosa recalled. They turned to see the tears flowing down the child's flushed cheeks, and consternation gripped them all at the sight of the little one weeping as if her heart would break.

"But what is the matter?"

"Are you ill?"

"Are you frightened?"

"What is it with you? Say!"

The questions came in a rush, now from mother, now from father, now from brother. But the child only pointed from her seat on the trolley to the buildings they were passing. In between sobs, she cried out, "Is this the land of the plague? Look at all the wreaths of the dead hanging on the doors."

Alfredo leaned across to her and enfolded his little sister in his arms. "No, sweet sister. Those are not wreaths for the dead. In America the good Christians here hang wreaths of green on their doors to signify the coming of Gesu Bambino. It is the Christmas season here too."

Rosa smiled to herself as she recalled the laughter they all had shared after Alfredo's explanation, and the sigh of relief little Gilda gave. Over the- years, they too, would come to hang a Christmas wreath. But the focal point of every Christmas in the Alanga household would never be replaced by wreath or tree; it would be the prespio. That, they would never give up.

Chapter Thirty-six

Rosa broke off her remembrance of that day long ago. Without disturbing Giuseppe, she got out of bed. It was 5:30. Quietly she moved across the room in her slippered feet, ever so careful not to bump her toe. She went to the heavy mahogany armoire and opened its full-length door. She took a long, black day-dress off its hanger. She had only the dim light from the vigil candle to see by; but her hand knew just where to go to get her clothes.

She slid quietly into the bathroom between the two bedrooms of the house and closed the door. On the opposite wall of the bathroom, the door to the other bedroom was shut. In that bedroom, Gilda and her sister Eleonora were asleep in the bed they shared. Under the door, a dim light shone, given off by a vigil candle burning before the plaster statue of Saint Anthony.

Rosa washed and dressed in the bathroom, left it, and passed silently through her own bedroom, through the living room, and into the kitchen. She lit the gas jet on the wall above the table, and soon the room was bathed in a soft light. She could feel the cold drafts coming from the window, in spite of the rags stuffed into the spaces along the sills. Lifting the lid on the surface of the cast-iron stove, she poured in a shovelful of coal.

Rosa looked at the clock on the wall. It was almost six o'clock, and soon the three others of the household would be out of bed and out of the house off to work. Her husband, to his job at Sargent's, and the two girls to the garment factory on Wallace Street, where they sewed sleeves and cuffs onto men's shirts. In moments, Rosa had the coffee pot on the fire, and by the time the two girls entered the kitchen, the pot was already bubbling away and sending up fragrant wisps of steam from its spout.

"*Buon giorno, Mama*," they both chirped. Gilda, a beautiful young woman now of seventeen years of age, went to the table and began cutting thick slices of bread to toast on top of the stove. Eleonora, whose name everyone had shortened to "Nora," began packing lunches for herself, Gilda and Papa. Into each brown paper bag, she placed a sandwich of salami spread over with marinated eggplant strips; then into each bag went a hunk of provolone cheese and an apple. The biggest sandwich was for Papa.

A few minutes after the girls, their father came into the kitchen, tucking his blue flannel shirt into his trousers, then swung his suspenders over his shoulders. He went to the window and peered out into the darkness. "Eh, another day of snow," he mumbled. "Will it ever end?"

They all sat at the table, except Mama who went to the stove, picked up the coffee pot and proceeded to pour the hot brew into their cups. Mama then sat down too, and the family began eating their breakfast by dunking chunks of bread into bowls of caffe-latte. The spoonfuls of coffee-soaked bread, "zuppa," warmed their insides and worked wonders on the vocal cords; they began talking.

"Have you told the Agnellis upstairs yet, that they will have to move by April, Papa?" Eleonora asked in between mouthfuls. She was getting married on the fifteenth of that month.

"Not yet, *piccina*, for if I tell them now—it is only December—they might move out sooner than needs be, and we will lose a month or two of rent. I will wait another couple of months before I tell them. That will be enough time for them to find another place. Do not worry, my daughter, you will spend your wedding night under your own roof." Gilda began to giggle. Mama looked at Eleonora, a woman now, and ready for the marriage bed. Twenty-three years had passed from the day she had first held her in her arms as a new-born infant. The years had flown by, and she was a woman now, ripe for a man. Such was life.

The mention of her "wedding night," and the sound of Gilda's giggling brought a slight flush of color to Nora's cheeks. And as she began calling to mind the few stolen kisses she and Giovanni had managed, and the ardor of his embraces, the color heightened the more. Gilda noticed her blushing, and giggled the louder.

"Hush, Gilda, leave off with your silliness. Your time will come soon enough. Now all of you, off to work. You girls will miss your trolley," Mama scolded. As Papa and the girls trooped out, the sun was just beginning to light the new day with its feeble rays. Alone in the house, Rosa treated herself to another cup of the hot coffee and then made ready to begin the day's work. It was Saturday; the bed linens had to be changed. There were beans to put to soak all day in preparation for tonight's meal. A hot, filling dish of *pasta e fagioli* would go down nicely on this cold, winter's eve. Besides, Giovanni Venturino, Nora's husband-to-be, would be stopping by for supper, as he did every Saturday night, and the dish was one of his favorites.

Then too, there was fresh, crusty bread to bake, to go along with the beans. The clothes from yesterday's wash had to be pressed. There were socks to be darned. Rosa decided not to go to Confession today, although it was the Saturday of the month, that she and Mrs. Baldassari from across the street made the trip together on the trolley to Saint Michael's Church to make their confessions to the Italian-speaking priest who would understand them. To go to Confession at Saint Rose's Church, just a minute away from the house, was out of the question for her and Mrs. Baldassari. The priests of Saint Rose's were Irish; the women would not understand the priests, nor the priests, the women.

The day was no day to go out, anyway; it was cold and snowing and Rosa's foot had begun to throb again. By morning's end, she had put the beans to soak, had changed the beds, and baked some loaves, with an extra one for Giovanni to take home with him when he left that night. A nice, young man, she thought to herself, that Giovanni Venturino. A carpenter, a good one, and a good man. A good husband for her Nora. She took a few minutes to reflect on this man that was soon to be a member of her family.

His people were from the city of Naples itself. All of them, tall and blue-eyed with light hair, the color of beach sand. They looked more like Northerners than Napolitani. But Neapolitans they were, for sure—warm-hearted, effusive, musical. Both Giovanni and his brother Rocco played the guitar. Another brother played the mandolin, and the father, the accordion. His two sisters had trained voices, and when they gave out with the old songs, tears welled up in many an eye.

Chapter Thirty-seven

The day flew by. Rosa finished her chores and supper was cooking on the stove when Giuseppe and the girls came in from work. Soon after, Giovanni popped in, and as always, he brought a box of pastries for the after-supper coffee. The girls set the table, and soon everyone was seated eating Mama's delicious *pasta e fagioli*. After they had wiped their plates clean with chunks of Rosa's freshly-made bread, and had drunk a glass or two of Papa's home-made wine, they ended the meal with coffee and the sweets Giovanni had brought.

All through the meal, Nora had sat opposite her beau. No chance for stolen kisses. The conversation had centered around work, and when that topic was exhausted, their talk turned to the latest news as reported in the papers; Fiume, on the Capodistrian Peninsula was back in Italy's hands, thanks to Gabriele D'Annunzio; President Wilson was in the throes of a nervous breakdown; the United States had rejected membership in the League of Nations, and the poor man had lost heart over it. He'd never be the same, the way Giovanni saw it. In between puffs from Giuseppe's cigars and Giovanni's cigarettes, the talk went on. The women cleaned up and engaged in their own chit-chat; the subjects of their men's conversations held no interest for them.

At nine o'clock, Giovanni made his goodbyes and left, and Papa extinguished the lights. He and his wife went off to their bedroom, and the girls to theirs. Another day was over. In bed Rosa and Giuseppe talked quietly together as they lay under the covers.

"He's a nice young man, that Giovanni," Papa said. "He's a carpenter, a good trade to have these days. Anything that has to be done upstairs after the Agnellis leave, he will do up first class." Giuseppe was speaking more to himself in a monologue because his wife, her mind full of her own thoughts, scarcely was paying much attention. "He should rip out those old cupboards in the pantry," her husband continued, "and build some new ones. They need a new floor in that back bedroom; the floor-boards are all warped."

Before he could go on any further with more of that kind of talk, Rosa gave voice to what she had been thinking. "Ah, I am so happy that the two of them will be living in the same house with us. It will be life's breath to me to have our daughter in the rooms upstairs, so close to us. And when a child comes, ah—to hold and kiss a little bambino, again, a grandchild of ours. The ones in Italy, I fear, we will never see, only in pictures. She turned her head automatically to the night table by her bed, but all her eyes could make out in the darkness was the frame of the picture that held the images of the three grandchildren she had never seen in the flesh, never held in her arms, Filumena's three children.

Then Rosa began to cry, and Giuseppe heard her soft sobs. He thought at first her tears were because of her longing for the grandchildren she had never held. No, the tears were for Francesco, he knew. He had heard her. "My Francesco, my little Ciccillo, dear mother's son. You are here in America, and we do not see you. Come to me, Ciccillo, come to Mama."

Giuseppe had heard, but said nothing. Her words stung him with a pang of sorrowful remorse. Over the years father and son had become strangers to each other. And from that day in Matteo's house when he had flung the boy's money to the floor and had struck him, the breech had not healed between them.

His mind was agitated now, and as he lay in bed, he began to argue with himself. "Am I not the boy's father? He is the issue of my loins. I am the one who has given him life, not this Don Luigi, and it is to me he should give his loyalty, me, whom he should obey. All my life I have set the example for my sons, so as to become honest, decent men. Look at Michele and Alfredo decent men who learn their daily bread honestly through the force of their hands and learning. They make me proud, these two.

"But this little one, he brings shame to the name of Alanga. He has chosen the way of the *mala vita*. He is a thief and a gangster, and I will not take the money he offers. It it ill-gotten." He thought of the attempts that Francesco had made over the years to give him money. Time and again he had refused, until his son finally never made any more offers, and the visits to New Haven had become few and far between. And, when they did meet, words between father and son were as few and far between. But with Frankie and his brothers and sisters and Mama, it was different, on the occasions when they were together. Happy-go-lucky, charming, lovable Francesco . Of course, the father perceived the difference in the relationship between himself and the boy, the boy and the others, and he was pained by it more than he would admit. Yet, let the boy come to his senses, be like his brothers, and earn an honest living. Then all would be well.

"Let him come under his father's roof. That is where he belongs, in this house that I paid for with honest money, money that I earned through the sweat of my brow and by the strength of my hands." He smiled to himself. He left off thinking about Francesco, and instead he began thinking about this house, this house that he and Rosa loved so much, this beautiful house that was his own. His irritation over Francesco subsided; his thoughts went back to the past, to the time when, with pride in his heart, he had said to his wife and children, "This is our new home, our very own house; every brick and every stick of it belongs to us."

Giuseppe bought the house in 1916, seven years after Rosa's arrival in America. He and Rosa knew the house well, for it had belonged to Cosimo and Anna Perrelli, with whom they had formed a lasting friendship early in their days in New Haven. As the Perrellis had taken Giuseppe to heart after their first encounter years before, so too, they had welcomed his wife. Many a summer afternoon the two families spent under the grape arbor in the Perrellis' backyard. There, in the company of Cosimo and Anna and Antonio, the little boy the Perrellis had adopted, they ate and drank, laughed and talked together. The love that Anna and her husband showered on the boy was unmistakable, and the happy little boy, it was easy to see, adored his parents. The Alangas never came without a little something special for Antonio, whom they came to love as if he were their own grandchild. Rosa, without grandchildren of her own in America, cuddled him, kissed him and always made sure she came with candy or a toy; whenever the boy saw Rosa and Giuseppe coming, he ran to greet them with a hug and called them Zio Giuseppe and Zia Rosa.

Rosa would never forget the horrible, sweltering July afternoon when she learned that the boy, little Antonio, had drowned in the morning in the Mill River where he had gone to swim with a gang of boys. It was the usual pastime for the neighborhood kids during the carefree days of summer, when the schools were closed, and the days were torrid, to dive into the cool water of the river, off the half-rotting piers that line the bank.

She and Giuseppe were living in a rent on Chestnut Street then, not far away from Angelo's, where Giuseppe and his sons used to board. Their first home in America was a small flat of four rooms on the second floor of a house that had seen better days. But, the place sufficed to house them all. The kitchen, the largest room in the flat, was not only kitchen, but living room, too. It was there, they all ate, and spent time together. The other three rooms were used for bedrooms: one for father and mother; the second for the two girls, and the last, for Michele and Alfredo.

On that afternoon in July, as she was on the back porch hanging out the wash, Mariuccia Greco had shouted across the yards to tell her of the *disgrazia*, the terrible happening, that had taken place—a little boy, a paesano, had drowned in the river in the Fair Haven neighborhood. Mariuccia had heard of it moments ago from the peddlar who had been peddling his vegetables on lower Chapel Street, where he had seen a crowd of people gathered around some men carrying the dead boy from the river.

His name? Did Mariuccia know?

"Antonino Perrelli."

When she heard Mrs. Greco call back the name, Rosa dropped the clean sheet she was unfolding to spread on the clothesline. The color fled from her face, and she had to hold onto the porch railing to steady herself. Throwing on her shawl, she raced from the house, forgetting to close the door behind her. She only remembered that she hadn't, when she was already on the trolley. She got off the car, walking, almost running up the block from Chapel Street. As she turned the corner onto the Perrellis' street, her heart began to thump rapidly. A small crowd of women, a few men, and some children were clustered in front of Anna's house. A policeman was standing on the stoop. As Rosa got closer, she could see that some of the women were dabbing at their eyes with handkerchiefs.

It was true, then; the boy was dead. Little Antonio.

For the next three days that the boy was waked, Rosa had remained by Anna's side. She sat holding Anna's hand, and mourned with her friend. She prepared food; she brewed pot after pot of coffee; she greeted those that came to visit and led them to the parlor where the little body lay.

Even now, years later, whenever Rosa went into that very parlor, now her parlor, it seemed as if she could detect the faint scent of flowers. Where her own couch now sat, the little coffin on its bier had rested those many years ago. Sometimes when Rosa went into the parlor, instead of her own couch, she saw the white coffin, and the corpse of the boy who lay in it back then, dressed in a white jacket and white pants.

There he lay, cleaned of the muck and ooze that had covered his face, legs and arms when he was taken from the river. To the mourners who had come to look down on the still and silent boy, he seemed like an angel sleeping. Rosa still remembered how a long curl had hung over the forehead, and the long black lashes of the closed eyes that contrasted so sharply against the awful paleness of the face.

After three days of holding wake, Rosa and Giuseppe rode with Anna and Cosimo, in a carriage behind the hearse on the long, slow ride to the Catholic cemetery. There they laid Antonio to his eternal rest. But for his parents, there was no rest, no solace, overwhelmed by a grief that did not wane with time.

One evening months later, Cosimo confided to Giuseppe that he and Anna had decided to leave America.

"Giuseppe," he said, as the two of them sat alone in his kitchen over a glass of wine, "Anna grieves too much here. This house, this America, no longer gives her joy or peace. While she had Antonio, she was happy, she was able to forget her loneliness in this land. It was the will of God that she could bear no children of her own flesh and blood, but with Antonio, she had come to know the happiness of being a mother. The good Lord, with one hand gave her a son, and with the other, He took the boy away. In Italy, back in Scafati, there are her brothers and sisters, and mine. There, there are nephews and nieces; here there is no one of our blood.

"What is there here for us, she says. A house, some dollars. We are like two fish in a bowl, swimming round and round. In Scafati, at least, we will be among our own again. There, we are aunt and uncle."

After a short pause, another sip of wine, Cosimo went on. "The only joy she had found here was in that little boy. Here, she is an alien in a land of strangers, with no roots to hold her down. Before, when the boy was living, she had reason to sacrifice her own wants, to stay in a place she never really liked or felt at home in. But, for the boy, she stayed. Now that he is gone, she wishes to return to Italy, where she can see and touch the blood of her blood. I am of the same mind."

Cosimo stopped, and for a long minute he said nothing. Giuseppe, not knowing what to say, remained silent. Suddenly his friend put a hand on his shoulder. "Giuseppe, my friend, do you like this house? Would you think of buying it from me? I tell you first, because you are my good friend and my paesano. It is a good house. You and Rosa, with your children, can bring life again to these rooms. For Anna and me, it is a tomb. But you, you and yours, can make these walls ring out once again with laughter. Tell your Rosa."

When Giuseppe told Rosa, she balked at first at the idea of living in a house where such a tragedy had occurred. But the price for it was a good one, and Giuseppe knew a bargain when he saw one. He bought the house. And so he came to own a piece of America. New paint on the walls, new curtains on the windows, their own familiar furniture and some new pieces, and Rosa soon lost her malaise. This house came to be her home, her world.

The house, after all, was a nice one. It was of two storeys, with five rooms identically laid out in both flats. The cellar was large, and in its cool expanse, was plenty of space to store the kegs of home-made wine Giuseppe knew so well how to make. And then, there was an attic, a large one, partitioned off into three, big rooms with windows on all sides. Plenty of light.

It was in the attic rooms that Alfredo and Michele used as their sleeping quarters for the two years they remained under their parents' roof. True, in the winter the attic was a deep-freeze, and in the summer, a sweatbox. But the boys were young and hardy. They coped without complaint. On those arctic nights when the cold was bitter, they lay under quilts of down, from head to toe, in woolen underwear. On those torrid nights, when the heat in the attic was stifling, they lay on the sheets in only boxer shorts in order to feel any slightest, cooling wisp of air that should come in through the wide-open windows.

Every Saturday, the two of them, for the two years they stayed with their mother and father, handed over without fail, a share of their earnings from their pay envelopes. So too, did Nora and Gilda. When the day came that the boys decided to leave the house and bach it together on their own, the biggest hardship was for Mama. "Who will cook for you? Who will clean for you? Who will wash your clothes?" she had protested. The boys laughed and pinched her cheeks. "We're grown men, Mama, not little boys anymore. We can take care of ourselves. Besides, it will be easier for you, not having to cook and clean for two big galoots like us. And we're not going to the moon, you know. Just to North Haven, fifteen minutes away. We'll always be around, don't you worry your head about that."

And on a hot summer's day in July, 1919, the two of them took their clothes from the attic and moved into a neat, little four-room bungalow in North Haven Mike had put a down payment on.

Chapter Thirty-eight

April 15, 1920 dawned clear and bright. This was Nora's wedding day. Rosa's heart was replete with joy, as she stood outside Saint Michael's Church on Wooster Square, in a circle of her friends and neighbors, well before the hour to enter the church. The men were off together in their own little circles busy smoking and exchanging jokes.

Rosa happened to look up; her heart gave a leap of joy. Coming down the walk at a fast pace toward the church, was her long-absent son, Francesco. Mother and son caught sight of each other at the same moment, and the boy ran straight to his mother as she started to break away from the group of women, met her advance, and enfolded her in his arms.

"*Mama bella*," he shouted with emotion. He kissed her on the forehead and pressed her ever more tightly. Rosa's eyes glistened with tears as she framed his face in her hands. "Francesco, Ciccillo *caro*, my son, my son." She kissed him on the cheeks and the tears spilling over the rims of her eyelids, wet his face. Then she stepped back to take him all in. She had not beheld her youngest son for so many months. Now, there he stood, handsome in his black pin-striped suit with its neatly folded silk handkerchief showing above the lapel pocket. On his head, a new gray kelly with a feather stuck in the band, crowned the black, shiny hair that showed along the sides of his head, and a black, silky lock of hair fanned out across his forehead.

Now their tears mingled, because Francesco could not hold back the tears that had formed in his eyes.

Catching sight of their brother, Michele and Alfredo bounded over to where he and Mama stood. When they reached their brother's side, each of them kissed him at the same time on a cheek, in the manner of the old country. Then they shook his hand in the manner of the new country. All four of them, mother and sons entwined their arms around themselves in a circle of love.

"All my sons, all my sons together," Rosa kept murmuring. They hadn't noticed Giuseppe's approach, and when they did see him standing outside the circle, there was an awkward silence for the span of a moment as his eyes met those of his estranged son, his prodigal. But Rosa's joy would know no restraint. This moment of happiness she would not let be dampened. In a flash, and with force, she grabbed her husband's hand and pulled him into the circle.

"Our Francesco is here, Giuseppe. Look at him, how fine he looks, how handsome." As Alfredo and Michele broke away, their mother pulled their father closer towards Francesco. Without a word, Francesco extended his hand to his father. All eyes were riveted on that hand. Would Papa take it?

It is said that when a man is drowning, his whole life flashes before his eyes in a split second. So it was with Giuseppe at that moment. The father found himself drowning in a sea of memory, looking at his son, this nattily dressed young man decked out in expensive clothes, handsome, virile, polished, American-looking. This was the son whose naked new-born flesh the midwife had placed in his callused, rough hands, and whose cries of protest at the father's touch, rang out again in his ears.

The image of a small barefoot boy running across the fields to bring water to his father and his big brothers, next flashed across his eyes. Then, again, he saw the boy laughing, excited and full of wonderment, scampering along the decks of the ship that had carried them across the Atlantic Ocean. This was the Francesco he was remembering. Who was this stranger standing before him now? Was this his son, his Francesco? No, this was a *scelerato*, an American gangster.

Slowly Giuseppe raised his hand to touch Francesco's outstretched hand. He did not shake it; rather; he carefully examined the palm. Then, turning it over, he scrutinized the surface of the hand. He lifted his gaze from the hand and looked squarely into the face of his son. There was a look of puzzlement on the boy's face, and Rosa's, and Alfredo's, and Michele's. At last Giuseppe opened his mouth to speak. "This hand is dirty, not by honest labor, but by dishonest and shameful acts. When next you offer it, let it have the look and smell of honest work, and I will take it in mine."

A flush of—what was it?—anger, shame, disbelief—reddened Francesco's cheeks. He turned to his mother, whose face was pale with pain at her husband's words. "Mama," the boy said, in a dry, cracked voice, "This is my sister's day of joy, but I will not stay if I am not welcome." Swiftly, he pulled a bulging envelope from his pocket and pressed it into his mother's hands. "Here, Mama, take this. Give it to my sister, and say that her brother wishes her happiness." He bent forward, picked up his mother's hand to his lips and kissed it.

He dropped the hand, darted into a crowd of people, and was gone before she was even able to say his name. She turned to her husband. Her eyes were moistened by tears. Half in a whisper, she said to her husband: "From my son, your son, the flesh of your loins, you have turned your face. What is in you?" Before she could say anything more, Alfredo, watching his brother running across the square, turned to his father. "Papa, let me go bring him back, before he is gone altogether." Alfredo's words were almost a shout; his eyes never left his father's face, and the frantic look of urgency in Alfredo's eyes pleaded for his father's consent.

The look of pain on his wife's face, the sting of her words to him, and Alfredo's anxious plea, took Giuseppe aback. For a moment he said nothing, but then, with an almost imperceptible nod that said, "Yes, go after him," he lowered his head. Alfredo broke away and ran off to catch up with his brother.

In his heart, Giuseppe had not wanted this unexpected meeting with his son to turn out the way it had. In fact, when he had first laid eyes on Francesco, it was with a feeling of surprise and then pride, that he looked upon the suave, good-looking young man standing there, that was his youngest son. Francesco certainly appeared sophisticated, prosperous.

But with every step the father had taken as he walked up to the place where his wife and sons stood, the more his old anger, his hurt at the boy's cockiness and defiance rose in his gorge. This son of his was nothing more than a racketeer, a hoodlum who respected more this Don Luigi, than his father. With such thoughts going through his head, his resentment had built up to such a pitch, that he had lashed out as he did. A feeling of fear and panic gripped him as he watched Alfredo racing after his brother. Had he been too severe with the boy, had his words so wounded Francesco that he would never come back to his father? Had he lost his son? Over and over in his mind, he kept repeating, "Catch him, Alfredo, don't let him out of your sight. Catch up to him." His eyes never lost view of the two boys, and he only breathed a sigh of relief when he saw the two of them together, Alfredo holding tightly onto Francesco's arm. He saw his two sons deep in excited conversation. Giuseppe turned away to look at Rosa, but she was gone, and he spied her a little way off, walking up the steps of the church. A white handkerchief hung limply in her hand.

Chapter Thirty-nine

Before Giuseppe began the ascent of the steps in order to reach his wife's side, he gave one more backward glance to reassure himself that the boys were still together. The blood began rushing through his veins in a mad course, as he spied both the boys, arms locked together, coming from the square towards the church. He quickened his pace up the steps to tell Rosa.

When Alfredo had caught up to his brother, he grabbed him by the arm. "Hold on, Frankie, hold on. Wait a minute. Wait a minute." Francesco did stop, his momentum halted by his brother's restraining grip on his arm. Then he angrily threw off Alfredo's arm, turned to face his brother, and blurted out: "What the fuck, Al. That old man is still in the old country. This is America. You can make your own destiny here; you got the chance here to grab life by the balls and squeeze until life yells 'uncle.' You can get out of it what *you* want. I don't kiss anyone's hand and then thank the son of a bitch for the measly crumbs he throws you. This is America, Al, the land of opportunity. Isn't that what they say? What the fuck!"

"Easy, easy, Frankie. Calm down. You're getting excited. You're right, you're right in a way. But you've got to understand Papa, the way he thinks. His ways are set; he thinks like his father thought, and his father before him; over there they all live and think the way their grandfathers did, and..."

Before Al could finish, Frankie interrupted. "Yeah, they all live the way their grandfathers did, that's why the fucking country is two hundred years behind the times. But this is 1920, Al, and this ain't Bosco. The streets *are* paved with gold, brother, if you know where to look for it. But you won't fucking find it with a pickaxe. His anger was spent, and the tone of his voice changed. He said quietly, "The old man hates me, Al."

"No, Frankie, Papa doesn't hate you. He loves you; he's just afraid for you. You don't know how many times, when just he and I and Mike are talking together, he's almost come to the brink of tears, worrying that you'll wind up in prison, or hurt—or worse. He loves you, Frankie. Don't you ever say again that he doesn't."

"You're not shitting me, Al?"

Al clapped an arm around his brother's shoulder and pulled him close. He smiled and said, "You stupid little bastard." He kissed Frankie on the cheek. "Come on, let's get to the church. For Mama's sake. Don't spoil the day for her, or for Nora, by being a thick-head. Shut up and put a smile on your face. It's your sister's wedding day."

Arm in arm the two of them started back, and then out of the blue, Al burst out: "Christ, Frankie. To say that Papa doesn't love you. Jesus! Deep down the old man has been hurting over you for a long time. He's missed you. And Zio Matteo, too. He's too proud to admit that he made a mistake about taking it out on his brother, I mean the words they had over you. But one of these days he'll make it up to both of you; he'll come around. By the way, how is Zio Matteo, and Zia Graziella, and the kids?"

They had arrived at the steps of the church. As they began going up, Al said: "Tell me tonight. We'll talk at the house afterwards, you, me, and Mike. We got a lot of catching up to do, brother."

They had just time enough to slide into the pew, before the bride began her march down the aisle. At the sight of her two sons, Mama's face lit up with a smile that outshone the light from the candles on the altar. There was a smile on Papa's face, too.

Chapter Forty

After the ceremony, and the reception in the church hall, the newly-weds, the families and some friends went back to the house. Food and drink were piled high on the tables under the grape arbor. While Giovanni's brothers plucked out all the old favorites on mandolin and guitar, those gathered around the tables gorged themselves as they talked and laughed and joked. Every now and then some of the old timers who were feeling "good" and a bit nostalgic, joined in chorus to bellow out an off-key rendition of the words of the song being played. The festivities went well into the evening, until the musicians announced one last song, then twanged out the strains of *O Sole Mio*, and laid down their instruments. In one's and two's the guests began leaving the yard, until only the families were left, the Alangas and the Venturinos, enjoying another round of drinks and chitchat together under the arbor.

The new husband took his new wife by the hand and discreetly broke away and started making his way to the back of the house and up to his wedding chamber. One of Giovanni's brothers spotted the couple just about to enter the back door. He yelled out across the yard: "Brother mine, you're a good man with the saw. Saw well tonight!" He roared out in laughter, and the whole arbor rang out in an explosion of chuckles.

The laughing died down, and Giovanni's family began saying their goodbyes. When the last *"Buona notte"* had been exchanged, only the Alangas remained in the yard. Mama was alone with her sons. For her, this day of her daughter's wedding, had been a day of unforgettable, limitless joy, a day not to be marred by the remembrance of bitter words between father and son. She dismissed from her mind, the morning's unpleasantness between Francesco and his father. Her happiness was complete. This day had seen the marriage of her daughter to a good man, and her sons were with her. Countless times this day, her eyes had wandered to take in the sight of her three sons, together, eating, drinking, laughing, joking, and her heart had been made full with happiness. And this night, for the first time in years, all her sons would be with her, under the same roof.

Rosa got up from the bench. "My sons, your beds are ready for you in the attic. Gilda has made them up fresh but a while ago."

"All right, Mama. *Buona notte.* We are going to stay here a while to talk and have another glass of wine." Alfredo rose from the bench and kissed his mother.

"*Buona notte, Mama,* we'll see you in the morning." Michele went over to her and kissed her.

"*Buona notte, Mama bella.*" Frankie enfolded his arms around his mother. Rosa pressed him close for long moments, reluctant to leave his embrace. When she finally let him go, there were tears in her eyes. She walked up to Giuseppe and took his hand. "Giuseppe, come to bed. Let the young ones be by themselves. They have things to say to each other, the talk of young men. They don't need an old rooster hanging around. Talk, talk, my sons. Talk together, you three brothers."

Giuseppe turned to the boys. "She's right. I leave you young ones to yourselves. Besides, I am tired. And too much wine. *Buona notte, Michele. Buona notte, Alfredo.*"

He left Rosa's side and walked slowly towards Francesco. He took the boy's hand in his and then kissed his son on the cheek. "*Buona notte, Francì. Stay well.*" The old man tried to pull his hand away, but Frankie held it tight. He returned his father's kiss, saying softly, "*Buona notte, Papa.*" Frankie let go his father's hand, and as Giuseppe began to walk away, Michele, with a big smile on his face, brought a loving tap with his clenched fist to Frankie's chin. Alfredo grabbed his little brother across the shoulder and pressed him close.

After Mama, Papa and Gilda left the arbor for the house, the three brothers were alone. Frankie walked back to a bench and sat down. He called to Al and Mike, "Park your asses over here and tell me what you guys have been up to." As they took places on the bench, Frankie said, "You know, the old man looks pretty good, but Mama looks kinda pale, tired. She walks pretty slow, I noticed. She okay?" Then without waiting for their response he answered his own question. "Must've worked too hard getting ready for the wedding, I guess. She sure put out a beautiful spread." In the dim light cast by the moon, he reached across the table, littered with fruit and bottles. He picked up one of the bottles of Papa's home-made wine and filled three glasses.

Spring was just around the corner. The night air was warm, and now and then a cool little breeze gently rustled the budding leaves climbing along the arbor. Mike lit up a cigarette and threw the pack on the table. "So tell me, big shot, what's up with you, Frankie? You look like you're doing all right for yourself. Nice suit, nice shoes, big gold ring on your pinky." While he waited for his brother's answer, he took a sip of wine.

"I'm into something big, so big, that I'll wind up with more money than the Bank of Naples. I'm in the big time now. No more penny-ante shit for me. No more shake-downs or hustling goods off the docks. Don't get me wrong; I did all right with that crap, but now I'm on to something that'll make the Vanderbilts look like pikers by the time I'm through." He smiled a wide grin, and with pursed lips, let out a round ring of smoke. "As long as this country keeps fucking Prohibition on the books."

"You're bootlegging. You're making bath-tub gin. That's it, right?" It was Al speaking this time.

"You've got it right, brother. As soon as the government passed the Eighteenth Amendment last year, I go up to Don Luigi. 'Don Luigi,' I say, 'listen,' and then I lay out the whole operation to him—how to cop the real stuff from Canada, how to make our own rot-gut and keep all the boozers happy while we rake in the dough. Presto! He claps me on the shoulder, gives me the go ahead. Already I got a still set up in the backwoods of Long Island, and another one in the Adirondacks in upper New York State. We're supplying all the night clubs and speakeasies in Manhattan, Broadway and off. We got more demand than we can handle. I gotta set up more operations. And get this—a third of all the take is mine. There's no end to this thing. I've struck a gusher; I'm on my way to the top of gold mountain." He slapped the table with his hand and shot up from the bench. Even in the pale moonlight Mike and Al could see that his face was flushed with excitement.

Frankie lifted his glass off the table. "Here's to Prohibition. Long may it last." He took a long sip of wine and laughed out loud.

With a note of sarcasm in Mike's voice that couldn't be mistaken, Mike said, "And the Feds. They're just shaking their finger, 'naughty, naughty' at the wop from Bosco, and not doing anything but sit on their hands."

"The Feds. The stupid bastards!" Frankie shot back at his brother's remark. "They smash in a few cases of booze, get their pictures in the paper doing it, and the country calls them heroes. Shit, for every bottle of rot-gut they grab, we put out a hundred more. As long as the assholes keep away from the stills, we're in business, no matter how many bottles they smash in the gutters."

He lifted his glass again and laughed. "Here's to America, boys, the land of opportunity. You said I was right, Al, back there in the square this afternoon. Remember? Now you know how right I am. You don't see me breaking my ass fifty, sixty hours a week to slap a lousy twenty dollars on the table on Saturday night. That may be okay for Papa. And if he thinks that's good enough for him, let him. He thinks his ship has come in; but I've got the whole friggin' fleet!"

Mike took a long drag on his cigarette and said, "You're pretty cocksure of yourself, little brother. You think Pop is a *ciuccio*, a mule, but he's got it better here than he ever had it in his life. He's satisfied. And he's proud of himself. Proud of having a house of his own that gives him an income, proud of having a steady job and the money he gets from it. And, he doesn't have to keep looking over his shoulder to see if someone is going to put a bullet in his back."

"Don't you worry about me. I got my ass covered at all times. And I get respect; they all tip their hats to me," Frankie replied hotly. "You've been watching too many goddamn movies about mobsters and G-men." He jabbed his thumb against his chest. "Me —I can take care of myself. I don't have to worry."

"That's just it. You don't worry about yourself, but Pop does." Mike jumped up from his seat and pointed his finger in his brother's face.

Al could see that an argument was about to brew. He stepped in between the two of them. "Enough of this," he said. And he changed the subject. "Tell me, Frankie, how's Uncle Matt doing, and Aunt Graziella, and the kids? They're one great bunch, and I'm sorry that Pop is on the outs with Uncle Matt. I hope that..."

Frankie didn't give his brother a chance to finish. In a subdued tone of voice he answered: "Uncle Matt and Aunt Graziella are the greatest, and the old man is wrong in getting pissed off at him. What I did, when I was living with Uncle Matt, I did on my own. Uncle Matt is just that, my uncle, not my father, but he always treated me like his own son.

"In the first place, none of us, Pop more than anybody else, should forget that we're all here in this country because of Uncle Matt. We should all be kissing his ass for getting us here, taking us in, feeding us, and housing us. He gave us our start, and if it wasn't for him, you and me and all of us would be in Bosco right now, scratching dirt and riding a donkey cart.

"I know, I know, nobody could hold me back. You tried remember, Al? And neither could Papa. It was easier for him to palm me off on Uncle Matt, who was smart enough to let me make my own way. I got to know the ropes, and Uncle Matt knew I knew the ropes. He could have kicked my ass all the way from New York to New Haven, back onto Papa's lap.

But he didn't, and now Papa is blaming Uncle Matt for not making me into an altar boy.

"What the hell! After fourteen years in this country, does he, or you two, for that matter, still look at this place through rose-colored glasses? Don't make me laugh! To the Americans, Italians are a bunch of wops, mules good enough to break their backs building their roads, their bridges, their tunnels, but not good enough to shake hands with. Every day in New York, I see those sons of bitches, the cops, harassing and pushing around the poor old ghees who don't know what the hell they did wrong. So much for all that bullshit about living the life of a *signore* in America." He spit the word out again between his teeth: "*signore*"

When the harangue was over, Al stood up. He stretched and gave out a yawn. "You've got a point, Frankie; you're right and you're wrong, too, at the same time. You still haven't said how Uncle Matt is doing."

"Always the philosopher, huh, Al? 'You're right, you're wrong.' The way I see it, it's one or the other." Frankie rose from the bench and stretched, too, and began again. "I'll tell you what I did for Uncle Matt. I set him up in his own business, really I did. Only six months ago, and he's going great at it. You remember what a tremendous cook Aunt Graziella is; you licked the plate clean of anything she cooked. Yeah, their own spaghetti and pizza joint; the *Vecchia Napoli* it's called, out on Mulberry Street. All the boys of the organization chow down there, and even the swells from the theater crowd. It's getting to be known around town as the best place to eat 'Eyetalian.'"

With a sardonic grin on his face, Frankie went on. "They call us greaseballs, but the sons of bitches break their asses to come down after the shows on Broadway to wipe their plates clean of all that greasy sauce. Then he picked up a spoon and fork and started to twirl imaginary spaghetti around the fork in the hollow of a spoon. "Oh, how elegantly they scoff it down," he said as he lifted the fork to his mouth and then patted his lips gently with the imaginary napkin tied around his neck.

Al and Mike couldn't help laughing at his antics, and when the laughter died down, Al said, "That's great, Frankie. I mean what you did for Uncle Matt. Really great. Why didn't you tell Mom and Pop?"

Frankie raised his voice, almost to a yell. "Don't mention a fucking word about it while I'm here. I don't want the old man to think I'm throwing it up to his face, that I did something for his brother that he couldn't. Promise me, you two, not a word, not while I'm here." He quieted down when his brothers nodded their heads in assent.

Chapter Forty-one

"Now what about you two? You guys haven't told me anything about what you've been up to. No dames? I didn't see either one of you in the company of a skirt at the wedding. Shit, what are you, a couple of monks?" He didn't wait for an answer, but went on after a moment's pause. "I haven't told Mama yet, but before the year is out, in fact, around Thanksgiving, you'll be at the biggest goddamn wedding you ever saw—mine.

"Yeah, it'll be something that'll knock your eyes out. Out on Don Luigi's estate on Long Island. Papa will think he's at the palace of the king of Naples when he sees that place. Fountains, fancy gardens, statues, a pool, and a house that looks like it belongs on the Bay of Naples. It's got terraces, tile roofs, cypress trees all around, everything like a villa."

Both Al and Mike were taken completely by surprise, Mike so much so, that the cigarette he was smoking dropped from his mouth. Al was shaking his head: "Christ, you're full of surprises tonight. But that's, that's wonderful. Mama will be tickled pink."

"Don't say anything to Mama about it. I'll tell her myself; when it gets closer to the big event, I'll be down and spring it on her. I want to make sure everything is in the works before I open my mouth about it to her. A few loose ends I gotta wind up first."

Mike leaned over the table. There was a big smile on his face as he pulled Frankie's cheek. "Great, Frankie. Maybe you'll settle down. I'm happy for you. What do you say, we call it a night. It's got to be close to twelve o'clock."

"Yeah, it is late. I've got to catch the 9:30 train back to New York tomorrow morning. I've got to get up early enough to say goodbye to Mama." Then after a pause, "And to Papa." The three brothers started walking to the back entry of the house. Quietly they ascended the stairs leading up from their parents' first floor flat on their way to the attic bedrooms. When they got to the second floor landing, Frankie stopped and cocked his ear to the apartment door of the newly-weds. He whispered,

"I think I hear the bed squeaking. Giovanni must still be sawing away. He began laughing; Al gave him a shove on the shoulder. "Get out of there, get on upstairs." But he was chuckling too, and so was Mike.

In the dark they tip-toed across the attic floor. That's your room, Frankie," Al said, pointing to a side room. "Good night. Catch you in the morning before you leave."

"Yeah. Good night, Al, Mike." He entered the side room and Al and Mike proceeded to the larger front room facing the street. It was the same room they had shared together when they were still at home. The two twin beds were turned down, and the moonlight lay soft on the white sheets Gilda had put on fresh, earlier in the day when Mama had told her that her brothers were staying the night. Gilda had opened all the windows, and a refreshing breeze, coming through, made the rooms comfortable.

Stripped to his underwear, each one got into his bed, and it was a while before they fell to sleep, any of them. It had turned out to be quite a day. There was a lot to mull over. Lying in his bed, his arms under his head, Frankie silently continued the conversation to himself, going over in his head the things he had still wanted to say to his brothers before Mike cut him short.

He had wanted to tell them that it was Don Luigi's own niece that he was going to marry—the daughter of the don's sister. When he had commanded his brothers not to tell Mama of the impending marriage, it was because he knew that she would inquire about his bride-to-be. Frankie wanted to forestall any further unpleasantness with Papa. He was sure the old man would put up some kind of fuss, and he had had enough of that today.

His thoughts turned to Concetta, the don's niece. True, he admitted, she's not a looker—a good pair of tits, though. But the important thing was, that she was the don's niece. Marrying her, he would really now be a member of the don's family. He smiled to himself. Don Luigi was crazy about him. He knew that. And marrying the don's niece, in fact, put him in the driver's seat, made him heir to the throne, so to speak. He saw himself sitting in Don Luigi's big, mahogany chair, the whole of the organization under his command. With that picture in mind, he drifted off to sleep.

Chapter Forty-two

In the next room, Mike lay awake in his bed. He hadn't been able to fall asleep either. His thoughts were about Frankie. Was this the same kid brother he used to carry home on his shoulder from the fields back in Bosco? Had it been that long ago? He pictured them as they were then—himself, walking home with the kid on his shoulders, with the feel of soil between the toes on his bare feet. One good suit to wear for the Sunday *passeggiata*; one good pair of shoes that would have to last and last. For the rest, a few rugged trousers and shirts for every-day wear and that was the make-up of the wardrobe. A few lire in the pocket to spend on tobacco or treats on a feast day, and you were on top of the world. Mike almost laughed out loud thinking about the simplicity of it all, the innocence of those days back in Italy. Life was uncomplicated, unhurried, and one day was like the one before it.

He did laugh quietly to himself, thinking: "Now, here's this little big shot, the son of a peasant, grandson of a peasant, great-grandson of a peasant, talking about statues, and fountains and swimming pools and money to burn. He wears a pin-striped double-breasted suit with a silk handkerchief stuck in his lapel pocket like a medal of honor. Black-and-white shoes on his feet, stylish, expensive, smooth and shiny as glass. A gold ring on his pinky. It took America to put that handkerchief in his pocket. In the old country he blew his nose between his fingers and wiped them on his pants. America put shoes on his feet. Back in Italy he wore *zoccoli*, wooden clod-hoppers, to the fields. That is, when he wore anything at all on his feet.

Mike thought: "All well and good, little big shot. Reach for the golden apple, but don't get yourself killed trying." The idea that harm could come to Frankie because of the life he was leading was ever present in the back of Papa's mind, Michael knew. He knew that that thought was eating at his father, and he wondered how many sleepless nights it had caused the old man.

Perhaps more than anyone else, because he was the oldest and had grown up by his father's side, Michael understood his father's make-up.

In the very marrow of Papa's bones, lay all the values and strengths and weaknesses of the southern Italian peasant that he was, and always would be. On the one hand, there was always the idea in Papa's head, that with the help of God, that through honest toil and with honor, there existed the ability to strive for the betterment of one's lot.

Like the two-headed god of the Romans, Janus, whose one face looked to the past, and the other to the future, so too, did his father perceive life. All the old man's beliefs were founded on the past, the proven ways of his own father, and his father before him. Like all the past generations of his class, Giuseppe knew there were times when it was expedient to be submissive; that he was a little cog in a large universe, where the forces of nature and man could be overpowering. One had to bend sometimes in order just to survive.

But yet, the will to endure, to overcome those very forces lay buried deep within his father's soul. Like so many countless others of his kind, Giuseppe had come to this new land of America in order to challenge destiny. This America, with its promise of opportunities not to be had in the old country, had lured him to its shores, and he found himself in a whirlwind. His father had come too late in life Michael realized.

To a certain degree, but not completely, Mike understood that he was much like his father, and so, too, was Al. But there was a difference. It had been easier for the two young ones to make the adaptation to a new way of life, and yet still hold on to a little bit of the ways of the land where they were born. They had managed to take the best of both worlds and come to a nice balance. With Frankie, it was different. Just a kid, the tough, crowded streets of New York had made him into the cocky, little scrapper he had become, getting what he wanted by being tough.

Mike hadn't had the chance to tell him that he was making something of *himself*, too, and in a way that brought a feeling of pride to Papa. The truth was, that Mike was doing great, really on his way up the ladder of opportunity. In just the two years since he had left working with Angelo, with the experience and know-how of the trade he had learned working with him, Mike had decided to strike out on his own. He had a business now, a business that was taking off.

All the time he had worked with Angelo, he had squirreled away what he could of the money he had earned on Job. Like a miser, every penny, every dime that he could spare, he had stashed away. Over the years he had saved a goodly amount, and when he felt the time had come, with what he had saved and what he had been able to borrow from the bank, he bought a piece of scrap land along the railroad tracks in North Haven. With his own hands, using used lumber which he had bought cheap, he added on to the old shack that stood on the property. In that expanded shack, he set up forms and began turning out building blocks, building blocks that were durable and that he sold at a low price. From a friend of his who worked in a foundry in the town of Ansonia, he had learned about the tons of slag, the waste ash and cinders used to mold the metal products the factory turned out. The foundry, and others like it, were only too glad to be rid of the dross.

So Michael rented trucks to haul away the debris to his yard by the railroad tracks in North Haven. There he concocted a mixture of ash, cinders and cement and began the production of his "Easy Blocks," as he named them. They were: "Easy to handle, easy to use, easy on the pocketbook." Before long, contractors, homeowners and do-it-yourselfers created an expansive market. Within a year's time, with hired paesani as a work force, and in an enlarged plant constructed of his own blocks, Mike had trebled his output.

He purchased three used trucks and with them, he was able to service towns farther and farther into the surrounding areas in and around New Haven. Business was so good in fact, that he was thinking of establishing soon another production site further down the coast, in the Bridgeport area.

Yes, *The Michael J. Lang Co. Inc.*, maker of *Easy Blocks*, was an up-and-coming firm. Mike had early perceived the advantage of anglicizing his name. A name ending in a vowel, he reasoned, was a drawback. Had he opened a restaurant and called it "Mama Rosa's," there would have been patrons enough. Americans didn't mind going down to a restaurant in Little Italy to absorb a little foreign color and enjoying a plate of spaghetti and a glass of wine. But when it came to an Italian running an industrial firm, or attempting to find a place in the political arena or in the professions, that was a horse of a different color. Mike wanted to avoid the hurdle of having to buck up against being boycotted because of his name. He changed it to Michael J. Lang.

At first, he had hesitated in taking such a step. He was not ashamed of his name or his heritage. But he remembered the old adage: "When in Rome, do as the Romans do." With what he had seen and experienced as a greenhorn in New York, and in New Haven, too, he became convinced that he was right in making the change to an American sounding name. American resentment towards the immigrants coming to the country in ever increasing numbers had likewise increased, especially towards the immigrants from southern and eastern Europe; and Mike had felt its sting.

Just before Mike dozed off, he smiled, saying to himself: "Michael J. Lang, you're doing all right for yourself."

No sooner had Al hit the bed, he fell asleep. But it was a fitful sleep. Then, after an hour's uneasy rest, he woke up. "Mike, you awake?" he called out in the darkness. Receiving no answer, he sat up on the side of the bed, reached over to the night table and picked up the half-empty pack of cigarettes. He pulled one out and lit it. By the light of the match, he picked up the ash tray and took a couple of steps to the chair by the front window.

Sitting in the chair, the ash tray in one hand and the cigarette in the other, in the moonlight, he could see the outline of the church across the way, standing dark against a silvery sky. Nothing except the slight whoosh of the rustling tree limbs, and his own exhalations of smoke, broke the stillness of the night. A jumbled confusion of thoughts was racing through his mind, and Frankie's sarcastic reference to him as a philosopher rankled him. He hadn't made a retort to his brother at the time, and now his mind was putting together the words he should have come back with. But Al was the type that did his best thinking after the fact. For him, precise and methodical in his ways, ideas had first to germinate, be analyzed, and then come to a conclusion; and that required a lot of thought. The trouble with himself, Al realized, was that he could always see both sides of a question at the same time.

When he had told Frankie that the kid was right and wrong at the same time, he didn't feel that he was being ambiguous. Al was able to understand his kid brother's aggressiveness and impetuosity; but at the same time he could understand his father's conservatism and complacency. The kid was young and daring. Papa was old and tradition-bound. Frankie was disdainful of consequences; Papa was cognizant of them. The boy had learned early on the streets of New York, that when you are wronged you fight back, then and there, fast and furiously. Papa, on the other hand, was patient and willing to wait for his chance to use one of the many ways there were to skin a cat.

Yeah, Frankie was right in seeing that opportunity existed here, but wrong in thinking that Papa didn't. Their father did; that's why he brought them all here in the first place; but Papa was only able to pursue opportunity in the only way he knew how, through the strength and toil of a pair of honest arms. And Papa was thankful for just the chance to exercise that strength of his and reap the rewards. It was the only accomplishment he could boast of, the ability to toil. Here, as the old man saw it, in America the rewards of his toil made it possible for him to improve his lot in life. Here Papa had Job, a house of his own, decent food, decent clothes, and amenities unheard of back in Bosco. And all as the recompense of the labors of his hands. Papa was content with himself and what he had been able to achieve.

On the other side of the coin, Al could see where Frankie was coming from. Here, in this country, his brother was like a kid let loose in a candy store, trying to stuff his pockets with as many goodies as he could without having to pay for them. America had always been touted as the land of the free. Frankie though, well, Frankie interpreted the word "free" as free for the taking. If only he could make his brother understand how wrong, how stupid, that kind of thinking was. Al ground out the cigarette in the ash tray. He was almost tempted to walk into his brother's room, wake him, and talk it all out with him. "Too damn late tonight," he murmured to himself. He slipped into bed, feeling more relaxed now, now that he had said to himself, what he should have said to his brother.

Chapter Forty-three

The following morning dawned bright and beautiful. Mama had already been up for hours. At seven-thirty she sent her husband up to the attic to shoo the boys downstairs. When they did troop in, the warmth of the kitchen and the aroma of percolating coffee greeted their noses. The table was set with cups and plates. Mama's face was beaming at the sight of her three sons as they entered the kitchen with their father. It was like old times. And, as in the days when they were her three little boys, she shooed them off to get washed.

Frankie was the first to go over and kiss his mother on the cheek. He was laughing. "Just like when we were kids. We'd better watch out, guys, or she will slap us on the *culo*."

"Yeah, I remember, Al chuckled as he rubbed his behind with his hand, and they all broke out in laughter, even Gilda who was at the stove, toasting bread. After a leak, and a quick washing of hands and face, one by one, they came out of the bathroom and into the kitchen and took their places noisily around the table. The room rang out with their bantering and laughter, and Mama was in her glory, basking at the sight of her reunited family around the table. "*Mangiate, mangiate, my sons,*" urging them to eat as she began pouring coffee into the cups. The boys dug into the huge platter of eggs and potato omelet. Mama herself piled Frankie's dish high, poking him at the same time with her elbow to start eating. "We all know who rates around here, huh, Mike," Al said to tease his mother. In response, she gave Al a playful rap on the head with her hand, and gave him a smile and a wink.

Gilda brought over a mound of toast on one plate and a platter of cooked ham on another. From all sides of the table, forks reached over to spear the fragrant meat and the golden bread. For the grand finale to the meal, there was a jumble of chocolate, almond, and anise cookies left over from yesterday's wedding table.

At the same moment Gilda was laying the cookies on the table, a knock on the door, ushered in the newly-weds from upstairs. At Mama's invitation, the two newcomers came to the table and squeezed in. The boys renewed congratulations and came out with a few wisecracks that brought a blush to the face of the bride, and a coy smile to the dimpled face of the groom.

"Let's see, now. April, May, June," and on to January, Frankie counted off the months. "Then there should be another tenant upstairs, eh, Mama? If this Giovanni is as good a man with the saw as they say he is."

Mike chimed in: "He'd better not be that good, that the little rosebud or the little fish comes before then!" The three brothers laughed in unison. Keeping a straight face herself, and giving Mike's head, this time, a gentle tap with the back of her hand, his mother exclaimed, "*Zitto, zitto*, now. Stop teasing your poor sister. You sound like the old gossips around the public fountain back in Bosco." She placed another handful of cookies in front of Frankie.

"Whoa, Ma. I gotta leave. If I eat any more, I won't be able to move from the table." He took another sip of coffee. "I've gotta make that train." He leaned over to kiss his mother. "I'll be back in a little while to visit again, Ma. I won't stay away so long again." He shot a quick glance at his father's direction. Giuseppe and the others rose from their chairs. Frankie walked over to his father. The two of them embraced. "The door is always open, my son."

"We'll walk you down to the trolley stop, Frankie," Al said. After another round of hugs and kisses, the three brothers made for the door. Once away from the house, Frankie blurted out with genuine feeling in his voice, "It's been great seeing all of you again. I really meant it, I won't stay away so long again. And you two, take a ride up sometime. I'll show you around, take you to Zio Matteo's restaurant. They'll both be so glad to see you, and I can already see what a spread Zia Graziella will put out for you two at the restaurant."

They reached the trolley stop on Chapel Street. "Shit," Frankie swore, "I'm sorry I didn't drive down. I've got a beauty of a Packard." He kissed his lips with his bunched up fingers. "Black, with whitewall tires. But I let Concetta's kid brother take it for the weekend, so he could play the big shot with his girlfriend. Remember, guys, nothing to Mama about Concetta."

The clang of the approaching streetcar stopped him short. "Be good, kid," Mike said, giving him a hug.

"I'm glad that you and Pop came around," added Al. He and his brother embraced.

"Yeah, me too. I'm glad." Frankie turned and climbed onto the trolley. The two older brothers remained at the corner until the car disappeared up the line.

"Well, things turned out okay, I guess. Come on, Al. Let's get back to the house. I've got to use the *baccauso*, or I'm going to shit my pants."

"Me too. Both of them began the walk to Mama's at a fast clip.

With the promise to return next Sunday for dinner (Mama was going to make lasagna), the boys took their departure from their parents' home. They headed for the little four-room bungalow they called home in North Haven, just over the New Haven town line. The place had a little kitchen where they prepared their meals, a bedroom each, and a den with a couple of armchairs, a sofa, and bookcases where Al shelved all his books.

They had been baching it now for two years, ever since they had decided to leave the family nest and go it on their own. Mama still found it difficult, even now, to understand their reasons for leaving. Had it been to leave for a new home with a new bride, that, she could have understood. So back then, she had used every motherly argument in her arsenal to dissuade them from going. It had been no easy task to convince her of their reasons for going. "Ma, we're grown men. We can't stay tied to your apron strings forever. Michele is starting his own business," Alfredo had protested, "and I have a dozen irons in the fire. The girls will still be home with you. The house will be less crowded. You'll have less to do without us underfoot. This is the American way, Ma." So they won her reluctant acquiescence.

And in fact, in the long run, it seemed as if nothing much had changed. The two boys made it a point, as much out of homesickness as out of filial devotion to stop by Mama's house often. Sometimes only for a hurried cup of coffee during the week, and almost always on Sunday for a meal together. The Sunday noonday meal had in reality become routine. And Mama made. sure they ate when she had them in her clutches. She stuffed them to the hilt with her good food. To her, they always seemed to be nothing but skin and bones. When they left, she always made sure to load them down with some of this and a little bit of that. Al and Mike never refused.

Chapter Forty-four

When Al had first come to New Haven to work alongside his father at the Sargent Company, he found the work more to his liking than the construction work he had done in New York. Stacking and loading crates and making out invoices, was a helluva lot easier than working with cement. He swore to himself that he would never carry a hod again, or wield a pickaxe. So, for the time he worked in Sargent's, he hadn't minded the work he was doing there. But he vowed that this factory job was not going to be his life's work, either. He had set his sights higher. The one great boon that America offered, was the opportunity to get an education, and so he set about relentlessly in pursuit of knowledge. It would be through the efforts of the mind, rather than the hand for him, that would fill his pockets with America's gold. He took every advantage to achieve this aim.

During the very first week after his arrival in New Haven, he enrolled in night school to continue learning English. No matter how exhausted after a day's work, no matter what the weather, he attended those classes faithfully. He made good progress, and once he had become more confident in his ability to manage English, he took out a library card. The library became a second home to him. He borrowed books, bought his own, so that in time, he had amassed a sizeable collection of his own volumes. He read and read, sometimes so late into the night, that he barely had four or five hours of sleep.

To a great degree, he had educated himself through the use of self-teaching texts that he borrowed from the public library, or bought. From astronomy to zoology, there was nothing he did not find interesting enough to study in his quest for knowledge.

On one occasion in those early days in New Haven, he even had participated in a free course in bible studies, offered by one of the Protestant churches of the city. He partook of the free coffee and donuts, profited from the lectures about the Old Testament and the New. He sloughed off the proselytizing efforts of the ministers and teachers who ranted and raved against "Romish superstitions" and "papist plots to overthrow America." He could no longer abandon his belief in the

Madonna or the saints, any more than he could abandon his own mother.

In time, the degree of proficiency he attained from all his studies, came in good stead. His English was faultless, grammatically perfect, and of an extensive vocabulary. Neither was it only his English that he was able to perfect, but also his Italian. There were shelves and shelves of books in the Italian language in the public library, and Al withdrew on his library card as many books in Italian as in English. In a short while he was able to read the classical works of Italian literature in great depth. The Neapolitan dialect that once had been his main language of conversation, he used only in speaking to Mama and Papa and the unlettered paesani who spoke nothing else.

Often he was the salvation of some poor greenhorn that had been snagged by a cop for some infraction of which the fellow was completely ignorant or innocent. More and more, lawyers availed themselves of Alfredo's services in the translation of all kinds of legal documents from one language to the other: land deeds, immigration forms, naturalization papers, birth, marriage and death records, medical records, criminal records, and a host of other types of documents, Alfredo translated them all. Non-Italian officials who found it so difficult to decipher transcriptions written in the peculiar calligraphy of Italian script, resorted to Alfredo for clarifications.

In order to expedite his written translations, Alfredo had even learned to type. On a second-hand typewriter he had bought at a pawn shop, he turned out reams of neatly printed documents, much to the appreciation of lawyers and officials.

Impressed by his language skills, both written and oral, one of the lawyers who had repeatedly used his services, brought him to the office of the editor of *Il Tempo*. This was the local Italian language newspaper for the city. In short order, thereafter, Al was engaged in writing a weekly column on practical advice to newly arrived immigrants. The topics he wrote about, covered everything from how to use a public conveyance, to how to apply for a loan from a bank. Even those paesani who had been in the country for some time, read his column with interest.

Alfredo did all this in order to earn some extra money, while he still continued with his job at Sargent's. One day Mike asked him to come in with him as bookkeeper in his business, and Al left Sargent's. Mike's business was flourishing, and he needed someone to tally the accounts, record and check invoices and manage the payroll while he himself took care of production.

So Al was making good money now, from his work as interpreter for the courts, translations, work on the paper, speaking engagements and as bookkeeper for Mike. In the Italian community he was making a name for himself.

Chapter Forty-five

On the second Sunday after Nora's wedding, Mike woke up to the smell of coffee coming from the kitchen. "Holy Christ!" he yelled out, "it's almost eleven o'clock." He put on his pants and shuffled in bare feet to the kitchen table where Al was reading the Sunday newspaper.

"What the hell time did you come in last night? I was in at midnight, and you weren't here then," Al greeted him. Mike ignored his brother's question and went over to the stove and poured himself a cup of coffee. He always took his black, no milk no sugar. He took a sip. After that one sip, he spoke. "If anything will bring the dead back to life, it's this coffee. What did you do, shit in it, it's so goddamn thick!"

"And what do you want? It's been cooking there for an hour." Al hadn't even bothered to look up when he answered. His eyes never left the paper. "Son of a bitch! Look at this. On the fifteenth, somebody heisted the payroll from a shoe factory in Massachusetts. A couple of guards got shot. But get this. The robbers were "foreign-looking men. Yeah, foreign-looking. You know what that means—Italians. Watch and see if they don't put the rap on a couple of paesani. What's that little ditty old Barletta down at the yard spouts now and then:

Quante vote a Colombo jestemmammo
che scoperse sta terra 'e liberta!
La liberta, se 'ntenne,
ca i' no vedo li frutte!
Vene lu pulizzio
e se li piglia tutte!
Se parla, se arrestato,
e...zitto...Ca pe niente
ti mannano a la seggia!

(How often we curse Columbus
who discovered this land of liberty!
Liberty remains hidden
because I do not see its fruits!

189

Comes the policeman and
he takes all!
If you speak, you're arrested.
Keep your mouth shut...Because for nothing
they send you to the chair).

Al threw down the paper with a slap that echoed his disgust. His gesture reflected the anger at the injustice of the anti-immigrant prejudice, especially the anti-Italian prejudice that he had come to experience since first stepping on American soil.

Mike put down his cup. "You sound like little brother," he said. There was wry smile on his face.

"I may sound like him, but I won't act like him. You don't right a wrong with another wrong. It will take a couple of generations for the immigrants, all of them, Italians, Jews, Poles, Greeks, to gain their rightful place as Americans. And they will do it, too, through assimilation. They will have to learn to talk, dress, think like Americans. It will be up to the kids born here to change the image of the Italian, the Jew and the rest of them, as an alien species. Once those kids get educated, get into the political, social and business arena, no one will be able to abuse them. They will be as American as the ones whose people came over on the Mayflower."

"Whoa!" interrupted Mike. "I'll go get you a soapbox."

Al laughed. "Do you think I'd be afraid to get on it? The beauty of this country is that you can get on one without getting yourself shot full of holes. And there is always somebody to listen. In spite of the small-minded bigots, this country was founded on the premise of justice and equality for all. In the long-run, everybody has rights. That's the saving grace of this America. Frankie thinks that gun power is the great equalizer. I say that it is brain power."

Mike broke in again. "Okay, okay, Thomas Jefferson. But, Jesus, Al, Mama is expecting us for dinner. She wants to get something going for the old man's birthday. It's coming up in a couple of weeks, remember? He's gonna be sixty-one, and still going strong, thank God. But hell, with what he's got stashed away from the money from Job, the rent upstairs, and with what I slip Mama every week, and with what Frankie can do for them, he ought to quit the factory, take life easy. You know plant his garden, make his wine, play bocce and cards at the Re Umberto Club with his old cronies."

"He won't quit work until the day he dies," Al responded.

On his way to the bathroom, Mike shot back, "Cripes! he could even go back with Mama to the old country for a visit, see the kids and grandkids they've got over there."

Al shot up from his chair. "That's it, Mike. That's it! Let's spring for it, and put the two of them on a boat for a visit back to Bosco. That would be the best birthday present we could give him."

Mike stopped short at the bathroom door. "Perfect, perfect, Al. That's what we'll do. We'll slap the tickets in his hands, and he won't be able to refuse. And the thought of seeing Filumena and Carolina and the grandkids will sure put a sparkle back in Mama's eyes. I don't know, maybe it's my imagination or something, but lately, I can't put my finger on it, but lately Mama doesn't look right to me. Even Frankie noticed it when he was down for the wedding. But the few times I've said something to her about the way she looks, she always laughed and shooed me away with that old saw, 'old age is carrion.'"

"Yeah, the old-timers have sayings to explain everything away. Those old-timers live by them. Maybe, though, you ought to say something about it to the girls," Al said. "Ask them to keep an eye on her. If they see something, tell them to tell us. We'll haul her to a doctor." Then he laughed. "Whew! what a battle that would be. Remember, Mike, that winter when she almost had pneumonia? Wouldn't let the doctor check her chest. She gripped her nightgown so tight around her neck, he finally ended up by putting the stethoscope over it."

In his turn, Mike burst out with a laugh, almost choking. "Yeah, and remember how Papa used to joke about their first night? She made him put out all the candles and turn his back while she undressed. Then she crawled in bed with her nightgown and drawers on!" They both roared, and then Mike gave Al a wink. In between chuckles he managed to say, "Huh! The old man must have got her out of that habit pretty quick. Seven kids! Boom!"

Al grinned broadly. Then he said, "Hey, listen, Mike. Make my excuses to Mama, but I can't make it to eat. I hate to do it, but I really can't make it today. I have a little something to do, that won't wait. Will you?"

"What? Is it because of the girl you're seeing, that Irish girl?"

Al didn't answer, and Mike left him and went into the bathroom. Fifteen minutes later they left the house together. "Mike, drop me off at the trolley stop on Chapel Street before you go to Mama's." They both got into the cab of Mike's truck. Al was all spiffed up, dressed to the nines. His straight, light-brown hair was so shiny in the sunlight because of the coating of pomade he had plastered it down with, that it looked like glass. Mike took the keys from his jacket pocket and was about to start the ignition. Looking at Al, he said kiddingly, "You look like you're going to a wedding."

"As a matter of fact, I am," Al answered his brother, "mine." The tone of Al's voice was serious, without a trace of flippancy in it. The keys in Mike's hand fell to the floor of the cab. He stared at his brother's face to see if he could detect something that would tell him that Al was joking. One look at Al's unsmiling features told him that this was no joke. He found his tongue and managed to blurt out, with a note of incredulity in his voice, "Al, that Irish girl? Not that Irish girl?"

"Yes. Maureen Donnell. We're eloping. It has to be this way. Her father would as soon have her marry a leper as marry an Italian. So we're running down to New York City to tie the knot, by a justice of the peace. Once we are man and wife, there's not much her father can do about it. He can go to hell, or beat his head against a stone wall, for all I give a damn. Who knows, maybe that whiskey-soaked liver of his will bust once he finds out that he has a "dago" for a son-in-law, and he'll drop dead. But Maureen and I love each other, and that's all that counts. Maureen knows that this is the only way we can ever marry."

Al was getting red in the face now, and he fairly shouted, "I'm not going to lose this one, Mike. I lost Angelina because of her mother; I'm not going to lose Maureen because of her father. I'll be damned if I'll let anyone stand between us."

Mike stretched over to his brother and put his arm around his shoulder. "You do it, Al, do it." He dug into his pocket and drew out his wallet. From it, he pulled out some twenty dollar bills which he jammed into Al's hands. "Take this, and have a real good time."

"Mike, I don't need it. Honest, I've got plenty."

"Shut up and have a few drinks on me. Now sit back, and let's get the show on the road. You don't want to be late for your own wedding."

On the way to the trolley stop, while they rode in the truck, Al began talking. He was relaxed and happy. "We will be back in a few days, Mike. We plan to set up house in a couple of furnished rooms for now. There are lots of them available up and around where the Yalies rent out. Then, I'll look for a flat some place, and we'll start buying the stuff we need."

"Like hell you will!" Mike shot back. "Al, take the bungalow. I can set up a bed and a hot plate in that little storeroom off the office in my plant. You're going to be a few days away? Make it a week. That'll give me time to move my things out of the bungalow, and then when you come back, you can move right into your little love nest. Shit! most of the stuff in the place is yours anyway, all those books and shelves and the desk. I'll leave everything the way it is, except for taking away my duds and a few personal belongings."

"No, Mike. I can't ask you to do that. The place is as much yours as it is mine. In fact, it's really yours. You bought the place."

"Shut up, and don't be a *capa tosta*." (thick head).

Mike drew up to the trolley stop and said to Al, "That is the end of it. Don't worry, I'll come up with a good excuse to tell Mama why you're passing up her lasagna. Now, you'd better get out. I hear the trolley coming." Before he got out of the truck, Al leaned over and grabbed his brother's hand. He shook it and at the same time, kissed him on the cheek.

"Best wishes, kid," Mike shouted out after him as Al got out of the cab. He waved and drove off.

Within twenty minutes, Al stepped off the trolley at Union Station. Inside the lobby, people were milling about, some at the ticket cages, others sitting on the benches or standing in small groups waiting for the announcement to board their trains. Al's eyes scanned the crowd. He didn't see Maureen, and a sense of panic began to overtake him. He walked hurriedly through the lobby from one end to the other, and he still didn't see the object of his search. Nervously, without thinking, he put his hand to his head and passed it through his hair, messing up the neat part he had so meticulously put there. A bead of sweat moistened his brow. He turned, and then with a sigh of relief, his shoulders drooped in relaxation.

Coming out of the coffee shop, he saw her, her gleaming tresses shining like burnished copper and framing the porcelain whiteness of her face. Maureen! Thank God; it was Maureen.

They caught sight of each other at the same moment. They quickened their steps towards one another. Not even aware of the hot tea spilling over the paper cup in her hand, she smiled and hastened towards Al. Her blue eyes were sparkling as he reached out to take her free hand in his.

"Alfred," she whispered, as his hand touched hers. He leaned over with a quick thrust of his torso and lightly kissed her on the forehead. She blushed slightly, thinking that the people around them were watching.

"Let's sit down, Alfred. My valise is on the bench there." A few steps away, they reached the bench and sat beside the bag.

"Alfred," (she always addressed him formally, never "Al"). "are we doing the right thing?" Her voice had a tremor of uncertainty. "My father and brothers will be furious. I am afraid, dear Alfred." Then she added: "Afraid for you, not for myself." Al put his arm around her waist and drew her close.

"Rina, darling. We love each other, and that's all that is important. I have no fear of your father or your brothers, or all the Irishmen in Christendom. There's an old saying in Italian that goes like this: 'Only death closes the door.' In other words, so long as we draw breath, we have the ability to overcome any obstacle. It's the same I guess, as the American saying, 'Where's there's life, there's hope.' Today is going to be our wedding day. Let's forget everything and everybody. It's you and me, Rina, for the rest of our lives." Al no sooner had finished speaking, when the announcement from the loudspeaker blared out for passengers to board the trains. They rose from the bench and walked to the boarding platform. Once in their seats, they sat hand in hand, and engaged in small talk as the train sped on its way to New York City and their union.

Chapter Forty-six

After a while, lulled by the gentle swaying of the rail car on the tracks and the soothing rhythm of the monotonous melody being played by the wheels, they both fell into silence. Al leaned against her with his head on her shoulder, as if to reassure himself that she was really there. Just for a moment, Angelina's face flashed before his eyes, but he blinked her image away. He looked up to gaze on Maureen's beautiful face, and he began to think back to the time he first had laid eyes on her.

That had been shortly after arriving and settling in New Haven, and his first trip to the public library there. He remembered walking across the Green that day and stopping to take a moment to admire the beautiful edifice before he entered. Once inside, he had crossed the marble floor of the foyer, flanked with busts of the great giants of western literature—Shakespeare, Milton, and others. He proceeded into the reading room with the same reverence as one entering a church. The very silence of the library, soft and comforting, like church, gave him a sense of being in a holy place. There were no images of saints in these rooms; instead, there were the images of some of the greatest minds in the world, in the form of the hundreds, the thousands of books lining the shelves.

He walked through the stacks slowly, running his hands over the volumes, caressing them, the beautiful, wonderful books on the shelves that were there to enlighten his mind and inspire his soul. And his for the mere taking!

Week after week he came to the library to read, study and write for hours and hours. At closing time he would depart, cradling in his arms the four books allowed to be withdrawn for the period of two weeks. In the ensuing weeks and months, Al followed a regular regimen of study, carrying away with him usually a grammar text, a mathematics test, or a history book or a literary work, all in English. For dessert, he allowed himself a book written in Italian, a work of one of the great masters of Italian literature.

To all the librarians, Al had become a familiar fixture, either prowling the stacks or writing at a desk every Saturday from five o'clock until closing time at nine. In time, even the head librarian, an old maid, whose hair was neatly rolled into a bun at the back of the head, condescended now and then to give him a nod of recognition, peering at him over her gold-rimmed eyeglasses.

All of the librarians were female; one in particular, was a stunning young girl, whose warm smile and sparkling, friendly blue eyes never failed to put Al at ease. So much so, that one evening, book in hand, Al approached her like a bashful schoolboy. With a trace of accent that he still had in those days, he asked if she would be so kind as to explain what was meant by an "adjective in the attributive position." Graciously, and with clarity, Maureen explained the grammatical concept to him; she seemed pleased to have been of help to him.

So, taking advantage of her kind willingness to help, Al more than once feigned ignorance just so that he could talk to her. She always responded to his requests with patience and gentleness. In fact, on the rare occasions when Al failed to appear, it was always with genuine concern that Maureen inquired why he had not been at the library.

In time a certain bond of familiarity had developed between the two; they exchanged names. He always addressed her as Miss Donnell. She always called him Mister Alanga. But within months, that formality ceased, as they learned more about each other in the conversations between them that had become less and less about books. She started calling him Alfred, and he called her Maureen.

One snowy evening after the library closed, Al waited at the corner a little way off from the front steps of the building. As she made her way down the steps and onto the snow-blanketed sidewalk, Al softly called out, "Miss Donnell.. Maureen." She wasn't startled. She had recognized his voice.

"Maureen, let me accompany you to the trolley stop. It's a long way across the Green, and it is dark, and.."

"That is very kind of you, Alfred," she interrupted, "but there is no need to trouble yourself."

"It's no trouble, Maureen. I would very much like to. I don't like to see you walking alone in the darkness and in the snow. You might slip and fall, you know."

She laughed. "Oh, I'll not slip. But I think it is very nice of you to be concerned. Very well, come." They walked side by side that night, not arm in arm, until they came to the trolley stop at the far end of the Green. Al waited until he saw her safely aboard the car. He waved her off with a smile. She returned both the wave and the smile. After that, it became the routine for both of them to meet at closing time and walk to the stop, side by side. Soon they were walking arm in arm.

As the weeks went by, the relationship between them grew to be something more than friendship; they had fallen in love. They began to meet on Sundays, too. Maureen, on the pretext of attending a movie with a lady friend, or of visiting another, would faithfully meet Al on the Green. In the little cafe where they usually met, over a cup of coffee and a pastry, they talked. Mostly they learned about each other; and they often spoke of their dreams, their aspirations, their hopes for the future, and their families.

Early on, after the relationship had developed into love, Maureen, with a note of pain in her voice, explained why she could never take Al home to meet her family. Her father, she told him, would never accept him. Al didn't ask why; he knew the reason.

But Maureen took it upon herself to answer the question that Al hadn't asked. "Alfred, my dear, perhaps we should go no further with this. I mean, I do love you, but I am afraid that the idea of us marrying is impossible." She lowered her head and gazed into her cup of tea. Then in a spate of words, rushing to get through something unpleasant, she began to explain herself.

"Alfred, it hurts me to say this, but I can say it no other way. My father, well, the truth is, my father does not think highly of...of"

"Italians?" Al finished the sentence for her. Maureen's face took on the color of a pomegranate. Al reached across the table and took her hand in his. "Listen, Rina, you don't have to say more. I'm no stranger to that kind of feeling about Italians in this country. I doubt if there is an Italian alive in America who at one time or another, hasn't been the object of an American's scornful look or insulting word, or worse. But that will all change in time, and maybe, your father too, will change his ideas about us. Why, he might even get to like me once he meets me." Al was smiling. Maureen raised her eyes from the cup. Her eyes mirrored both pain and embarrassment.

"No, Alfred. You don't understand. My father and you will never meet. I know him, and I know how strongly he feels about, about. Oh, he will never change his ideas." Al reached over to her face and wiped a tear that was trailing down her cheek. Then he raised here chin and looked into her eyes.

"Rina, look at me. I love you. It's not your father or your brothers that I love. As long as you love me, what they think of me doesn't matter. I am not afraid of them; they can never do anything that will make me stop loving you. I want to marry you, Rina. I believe that you love me. We can build a life together that will be happy and good, in spite of your father." Suddenly he rose from his chair, almost knocking it over.

"Let's get married right now!" he blurted out.

"Sh, Alfred, please. People are looking." A smiled crossed her face. "They say that Italians are impetuous. They may not all be, but I know one that is." In a moment the smile left her face, and the bantering tone of her voice faded. "I've got to get home, Alfred. I'll be missed if I come into the house too late. It is futile to talk of this matter now, in this place. Walk me to the trolley, dear. Please, let's go now. She picked up her purse from the table and rose from the chair. During the short walk to the trolley stop from the cafe, they walked in silence. At the stop, before she ascended onto the car, she turned and said, quietly, "Will I see you Saturday at the library?"

"Of course." Al's voice was strong and sharp.

As the trolley began moving, she waved to him from her seat. Al waved back.

Chapter Forty-seven

Maureen's ride to her Dwight Street home from the Green was a short one. Once off the car, she walked the few steps from the corner to the large, ornately Victorian house that was her home. She made her way noiselessly up the steps to the front door and quietly opened it.

"And how is Mary, the poor dear? The fever is it, that is bringing her low?" a voice heavy with brogue called out across the foyer from the front parlor.

"She is much better, Mother. Oh, she will be up and about in a week or so, I am sure. Maureen hung up her hat and coat on the coat tree as she answered her mother. Then she walked into the parlor and up to her mother who was sitting by the fire with her cup of tea.

"A cup of tea, dear?"

"No thank you, Mother. I had coffee just before leaving Mary's. Where is Father?"

"Pshaw! Where but at the lodge hall of the Order. Sure, now, they are all planning for the Saint Patrick's Day parade."

"Of course. Two months hence or so, and it is here. If you will excuse me now, Mother, I will go up to my room. Work, you know, tomorrow."

"Yes, Maureen. Oh, do stop by Helen's room. Your sister came in only a short while ago herself. She said she wanted to speak to you when you came in."

Maureen bent over the sitting figure of her mother and gave her a kiss on the forehead. "Goodnight." The girl left the room and proceeded to the stairway leading up the upstairs bedrooms. Once at the landing, she went to her sister's room and gently tapped at the door.

"Come in, Maureen," called out a voice from inside the room. Maureen opened the door and entered. "I knew it had to be you," her sister said, "since everyone except Mother is out of the house. Here, come sit by me." Helen was patting the cushion by her side on the chaise lounge on which she was seated.

Maureen walked across the carpeted floor to the bay window where her sister was sitting. Helen resembled more her father in looks, and was not as pretty as Maureen, but she was by no means homely. In her middle thirties, it was assumed by all, and not least by Helen herself, that she would remain an old maid. She seemed resigned to the fact, and to all appearances was content to remain unmarried and be a companion to her mother.

"So tell me, dear, and how is Mary getting on?"

"Quite well," answered Maureen. Her voice quavered slightly. "I'm sure that she will be up and about in a week's time or so."

Helen reached over to her sister sitting beside her now on the chaise, and took her hand. With a steady gaze, her eyes searched Maureen's intently. There was a little frown on Helen's forehead when she said, "Sister, where were you all afternoon? You were not with Mary, for you see, I spent the entire afternoon in her company. We chatted and had tea together, and passed a little while with our embroidering. You were not at Mary's at all, my dear. Why do you say you were, when obviously you were not? Do you wish to tell me? Whether you do or not, I will say nothing to anyone in this house. I will respect your wishes in the matter. But I shall be somewhat hurt if you feel that you cannot confide in me, Maureen. We have always shared our confidences. We have always been two peas in a pod."

"Oh, Helen, dear sister." Maureen leaned over and embraced Helen. There were tears in her eyes. Helen pulled a lace-edged handkerchief from her sleeve and dabbed the tears away from her sister's eyes.

"Now tell me. Is something wrong? Perhaps I can be of help. Don't be afraid to tell me, Maureen."

Like water rushing over a dam, Maureen's words gushed forth. For a full half hour she bared her soul to her older sister. She told her everything about the relationship, the love that had developed between herself and Alfred. She recounted the afternoon's events at the cafe and Alfred's proposal of marriage, the elopement he had proposed, her own fear of Father's anger. "Oh, the impossibility of it all!" Maureen cried out when she had ended speaking.

She seemed exhausted by the effort of the telling, yet relieved by sharing the burden of her anxieties that she had been carrying within her breast for so long a time. She sat with her hands folded in her lap, and her head bowed like a pathetic little schoolgirl expecting to be punished for some misbehavior.

For a moment Helen remained silent. Only the ticking of the clock on the mantel broke the silence in the room. Then noiselessly Helen rose from the seat. "Tell me, Maureen dear, does this Italian boy truly love you? And you, him? Is he a good sort, with whom you would spend the rest of your days?"

"Oh, yes, Helen. He is such a good man, caring and gentle, and handsome. We truly love each other, there is no question of that. But Father, Father will never accept him, that I know. Oh, Father's fury would be terrible, should he ever find out about Alfred and me."

"To hell with Father! The man is a bigot and a clod."

Helen's outburst brought a look of surprise to Maureen's face. Her amazement grew as her sister went on, her voice bitter and sharp. "He forgets when he was nothing but shanty Irish, and now that he is lace curtain, he thinks himself better than others. He has money now, and a house on Dwight Street and wears a bowler instead of a cap. Oh, the airs he puts on! He forgets that he came to this country in steerage and began his life in America laying railroad ties and working in a coal mine. Why, his first home was naught but a shack by the railroad tracks, whose very walls shook every time the cars rolled by."

Wide-eyed, with mouth agape at her sister's vituperative tongue-lashing of their father, Maureen suddenly found the words to say to her: "Helen, I've never heard you speak so. I never knew you harbored such feelings."

Helen threw back her head and laughed. "Oh, yes. Good old Helen. Why, she wouldn't say boo to a goose. Yes, Father, no, Father, of course, Father, certainly Father. Well, look at me, Maureen. What do you see? You see a thirty-five year-old old maid, And why? Because of that mean-spirited old man we call Father. I had my chance at happiness, but I was too simple and too frightened to disobey that tyrant and assert myself."

She was pacing back and forth across the room as she was speaking. She fluttered her handkerchief to accentuate every rise in her quivering voice. The color rose to her cheeks to shine vividly pink against the whiteness of her face.

"I had my chance for happiness, Maureen," she reiterated. "And I lost it. Because of him." Helen came up close to her sister. Her voice was forceful and commanding. "Don't make the same mistake I did. Go to your young man. Build a life together with him. This may be your one chance for happiness, your one chance to escape from Father's insufferable tyranny."

Limply she returned to her seat. There were tears in her eyes. Maureen went to her and put her arms around her sister's shoulders. As she did so, she heard Helen whisper softly to herself, "Oh, Kevin." In a flash the image of a tall, blonde youth sped across Maureen's mind, a face out of the distant past. She remembered, she was only a child of eleven or twelve then, and they had just moved into this house, this house that seemed so elegant, so magnificent, then.

Her thoughts jumped to the day soon after the move to the new house, and she seemed to recall the sad face of her sister weeping. Yes, Father had raged and stormed at her, and that was why Helen was crying. Maureen had been frightened of course at Father's outburst and her sister's tears, but the wonder of the new house with its polished floor and marble mantels had held more interest for her at the time. It had been yet another display of Father's temper, and she had never discovered the cause of the row between Father and Helen.

Helen leaned back in the chair. In a voice, soft, now, she continued, speaking, it seemed to Maureen, more to herself than to her. "Yes, I was in love once. Kevin, Kevin MacDonald. He was a fine lad, so tall and handsome and manly. He was a trimmer in the carriage trade, you know. But his family were Orangemen, Scotch-Irish from Ulster, and Protestant. That was enough reason for Father to dislike him so, to forbid I accept his proposal of marriage." She rose from her seat. With both hands, she lifted Maureen from the chair. With a fierce look of determination, lightning flashing in the blue of her eyes, she said, "Maureen, profit from my stupidity and weakness. Go, go, and be happy with this young man of yours. Do as I say, and when all of your plans have been laid out, let me know the day that you will be off with Alfred. Then, when you are safely away, I will tell Father that you have left, later, when it will be too late for him to do anything about it."

Maureen found her own eyes bathed in tears. She kissed Helen's cheek, still damp with her own tears. A smile crossed Maureen's face, and a rosy flush of joy tinged her cheeks. With a burst of elated enthusiasm she shouted out, "I will do it, Helen. I will do it. You have given me the courage to see what I must do. Oh, Helen, I cannot have you involved in this in any way. If you were the one to tell Father of my running off with Alfred, he will be sure to know that you had known of it. He would be furious with you." She stopped talking for a moment. Her brow was knitted over in thought. With a start, she clapped her hands together.

"I know. I know just how to do it. Mother is the only one who ever goes into the front parlor when she takes her afternoon tea. She always sits in her favorite chair by the fireplace. I shall leave a letter on that chair, and when she goes to sit, she will find it. By the time she reads it, it shall have been too late for anyone to do anything about my departure. Alfred and I will have been long gone, and wed.

"Oh, Helen, you are a dear. I shall ever hold you in my heart, for giving me the courage to know what I should do." Full of resolve and determination, she rushed across the room to the door. She opened it, then turned to her sister and blew her a kiss. Helen smiled broadly and waved her off.

Chapter Forty-eight

If ever a week seemed an eternity, it was the week following Maureen's talk with Helen. Now that she had made her decision to follow her heart and marry Alfred, she could barely wait to tell him. When she saw him come into the library on that blessed Saturday, she could scarcely restrain herself from running into his arms. With great control, however, she held herself in check. With the usual prim decorum of a proper librarian, as exemplified by the head librarian sitting next to her at the reception desk, Maureen dutifully processed the books Alfred was returning. Then, as if suddenly remembering, she said, "Oh, yes, Mister Alanga, I believe the book you asked for last week is on the shelf. If you will please come along, I will show you where it is to be found. Excuse me, Miss Evans, while I show this gentleman where the book is located on the shelf."

The old librarian assented with a slight nod of her head. Maureen rose from her chair and led Alfred across the reception hall and into a dimly lit alcove off the main stacks. Al followed her to the very end of a row of shelves. There, Maureen, her voice quavering with excitement, told him the good news.

In the weeks that followed, the two lovers made their plans in the little cafe that was their place of rendezvous. Maureen had insisted that they wait a month before they rushed off, and although Al would have run off that very day, he gave in to her wishes. The month, she told him, would pass quickly, and indeed it had. And now the day had come, and they were sitting on the train that was speeding them to the fulfillment of their dream.

They married the very afternoon they arrived in New York, and spent the week honeymooning. They dined, they took in a Broadway play, and they visited Ellis Island and the Statue of Liberty. They made love. Al was glad that he had taken Mike's advice, and stayed the week instead of the few days he had originally intended to remain in New York City.

When they returned to New Haven as man and wife, Al brought his bride to her new home. Inside the bungalow, everything was as neat as a pin. A vase of rather wilted flowers graced the kitchen table. Mike, true to his word, had cleared out his belongings and had readied the house for the new occupants.

"Oh, look, Alfred, on the table." A package, wrapped in silver paper and crowned with a silver bow lay next to the vase of flowers. Al picked up the little card and read: "To Mr. and Mrs. Alfred Alanga, congratulations. Mike."

"Open it, Maureen. It's from my brother, Mike."

"How thoughtful of him, Alfred. I must meet him soon." She peeled away the wrappings and lifted the box's cover. Inside was a silver tea set. Teapot, sugar bowl, and creamer, all on a serving tray. The gleam of the polished silver shone exquisitely bright in the afternoon sun coming through the windows.

"Oh my, how lovely, how lovely. Michael must be our first guest to dinner, so that I can thank him in person."

"You will meet him soon enough, Rina, if I know my brother. He will want to see for himself how beautiful you are, after all I've said about you. Believe me, he will be here first thing in the morning to see if we're back."

And in fact, hardly were they out of bed the next morning, with the coffee yet to boil, that a gentle rapping on the door announced Mike's arrival. Al, his hair all a-tussle, and still stuffing his shirt into his pants, began laughing. "Here comes your brother-in-law, Rina, just as I said."

"Gracious, Alfred, my hair is a mess. I haven't braided it yet."

Al pulled her to himself and kissed her. "You are the most beautiful woman in the world, with or without braids. Let him see what a copper mine of hair surrounds that gorgeous face of yours." He left her and went to the door and opened it. He lunged at Mike standing there, and gave him a big bear hug. "Come in, buddy. Come on in." Without letting go of his brother, he pulled him to the table. "Rina, meet my big brother." With a faint blush of embarrassment on her cheeks, Maureen came up to Mike with her hand outstretched.

"Michael," she greeted him. "Alfred has told me so much about you. I am so happy to meet you at last." She smiled and then added teasingly, "Really, it is so difficult now that I see you, to tell who is the better-looking." Al laughed and poked his brother playfully with his elbow. "She's Irish, you know, and kissed that damned Blarney Stone." Mike's face broke out in a broad smile. He let go Maureen's hand and planted a brotherly kiss on her cheek. The ice was broken; Maureen and Mike felt at ease with each other. Soon all three were chatting over coffee. All feeling of embarrassment or reticence evaporated; it was as if the new in-laws had known each other for a long time. Maureen sensed right off that she had found a friend, a brother, in Mike.

As soon as they had finished breakfast, Maureen began clearing the table, then went to finish tidying herself up. Once she was out of earshot, in the bedroom, Mike said softly to his brother, "Al, I told Mama, you know, about you and Maureen getting married. I didn't think it right not to let her know what was going on. I know that maybe you wanted to tell her yourself, but, well, I didn't want her to think anything was wrong. You know, why you wouldn't be showing up at the house for a week. I hope you aren't sore with me, Al."

He didn't give Al a chance to say anything, but went right on talking. "And you know, she's all hepped up to meet your wife. She's as happy as hell about you marrying. You should have seen her face when I told her. Now she's anxious to meet your wife, and so is Papa. So don't go to work today. Let me go now and tell her that you two are coming to lunch. This way, she'll have time to get up a royal spread. You know Mama. She'll want to do it up big. Okay? What do you say?"

Al went up to Mike and clapped his arm around his brother's shoulder. "I'm glad you told them, Mike. Now that I think about it, it's better she knows what to expect. In a way, I was feeling kind of bad about not telling Mama and Papa first about what I was doing. I never told them 'in the first place about Maureen, only you. She would have wanted a bang-up wedding like Nora's, but that would have been out of the question—no time, and besides, with Maureen's people feeling the way they do about me, well, I figured it was the best way—just to run off. I know I'll have some explaining to do to Mama and Papa, but now she knows I'm married, and is happy about it, so I guess everything is okay. Go ahead, Mike, tell Mama we're coming. Maureen will love Mama, and Mama will feel the same, I know. Go on, and I'll give Maureen the word."

That day Mama met her new daughter-in-law for the first time and although conversation between the two was minimal because of Mama's limited English, the look of pleasure in Mama's eyes spoke louder than any words. The first meeting of the two, and lunch were a great success. Once home, Maureen told Al how "sweet," as she put it, Mama was, and how "delightful" were his sisters.

Maureen's heart had been instantly won over the first moment she and Mama met. Mama, in almost slow motion, had stretched out her arms, and gently placed her hands on either side of the girl's face. And when Al translated what Mama had said—that Maureen had the face of a Madonna, Maureen's eyes glowed with happiness at the compliment. She took the old lady's hands down from her cheeks, pressed them tenderly in appreciation, leaned over and kissed Mama's cheek.

As Al knew it would be, his mother had laid an array of food on the table of banquet proportions. Maureen was simply overwhelmed; everything was so different from the "boiled dinner" of potatoes, cabbage and beef that was the usual fare at home. Mama beamed with pleasure at every mouthful her new daughter-in-law took. She was delighted seeing Maureen taste of every dish, and her joy reached the height of ecstacy when Maureen asked Mama earnestly to teach her how to make the delicious "little meat pies," that is, the ravioli that was Mama's specialty.

Back home that night, as they lay in bed, Maureen again expressed her delight to Al in meeting his family. She hadn't met Papa yet; he had been at his job in Sargent's, nor Frankie. But Al told her that meeting would take place next Sunday. It was Papa's birthday, and Frankie was coming down from New York City for the celebration.

Maureen put out the lamp on the night table. "Good night, Alfred, dear," she whispered. She put her arms around him as she lay next to him. She snuggled close and they kissed. When their mouths separated, Maureen said hesitatingly, "Alfred, is there something wrong with your mother's, Mama's, I mean, legs? At times I thought I saw her wince with pain as she walked. And she looked rather drawn to me."

Al bolted up from bed. "Damn! I forgot. Mike and I talked a while "back about her not looking well lately. The first chance I get, I'll get her looked at by the doctor. She'd never go to one on her own. I'll have Doctor Praiano stop by the house for a look-see. She probably needs a tonic or something. I'll stop by his office and arrange for him to come to the house."

"Do that, dear. Do it soon."

Chapter Forty-nine

The day of Papa's birthday party was a gorgeous, warm day. And what made it perfect was, that for the first time in a long time, the whole family was together. Not only had Frankie come down, but he had brought with him, Uncle Matteo, Aunt Graziella and their kids. Mama and Graziella were overjoyed to see their husbands, the two brothers, embrace and on good terms again. Flurries of hugs and kisses abounded in a tangle of arms and faces. And in the midst of the eating, drinking and talking that went on around her as the day wore on, Rosa's face beamed, absolutely glowed as she gazed upon all the cherished faces around her again. Her sons, her daughters, Nora and Gilda, and her new daughter, Maureen. Zio Matteo and Papa, and Zia Graziella. and the children, all grown up now. Their son Matteo, was no longer "little Matteo. He was a young man, tall and handsome, who never failed to catch the eye of the young ladies on whose tables he waited in the restaurant. And as for Marietta, already more than one young man's mother had approached Graziella about a son's ardent passion for her attentions. Even Graziella's Francesco, eleven years old now, was bussing tables at the restaurant.

To Maureen, the meal went on and on, never seeming to end. It lasted for hours, and just when she thought there could not possibly be anything more, out came Mama and the girls with more platters of food. Only when the demi-tasse cups were set out on the table, did she surmise that the feast had run its course.

After the last cup had been filled, Michael rose from his chair. "Mama," he said, "Papa, everybody, listen." Out of his shirt pocket, he pulled a long, white envelope. He turned to his father. "Papa, this is for you, and Mama, from all of your children." He hesitated before going on, and turned to face Al. "Hell, Al, I told you, you should be the one to do this. I'm no good at speeches. You're the one with words."

"Never mind," Al broke in, "you're the oldest. You should do it, so get on with it." Mike turned his gaze back to his mother and father.

"Papa," Mike resumed, "Papa, we know how hard you and Mama

have always worked for us. We know that your children always come first, that everything you two do, you do with our benefit in mind. Even to leaving the old country and coming here so that your kids could have the advantages of a better life in America." He stretched across the table and handed his father the envelope. "This is for you, from all of us." As Giuseppe took the envelope in his hands, a burst of hand-clapping broke out.

"Bravo, bravo, Michele," Uncle Matteo shouted.

"Well said, well said," Frankie added.

"Better than I could have done, Mike," Al called out.

"Papa, open the envelope," Gilda spoke out excitedly.

Their father pulled out the flap from the envelope. His fingers probed the inside, and he extracted its contents. A puzzled look came over his face.

"They're tickets, Pop," yelled Frankie. "Two tickets, one for you and one for Mama. To Italy. Back to the old country. For a whole month. What do you think of that?" Frankie turned to his mother. "You're going to see your grandchildren, Mama. You're going to see your daughters again, Filumena and Carolina. This time you're going first class, not steerage. A cabin all to yourselves. You sail on the *Conte di Savoia*. How's that for coming up in the world? You leave on the thirteenth of June, Saint Anthony's feast day."

It took a few moments for the enormity, the reality of what Giuseppe and Rosa had just heard, to sink in. Rosa's eyes began to flood with tears, and Giuseppe's hands trembled a little as he looked down at the tickets. The two of them had always harbored the dream of returning for a visit back to the land of their birth, to see Bosco once again, and their daughters and their grandchildren. But it was always someday—someday that had become more and more remote of fruition with the passage of the years.

All eyes were on Mama and Papa, waiting anxiously to see their reaction. Then when Papa's face broke out in a wide smile, and Mama clasped her head in her hands, wagging it from side to side, all the while murmuring, *che meraviglia* (what a wonderful thing), everyone's face put on a smile. This, then was the finest gift the children could have given their parents.

The rest of the afternoon and evening went on in a lighthearted mood of festive gaiety. Frankie and Uncle Matteo's family finally gave in to Mama's insistence that they stay the night. After all, there were so many matters yet to discuss—whom to see in the old country, what messages to relay to family and friends, what places to visit—the old forge, the church, the town piazza, the ruins of the old monasteries. Would they still be there? Did the *carrettieri* still drive their lumbering carts pulled by braying mules over the roads and byways of Bosco? Did water carriers still go through the streets and piazzas chanting about the delicacies of the lemon-scented water they sold for a *centesimo* a glass? And did the street musicians, the puppeteers still entertain in the piazzas and streets of Bosco? Or had modernism and progress wrought changes even in little Bosco, and had the old ways disappeared?

Back and forth the conversations went late into the night. Old names, old faces, old memories were dredged up out of the past. Places and faces long buried in the deepest recesses of their brains, once more surfaced to evince now a tear, now a smile, now a sigh. On and on went the talking, until at last, someone realized that it was very, very late. Frankie yawned and stretched. "Where am I sleeping, Mama? The attic?"

At that, Mike and Al got out of their chairs. "It's time for us to go," they said together. "Work, for me tomorrow. Maureen, will you get our things?" Al added. As his wife went off to retrieve their jackets, Al bent over and kissed his mother and then his father. Good-nights were said all around, and the evening came to a close.

At home that night, as she began to undress for bed, Maureen said to her husband who was already under the sheets, "What a wonderful evening it was for all of you, wasn't it, Alfred? Such fond and vivid memories that all of you have. Although, now that I think of it, I find it rather strange that Michael had so very little to say about his days back in Bosco. You, your parents, and even Francis had so much to relate." Laughingly, she added: "What was it? Did some pretty *signorina* break his heart there?"

In a soft, almost inaudible whisper, but heard by Maureen, Al murmured, "She was pretty." At that moment he saw Adelina's face as he remembered her when she had stood by the side of the road to see them off to America; he was sure that Mike had been seeing that face all night long.

"Someday, Rina, I'll tell you Mike's sad story. Not now, though. It's late. I'm too tired. Good night, sweetheart."

Chapter Fifty

The following Tuesday before he left for work, Al said over his last cup of morning coffee, "Oh, by the way, Rina. Listen. will you come with me to Mama's tonight? I spoke with Doctor Praiano yesterday. He's a good friend of mine. He promised to stop by and give Mama a check-up this evening at the house. She would rather take on the devil than have a doctor touch her. But with you there, she's not apt to put up a fuss." He laughed. "She thinks doctors are all quacks. She has more faith in herbs, poultices, salt and prayers to Saint Cure Cough and Saint Cure Ache, than any doctor."

"Of course, Alfred. I'll be happy to come with you. Now off you go. I shall be all ready this evening."

That night at Mama's house, when the three of them stepped into the house, Al, Maureen, and Doctor Praiano, Mama gave them a puzzled look. The doctor was a stranger to her, but she smiled seeing him with Al and Maureen, and was just ready to offer to make some coffee, when Al explained the reason for this unexpected visit, that he had brought the doctor, his friend, to check her over. Her face hardened to a frown. The welcoming smile disappeared from her face. She glanced at her son with a steady look, the kind of look she gave when ready to scold. But Maureen walked up to her with a big smile on her face, and took hold of her hand. Mama's features softened. She would not embarrass herself by making a scene before her daughter-in-law.

Al just smiled sheepishly at his mother's initial words of protest. "But I must finish cooking Papa's supper," she insisted. "He will be home any minute now. " With a smile still on his face, Al walked up to his mother and took the wooden spoon she was holding and gave it to Gild.a. "Here," he said to his sister, "you finish stirring." He turned around to face his mother again. "Mama, don't be a *capa tosta*. Let the doctor look at you. Come on, do it for me. Doctor Praiano is a nice guy and a paesano."

Al didn't wait for her answer, but instead went to the doctor's side. "Take her in there, Doctor Praiano." He pointed to the bedroom. "Take your time and look her over good." Maureen came up to Mama, took her by the hand, and gently started towards the bedroom, the doctor following. Just before entering the room, Mama called back, "Make yourselves some coffee. Gilda put the pastries on the table." Then she vanished into the bedroom, and the doctor closed the door behind them.

The minutes ticked by. First ten, then fifteen, then twenty. Just as Papa entered the kitchen from work, the bedroom door opened. Mama exited first. There was a look of pain on her face, and she was noticeably dragging her foot. She barely raised it from the floor. Papa was mystified, and Gilda quietly told him what was going on as the doctor led Mama and sat her down.

"I'm sorry Signora Alanga, if I caused you any pain when I examined that toe," Doctor Praiano said softly. "Never mind putting on a shoe. Just walk around in your stockings, not even a slipper. Better yet, keep off that foot altogether." He looked up from Mama to Al, and with a discreet wave of his head, Praiano beckoned Al to follow. The two of them left the kitchen out onto the back porch. Almost brusquely, the doctor grabbed Al's arm in a tight grip. Then lifting the forefinger of his free hand, he raised it to the level of Al's face. "Tomorrow, first thing, he commanded, "as early in the morning as possible, I want your mother at Grace Hospital. I will stop by at the hospital on my way home tonight and get everything set for her admission."

At the word "hospital" Al's face went white. He, in turn, grabbed hold of Doctor Praiano's arm. "What? What are you telling me, doctor? Why the hospital? What's the matter with Mama, what?" Al fumbled in his shirt pocket and withdrew a pack of Lucky Strike cigarettes. He jerked the packet upwards; a cigarette popped up, and he brought it to his mouth. Then he extended the pack to the doctor, who took one out, and they both lit up.

"Al, your mother, well, in the first place, I'm certain that she's a diabetic, you know, sugar. Tomorrow's blood work and urine analysis at the hospital will bear me out, I'm sure. The dizziness, the fatigue, the thirst she's been feeling for some time, and the excessive need to urinate, are all the classic symptoms of diabetes. All these symptoms, she admits to. But what makes me absolutely certain of my diagnosis, is the look of that big toe of hers. The inflammation is serious. I just hope that it is not gangrenous. If it is, and if the infection has gotten into the bone..." He stopped abruptly and put a fatherly arm across Al's shoulder. Then he continued. "Al, I've got to tell you straight out, if that bone is gangrenous, the matter is, well, it might mean serious surgery."

Al bit his bottom lip so hard, he almost bit through, and the dent on the lower lip became blood red as soon as the teeth let go. "I think I know what you are saying, doctor. Tomorrow, the hospital, she'll be there." He reached out and clasped both of Doctor Praiano's hands in his. Then, almost in a whisper, in a softness of voice that echoed both fear and pleading, he said, "Doctor Praiano, you'll do, I mean, I know you'll do everything and the money—no problem. Only, please..."

"Al, everything possible will be done to save the..." The doctor paused for a moment. "That is, well, that, toe, and I hope, it's just the toe that's badly infected. You see, your mother clipped her toe nail, and in doing it, she cut the skin of the toe. Ordinarily, in non-diabetics, the salt water bathing of the toe your mother resorted to, would have done the trick to mend the cut. That's what makes me almost positive that your mother is diabetic; that little nick got infected and the infection has spread to the foot, so extensively and so fast."

He shook his head and broke away from Al's grasp and started walking down the steps. At the bottom, he called back to Al, "The hospital, Al, tomorrow, as early as possible." Then he walked away into the darkness and to his car.

Chapter Fifty-one

In the several days following Doctor Praiano's visit, the worst of his fears were borne out by the examinations and tests conducted at the hospital. All the analyses showed a huge level of sugar. And worse, the toe was gangrenous. To save the foot, and indeed the leg, the toe had to be amputated at once. To his stunned father, Alfredo explained the immediacy of the decision and permission to operate that was required of him. He and all three of his sons were together in the surgeon's office at the hospital, where the surgeon had explained the procedure and formalities necessary for the operation to take place. Al had translated the surgeon's words to his father; the papers were lying on the desk awaiting Giuseppe's signature. The old man was filled with bewildered consternation. He was thinking: "Here there is a man and he wants me to say, yes, I give you my permission to cut away the living flesh of my Rosa. Is it possible that I must do such a thing? More than once he had picked up the form from the desk, and then laid it down again.

"Come, come, Mister Alanga. This matter must be attended to as quickly as possible. I would like to schedule the operation for tomorrow morning." The impatience in Doctor Wilson's voice, the surgeon, was obvious to Al, Mike and Frankie. Mike caught a glimpse of Frankie's face; it was turning red in anger, and his fists were clenched. Al knew his brother was beginning to boil, and he knew that Frankie had a short fuse. He stepped quickly up to the doctor, took the form he was holding, from his hand, and said, "Doctor, give us a few minutes to explain again all this to our father." Mike had to control his own antagonism he felt at the doctor's brusqueness towards his father.

"Yes, yes, please do. My time is very valuable, you know. Please see that I get the release form for the operation immediately." He turned away and walked hurriedly out of the room and down the hall.

Once alone in the room with his brothers, Frankie exploded. "That son of a bitch!"

"Shut up, Frankie. This isn't the time nor the place to get your nose out of joint." Then Mike went over to his father, and in Italian, in a calm but strained voice, pointed out the urgency of the matter. If Mama's leg, her life, was to be saved, the toe had to come off. When he finished, Mike put his arm around his father, and put a pen into his hand. He led him to the desk. "Put your mark here, Papa." Giuseppe signed by putting a shaky "X" on the line, and Mike wrote his own name in attestation of his father's signature beside the mark.

It was a forlorn and dejected Al that made his way home that evening. Over and over on the way home, he kept seeing Mama's drawn and pale face against the pillow of the hospital bed on which she lay. He had kissed her before he left, and in return, she had given him a weak smile. She was worn out by all the tests and probes she had undergone in the period of the last several days.

Never before had Al seen his mother lying in bed, looking so old, so helpless, so feeble. And tomorrow, tomorrow, what were they going to do to this poor old lady, his beloved mother. He shook his head violently in order to throw out of his head the images of knives and blood, and a severed toe.

Deep in such thoughts, he had almost reached the front door of the bungalow, when from behind the trunk of the enormous oak tree that spread its thick, leafy branches over the little house, two figures shot out at him. He felt a tremendous blow on his right shoulder. When he turned to face the direction from which it had come, another punch of a fist caught him square on the chin.

"Get the guinea bastard, Sean. Pin his arms behind him." Before Al could even manage to put up his dukes, someone pinioned his arms against his back in an iron grip. Punches from the fellow in his front began to jab, one after another, into his gut. With all his strength, Al jerked up his knee; it made contact with his assailant's groin. The fellow let out a howl of pain and doubled up, his hands cupping his genitals. At the same time, Al pushed up his arms, up and outward, breaking the hold on them. The odds were more even now, and he began to throw punches fast and furious straight to the head of his opponent.

"Kevin, for the love of Christ, help me!" But Kevin, in excruciating pain, lay flat on the ground with his hands still between his legs. He could barely lift his head, let alone a fist. Just as Al landed a punch that sent his attacker sprawling against the oak, Maureen came rushing out the door. In her hand she was holding a rolling pin. She recognized her brothers: the one, in spite of the contortions of pain screwing up his face, the other, in spite of the blood that was flowing from his nose and mouth.

"Oh, you vile creatures, you despicable louts," Maureen spat out at her brothers. Her face was red with anger, and as she saw Sean get up from the ground, she rushed at him with the rolling pin raised above her head. He backed off. "Easy, now Maureen, easy now. I just want to help Kevin. He's hurt."

"Good," she replied hotly. "Good, pick him up and get off with you. And if ever you dare to show your ugly faces here again, you will deal with me. Do you understand me, you besotted cowards? Oh, a brave lot you are. Two against one, and sneaking up like thieves in the night. A fine lot you are, the two of you. The sons of your father you are, and that's for sure."

"It wasn't my idea," protested Sean weakly, wiping the back of his hand across his bloody nose. "And it wasn't Kevin's idea either. It was Dad had us come after your man."

"Shut your mouth, lad, and leave Father out of this," the older brother yelled. "She's made her bed, now let her lie in it. Let her be, and let's go."

Maureen bristled at his words. "Yes, let me be, let us be. Now leave, both of you. I want nothing more to do with either of you. And as far as I am concerned, I have only a mother and a sister. You, Sean, and you, Kevin Donnell, can go straight to the devil."

She turned away from both and took her husband by the arm. She began leading Al towards the open door of the house. Only once did she turn to look back, to make sure that her brothers were leaving. She could make out her brother Sean supporting a limping Kevin. Both were heading away from the house in the direction of the street.

Inside the bungalow, Maureen sat her husband on a kitchen chair. She tipped his head backwards over the top edge of the chair and began washing his face. With a wet washrag, she stemmed the trickle of blood still oozing from his nose, then his mouth. She finished, put the blood-stained cloth on the table, and with her fingers, began smoothing his rumpled hair.

"My darling Alfred, look what they've done to your beautiful face; it's all cut and marked." Gently, lovingly, she began running her index finger along the length of his nose. "Thank God, it isn't broken. Oh! but that eye. It is already swelling and turning blue." Maureen turned away and came back to Al in a minute. In her hand she held a bottle of iodine. Carefully and gently she began to swab the cuts on his cheeks and chin with it. As she leaned over to dab on some more of the disinfectant, Al pulled her close and kissed her.

"That's all I need to fix me up." He smiled and took another kiss. Maureen playfully dabbed the tip of his nose with a dot of iodine. She gave Al a big smile. "Well, now. Here, I was feeling sorry for you. But if you can pucker up your lips to kiss, I need not worry." But then the smile faded from her face, and she said in a serious tone: "Oh, Alfred, my darling. I am so sorry that it was my brothers that did this to you."

Before she could say more, Al rose from the chair and started unbuttoning his shirt. He said, "Listen, Rina. I told you once before, it is you I love, you that I married. Not your brothers, or your father, or your family. All that matters to me is that you accept and love me. If your family does not, I don't give a damn. Come to bed, Rina."

Chapter Fifty-two

On the tenth day after the amputation of Mama's toe, Mike, Al, and their father brought Rosa home. Carefully, tenderly, the boys lifted their mother up the steps of the stoop to the open front door, where both Nora and Gilda were waiting to welcome their mother home.

The color blossomed on Mama's cheeks the moment the boys sat her on the soft armchair that had been moved into the kitchen from the parlor. The kitchen, they knew, was the room in which she would be the happiest, the most comfortable. The hearth was the center of her universe. Rosa was really home now, and the joy she was feeling being there, showed itself on her face. All the pain, all the homesickness of the past two weeks disappeared as her eyes fell upon all the familiar objects of her kitchen, and as she sat surrounded by all the beloved faces of her family. The warm breezes wafting through the open windows of the kitchen caused the curtains to wave and flap as if they were banners of salute on the joyous occasion.

The family's pleasure was complete as they watched Mama eat with evident relish, the food that Nora and Gilda had prepared for her home-coming. All of them had a good laugh over Mama's description of hospital food, *pappochia*, as she derisively called it. A milky mush fit only for babies being weaned, she described it, as she downed the last morsel of Nora's lasagna, and wiped the sauce from the plate with a chunk of bread.

Every day of the following week, either Al or Mike made it a point to stop by and spend some time with their invalid mother. A week to the day of Rosa's home-coming, however, when Mike came whistling up the steps of the front porch, the door flew open and a frantic Gilda rushed at him. "Michele, Michele," she practically screamed at him. "Come and see Mama, come and see Mama. Oh her leg looks so bad. Oh, God, oh God." Mike rushed past his near-hysterical sister and ran to the kitchen. His mother was sitting in the chair, and on the floor, lay the basin and wash cloth that Gilda had been using to sponge bathe her mother. Mike gazed down in horrid disbelief at his mother's foot. The suture had become inflamed and was oozing a bloody pus. Flaming darts of red were visible all the way across Mama's foot up to the ankle.

Within fifteen minutes, with Mama in the cab of his truck, and Gilda beside her, he was speeding up Chapel Street to the emergency room of Grace Hospital. That evening he, his father and Al found themselves again in Doctor Wilson's office. Mike's face turned the color of ashes when Doctor Wilson gravely announced that the leg had to be cut off. Al moaned audibly. Giuseppe's head fell like a stone to his chest, when the boys told him the awful news. The boys watched as their father slowly made his way across the room towards the window, where, in the dimming light of late afternoon, he saw his own image on the glass.

Beside his reflection, he saw the standing figure of a young beautiful girl, as he first saw her walking in the piazza in Bosco when he was a young swain, and Rosa a young maid. As Giuseppe stood at the window in that hospital room, the years rolled back to the wonderful Sunday when he first laid eyes on Rosa. The girl was tall and slim, and her hair was raven black. But the eyes! They shone like emeralds, green, in the shape of almonds. Sunday after Sunday, he remembered, he had lounged at the edge of the piazza, waiting impatiently to catch sight of her. One day, with his mother with him, he pointed out Rosa to her. "I will have *her* for my wife," and he pleaded with his mother to find out who she was, and where she lived.

He mooned and moped like a lost soul until his mother met with a matchmaker to present her son's proposal of marriage to the girl's family. Giuseppe recalled how his heart had been in his throat when her parents brought Rosa to his mother's house, for the girl to eye him, and he, her.

She was sixteen years old, and therefore, of a marriageable age. Under the ornate mantilia that covered her head, her raven hair contrasted against the stark whiteness of her headdress. And those two eyes, those two green eyes that she had directed at his face, mirrored both shyness and intensity at the same time. Even as she sat stiffly in the chair, one could see that she was taller than most of the girls in Bosco. The boy, Giuseppe, only surpassed her in height by an inch or two. She sat, her hands folded in her lap, fittingly silent and retiring.

Across from her, stiff as a board, handsomely dressed in his best clothes, sat Giuseppe, equally silent, equally proper. Never a word did either of them speak to each other. They sat silent while their parents and the matchmaker did all the talking. Surreptitiously now and then, the two young ones eyed each other. When their eyes happened to meet, they would both blush in embarrassment at having been caught.

On and on, the parents spoke; they paid each other lavish compliments; they sang the lavish praises of their offspring; they boasted of their wealth in goats, pigs, chickens, and acreage under cultivation. But the two major figures of the drama sat and listened, taking in the measurement of each other. Both of them drank the coffee, ate the pastries, but tasted nothing.

The ritual of the first meeting between the families came to an end. And Giuseppe was left in limbo. He would have to wait for the decision of the girl and her family. Did the girl like him? Did her family approve of him and his family? He would have to wait to find out the answers. He knew the rules of the game. It would be unseeming for a decision to be forthcoming right away. A proper length of time would have to pass; the family of the girl must not appear anxious to palm off a daughter. After all, this girl, this Rosa Rienzi was a pretty girl, from a good family, and a good catch for any of the young men in Bosco.

Two weeks of suspenseful waiting had gone by. During that time, Giuseppe, love-sick as he was, barely ate enough to keep a bird alive. At night he lay in his bed with Rosa's face ever before his eyes. Under those eyes, dark circles began to show from lack of sleep. His mother began to fret and worry. She hovered over him like a mother hen, practically spoon-feeding him in order to see him eat. His father just laughed to himself; he knew what the pangs of love-sickness did to a man. He knew how hot the blood coursed through the veins of a young man in love.

Finally, one blessed evening, as he walked home slowly across the fields from his day's labor, Giuseppe spotted the matchmaker approaching the door to his house. As swift as a deer being chased by a wolf, he bounded through the corn stalks, dropping his tools along the way. Breathlessly he stole quietly alongside the open window at the side of the house.

With his ear cocked to listen, he suffered all the tortures of the souls in Purgatory, while all the amenities occasioned by the matchmaker's visit were observed. First, coffee and sweets. Then, polite conversation about the crops, one's health, tidbits of local gossip, the illnesses of this one and that one.

Under his breath, Giuseppe swore to himself. Would they never get around to talking about the girl, about him? Then at last, he heard the matchmaker ask, "And your son, Giuseppe, he is well? This, then, was his mother's cue to recite a glorious litany of her son's virtues. She made sure to cover all the fine qualities the boy possessed. He was handsome. He was strong. He was honest and gentle. He was respectful. On and on she went until she ended proudly: "There's not a better boy in all of Bosco. Giuseppe had to smile in admiration of his own grandeur.

Not to be outdone, the matchmaker rose equally to the occasion. This girl, Rosa Rienzi, was a prize. She was virtuous, a virgin, a good cook, a good housekeeper, thrifty, sensible, mature for her age. And, here, the matchmaker nodded knowingly—a girl healthy and strong enough to bear children. Finally: "Both she and her family find favor in your son, and consent to the joining together of your two families."

Giuseppe, remembering how he had kicked up his heels in joy, was smiling to himself as the sunlight coming through the hospital window, warmed his face. Suddenly he felt an arm around his shoulder, and a voice broke into his reveries. "Papa, what is it? Are you all right?" Mike's voice caused all the visions to vanish, the figure of himself crouching by the open window of his house those many years ago, the image of his mother in the kitchen with the matchmaker, the beautiful, slender form of Rosa as she was then. The stark reality of the hospital room and the dread terror of the impending amputation of his wife's leg jarred Giuseppe back to the present.

Chapter Fifty-three

During the next three weeks after the removal of Mama's leg, life for all of the family became a roller-coaster of emotional ups and downs. Each day in those early weeks of June after the operation, some or all of them would go to the hospital, almost always with roses, Mama's favorite flowers. The room came to smell and look like a rose garden. The fragrance of the flowers masked the awful antiseptic odor of the dingy basement room where Mama had been put to recuperate.

During those first early days, in a stupor brought on by the pain and drugs, Mama was barely conscious of their presence. Her moans were pitiful to hear; she tossed her head from side to side, weakly calling out the names of Jesus and Mary. The little room grew stifling as the June days grew warmer. No fresh air circulated in the tiny, closet-like space in which she lay. Beads of sweat dampened her face and neck. When they saw her swimming in her own perspiration, all of them, even Giuseppe with his thick-skinned, rough hands, would wipe her face, neck and arms with a soft towel.

Gazing down on the form of her body under the thin cotton blanket, Al, Mike, and Frankie often bit their lips. One side of her was full and whole, and the other, where her right leg should have been, the blanket lay flat and formless. After the first time he visited her, Frankie always averted his eyes from the bottom half of his mother's body. He only riveted his eyes on his mother's face. The women, Nora, Gilda and Maureen were stronger than the men. After the first shock of the realization that Mama's leg was gone, they stoically accepted the reality of the fact. They did what had to be done to make her comfortable. With loving tenderness, the women exhibited no qualms about adjusting and smoothing the blanket, covering the remaining leg whenever Mama had kicked it off in nervous agitation. Once, with a very strong jerk of her leg, the blanket was drawn away from the stump of the amputated limb. Where there should have been a whole leg, the visitors saw a grotesquely rounded bump just above the knee. A bloody, stained bandage, speckled in blotches of brownish-red, flashed out at them against the whiteness of the hood-like covering that capped the stump.

The three brothers, (Frankie had come down from New York that day), felt sick to the pit of their stomach at the sight. "I'm going for a smoke," Mike said.

"Me too," echoed Al.

"Yeah," added Frankie tersely.

Giuseppe sat down in the chair by his wife's bed and took her hand in his as the boys left the room.

Once outside, on the steps of the hospital's entrance, the three sons regained their composure. The warm breeze against their faces felt good as it brushed their cheeks. They lit up. But even the refreshing breeze wasn't able to cool the anger that was mounting in Frankie's gorge.

"That rotten butcher. He's chopping up Mama piecemeal." The blood rose to the boy's face as he spoke. With his face contorted in a disfiguring scowl, he shouted: "I'd like to kill the bastard."

"For Christ's sake, Frankie. Wilson's a doctor, a surgeon. He knows what he's doing. He took off the leg to save Mama's life. Remember how Papa used to prune back the decayed vines in the vineyard and lop off the bad branches on the fig trees?" Al tried to reason.

"Yeah, well Mama's no goddamn fig tree," Frankie shot back with fire in is eyes. Al didn't answer. He turned away from his brother, flicked his cigarette to the pavement and said, "Let's go back. The important thing is, that we've still got Mama." He walked to the door, and his brothers followed. None of them spoke as they walked down the corridors and down to the basement to their mother's room. Mike hadn't said anything outside at Frankie's angry outburst, but as he walked down the halls, he couldn't get his brother's angry words out of his mind. Al was right of course. Still, he shuddered as they opened the door to where Mama lay.

The three boys stayed all afternoon, then one by one, gave Mama a kiss and left her with their father still sitting by her bed. Frankie bid his brothers goodbye and returned to New York. Mike and Al went to their own places.

That night in bed, in the comforting embrace of his wife's arms, almost in a sob, Al whispered to Maureen, "They'll never get to Italy now." He choked. "The one, big wonderful thing we were going to do for her and Papa, and now it will never happen. By now she should have been packing her bags and wrapping all the gifts she was going to bring for all of them back in the old country. To have walked along the streets of Bosco again, would have been a dream come true for her. And there she is, lying flat on her back, never to walk anywhere again."

He bolted upright out of Maureen's arms, threw back the covers angrily and got out of bed. Lighting a cigarette, he walked to the window to gaze out at the stars through the tears forming in his eyes. The droplets on his long, curling lashes, shimmered like diamonds. He blinked them away so as to clear his vision. Then he felt Maureen's arm around his waist. She rested her head softly against his shoulder.

"It does seem a cruel, awful thing to have happened, Alfred. But remember this. Your mother is a strong woman, and with the help of God and of her children, her life will go on, much as before. The love and devotion that her children, all of them, have for her, will give her the strength and the will to carry on. I know that all of you will be her legs, and her arms, and her eyes for as long as she may need you."

Al turned and kissed the top of her head. The sweet fragrance of her hair brought a smile to his lips. "You always know the right words to say." He took her hand and led her to bed. Her leg next to his was warm and soft. He touched it and ran his hand up the length of her thigh. Under the covers, Maureen took hold of his hand. She placed it tenderly on her abdomen. "Alfred, dear," she said, "you can't feel it yet, but I believe a new life is beginning in there. A little Rose or a little Joseph."

Al shot up like a bullet from his reclining position. "My God," he shouted. "Rina, you're pregnant? Are you sure? Is it true?"

"I'm almost certain, darling." Al turned on the light that was on the night table. A big grin illuminated his face. Grabbing her in his arms, he kissed her repeatedly, until Maureen pushed him away with a laugh.

"I haven't had my "friend" for two entire months now. And that queasiness I've been feeling in the morning lately, is not due to a spring cold, I will bet anything." Al raced to the table for his cigarettes. His hands shook in excitement as he lit one.

"If it is so, Alfred, I hope it is a girl, a Rose for Mama. Just think how happy she will be to cradle a darling grandchild in her loving arms."

"Rina, I hope you are right about this. If anything will make Mama want to live, it will be the joy of holding a baby in her arms, her own grandchild. Oh, go to the doctor right away and find out if it's really true, that you are pregnant. Oh, let it be a girl, let it be a girl."

Chapter Fifty-four

The day they took Mama home from the hospital, Al told his mother about the baby. What food, or flowers, or gentle kisses could not do to snap her out of her lethargy, listless and sedated as she had been, the news about the baby brought light to her tired eyes and a radiant smile to her lips.

The very afternoon of Mama's home-coming, the family were all gathered together in the kitchen. The smell of coffee and food filled the room. Giuseppe put his arms around Al and Maureen. Kissing first one on the cheek, and then the other, he said, "This is the medicine that will make your mother well." He pressed them close to his sides. "The best medicine in the world, this."

"Come, sit down and eat. Look at all this food Gilda and I have cooked," Nora called out. Then she started pulling chairs away from the table so they could come and take their places. After the meal, they began to leave, one by one. Frankie was first to go because he had to make the long drive back to New York. He promised to stop by Zio Matteo's house to give them all the news. Gingerly he slapped Al on the back and extended a congratulatory kiss to Maureen. As he walked to the door, he yelled back, "Don't forget. Keep me posted on Mama." As he was making his way through the front hall, he was whistling happily.

Before taking their leave, Al and Maureen opened the door quietly to Mama's room. They saw her lying peacefully on her bed, a rosary clasped in her hand on the blanket. She was still and unmoving, fast asleep. Without a sound, Maureen drew the door shut, and she and Al left the house.

Al was feeling more light-hearted than he had felt for months. His happiness showed itself in his voice as he talked to his wife in the car on the way home.

"Did you see how Mama's face lit up when she understood what we told her, that you're expecting? You could see the joy in her eyes, couldn't you, Rina? She's going to make it, Rina, just to see and hold that baby of ours in her arms."

He stopped talking. In his mind he was picturing to himself the image of his mother cooing and softly singing the *ninna nanna*, the age-old lullaby Italian grandmothers croon to their baby grandchildren. He smiled as he saw himself holding in his own arms that tiny, new life that he had engendered.

They had arrived home, and Al stopped the car. He left it parked by the curb, and the two of them began walking up the path to the house. Nearing the front door, Maureen glanced to the mailbox by the side of the door. White envelopes peeked above the lid. She darted away from her husband and raced to the porch. She yanked the mail from the box, and began flipping through the half-dozen or so envelopes. She let out a little shriek of delight. "Oh, Alfred. It's here, a letter from Helen, my sister. I wrote her a few days ago, and she has replied."

Inside the house, without even removing her jacket, Maureen ripped open the envelope and began reading her sister's note. Her eyes flew rapidly from line to line. When she had finished reading, she pressed the paper to her chest. "It's wonderful. She wants me to meet her this Saturday afternoon in front of the library on the Green. Oh, it will be so good to see her again, to talk to her, to hear about Mother."

Al walked to where his wife stood. "I'm very happy for you, Rina, happy that your sister cares for you. From all you have told me, she must be a fine woman. You will have to take the trolley downtown. I've missed so much work, that I won't be able to go with you. Will you manage?" Al was speaking the truth; he indeed had to catch up on his work; deep down he felt, too, more than just a little trepidation at meeting anyone of Maureen's family. He hoped that the excuse about his having to work didn't seem lame, and that she would not mind his not going with her.

"I understand, Alfred. And besides, to be honest with you, I'd like to be alone with Helen. Just the two of us this time. There will be so much we will want to say to each other, and you would feel out of place, I am sure. She will want to meet you, but that will come all in good time. Now let me fix you something to eat." In moments she was busy in the kitchen, humming softly. Already in her mind she was imagining the anticipated encounter with her sister on the coming Saturday.

Saturday came. Maureen boarded the trolley at the corner a little way from the house. Later she made the necessary transfer to another car and got off at the far end of the Green. She walked with a quick step across the grassy expanse, and as she drew closer to the library, she caught sight of Helen. Her sister was standing at the bottom of the white granite steps that led up to the library portals, the same library where she had once worked and where she had met Al for the first time.

Helen waved in recognition as her sister approached. The two of them were soon in fond embrace. Out of breath from her hurried pace across the Green, Maureen gasped, "Oh, Helen, it is so good to see you. I've missed you so, and Mother. How is she? You must tell me everything." Then taking her sister by an arm, she led Helen towards the Green. There, under one of the sprawling elms that grew throughout the park, they sat on a bench in the shade of the tree's branches.

The day was beginning to get hot under the noon-day sun, so that the shade of the tree was more than welcome. Flocks of pigeons were pecking at the ground, gobbling up the morsels of discarded scraps and crumbs of bread and popcorn. The sound of muted laughter from a group of young children playing tag on the grass in the distance, reached their ears. People strolled by along the paths that criss-crossed the turf of the park.

Off in the distance a knot of youngsters around a monument at the far end of the Green, were lined up to take a drink from the fountain housed in a niche at the base of the gleaming white marble structure. Just as Maureen opened her mouth to speak, the bells of Center Church behind them, began tolling the noon hour. When the clanging was over, she began to speak. "Tell me, Helen, how are things at home? How did Mother take my going off? I can imagine Father's displeased reaction, the fury of his temper, and his storming about."

"Truth to tell," answered Helen, "it has not been pleasant at home, especially during the first few days. His rantings were awful to hear, and I won't repeat his oaths and deprecations. But you have seen him more than once when his dander is up, so I need not go into detail. Pshaw! Enough of him and his bestial temper. I am so happy, Maureen, that you wrote me. It was very clever of you to disguise your handwriting on the envelope. Had Father come upon it and recognized your hand, I never would have seen your letter, of that I am certain."

Maureen answered: "I know only too well he would not have given you the letter. That is why I addressed the envelope with my left hand scrawl. Now tell me about Mother. She is the one I am most concerned about. Tell me truthfully, tell me honestly, does she think ill of me for running off, for marrying Alfred?"

Helen took her sister's hand and patted it gently. She looked straight into Maureen's tear-brimmed eyes. "The greatest hurt she feels, I think, is that she did not have the opportunity to see you walk down the aisle of Saint Mary's Church as a bride in white. The one thing that does bring a worry to her heart and a furrow to her brow, is that you are married by a justice of the peace, and not by Father O'Connor. She deems that ceremony no marriage at all. It pains her, Maureen. She has told me so in all confidence."

"Oh, but Helen, we are married by a priest. Shortly after our return, Alfred made the necessary arrangements with the parish priest of the Italian church. We were duly married, according to the rites of the church. In front of the altar railing, of course, but married as Catholics nevertheless. It was done one evening with Alfred's brother Michael and his sister Nora as witnesses. Relieve Mother's mind on that score, won't you?"

"How truly wonderful this news will be to Mother; it will give her a lift. It will set her heart at ease. You know how much the church means to her; it has always been her one solace in the hard life she had led with Father. She has been so longsuffering, and the church and her devotions have always been her refuge. And now about you, Maureen, tell me about yourself."

In answer, Maureen chatted on and on; there was so much to tell her sister—about the happiness she shared with her new husband, her little home, her new-found family, Mama Rosa's tragic loss of her leg. "And now, Helen, I've saved the best news for last. I shall be a mother! Yes, I am going to have a baby. Think of it, Helen. You are going to be "Aunt Helen!" Maureen's face was beaming, and Helen's eyes sparkled in surprise. She reached over and hugged her sister in close embrace. "Imagine! Me, Aunt Helen." She kissed Maureen on the cheek. "May I tell Mother?"

"Let me do it Helen, if you don't mind. In a few days it will be the Fourth of July. Say you wish to take her with you to view the parade. Father cannot object to that, and we will meet here. I do wish to see her and to talk to her. I want to see her face when I tell her that she is to be a grandmother." The two sisters made their plans to meet on the appointed day as they walked together, arm in arm, to the trolley stop. There was a decided spring to the steps they took as they made their way. At the stop, they embraced once more. "Until the glorious Fourth, then!" And they boarded their respective cars.

Chapter Fifty-five

The Fourth was a beautiful, sunny day. Hordes of people lined the parade route along Chapel Street. Little boys, waving flags and popping their cap pistols ran along the curbs as they followed the marching bands and the fleet of fire trucks. Shouts, hurrahs, and a frenzy of hand-clapping greeted each contingent as it approached.

Al and Maureen made their way through the thick crowds and started across the Green.

"There they are, Alfred, there they are. See them standing on the landing of Center Church? Mother and Helen." Maureen started to quicken her pace, but Al, holding onto her hand, halted her progress. "Rina," he said, "you go on alone. Suppose, suppose, well, that they won't like me? Suppose your mother should be angry, should resent me for marrying you, for the way we ran off?"

"Oh, you goose. How could they not like you? Just wait until they see you. You'll see that you have nothing to fear."

"Please, Rina. You go on alone. I'll wait here."

"Very well. I'll go on alone—first. I don't want you to feel ill at ease. I'll prepare the way, so to speak. But when I wave, I want you to come. I was rather ill at ease thinking of meeting your family for the first time, so I understand. But really, dear, you have nothing to fear from Mother or Helen. Do come when I wave to you."

Al let go her hand, and she began walking away from him. She turned once to give him a smile of reassurance. On the steps of the church, moments later, Al saw the three women together, Maureen, Helen, and their mother. He could see the older woman dabbing at her eyes with a handkerchief that she had pulled from her sleeve. They were in conversation, and now and then, Al saw one or the other smiling and touching each other's hand or arm. Suddenly he saw Maureen break a little away, come to the edge of the step and wave her arm in the air. She was beckoning him to come. He hesitated a moment before responding. Then summoning up his courage, he threw up his arm and waved back. He began his walk towards them. His mouth suddenly went dry, and he could feel a few beads of sweat forming on his forehead.

On the steps of the church, he could see that the women were intently watching his approach. He felt their stares, and he began to get red in the face. A slight breeze mussed his hair. He raised his hand to his head to smooth back the maverick locks of his hair. For a moment his arm blocked their stares, and he regained his composure. He smiled. When Helen smiled back at him as he started up the steps of the church where she was standing, she extended her hand to him. He lost all his fears and nervousness. "You are Helen," he said. "So nice to meet you," and he clasped her hand.

"Mother," broke in Maureen, this is my husband, Alfred." Al turned to offer his hand to Mrs. Donnell, whose eyes had never stopped scrutinizing him. For a moment, Al lost his ease when he perceived the mother's steel-blue eyes studying his face so fixedly. A feeling of panic raced through him in a momentary surge, and the thought crossed his brain: "She expects to see a swarthy, mustachioed ghee with a monkey and a hand-organ." He felt his face reddening even more at the thought.

But a pleasant smile broke out on the woman's face. She stretched out her hand to meet his, saying in a rather, hesitant, soft voice, "Alfred, how do you do?" She was as much uncomfortable as he was.

An exuberant Helen staved off any further feelings of uneasiness with a lively, "Come, all. There is a free bench across the way. It's so dreadfully hot today. Will you treat us to some ice-cream, brother-in-law?" she asked in a merry tone of voice. Al, only too glad to get away for the moment, rushed off to catch up to the ice-cream vendor a little way off from them. While Al was hurrying on his way, the women took seats on a bench. As they sat, Helen whispered to her sister, "Maureen, he is a charmer, a handsome man. Have no regrets. You've done the right thing." Maureen took her sister's hand and gave it a squeeze in acknowledgment of her sister's complimentary words.

"Well, Mother, now that you have seen him, what do you think of my husband, your son-in-law. Will you not accept him as such? If you knew him as I do, and how much I love him, you, too, would see how good and fine a man he is."

"That's just the thing, my dear. I don't know him at all, but I hope for your sake, that he is all you say he is." She let out a little, almost soundless sigh. Then she said no more. She had caught sight of Al fast approaching the bench. Clutched in his sticky hands were three dripping ice-cream cones which he speedily handed to each of them.

The women rose from their places on the bench, and along with Al, they started to walk slowly across the Green and were soon amidst the vast throngs of people who were watching the marching bands and floats. The sisters flanked their mother, chatting as they went along, and enjoying each other's company. They had so much to say to each other, and the afternoon sped by.

After some time had gone by, Al excused himself to go off to speak to a friend he had spotted. The three women were alone together, and it was at that time that Maureen disclosed to her mother that she was expecting the birth of her child in January. Mrs. Donnell stopped short, but only for a moment. She enfolded her arms around her daughter in a tight hug for a long minute. The mother's face wore a wide smile and her cheeks were tinged in red. "Oh, my dear, my darling little girl," she repeated more than once. Just as they embraced once more, Al, after a brief few words with his friend, appeared. Seeing him, Maureen's mother broke away and reaching out, took his hands. "God bless you both, Alfred, and the new one to come," she said with feeling. Al took her hand and raised it to his lips. "Thank you." Hesitating for only a split second, he added, "Mother. Thank you." Both their faces flushed as their hands parted.

The afternoon wore on, and the time to leave was nearing. The parade was over. The crowds began to thin out. But before they parted, the sisters and their mother made their arrangements to meet again clandestinely. The plan, was to meet every Wednesday evening. Under the pretext of attending a novena to Our Lady of the Miraculous Medal, Mrs. Donnell and Helen would be able to go off together without arousing suspicion. Their meeting place, they decided, was to be by Center Church.

Chapter Fifty-six

The succeeding July days were scorchers, but in spite of the searing heat, Mama continued to wear the long-sleeved, ankle-length, heavy linen black dresses she had always worn.

"This is America, Mama. Wear something with short sleeves, something cooler, like the American women do," Nora and Gilda pleaded, and often even the boys. But none of their arguments could make the old lady change her ideas of what was proper fashion. So she went on languishing in the heat; the dress she wore remained buttoned at the neck; the hem reached her ankle, and the sharp bones of her thinning wrists stayed covered.

It was Maureen who succeeded in bringing about the miracle. As always on a Sunday, a visit to Mama was the custom, merely to be together over dinner, to talk over a cup of coffee and enjoy the sweet ricotta-filled canoli someone was sure to bring from the Italian pastry shop. On the last Sunday of the month, when Michael, Al and Maureen arrived, they found the others under the grape arbor in the backyard of the house. The house itself was an oven, and because it was a little cooler under the arbor, they had assembled to eat the meal under the shade of the arbor. Frankie was there, too, having made the ride down from New York, especially to see Mama again. He brought her a bouquet of the roses she loved so much.

Even as the three newcomers were walking the length of the alleyway to the backyard, they could hear the laughter and the happy ring of voices chattering excitedly. Once Mike, Al and Maureen were in view, Nora's husband jumped up from the bench, rushed over to them and clapped the boys on their shoulders.

"Me too," he all but shouted. "I'm going to be a papa." Giovanni fairly raced back to the table in his eagerness to pour his brothers-in-law some wine from the jug on the table. All smiles, Mike and Al went to Mama and kissed her. Maureen followed and did the same.

"How do you like that, Mama? Babies falling from out of the sky," said Al.

"That's not where I heard they come out of," quipped Giovanni with a mischievous grin on his face.

"Oh, what a rascal," Nora scolded as she whacked the dish cloth in her hand across her husband's back. Amidst the laughter, Maureen beckoned to Al. Quietly she asked him to go to the car and bring back the bag she had left on the seat. During the minute or so that he was gone on his errand, she whispered something to Nora and Gilda. When her husband returned she took the bag from his hand, and before Mama knew what was happening to her, the old lady found herself being wheeled away and up the makeshift ramp on the back porch steps that Giuseppe had put together. The men looked on while the three young women whisked Mama away. The fellows shrugged their shoulders questioningly and went on with their talking and joking.

Twenty minutes went by, and then suddenly the men's attention was drawn to the ramp. They heard the rolling of the chair being wheeled down the incline. Maureen, Nora and Gilda were smiling sheepishly. Mama's face wore a shy grin that was caused either by embarrassment or muffled elation. It was hard to tell which.

Frankie let out a shrill wolf-whistle. "Hey, Pop, look at that beauty! You sure know how to pick 'em. Now, that's class!"

The women pushed Mama, clad in her new dress into the shade of the arbor. Gone was the funereal black; instead, the lightweight cotton dress she was wearing was the color of the summer sky. And, as clouds across the sky, a delicate band of pure white lace, edged the square-cut neck line, a good six inches lower than the usual high collars Mama always had worn. Gone, too, were the long sleeves. The whole lower arms, from the elbows on down, were exposed to the air. And instead of the dress reaching down to her ankles, it now crossed mid-way across her shins. One could tell that the old lady felt practically naked. She kept her stretched out hand across her exposed neck and the little bit of breastbone that showed.

A brand new pair of pendant earrings embedded with a little blue stone hanging on slender shanks, waved with every movement of her head. The small, dull-gold globes that had been a gift from Giuseppe years ago, and that she had worn in her ears ever since, were out.

"There now, don't you feel more comfortable and cooler, Mama?" Maureen asked. Without waiting for an answer, she turned to the others. "I made that dress especially for her. I knew that she would look beautiful in blue."

Proud of his wife for her kindness and her love for his mother, Al put his arm around Maureen's shoulder. Frankie came up to his sister-in-law and blurted out irreverently, "How the hell did you manage it, to get her out of that damn black, I mean?" He smiled at Maureen, and she smiled in return.

"It wasn't easy," she said, "but all three of us just drowned out her protestations; she couldn't fight us all off. But you know, after it was all over, I think she is pleased with her new look. I saw a little smile cross her face when we brought her to the mirror. All beautiful women are a little vain, you know."

"I hope I never see her in black again," Frankie said softly as he left Maureen's side and went to his mother. He kissed her on the cheek. "You're beautiful, Ma. Just like the Madonna; she's always in blue, and from now on, I always want to see you in blue, or green, or purple, or in anything but black." He pinched his mother's cheek playfully. "*Capisce?*"

His mother gave him a little slap on the hand, and she let out a laugh.

"You look nice and cool, too, Ma," said Al. "Rina made that dress herself, just for you. She's one good dressmaker, huh?" Rosa gave her daughter-in-law an appreciative glance and murmured a soft, "*Grazie, cara.*"

Now everyone could see how pitifully thin Mama's arms really were. And where her leg was missing, the new dress lay flat and shapeless against the chair. But, as the afternoon wore on, however, more color came to Mama's cheeks, brought on by a glass of Papa's hearty red wine and the warmth of the love she felt emanating from those surrounding her. Their solicitude and genuine concern for her every comfort brought smiles of gratitude to her face. She was happy.

Her own children, and Maureen, and Giovanni, she thought to herself they were all as good as bread. That lovely wife of her son, going through all the trouble of making her a dress. How then, could she have denied the girl's gesture of generosity, by not accepting the dress and the earrings? The dress, it was so carefully made; and she did feel cooler in it. That night after Nora and Gilda had helped undress her for bed, she lovingly ran her hand over the fabric draped over the chair by her bed.

Before drifting off to sleep, she began to think of the days of her girlhood, back in Bosco. Then, she wore the bright reds and blues and yellows of the traditional costume of her native region. She saw herself as a young girl on the days of *festa*, a pretty young thing with her head covered by a sparkling white *tovaglia*, her slender waist girded by a black bodice that contrasted with the white of her blouse and the bright red of her skirt with its horizontal bands of yellow and blue across the bottom. She smiled to herself, thinking of the pendant earrings of delicate filigree, hanging long below the lobes of her ears; how they spun and twirled when she danced the tarantella!

With a quick shake of her head on the pillow, the vision vanished and she returned to the present. Dancing! But what! She wasn't even able to walk now. She closed her eyes, crossed herself, and said a silent prayer. She must accept the loss of her leg without feeling rancor. For this is what God had willed. His ways are inscrutable. She was tired; the day had been a full one. No more thinking. Soon she was asleep.

Chapter Fifty-seven

It was Mike's idea that Gilda quit work at the garment shop in order to stay home and take care of their mother. "Look," he explained, "Nora's pregnant now, and she won't be able to keep coming downstairs to look after Mama while you are at work. Gilda, I'll give you whatever you're earning now as wages, and more. This way, you won't be losing anything, and Mama will get the care she needs. It'll just be for the time she needs to get her strength back and learns how to get around on her own. Papa can't do it. Mama needs a woman, you know, with all the personal things. And she can't manage yet to do all the cleaning, cooking and other stuff she used to do. What do you say, sis?"

Gilda agreed. She quit her job and stayed home to care for their mother. For Mama, Gilda's help and company all day long were like a breath of fresh air, and by the end of the first two weeks of August, it was plain for all to see, that Mama's spirits had revived. Her strength was returning bit by bit, more and more, with each day that passed. Her old vitality, her characteristic independence was beginning to show themselves once again. Little by little, Rosa began to take on a greater share of the household work. She insisted on doing things for herself. With a colander in her lap, she shelled peas, she peeled potatoes, she skinned the peppers Gilda roasted.

So much like her old self once again, one day she had Gilda crank up the victrola. She wanted music in the house. So Gilda went to the stacks of 78's, those discs of heavy plastic with their labels in red, white and green, the colors of the Italian flag, and chose some of the old Neapolitan favorites her mother loved to listen to. The voices of Fernando de Lucia, Beniamino Gigli, Ria Rosa, and Gilda Mignonette, echoed throughout the house once more. The day came when Mama even started to sing again, along with the music. When Mike heard about that, he came loaded down one Sunday with a dozen new records he had bought for Mama. With just a few playings on the turntable, Rosa learned both the tunes and the words to every new song. Song and laughter were returning to the house. Mama was getting stronger and happier with each day that passed. Things were back to normal at Mama's. The expectation of the babies to come, and music, had worked their wonders. Mama was the old, full-of-life Mama again.

A few nights later, Al was explaining to Maureen why he had been late for supper that evening. It was August 27th, a day that afforded a beautifully cool break in the heat of the past week. Mike, he explained, had happened to mention that he had bought some records for Mama, and how happy she had been to receive them. "So I went to the music store on Greene Street, Rina, and bought a few more for her. I stopped by the house and gave them to her. You should have seen how delighted she was to get them. I had to stay a while to listen along with her. She loved especially, a song called *A Vuchella*. The melody is really pretty; the words are all about an ardent lover's desire to plant a kiss on his girl's sweet little mouth. That's what *vuchella* means, sweet, little mouth. Even as I was leaving, I could hear Mama la-la-la-ing along with the singer, as I went out the front door." He came close to Maureen. "Now, how about a kiss by this ardent lover on that pretty *vuchella* of yours?" And he had his mouth on hers before she could say, yes, or no.

She pulled away from his kiss. "I'm so glad you took the time to do that for Mama, Alfred. It's good to hear that her spirits are perking up, and there is nothing better than music to help raise them. Now eat your supper. I hope that the eggplant hasn't dried out."

"Rina, it's as good as Mama makes." In between mouthfuls, he reiterated his regrets for being late. "It was just an impulse to stop by Ricci's Music Emporium and pick up a few records for her. After Mike told me how much she really enjoyed the ones he had gotten for her, I had to do the same, just to hear her sing again."

"I never doubted for a moment that she would not come around," Maureen replied. "With her simple faith in God and that Italian fatalism—what is it now? *Che sara, sara.* What will be, will be, isn't that the meaning? I knew she would rally; her children need her." Maureen smiled and poured more coffee into her husband's cup. Just as Al encircled her waist with his arm to draw her close, there was a loud, persistent rapping at the back door.

"Now who, at ten o'clock at night, could that be?" Maureen exclaimed. She made her way across the kitchen and opened the door. There stood Mike. His face was flushed; she noticed it at once. She saw too, the look of absolute pain on his face, and the look of panic in his eyes. She put a trembling hand to her throat, expecting him to utter some terrible announcement about Mama. Mike just nodded to her without saying a word, and walked across the kitchen to the table where his brother was sitting, cup in hand. He pulled out a chair and sat, his head making a sudden bow to his chest. Al jumped up from his seat in alarm and went to him. "Mike, what the hell is the matter? Is Mama?" He hesitated, then screwed up the courage to finish, "Is Mama okay? Has something happened to her?"

Mike lifted his head, and Al could see that his eyes were wet with tears. "It's not Mama, Al. Frankie. Frankie's dead, Al." The tears in his eyes flooded over the lids in a torrent and were washing down his cheeks. Al's face lost all its color, and Maureen cried out, "Oh, no!" In a second she regained her composure and went up to her husband and gently brought him back to his chair. She turned to Michael. "Let me get you a cup of coffee, Michael."

Al looked at his brother across the table. Tears were now welling in his own eyes, and his heart was pounding. The first thought that had come to his mind, was that his younger brother had been shot, killed by some rival gang member. Before he could ask how Frankie had died, Mike blurted out: "He got burned to death, Al. Oh, Jesus, what a death, what a death! Al, Frankie is gone. He's gone, he's gone, he's dead." Mike could say no more for a moment. He broke out in agonized sobs that reverberated throughout the room. To Maureen, the sobs sounded like the death throes of a wounded animal, and her own eyes became filled with tears. Al's throat tightened. Not a word could he say. Maureen wiped the tears from her eyes and came to the table with the coffee pot. She placed a cup before her brother-in-law and filled it, but Mike took no notice.

Mike wiped his eyes. His voice hoarse, he started to speak. "Late this evening a big, black Cadillac with New York plates drove into the yard. As soon as I saw those three guys get out, with their black, pin-striped suits, white ties, and fancy fedoras, I knew they had something to do with Frankie. My customers don't look like that. "Michael," they say. "Michael Alanga?" and when I answer them, one of them puts his arm around my shoulder, and they begin introducing themselves as friends of Frankie. They offer me a cigar and tell me to sit down. " ' *Mi dispiace*,' one of them says." Mike's voice broke for a moment. " ' We've got some bad news to tell you.' " And then they went on to tell me that Frankie died this morning, and how it happened.

238

"A couple of nights ago, Frankie and some of the bootleggers were making moonshine booze at one of their operations deep in the woods on Long Island. Frankie's girl drives up, you know, Don Luigi's niece that Frankie told us about, the one he was going to marry in a couple of months. She's all excited about some pictures she had had taken, and wanted to show him. Because it's dim in the shed where they're distilling the stuff, she lights a match so he can see better."

Mike stopped. He couldn't go on. But he didn't have to put into words the scene that Al was already picturing in his mind, the inferno that must have resulted as the fumes from the alcohol ignited in the closed shed.

After a minute, Mike continued. "The fireball just blew the whole place up. Only one guy who was standing by the door was able to make his escape. The others didn't have a chance. The girl, Frankie, two others, all gone." He shot up from his chair and slapped his forehead. "Jesus, what a way to die!"

Al visioned his kid brother engulfed in flames, and he let out a moan that came from deep within. The anguish of both brothers caused Maureen to shiver visibly, and tears began to fall afresh from her eyes. She had come to like Frankie very much—his boyish impetuosity, his ready laugh, his generous heart. Frankie—dead. Frankie, the wild, untamed, cocky, tough-spirited, independent little brother, was dead. Frankie whose love and adoration and tenderness towards his mother had always made her have a soft spot in her heart for the boy.

Her thoughts were interrupted by the sound of Michael's voice. "Al, what are we going to do? We can't tell Mama now. This'll kill her. The way she is now, she won't be able to handle it. She's just starting to bounce back. The loss of her leg she can take, get used to. But the loss of Frankie, the way he died, it'll kill her. And Papa? Him, we've got to tell. How are we going to do it, Al?"

Chapter Fifty-eight

It was Maureen who provided the solution. Yes, Papa had to be told straightaway, of course. And the boys would have to go with him to the funeral on the coming Sunday. "It would be unthinkable," she said, almost weeping, "but the pain would be great for him not to have said his last goodbyes to his son. You must meet him as he leaves work tomorrow. Tell him as gently as you can, and then all three of you go to New York Sunday. You will have to think of something to tell Mama why you are going; say, perhaps, that Uncle Matteo is sick, or has been in an accident. It is the only thing I can think to do, unless either of you has something else to suggest."

Al passed his hand over his brow. He looked and felt uncomfortable. The agony he was experiencing in his soul was mirrored by the dryness in his voice when he spoke. "I don't know if it is the right thing to deceive Mama this way. She has to know. When Frankie never comes around any more, she'll suffer worse for his absence, than knowing now, outright." He stopped and threw up his arms in a gesture of futility.

"No, Al," Mike answered. "Your wife is right. To tell Mama now, when she's only just beginning to get her strength back, would knock her for a loop. With the condition she's in, it is too early to kick her in the gut with such a blow. Frankie is, er, was, her baby son, the apple of her eye. Yeah, I know, she loves us all. But Frankie, well, Frankie was special to her. You know it, and I know it. In a month, two months, it will be up to Papa to tell her. He's the one that has to do it. All their lives they have shared everything together, the good and the bad. I'm not saying that it won't be rough for him, too, but he's a man, and he's her husband. He's the one that must tell her. He'll know when and how." He stopped. He puffed out a blast of breath from his pursed lips. Then he looked first at his brother, and than at Maureen for a sign of acceptance.

Maureen went up to her husband and gently placed an arm around him at the window where he was standing. Al was gazing out at the moon, so that no one could see the pain on his face and the tears that had again began filling his eyes.

"Alfred, dear, as hard as it may seem now, you are not deceiving your mother. I do believe that in the long run, it is best not to let her know now about Frankie's death. Let her get all her strength back. After the awful ordeal she has just been through, I don't believe it would be wise to have her undergo another trauma. Your father will know, as Michael has said, when the time will be best to tell her. Tomorrow, both of you fetch your father as he leaves work, and let him know in the gentlest way you can, about Frankie's death. Tell him what you have in mind to do in order to spare your mother."

Then she turned to Michael and said, "It is very late, Michael. You are welcome to stay the night. Sleep here if you wish. I'll make up the couch."

"Thanks, Maureen, but I'll go to my place. I'd rather just be alone. I appreciate your asking, but I'll go now."

"I understand," Maureen replied. Mike walked across the kitchen and went out into the soothing darkness of the night.

Chapter Fifty-nine

Al locked the kitchen door after his brother. Then he put out the lights, and he and his wife went into the bedroom. There, Maureen walked to the sewing machine in the corner of the room where she did all her work. As her husband began to disrobe, she picked up a folded length of cloud-gray material. Half to herself, she said, "I guess I won't finish this. It was to be a new dress for your mother. She would never wear it now. She'll wear nothing but black for the rest of her life."

Saturday morning dawned bright and clear with a blazing sun already in ascendancy. When Maureen awoke, she found her husband up and out of bed and in the kitchen sipping his third cup of coffee. She saw at once that his eyes were red and glassy from lack of sleep. "What a terrible night he must have had," she thought to herself. And indeed, Al had lain awake half the night, his brain tortured by images of his dead brother, his mother, his father. Over and over, a hundred times, it seemed, he tried to frame in his mind the words he and Michael would have to utter to their father. How do you tell a father that his young son has died a horrible death? He had prayed that the night would never end, that day would never come.

But it had come. It was here. He dreaded what he had to do today. He refused to eat the breakfast Maureen had prepared for him; and Maureen, after a few coaxings, gave up trying to have him eat something. He sat alone in the parlor, at times breaking out in a cold sweat, as his mind jumped from one thought more morbid than the last. At times during the long morning, he fell into a fitful sleep, only to be awakened by the nightmares that raced through his mind.

Noon time came, and Maureen, seeing him asleep, did not rouse him to come to the table for the lunch she had laid out. He would benefit more from the rest than the food, she thought. She moved about quietly on cat's paws so as not to disturb his slumber. Suddenly, sensing her presence, Al woke up with a start to find his wife gazing on his pale face as she stood above him.

"Rina, oh, Rina. It's you. I suppose I must have dozed off."

Then the realization came to him why she was standing there with that sad face, looking down at him. He leaned over and put his elbows on his knees. He covered his face with his hands. Maureen came to him and gently pushed back his tousled hair from his damp forehead.

"It's no shame for a man to cry, you know, my darling," she said in a sympathetic whisper. Al took his hands away from his face. He buried it in her bosom. She could feel the vibrations of his sobs against her chest, so pitifully heart-rending, that tears came to her own eyes. She said nothing, but began stroking the top of his head, as she pressed him close to her body. For a minute he remained in her embrace. The only sounds to break the silence of the sunlit room were the agonized sobs muffled by the closeness of her own heaving breast.

With a jerk, Al broke away. "What time is it?"

"One-thirty, dear," Maureen answered. "Michael should be arriving soon. Why don't you get yourself ready? I will warm up something for you to eat. Come now, do as I say," and she led him to the bathroom.

By a quarter to three, Al found himself in Michael's car on Water Street, waiting for their father to exit from work. Both of them smoked cigarette after cigarette while they waited. The two knew just where to watch for their father, as when in the past, they sometimes picked him up on a snowy winter's day in order to spare the old man the walk home from the factory.

"There he is, Al, just coming out the gate." Mike got out of the car. He called out to his father, and when Giuseppe saw him, Mike was motioning to the old man with a wave of the arm. "Papa, over here. I'll give you a lift home." Giuseppe smiled as he recognized his son, and waved back. Approaching the car, and wiping his brow, he said, "One can die from this heat."

"Get in, Pop." Mike opened the back door of the car. "I've got something to say to you." He started up, and drove away, a short distance up the street, away from the crowd of exiting workers, and stopped. Under the shade of one of the few leafy elm trees that remained on the street lined with factories, Al and Mike broke the news of Frankie's death to their father.

Although it hadn't been an easy thing to do, what they had to do, they did. As one struck by a blow to the heart, Giuseppe fell back in the seat. His face lost all its color. His hand trembled as he passed it backwards over his head and through his hair, as if to clear his mind of some evil. For just a moment, his mind went blank, devoid of all thought.

When the sense of what his sons had just told him brought him out of the vacuum, he said: "How? How? They killed him! Those of the *mala vita* killed him! They killed my son."

"No, Papa. It wasn't that way. No one killed Frankie." Mike began from the beginning, from the first moment he himself had learned of it from the guys from New York. Where he left off the narration, Al continued until their father knew everything of the events that led to Frankie's death. Al asked his approval of their intention not tell Mama now. Both told him they thought it best to proceed to New York now, right away. Mike and Al had concocted a story to tell Mama the reason they had to go there.

Giuseppe agreed with his sons. "Let us go home now. We will say nothing of Frankie at this time to Mama." At the house, however, it took all the inner strength they possessed to carry through with the pretense. Mama had at first been somewhat surprised to see the three of them walk in together. And then Mike, with as much evenness of voice and outward calm as he could manage, told his mother that they were going to New York as soon as Papa cleaned up. Zio Matteo had been in an accident.

Chapter Sixty

It was only right of course, that her husband should go to New York now to see his brother, to be by his side after the terrible accident that Zio Matteo had suffered. She understood that the call of the blood was strongest at times like this. Giuseppe and Matteo were brothers, after all. In spite of any differences that had occurred in the past, in a time such as this, such differences were forgotten. "Go," she said, "and I beg the Madonna that you find poor Matteo safe in her care."

While their father was busy washing himself and changing into his good clothes, Mike and Al filled in for Mama the details of what had happened to Zio Matteo. An automobile driven by a drunken driver had struck Matteo when the car jumped the curb. A broken arm and leg were nothing much to be concerned about; but possible internal injuries made his condition more serious. The boys promised Mama that they would be sure to let her know everything about Zio Matteo and his family upon their return.

Before they left, Mama and Gilda loaded the men down with bags of sandwiches and fruit to eat on the way to New York. In spite of their protests that they would stop on the road if they were hungry, Mama insisted on having her way. Michael and Al knew now that Mama was on the mend. There was no mistaking the commanding tone of insistence that resonated in her voice, just as it used to be in the past. The sound of that old resoluteness in her voice eased their conscience a little. They were convinced now of the correctness of their decision to say nothing of the real purpose of their trip to the city. Nothing must jeopardize her road to recovery.

The only thing to bring a sense of uneasiness to Rosa, had been the somber and quiet demeanor of her husband. But she dismissed her concern and attributed his dark mood to worry about his brother. Besides, Giuseppe was a man of few words. When it came time to leave, Al and Mike leaned over to kiss Mama goodbye. Then their father did a strange thing. He, too, bent over his sitting wife and kissed her on the forehead. Never before had their children ever seen such a physical demonstration of outward affection between them. One kissed one's children, even as grown adults; children kissed their parents. But before the eyes of others, it was a rare event indeed, for such a display between husband and wife. A look of surprise came over Rosa's face. But her husband had-straightened up, turned away, and was motioning to the boys to follow, as he headed towards the door.

Once in the car, Michael explained to his father and Al that there would be a car waiting for them at the old barber shop where Frankie had worked as a young boy in the neighborhood. From there, Don Luigi's driver would take them to the don's estate on Long Island. That's where Frankie was lying in state.

After that explanation and a little bit of talk, the rest of the trip was completed in virtually funereal silence. Few words were spoken by any of the three. Al, exhausted by the restless night he had spent, was lulled by the quiet motion of the moving auto, and dozed off in brief catnaps. Mike smoked cigarette after cigarette in silence as he drove. Their father, alone in the back seat, it was obvious to Mike, did not want to speak or be spoken to. Mike was just as glad to have it so.

Along the way, they stopped once so that Mike could buy a pack of cigarettes, and for all of them to relieve themselves. After that stop, it wasn't long before they reached their destination. The time was about seven in the evening. It was still light out, although in a short while, dusk would begin dimming the brightness of the evening sky.

Mike drove up to the front of Peppino's barber shop. Don Luigi's driver was there, leaning against a Cadillac and smoking a cigar. Mike recognized the guy as one of those who had come down a couple of days ago to tell him of Frankie's death. Greetings were short and sweet. After a few perfunctory words, they were all on the road to the Island, but in two vehicles.

Giuseppe would not enter the Cadillac. Mike had no choice but to follow Don Luigi's man to the estate. The traffic was light, so Mike had no difficulty in trailing the Cadillac from the East Side to Long Island. The short ride came to an end on the circular driveway in front of the pillared portico of the don's estate. One of the don's captains waited by the steps, and as Al got out of the car he was embraced and greeted. Giuseppe pulled away from the offered embrace, and the man gave him a hard look, which Giuseppe returned in kind. When father and sons were all out of the car, the captain led them up the six semi-circular steps to the huge front portals which were flanked by marble statuary of fig-lead clad Roman gods.

Al's first impression of the place was that it was unreal, some left-over Hollywood movie set. Once they all walked through the doors and onto the marble floor of the foyer, the sickening scent of gardenias and the soft murmur of the Rosary being recited in the distance, jolted him to reality. Sal, their escort, led the Alangas across the feather pattern of the green and white marble floor to a grand salon on the left. An archway, supported by two acanthus-crowned columns framed the entrance to the salon. Atop the arch, a tiffany glass panel, designed with grape clusters, connected by vines and leaves, shone with suffused light.

The two brothers and their father did not enter. A priest was droning the last decade of the rosary prayers.

The salon measured at least twenty-five feet by twenty-five feet in area. On both sides of a wide center aisle leading to the back wall, dozens of ponderous chairs in gilded framework and with tapestried backs and seats, were occupied by quiet mourners. Soft sobs from some of the women punctuated the somber silence. Against a backdrop of dozens of floral arrangements, and flanked by two huge electrified candelabra that cast an eerie aura of orange-yellow light, two caskets lay side by side.

The priest finished his recitation of prayers with a decorous sign of the cross. Giuseppe started a slow walk down the aisle to where the body of his son reposed in its last sleep. Behind him, his two remaining sons followed. Mixed with the subdued sobs of the tearful women, people whispered: "Frankie's father. His brothers."

Chapter Sixty-one

At the end of this sad road to Calvary, father and sons came to their Golgotha. Both caskets were closed. One of the caskets was mounted with a gold-framed picture of a girl. In a matching frame, on the other coffin, the image of Frankie stared out at his father and brothers. There was just a hint of a breaking smile on the handsome face. Father and brothers riveted their eyes on the face of the boy. Motionless, they stood transfixed by Frankie's face gazing back at them with eyes that did not blink, lips that did not move. After what seemed an eternity to Al, his father lowered himself to the prie-dieu and made the sign of the cross. Al took a place by his father's side on the kneeler. Mike remained standing behind them; his mind could not form the words of the prayers he had known all his life, neither a simple "Hail Mary" nor the "Our Father." Only Frankie's name kept going through his mind, over and over again—Frankie, Frankie, my kid brother, Frankie.

Five, ten minutes passed until finally Mike tapped Al's shoulder. Al rose, and his movement stirred his father to do the same. One by one, they bent over the casket, kissed it, and turned away and slowly made their way out of the salon. Sal met them as they reached the foyer. "The don would like to meet you," he said to father and sons. His terse comment had a note of command in it, that none of them missed. Sal began to move away, but none of the three followed. Sal retraced his steps. His face had a stony look on it as he stood in front of them.

"I will not see this man of the *mala vita*, this murderer of my son." Giuseppe's words cut through the scented silence with the swiftness of a stiletto thrust. Sal's face turned to the hardness of granite for a moment, then softened. "The don is grieving too, Signor Alanga, as much for Frankie as for his niece of the blood. To him, Frankie was like a son." The blood began coursing through Giuseppe's veins like a flash of fire when he heard Sal's last words. Mike saw immediately the effect of those words, on his father's face. Seeing his father's rage starting to mount, he stepped in between his father and Sal.

"Come, Papa." He took his father's arm. "Al, you go with Sal. I'm going to take Papa outside. Go ahead." He turned with his father toward the front doors. Briskly Al and Sal began their walk across the foyer. Just before they reached the door to Don Luigi's study, Sal said suddenly, "I'll say this for your old man. He's got balls." Then he opened the door and led Al into the room. At the other end of the foyer, just before reaching the entry way, Giuseppe stopped a moment and turned to Mike. "I want to sit with my son." He started to retrace his steps to the salon where Frankie's body lay. He and Mike sat down in two empty chairs and stared at the casket and Frankie's picture.

Once inside the don's study, Sal's hand steadied Al from proceeding any further. He walked to the figure sitting in a leather easy chair by the French doors that opened onto a terrace. Sal whispered something to Don Luigi, and in a moment, came back to Al. He motioned him to come forward. The room was shrouded in semi-darkness. The only light came from a solitary lamp placed on an end table.

Sal pointed to the vacant chair by the one being occupied. "Sit down," he said, then walked away and left the room. As Al neared the chair, a voice, husky, as if it were in need of a drink to clear away the dryness of the throat, repeated: "Sit down, Al, sit down. So, your father won't meet with me. Too bad, too bad. I'd have liked to talk to him about Frankie, and what that kid meant to me." The voice coming from the chair paused a minute and then resumed. "How's your mother?"

"Coming along," Al said as he sat down. Now he was able to see the face of the voice. It was covered in gray stubble that looked like little pins stuck across the man's ash-colored skin.

Two bleary, blood-shot eyes studied Al as he sat in the chair.

"You're Frankie's brother Al—I know you. I never met you before, but I know you. Like I know Mike and Nora and Gilda and your sisters in Italy, your mother, your father. Frankie *buonanima*," and Don Luigi's voice cracked, "told me all about all of you." The don stopped and rubbed his hand across his throat. "Fix me a drink at the bar there, Al. Scotch and soda. Help yourself to whatever you want."

Al rose from the chair and went to the bar, a long, ornately carved mahogany counter with mirrored shelves behind it. The shelves were stacked with bottles of every kind of liquor made. Al stopped short as he came up to the bar. On one of the shelves in the middle of the unit, sat a silver-framed picture. Side by side, arms across each other's shoulders stood two smiling figures. Frankie and Don Luigi. Scrawled at the bottom of the picture, Al was able to make out the words: *Al mio benamato padrino, con affetto, Frankie.* (To my beloved godfather, with affection, Frankie).

To Al, it seemed as if Frankie was suddenly standing before him, ready to step out of the frame and slap him on the back. He was alive again, and at that moment Al found himself smiling back, ready to give his brother a hug, so real to him was the apparition. Al's eyes became clouded over with mist; he blinked and the vision was gone. He was staring at an eleven-by-fourteen black and white picture, only a picture.

It took Al a few minutes to mix two drinks, and he walked back and handed one drink to Luigi, who said quietly, "You like that picture? I love it; I love Frankie." The old man choked up with apparent emotion for a moment, and then continued. "That kid was the son I never had, the kid brother of mine who died too young because he never had an even chance at life. Maybe that's what I wanted to give Frankie, the kind of life my kid brother never had the chance to live. Go to that desk there, and open the right-hand drawer."

Al did as he was told. "Open it. You'll see a picture on top. Look at it," Luigi commanded. When Al lifted the photo to the light, he was amazed to see a young fifteen or sixteen year-old boy who looked so much like his brother Frankie at that age, the he let out a muted whistle.

"Jesus! This is your brother? Madonna, he looks enough like Frankie to be his fraternal twin. The nose is a little different and the lips fuller, the hair curlier, but the resemblance is there."

"Yeah, Frankie was about that age when I saw him for the first time, working in the barber shop, and then one time in an alley beating the shit out of some Irish toughs who were tormenting some poor, feeble-minded friend of his. I saw him in that fight, and I liked the way he handled himself. Frankie had guts, and I knew right then and there, that I wanted that kid around me, that I wanted to do something for him, something that I didn't have the chance to do for my own kid brother.

"Never had kids of my own; too busy making it in this fucking rat-race. No mother, no father, no brother. Only my sister, the mother of my niece, the girl Frankie was going to marry. I brung you here to tell you these things, because I want you to understand this: that I loved Frankie like my own flesh and blood. Maybe I did wrong, I don't know. But I wanted him to have an easy life. No pick and shovel for Frankie, no kissing ass to put a cheap shirt on his back, and day-old bread to eat. You don't fucking get along in this country that way. If you don't kick and punch and bite, you always stay a little guy, a little greasy wop, breaking your balls and your back, doing the shit the Americans don't want to dirty their hands doing.

"Frankie told me a lot about all of youze, and the trouble he had with his old man. Frankie was smart; he didn't buy all that bullshit, all the crap about earning your bread by the sweat of your brow. My old man was the same as your old man, believing all that baloney about gettin' ahead by working. He worked all right, my old man. He worked himself to death, breaking his back every day, pushing a cart up and down the streets. He died young and lies buried in a pauper's grave, I don't even know where, no stone with his name on it. And he left my mama with a kid still in the old country until I brought 'em over; and I didn't get the money to do it by pick and shovel. That's my story, and maybe you don't give a shit about it. But Frankie, Frankie, like I said, was a smart kid, and he didn't want that kind of a life for himself or for none of youze.

"Now listen. Maybe your old man will understand better where Frankie was coming from if you tell him everything I just told you. Anyway, what's done is done. Words don't mean shit at a time like this. But thanks for coming, Al. You can go now. I'm tired."

Al rose from the chair to go. As he said "Goodbye, Don Luigi, I'm glad you told me all this," the old man reached over to the table by his side. He picked up a black leather box and handed it to Al. "Take this. I want you to have it. I was going to give it to Frankie to wear on his wedding day." Al took the case, nodded to the don, then picked up the man's hand and shook it. He turned away and left the room. In the foyer, Al opened the box. On a thick, gold chain hung a crucifix. The cross was of solid gold. The corpus was of silver. The bent head of Christ was encircled by a crown of diamonds, and droplets of blood in rubies dripped from a ruby heart.

Chapter Sixty-two

Mike, Al and their father spent the night in a cheap hotel in the little village not far away from the don's estate. The next morning, amidst a huge throng of mourners, the three of them said their final goodbyes to Frankie. At the graveside, two caskets lay next to each other; the priest said his last blessing, sprinkled holy water over the coffins, and one by one, people placed a flower on the caskets. Then they walked to their cars.

The don was nowhere to be seen. The three Alangas were the last to leave. At their car, Sal stood waiting. Addressing none of them in particular, he said, "The don had a stroke last night. After you left."

For a split moment Al was sincerely taken aback. "Sorry to hear that, Sal. Really sorry." Sal nodded his head and walked away from them. Mike, Al and their father got into their car.

"No, we go home. We go home," Giuseppe reiterated. Mike knew well that commanding tone of his father's voice, so he did not repeat the suggestion that they stop by Uncle Matteo's. He and Al, both, would have liked to have seen their uncle and aunt. Neither of them had come to the wake or the funeral; obviously they knew nothing of Frankie's tragic death, or they would have been there. Besides, it only seemed right to the boys that they should stop to visit with their uncle. They were only a half-hour's drive away, and their aunt and uncle had always been so close to Frankie.

On the road back to Connecticut, Mike began to think that perhaps his father had a point in wanting to get home as soon as possible to Mama. She'd be sick with worry if they delayed their return, and begin to imagine all sorts of things, if not about Zio Matteo, about them. The boys knew that for Mama, the trip to New York was like going to another country. To her, back in the old country, a trip to the next village was like going on a journey. "I guess in the long run, Papa is right. Al probably wants to get home to Maureen, and I couldn't take all the crying at Zio Matteo's." He sped along the highway at a fast clip.

All the first half of the way home, none of them said much; each one remained silent, his mind busy with his own thoughts. Only after half the distance to New Haven had been covered, did Al begin to recount his meeting with Don Luigi. The silence in the car had begun to wear on his nerves, and he had more or less promised the don that he would let his father know what the don had felt and said about Frankie. Hesitatingly, he showed his father the crucifix that was to have been Luigi's wedding present to Frankie. Giuseppe held the box in his hands, his eyes staring vacantly at it, and without a word, he handed it back to Al. Al regretted having shown it to his father. He knew what the old man was thinking: a wedding present for a son who would never have a wedding, never wear the cross around his neck.

Al placed the box in his pocket, and he thought to himself: "I like the guy. He loved Frankie." The don really loved his kid brother, "like a son," he had said. But Al would never repeat those words of the don to his father. Those words would have caused too much pain to his father.

It was just past one-thirty when Mike pulled up in front of his parents' house. Putting on their best face, the three of them entered the house to find that Sunday dinner was just about finished. Gilda and Nora were clearing the table. Nora's husband was picking his teeth with a straw from the broom. Mama was brushing crumbs of bread into her hand from the table.

As soon as the men came into the kitchen, Mama's face lit up at seeing her men home. Al and Mike put on a phony smile, came over and kissed her. Giuseppe nodded to them all, took off his jacket and hung it on the hook of the kitchen door.

In no time at all, Mama took charge. "Sit, sit. Gilda, bring some pasta for your father and brothers. Giuseppe, how is Matteo?"

"Eh!" was all Giuseppe answered. Al, knowing that it was going to be hard for his father to carry through the deception, began filling in the details of their trip to New York. He gave a realistic account of the visit to the hospital and the stop-over to Graziella and the kids. He lied convincingly; Uncle Matteo was going to be all right. It was just going to take some time, that was all, until he was on his feet again. The broken bones would mend. There were no serious internal injuries after all. When Mike and Al left the house, they were satisfied that they had carried off the ruse well. Mama suspected nothing.

Late that afternoon, his shoes kicked off, his shirt unbuttoned, and sipping a cold beer, Al sat on the couch with his arm around Maureen.

All the heightened emotions of the last twenty-four hours were drained from his mind. He was too tired physically, and too tired mentally to think of anything. He was beginning to feel a sense of relief, that the worst was over. The restraints he had felt in his father's somber presence were gone. The first sharp shock of grief was over. He was away from caskets and flowers and the sound of sobbing and weeping. He was home again, home again with Maureen. The warmth and softness of his wife sitting next to him on the couch, the sound of her sweet voice acted as a palliative for him. He pressed her close.

He found it easier to talk now, to unburden himself. Quietly, slowly he began telling Maureen all the details of everything that had taken place in New York. His voice was calm, even dispassionate as he told her about the wake, the funeral, his talk with Don Luigi. He reached over to the jacket he had thrown over the arm of the chair. From its pocket he withdrew a black leather box, opened it and handed it to his wife. The crucifix gleamed bright in the light still streaming through the window. "That's all that's left of Frankie," he said in a flat, quiet tone. Maureen gazed at it admiringly, then closed the case and silently handed it back to her husband.

"Someday, when I work up the courage, I'll give it to Mama." He put the case on the table by the couch. Covering Maureen's face with his, he kissed her. "I'm so glad I have you, Rina. What would I have done without you? Poor Mike, he's all alone. I've got you to help me through things, to share my heartaches and my joys. The old guy up there knew what he was doing when he created woman for man. How does the Bible say it?— 'to be a helpmeet unto man.' Poor Mike."

"Speaking of Michael, Alfred, you promised me once to tell me about him. Why hasn't he ever married? It's something that happened in the past, in Italy, isn't it? That much I gathered from the few hints I've picked up. He's a wonderful man, a good man, and quite good-looking. Of course, not as handsome as you," and she broke out into a little chuckle and pinched Al's cheek. "But really," she continued, "he should be married, and with children of his own."

"Mike has a kid."

Maureen let out a gasp of surprise. A puzzled look crossed her face, and as she opened her mouth to speak, Al didn't give her the chance either to pose a question or make a comment. He went on, "He's never openly admitted it, at least to me. He's like Papa, close-mouthed. He keeps things to himself. But still the family knows, although no one says anything to him." Then Al went on to explain about Adelina, the girl he left behind in the old country, back in Bosco.

Al told Maureen all about how just before leaving for America, Mike and Adelina had stolen away to be alone together in the field that day so long ago, how he had whistled out to warn Mike that Papa was coming across the fields. "That had to be when it happened," Al said. He surmised to Maureen that the two lovers had been overcome by passion and the thought of the impending separation, and must have coupled then. It had to be then, Al was sure. He could see his brother's face as if it were yesterday, as Mike came back across the field, his face all flushed, and adjusting his shirt into his pants.

"The old story, huh, Maureen? Affairs like that happen every day. Anyway, a letter from Mama came one day while we were still living in Uncle Matt's house on the East Side, that Mike must forget about Adelina. Her old man, finding out that she was pregnant, married her off to spare himself the disgrace of being the father of a young, unmarried, pregnant daughter. That's the way things like this are handled by fathers in the old country when daughters go astray. And what could Mike do about it? Nothing. He was in America, Adelina in the old country, married off to an older man who took her away to his own village, away from the shame she would have had to face in Bosco. But that girl has never faded from Mike's memory or heart. He's been hurting all this time, if I know my brother.

"But you know, Rina, I know my brother. I know the way he thinks. As long as Adelina is alive, and there's a kid of his out there, he'll never marry. He's been biding his time. Some day he's going to go back and find them. And when he finds them, I don't know what the hell he will do. But he will do something, mark my words. That's the story, Rina." Al got up from the couch. "I've got to get some sleep," and he started to walk away from her and towards the bedroom.

Chapter Sixty-three

The following Sunday, precisely a week after Frankie's funeral, was a day that none of the Alanga family would ever forget. As soon as Mike, Al, and Maureen opened the door to the front hallway, on their customary Sunday visit to Mama's, they knew something was terribly amiss. The sound of women wailing, punctuated by the hysterical voices of Gilda and Nora calling out Mama's name, Frankie's and the Madonna's, slammed across their ears.

Mike's jaw, and Al's too, dropped to their toes. There stood Zio Matteo, a black mourning band on his arm, hale and hearty. Zia Graziella, too, was there weeping inconsolably and passing a damp cloth over Mama's forehead. Their mother's head was tilted back in the chair. She was as white as a corpse. In fact, except for the fluttering of her eyelids and the heaving of her chest, she might have been mistaken for one. Giuseppe and his brother stood apart from each other, a little distance away while the women ministered to Rosa.

Intuitively, the boys knew, of course, what had taken place. Somehow, Zio Matteo, had learned of Frankie's death and had come down to New Haven to be by his brother's side and to share his grief. As it had happened, a couple of the don's men had come to the restaurant, and Matteo learned of the tragedy from them.

Off to the side, Gilda, in between sobs and tears, explained to her brothers the events of the morning. Upon her entry, Aunt Graziella had rushed to Mama's side and embraced her, her face streaming with tears.

Gilda went on: "At first, Mama thought that something awful had happened to Zio Matteo, but when she saw him come in and walk over to Papa, and a mourning band on his arm, Mama turned white. All Zia Graziella kept murmuring in between her sobs, was Frankie's name— 'poor Frankie, poor Frankie,' and something about a fire. Papa rushed forward like a madman and roared at Zia to shut up. Then he started to pull her away from Mama by the arm. I thought the poor woman was going to die of fright, right then and there. Zio Matteo ran to auntie's side, and for a minute, I thought that he and Papa were going to have a fight when he shoved Papa away from Zia. Then Papa, with a look of despair in his eyes, put his arms down by his side and just folded into one of the kitchen chairs.

"Soon Papa told us all that Frankie was dead. When Mama heard that from him, she let out a scream and passed out I guess, or near to it. That's when you came in, when Nora and Aunt Graziella were trying to bring Mama around." Gilda ended her words in a flood of tears and wiped her eyes with the corner of her apron. In between sobs, she kept calling out Frankie's name. The girl covered her face with her hands, then lowered them and took Al by the hand. She pulled him into her bedroom. "Tell me everything, Alfredo," she begged.

She and Frankie, as little children adored each other. As toddler playmates they had been inseparable. Where one was, the other was sure to be. Mama always referred to them as the "twins." They were the babies of the family, the last of the brood to be born. If Frankie should get hurt, it was usually Gilda who cried, and not Frankie. When they got older, and Frankie went out to labor with his brothers in the fields, Gilda had to stay at home with her sisters and Mama. But it was always Gilda who ran out first to greet Frankie at the end of the day.

Al tried as gently as possible to tell his sister about the manner in which Frankie had met his end in the burning shed on Long Island. As she listened to Al, Gilda's heart died within her. Neither the resilience of youth, nor time would ever be able to erase from her memory, the loss of her brother, or the way in which he had died. Al realized that. He then did something that he had never done before. He took her in is arms, pressed her close in embrace and began stroking her hair.

They had grown up knowing that physical contact between brother and sister was a thing only of childhood days. But with the coming of age, a brother was to regard a sister as someone to be respected and protected; and maybe at times have the prerogative to chide and command. But anyone who took liberties or impugned a sister's honor, always had a brother's anger to contend with.

After a while, Al released his sister from his embrace, and just at that moment, Maureen came up to them and she said, "We have put Mama to bed. Your father is with her now." Even as Al and Gilda and Maureen came into the kitchen, from Mama's bedroom they could hear her anguished moans and the crying out of Frankie's name. Even in the worst moments after the loss of her leg, no one had heard her cry out. But the loss of her son, that was a pain too awful to bear in silence.

Uncle and aunt made an early departure. Their grief was deep, too, and in addition, the events of the visit had made them ill at ease; and Aunt Graziella especially, was filled with remorse because of her unwitting disclosure of Frankie's death to her sister-in-law. On his part, Matteo had felt the sting of his brother's anger. And although the nieces and nephews implored the two of them to remain, they would not. It was painful to Al to think that perhaps the rift between Giuseppe and Matteo had widened.

Chapter Sixty-four

The weeks that followed were ones of tangible, oppressive sorrow for everyone, especially for those in the house of Giuseppe Alanga. The only thing that prevented Gilda from having a complete collapse into listlessness and grieving was her need to attend to her mother. Often enough Nora came downstairs with a dish of food or to give her sister a little relief and a little company. Although her swelling belly caused her discomfort, Nora often came down to be with her sister at their mother's bedside. For the most part, however, it was Gilda who carried the burden of looking after Mama. The young girl bathed her, changed the bed linens, cooked, and cleaned. Persistently, she coaxed her mother to eat, and at times spoon-fed the invalid mouthful by mouthful. At times, Gilda merely sat by the bedside, wiping Mama's face with a damp cloth.

During the first week, Rosa lay feverishly in bed. She said little and was only able to get a little rest if the room was darkened. So Gilda, at her mother's insistence, had to draw down the shades; the only light permitted in the room came from the vigil candle burning in front of the statue of the Virgin. Shrouded by darkness, and in silence, Mama did her grieving alone. Sometimes the name "Francesco" escaped from her lips, sometimes a moan.

It was a relief for Nora to return to her own flat upstairs. She did have a husband to cook for and a home of her own to look after. Giuseppe returned to work at Sargent's and Mike and Al too, had their work to go to. The days went by, and the first acute shock and the numbness they all had first experienced at the time of Frankie's death, dulled. The routine of going and coming, working and keeping busy fell into place again. Life went on after all.

Finally, through the insistent urgings of both Nora and Gilda, their mother was persuaded to leave her bed one day. Carefully the girls helped Mama into her wheelchair. Once more Mama took her familiar place in the kitchen. When Giuseppe came home that evening, he found his wife neatly folding towels and napkins. For the first time in days, Rosa ate her supper at the kitchen table with the rest of the family. Even

Nora and her husband had come down to join in the meal. Again the sound of voices around the supper table filled the kitchen.

The next Sunday, dinner was like old times. Mike, Al and Maureen, who even though she didn't feel quite well under the pressure of her burgeoning waist, all came down to be together around the altar of the table. Life had returned as normally as could be expected. The family was the family again. More than anything else, perhaps, the one thing that lifted Rosa's spirits was the sight of her daughter and her daughter-in-law with bellies full with the promise of new life to come. They were like two stems of the roses she loved so well, with buds ready to burst into bloom.

But her Frankie—a blossom plucked too soon, before its full flowering, would never fade from her memory. He would always be alive in that memory.

On Wednesday night of that very same week, Maureen kept her rendezvous with her sister and her mother at the "novena." Every week without fail, she had been doing so. Only one more Wednesday, and the novena would be completed.

Al knew immediately that something was wrong, as soon as his wife stepped into the house upon her return from seeing her mother and sister. She had been crying. Her eyes were red, and the beautiful, milky-white skin of her face was blotchy. She had not entered the house with her usual bounce and cheery, "Hello, my darling. Did you eat the supper I left for you?" Instead, she went straight to the sofa by the entrance and threw herself down. She tilted her head back and closed her eyes.

"Rina, what's wrong, are you okay?" She did not answer, and Al with a little note of alarm in his voice asked, "It's not the baby, I mean, everything is all right in there, isn't it?"

"Oh, I'm just tired, I guess. Everything is fine, really. I'm just tired."

"No, everything is not all right. You were crying. I can tell by your eyes. Tell me what's wrong. Al sat beside her and put his arm around her. Gently he pushed her head to his shoulder and began to stroke the hair away from her face.

"Oh, that feels nice, so soothing."

Al brushed away a tear that was making its way down her cheek. "Okay, what's the matter? Out with it. Maureen heaved a long sigh. "Oh, Alfred, my father knows that Mother and Helen have been meeting with me. There was a terrible row between him and Helen. He even struck her in his rage.

"When I went to meet with them at the usual place, only Helen was there. She told me what had happened. That old snoop, that horrid Mrs. Murphy saw the three of us together last week. Of course, she noticed, too, my condition. When she later chanced to meet Father, the old gossip told him about seeing us; she had not seen me about for so long a time, she said, and was happy to see me in the company of Mother and sister. Oh, with what glee she must have told him of his obviously pregnant daughter. She knows nothing, of course, about my marrying, and has no doubt spread vicious rumors throughout the neighborhood.

"Storming into the house like a mad bull, and screaming like a banshee, Father confronted Mother." Here, Maureen paused for a minute to explain to Al what a "banshee" was. Then she continued: "I know how terrible Father's rages are, how terrified Mother must have been. Helen tried to divert his fury from Mother, and he turned on her as well. He was so furious, that when Helen intervened, he slapped her.

"He said some simply horrible things in between his curses. I won't repeat them, but the upshot of it all is, that he has forbidden Mother ever to see me again. It is only because he was in a drunken stupor tonight, that Helen was able to come out and tell me all this." She stopped and pressed her wet face into her husband's chest, trying to stifle her sobs. She lifted her head and dried her eyes with her handkerchief. "Oh, poor Mother! He would have her disown me, as he has." She burst out into another fit of weeping.

Al put her head again on his chest and held her tight. The blood was beginning to boil in his veins. He controlled his first impulse to curse the old devil aloud. But, the man was Maureen's father after all was said and done. And he did not want to add to her unhappiness by an angry outburst. Mustering up as much calm as he could manage he said, "Look, Rina, if your father doesn't want to be a part of our lives, that is his choice, his loss. Not yours. We've got each other, and now this baby that's coming, our own flesh and blood; that is all we need be concerned about. Maybe someday he will come around when he realizes what he is missing—his daughter and his grandchild. And don't worry, you will see your mother and sister. Christ! they aren't on the moon. There will be plenty of opportunities to get together with them; we will make those opportunities. You will see. Come on now, cheer up."

To himself, he said, "The old bastard won't live forever."

Chapter Sixty-five

September passed, and then October, and winter loomed on the horizon. The gray skies of November brought with them the first falling of snow. With the cold, Mama seemed to spring back to life. It was as if the cold stirred her from a dulling lethargy induced by the closeness, the darkness and the isolation of the cocoon that was her bedroom. She had come out of that cocoon into the kitchen, the place where she had always loved to be, the one room in the house, that was her domain. Now that the season had begun to turn cold, she stayed mostly by the stove with a shawl over her shoulders and a blanket across her lap. There she passed the hours sewing, darning and tatting. The little shuttle loaded with its colored threads flew between her fingers. Pillow cases, napkins and handkerchiefs, she edged with the intricate lacey borders that her imagination created. Shades of blue, pink, violet and green brightened the starkness of the white pieces she attached them to. In the corners of each piece, she wove the shapes of little flowers surrounding a fancy, curlicued letter "G."

Later, in her chair drawn up to the kitchen table, she ironed each piece, folded it with care and precision, and gave them all to Gilda. "Put them in the chest. These are for you, because someday you will marry, and you will take them with you to your own house."

"Oh, Mama." But obediently Gilda would take them from her and place them in the cedar chest in her mother's bedroom.

At other times, on the kitchen table covered with a coating of flour, Rosa mixed and kneaded dough, and from it cut the homemade pasta the whole family loved to eat. No one could make it as well as Mama. Sometimes it was the *cavatelle* she made, the little shell-like pasta that she rolled off her thumb. Sometimes it was the *tagliatelle*, those long strands of noodles, and sometimes it was the *gnocchi*, the dough and potato dumplings that she rolled out. If the *gnocchi* weren't made just right, they sat in the pit of your stomach like little balls of lead. But Mama's *gnocchi* were the best in the world.

With the approach of Christmas, the activities in the house increased as the spirit of the season took hold. All must be in readiness for the culmination of the holiday. Christmas Day itself, for Giuseppe's family, was an anti-climax. It was the Vigil of Christmas, Christmas Eve, that brought the whole family together. That was the night to bask in each other's company, to share the good things of life in a special way—the food, the drink and the love of one another heightened by the coming birth of Gesu Bambino.

The whole week before Christmas Eve, Giuseppe, happy once more to see his wife more and more on the road to recovery, and while the women went about cooking and baking in preparation of the coming festivities, spent his free hours assembling the traditional *presepio*.

A light, powdery snow had just begun to fall that Christmas Eve, when Mike, Al and Maureen drove up to the house. The snow catching the light of the moon, shimmered like so many tiny diamonds falling from the sky. The moment the three visitors opened the front door and were in the front hall, their noses caught the smell of fish frying on the stove in the kitchen.

"We will be eating good tonight, Rina," Al said merrily.

"And when don't we ever, in this house," quipped Maureen laughing.

"Yeah, but tonight is something special. Wait'll you see what Mama and the girls put on that table!" chimed in Mike.

They trooped into the kitchen. Everyone was there, Mama, Papa, Gilda, Nora, Giovanni, and as soon as the new-comers were in the room, a flurry of *Buon Natale*, kisses and handshakes were exchanged in accompaniment to excited laughter and the merry sizzling sounds of frying fish cooking on the stove.

"It's beginning to snow outside. We are going to have a white Christmas after all, but we don't have to go out and shovel it to make a few bucks like we used to have to do in those days in New York, eh, Pop? Remember?" Mike shouted out.

Yeah, I remember," Al piped up, "but you had to do it if you wanted to eat. Thank God those days are gone. Those days were *miseria*."

The men went on reminiscing for another quarter of an hour, until Gilda gave the welcome call to come to table. They all gathered around the supper table, and there, the joy of the holiday mood manifested itself to the fullest. The array of platters and bowls filled with good things to eat, was a feast not only for the palate, but for the eyes. Papa's best home-made wines brought up from the cellar, sparkled through the glass decanters, the white wines the color of pale gold, the reds, the color of garnet. The aromas issuing from each steaming bowl and platter filled the whole kitchen in a symphony of smells to tease the nose.

Gilda and Nora served the meal of meatless food in a sequence of tantalizing courses one after the other. Because it was the Vigil of Christmas, a day of abstinence from meat, all the main courses consisted of fish dishes. First, though, came the antipasto, made up of a bed of lettuce and topped with anchovies, capers, strips of raw peppers, cheese cut thin and olives green and black. Then a salad of boiled calamari with its oil, lemon and garlic dressing. After that, they piled high their plates with spaghetti covered with the tomato sauce made with crab legs and lobster tails in place of meatballs and sausage. Not a drop of that sauce did any of them let go to waste; with chunks of bread broken from the crusty loaves that Gilda and Nora had baked fresh that morning, they all wiped their plates clean. Fried shrimp, fried scallops, and calamari fried this time, completed the meal.

During the whole time of the meal, they sat around the table, elbow to elbow, eating, drinking, talking. They were family, that union of love and blood which bound them all together as one. The one vacant place around the table that evening was Frankie's. No one mentioned his name, but at one time or another in the course of the evening, the image of his young face appeared in the mind's eye of each of them. No one gave voice to the ache in their heart as the thought of him crossed their mind. But their silence did not mean that he was not there with them. The wounds caused by his untimely death were still too fresh in all their hearts to be opened by the utterance of his name. His name was best left unspoken.

The men unloosened their belts, leaned back in their chairs and pulled out their smokes. The young women cleaned the mess left on the table. Off came the stained and spotted tablecloth, and on went a clean, white one, and Gilda set the demi-tasse cups in their saucers at each place around the table.

Then in a while, when enough time had elapsed to give the digestive system a rest, Gilda filled the cups with steaming, black espresso coffee and set the bottle of anisette liqueur on the table for those who like a drop of it in their brew. In between sips, they bit at the *canoli*, those Sicilian tubes of blistered pastry filled with rich, sweet ricotta embedded with pieces of citron, pistachio nuts and orange peel. For anyone who felt the need to "pick," bowls of figs and other fruits, roasted chestnuts and hazelnuts, almonds, and walnuts were on the table.

And so the hours passed, until the midnight hour arrived. Papa rose from the table. All of them, with the exception of Maureen, knew what that meant. They got up from their chairs and followed Papa into the parlor. Al took his wife's hand and brought her along. She saw Papa go the china closet, open the glass door, and take out something wrapped in a handkerchief. Then he started walking to the presepio, where he carefully unfolded the cloth in his hand to expose the little plaster figure of Gesu Bambino. Reverently he placed the Christ Child, bound in swaddling cloths, into the manger between the kneeling figures of Mary and Joseph.

Then, for the first time since Frankie's death, the sound of music once more resounded throughout the house. Mike had gone to the victrola, placed a record on the turntable and cranked up the handle. In a moment the wailing of bagpipes filled the room. The voice of a male singer began bellowing out the words of the traditional Neapolitan Christmas hymn, *La Pastorale di Natale*. A misty film clouded the eyes of Mama and Papa. Nora and Gilda, too, as well as the boys, found themselves affected by the haunting strains of the bagpipes, transporting them back in time to the days of their childhood in Bosco and Christmases past.

As they waited for the tune to end, in a quiet whisper, Al explained to Maureen, how, back in Italy at Christmas time, the shepherds came down from the pasture lands in the hills. Playing the *pastorale* on the pipes, they made their way from house to house in the villages. After each serenade, in the generous spirit of the season, the housewives gave them gifts of wine, food or coins.

When the scratching of the needle on the record signaled the end, the family went back to the kitchen. All, except Maureen. She stood entranced in front of Giuseppe's *presepio*. Not even in church, had she ever seen such a wondrous display of the nativity scene. With his Neapolitan love of detail, Giuseppe had placed every item of the scene just so.

On a realistic landscape replicating grottoes, mountains and cliffs made of papier-mâché, scores of little terra-cotta figures dotted the paths through hills and valleys that led to the cave where the holy family was the focal point of the panorama.

When Maureen finally came into the kitchen to join the others, her exclamations in praise of Papa's *presepio* brought a smile to her father-in-law's face. "Yeah, Rina. Papa does a real bang-up job, and every year he manages to add something more to it. Pretty soon the thing will take up the whole room."

"Is that why there is no Christmas tree, Alfred—no room?" Giuseppe threw up his hand in a gesture of disgust. "But what Christmas tree!" he blurted.

Mike and Al burst out laughing. "You said a naughty word, Rina. Papa thinks a tree in the house is a stupid idea. The true significance of Christmas is the *presepio*, not a tree decorated with balls of colored glass hanging from its branches. The closest thing to the idea of having a tree in the house, for him is the *ceppo*, what you would call a Yule log. In Italy, they burn one in the fireplace all night to give off warmth and light, and the light it gives, symbolizes the new-born Christ, the Light of the world. That makes sense to Papa, not a tree standing in a corner of the parlor. He's been in this country for fourteen, going on fifteen years now, and he won't let one in the door." Al finished with a laugh.

"He can be a thick-head, this old man of ours, hey, Al?" Mike asked with a smile. Everyone joined in with a chuckle or two, their father himself. "Never mind all the talk. Come to the table now. It's Christmas Day! And at Gilda's words they all took their places around the table again. This time the table was graced with platters of sausages, meatballs, chicken and veal cutlets. It was past all comprehension for Maureen to think that they were going to eat again. Another frenzy of feasting began, and while the others gorged themselves anew, all she could manage to eat, was a small piece of chicken that she nibbled on. When all was over, there was very little food remaining on the table.

The end of the second sitting brought a finish to the get-together. With the last exchanges of *Buon Natale*, the party broke up. Nora and Giovanni went upstairs to their own flat. Mike, Maureen and Al made their last goodbyes to Mama and Papa, and then started to the front door. The snow was falling heavily now; everything was covered over in white. Holding on to Maureen securely, Al led her down the steps of the front stoop and into the car. The brisk cold of the night air revived the three of them out of the torpor brought on by the food and warmth they had enjoyed inside.

Chapter Sixty-six

The new year came, and with it, the snow, ice and cold of the New England January. Maureen, big now with child, did not stir from the house, not even to go to Mama's for Sunday dinner. Al insisted that she stay put. "You're safe and warm in the house," he declared. "We're not taking any chances of you falling or catching cold. No one would expect you to be out gallivanting, least of all, Mama. Not in your condition. Mike and I will keep dropping by there to see the folks. Mama's feeling a helluva lot better, anyway. You could see how good she was at Christmas. I tell you, Rina, those old folks from the old country are made of iron. No matter what dirty handouts and hardships life dishes out, all those old women like Mama pick themselves up and go on, no-matter what pain they're suffering."

Maureen smiled. "My, you are waxing poetic." Then, in a split second her face took on a serious look. "But, there is a great deal of truth in what you say. I see it in your mother," and then with a note of sadness in her voice, she added, "and in mine."

"My mother had had her knocks, too, you know. She came to this country from Ireland to Pennsylvania when she was just a wisp of a girl. Her own mother had died giving birth, so her father left the old sod with his three young children in tow. They came to find a better life here, away from the poverty in Ireland. He went into the coal mines, and Mother, at sixteen years of age, went into service. For a few dollars a week, a room in an attic that sweltered in summer and was freezing cold in winter, and a bit of food that she had to eat in the pantry, she slaved away scrubbing and cleaning in one of the big houses on the hill. All the rich lived on the hill, you know, away from the 'flats.'

"I think she thought she would be escaping from that kind of servitude when she married Father at the age of nineteen. He was older than she by nine years. He worked alongside her own dad in the mines, too. And his life hadn't been easy, either. His parents had died soon after coming to America, and he was knocked about a good deal.

"He was a hard man and a hard drinker. When he was under the influence, he became a terror towards Mother and us children. He rapped us all about, and especially Mother, when he was in his cups. Age has worn down the violence somewhat, but he is still someone to fear when he is in a rage. In the early days, when we lived in a shanty down by the 'flats,' things seemed to go from bad to worse. Many Poles and Slovaks and Italians came into the coal pits to work. Wages went down. The great majority of the miners were Irish and Welsh, and they blamed the foreigners who were willing to work for less. There were many bloody confrontations between the old-timers and the new-comers. One night, Father came home with a bloody knife wound in his side. An Italian had stuck him with a knife. He then had to leave the mines after that. His lung had been punctured. If it hadn't been for Mother taking in laundry and ironing, we would surely have known great want, and have starved, I think.

"Mother's father died shortly after, leaving a bit of money to her. With that, Father decided to leave Pennsylvania and start afresh somewhere else. They came to New Haven to live with Father's older bachelor brother. Dad was able to find work here in the carriage trade at the Hooker Carriage Works on State Street. With what he earned, and with what Uncle Daniel had, they pooled their money and opened a saloon on Wallace Street. Things were better after a while." Maureen laughed. "We went from rags to riches, as they say.

"Father got to smoking expensive cigars and wearing a fine bowler hat. And then when he was able to buy the fine house on Dwight Street, well, one would have thought him lord of the manor. He no longer threw his hands, but he browbeat us all with his shouting rages. And poor Mother, poor soul. All her life she has been dominated by men. First, her father and brothers, and when in service, by the master of the big house on the hill. Always commanded about and having to answer meekly, 'Yes, sir. No, sir. Immediately, sir.'

"And then, of course, Father. She has been so long-suffering. She has had the patience of a saint and the resignation of a martyr. Always so timid. Thank God, neither Helen nor I are so soft. We had to learn to arch our backs. Now that we are older, we are not as afraid, as we were when we were children. And of course, he is not as fierce as when he was in his prime."

She stopped talking, and a dreamy look came into her eyes. A myriad of scenes from the past popped into her mind, as if someone were operating a slide viewer, flicking one slide after another across the screen of her mind. Pictures of those early days when Mother would stand between Father and children taking refuge behind her skirts. Or, Father slapping Mother in his drunken rages. Or, Father cursing and smashing crockery and overturning furniture. And then, his final collapse into a disheveled heap on the kitchen floor, and Mother with the help of the boys, dragging him off to his bed to sleep off his stupor.

Al broke into her reveries. "All mothers are like that I guess, Maureen. I mean, they suffer in silence, no matter what raw deals life hands them. They go on for the sake of their children, and sacrifice their own well-being for the ones they love. You know, women are a helluva lot stronger than men. A man thinks himself strong because he can lift a hundred-pound sack of coal, or not flinch under physical pain. But it is the pain that women carry in their hearts where the real strength lies. Your mother, and mine, Rina, they're strong women. They go on with the business of life, in spite of their pain, for the sake of the family, no matter what heartaches they suffer.

"And what a mother you will be. Kid," he said, patting Maureen's stomach, "you are going to have a great mom. The best in the world. Gee! Rina, just think. Any day now—what, two weeks, three weeks, and we will be Mom and Dad. A kid of our own. Can you beat that!" Then, winking his eye, he chuckled, "I hope we have lots of babies!"

Chapter Sixty-seven

The dreary days of January seemed to go on forever. Alone in the house each day, snug and warm, Maureen waited anxiously in joyous anticipation of Al's return from work. She spent the lonely hours of every afternoon sitting by the stove. Needle in hand, she worked at completing the baby's layette that she had started months ago. She added more items to the buntings, blankets, diapers and caps already made. With her fat belly in the way, she had found it too uncomfortable to sit hunched over the sewing machine. Besides, it was more relaxing to work slowly and quietly without the whirring noise of the machine. Not having to work the treadle of the machine with her foot, and stretch her arm to turn the wheel of the machine's arm, was less tiring to her.

There was no such strain plying the needle, and so, hour after hour, Maureen stitched away with calm precision.

Or, sometimes with a skein of yarn in her lap, and knitting needles in her hands, she clicked away with deft fingers that needed no thought to guide them. Even with eyes closed and head tilted back, her able fingers knew how to fashion the little woolen booties and sweaters she turned out. When the work was finished at the end of the day, she placed each article in the bassinette at the foot of her bed.

Routinely, each afternoon followed another in the same way. But today, she was so tired, so uncomfortable, she lay her work aside and put the tea kettle on the stove. She felt the need of a nice cup of the hot tea she loved so much. The last days of the month were coming to a close. It was already the twenty-ninth. She looked at her stomach. Would she go into February, she wondered. How impatient she was now, for the miracle that lay within her womb, to come into being. Her arms ached to hold the baby, her baby, and Al's.

The strident whistling of the tea kettle jolted her from her thoughts. She set the tea to steep, and walked into the bedroom to the night table. Opening a drawer, Maureen drew out a little bundle of envelopes. Back at the kitchen table, the tea cup beside her, she read again, one by one, the six letters before her. They were letters from Helen, and Maureen never tired reading the contents over and over. She cherished every little bit of news about Mother and her sister, and took satisfaction in the assurance that all was well with them at home. It gave her some little degree of comfort to learn that things had quieted down there, after the strident argument when Father had discovered their subterfuge and that she, Mother, and Helen had been meeting secretly.

In one letter, Helen had informed her sister that a kind of icy truce prevailed. Few words were being exchanged between any of the family, especially between Helen and Father. And Mother, in her calm and timid way, went about in her usual, quiet manner performing her household tasks—preparing Father's meals, washing his shirts, ironing his clothes. And the few conversations Mother had with him were innocuous and innocent of anything that could cause an angry outburst. Only when Mother and Helen were alone together, did they speak of Maureen.

So for Maureen, it was a great relief to know that a measure of peace had returned to the old house. As Helen informed her in her letters, the furious first days of their father's rantings and ravings were over. Mother sat as usual by the fireplace with her knitting and her thoughts. And as for Helen herself, she had the refuge of her work, where amid the laughter and chattering of the children she taught in her third grade class, she was away from the gloom and mirthless atmosphere of home.

Maureen finished her tea and her reading. At first she had the thought to write a letter to Helen. But she was exhausted and her back was aching. Letters in hand, she got up from the table and walked to the bedroom once more. She replaced the letters in the night table drawer. How clever, she thought, for Helen to have arranged for Maureen's written replies to be addressed to Mary O'Leary, her sister's good friend, a teacher in the same school building where Helen taught. When the postage stamp that Maureen affixed to the envelope was in an inverted position, Mary knew that the missive was meant for Helen. She then would bring it to school and give it to Helen. In this way, Father could not know of the sisters' correspondence to each other. The deception was working beautifully.

On her way back to the kitchen from the bedroom, Maureen glanced at the clock. It was time to prepare supper. Before long, Al would be home. She shrugged off her weariness. She wanted her husband to have warm food when he sat at the table. A nice, hot stew was just the thing on a cold evening like this.

When Al did walk into the house a few hours later, the aroma of the onions, potatoes, carrots and beef simmering in the pot on the stove, was as welcome to his nostrils as was her kiss to his lips. "Hmm, that smells good, Rina. And how's the little mama tonight?" He stood behind her, his arms enfolded around her waist and nuzzled her neck. "Sit down," he told her. "I will set the table. You sit. When the food is ready, I'll serve." He pointed his finger at her stomach. "Anything budging in there yet?"

She smiled back at him. "Everything seems the same," she said, matter-of-factly. "But I do feel very tired, dear. That stew is done, Alfred. Shall we eat?" Al brought the pot to the table and ladled out the stew into both their plates, and then as they ate, they chit-chatted about this and that. When the meal was done with, Al cleared the table. The winter darkness outside made it seem like midnight, although it was only a little after seven.

"You go to bed, hon," Al told Maureen. "See if you can get some sleep. With that load you've been carrying, no wonder you are tired. I'll finish up here. I want to figure up the bills and read the paper. "I'll be in in a little while. Good night."

"Good night, Alfred." Maureen went into the bedroom. Al could hear her move about as she readied herself for bed. He heard her get into bed, and then nothing more. Quietly he went about his business. It was ten o'clock when he came to bed. Maureen was sound asleep. He placed another blanket over her sleeping form and slid in noiselessly beside her.

Chapter Sixty-eight

Al awoke with a start. Maureen was moaning. He heard her breathing in short gasps. When she moved and sat up in bed, Al knew something was not right. "Rina," he almost shouted, "what is it, is it time?" There was a note of mounting panic in his voice. "Shall I go for Maddalena? Shall I go for the midwife?"

He jumped out of bed, turned on the lamp, and started for his pants.

Maureen called him back. Letting out a long breath of air, she said in choppy spurts, "No, there is a lot of time yet." Laying her head back against the headboard of the bed, she said "The pains have just begun. It will be hours yet. What time is it?"

Al looked at the clock on the night table. "Just about two in the morning." He went over to her side of the bed and put a couple of pillows behind her back. "I'm getting dressed. I'm going for the midwife."

"Get dressed if you wish, but don't go yet for the midwife. It would be a shame to rouse her at this time of night, only to sit here, for God knows how many hours. Please do as I say. Just stay with me. I will tell you when to fetch her, when the spasms come regularly, when they come one after another."

"Rina, are you sure?" Al sat on the bed beside his wife and took her hand in his. She smiled at him reassuringly. "Get dressed. You will catch yourself a nice cold, just clad in your underwear. I'm fine. Make yourself a cup of coffee, and me a cup of tea. They will do us both some good."

Al was only too happy to be told what to do, to be useful in some way. His wife's calmness now, her seeming control, put him at ease and helped take away the anxiety he had first felt. He shoved a cigarette into his mouth, dressed, and went into the kitchen. In minutes, he had the coffee pot and the tea kettle on the stove.

Just as he was entering the bedroom with a cup of tea, he saw Maureen writhe in pain as she underwent a sharp contraction. He nearly dropped the cup. Her moment's pain passed, and she sank back into the pillows. "Let me have my tea," she said quietly. "And comb your hair.

You look like a hedgehog." She grinned, and Al obediently ran his fingers through his hair.

A dozen times during the wee hours of the morning, Al popped into the bedroom. Then back to the kitchen. Then back to the bedroom. When dawn finally arrived with its promise of sunlight and visibility, Al began feeling a sense of relief. He didn't feel so alone and so helpless now that the gloom and heaviness of the darkness vanished. He regained enough of a sense of ease as to be able to cope more confidently with what was going on. Still, he began to champ at the bit, waiting for his wife to give him the word to go for the midwife.

At last, at eight-thirty, Maureen told him to leave the house and bring back the midwife. He flew out the door. "Put on your coat," she called out after him. But he was already gone. By a little before nine, Al burst through the front door, leaving the midwife huffing and puffing up the path. He left the front door open for her to follow in, and ran to his wife. "I'm back, Rina. Are you okay?" When he reached her bedside, he saw beads of sweat on Maureen's forehead. He ran to the front room and called out to Maddalena: *Subito, subito.* Hurry, hurry." Although he knew the woman understood a little English, he was taking no chances on her not understanding him. After all these fourteen years in America, even though he spoke and understood English perfectly, he often broke out into Italian when his emotions were running high. It just happened, without his even thinking.

The midwife, a woman of about forty, a little on the fat side, just waved him off, and out of breath, she slowed her pace. Once in the house, she removed her coat, scarf, and boots, slowly, while Al kept urging her to hurry. She was thinking, how foolish, stupid even, men were at times like this. What did they know about babies, only how to make them. How many babies had she brought into the world, that she needed a man to tell her what to do? When she did finish removing her things, she went to his wife's side in the bedroom. With a corner of the sheet she wiped the moisture from Maureen's damp face. Then she shooed Al out of the room and ordered him to bring her some clean towels and to put some water to boiling on the stove.

As Al reentered the bedroom with the towels, he blurted out, "I'm going to get Gilda, Rina. Somebody from the family ought to be here with you. Someone to help out."

"No, Alfred, it isn't necessary. Besides, she has to be with your mother."

"Mama can manage now. Papa's there. Nora is upstairs." Then to Maddalena, in Italian, he explained where he was going. He waved to Maureen, and before she could protest, he was gone.

It was slow-going to the city. The roads were rutted with patches of ice as hard as concrete. Well over an hour passed before he returned with his sister. Immediately, Gilda went into the bedroom. Al felt better now that his sister was here. He heard voices coming from the bedroom, and then someone closed the room's door. From behind it, he could hear Maddalena commanding Maureen, now in English, now in Italian, to push. Gilda, too, sometimes repeated: "Push, Maureen, push." For twenty minutes Al's ear was attuned to every agonized gasp, every strained moan escaping from his wife's hoarse throat.

Then one last cry from Maureen, and a loud explosion from Maddalena, "*Ecco! allora!*" (It's here, well now!). On the wake of her words, Al heard an audible slap. Then a baby's wail, and he knew the ordeal was over for Maureen. His child was born. The door still remained shut, and he heard the movement of footsteps going back and forth across the floor. The door opened. The midwife beckoned him to come with a wave of her hand. As the new father approached her, she murmured, as if she were too embarrassed to say it: "*E femmenella.*" (It's a little girl).

Al bounded into the bedroom. Gilda was neatening up the bed clothes. He saw his wife propped up against the headboard, smiling. Nestled in her arms, she held a bundle wrapped tight in a blanket. A little red face peeked out, the little head jerkily moving from side to side. Little lips opened and closed, up and down, up and down, as if sucking on a nipple. Gilda picked up a basin of bloodied water and left the room.

It was Sunday, January 30, 1921, and almost the noon-hour. Another Rose, another Rose Alanga had come into bloom.

Chapter Sixty-nine

Gilda stayed the week. She cooked the meals, cleaned the house, washed the diapers. The two women, she and Maureen, kept each other company. In a few days' time Maureen was strong enough to be up and about. She and Gilda spent the days chatting, eating their meals together, and tending the baby. By the warmth of the stove, in her rocking chair that Al had rushed out to buy, the new mother breast fed little Rose. Then like the good little baby that she was, the infant napped for hours until the next feeding. Fed, cleaned, and diapered, the baby lay contentedly in the bassinette, wrapped tight in bunting, only her tiny face uncovered.

The day before the week was up, Gilda and Maureen were at the table having lunch. The baby was asleep. The house was quiet, except for the sounds of their muted voices. Bright sunlight streamed through the windows of the kitchen. When the two women had exhausted the topic of the baby's beauty, her well-being, and Al's rapture over his new-born daughter, Gilda spoke of something she had never mentioned before to Maureen.

"Why is it," she asked, "that your papa hates Alfredo so?"

She was aware of course, as was everyone else in the family, of the great displeasure and bitterness of Maureen's father about the marriage of his daughter to her brother. Maureen sighed. With a note of sadness in her voice, apologetically almost, she tried to make her sister-in-law understand about the bigotry and prejudice that consumed her father. She was not attempting to excuse his unreasoning intolerance. He felt the way he did, she explained, not just towards Italians, but he was equally intolerant of all the non-English speaking immigrants coming to these shores. He felt threatened, she told Gilda, by people he had nothing in common with, and whose ways and languages he did not understand. She told of her father's bitter experiences in his early days in America when he was vilified and ridiculed for being Irish and Catholic. Maureen supposed that having been bullied and despised for just being what he was, he found it easy to do the same to the new foreigners, to join the bandwagon. Once he had been scorned. Now he was doing the scorning in the hopes of being as "American" as those who had once taunted him for being a greenhorn. There were new greenhorns now—Italians, Jews, Greeks, Poles, and all the other alien nationalities—all fair targets for derision by the establishment.

When Maureen had finished speaking, there was a long moment of silence. Then Gilda, with a puzzled look in her eyes that mirrored her incomprehension of such a shallow basis for hatred of people—their language, their looks, their dress, shook her head. "We are all children of God, are we not?" She got up from the chair and began clearing the table, and no more was said about the subject.

The following day, Al brought his sister home to Mama. Maureen was able to manage on her own now. There was no need for Gilda to stay. Others needed her, too. Nora's time was getting close. Once home, Gilda regaled them all, Mama, Papa and Nora with exuberant and detailed descriptions of Mama's new granddaughter. Each time she mentioned the baby's name, Rosina, little Rose, Mama's face beamed with joy and pride. The baby was named after her; but that was no surprise to anyone. Italian sons almost always named their first-born after their mother, their father.

With her woman's keen eye for detail and color, Gilda gave them all a picture of little Rose's every feature—her tiny, well-formed nose, her pretty mouth, the hair the color of copper, like Maureen's, the skin the white of milk. The eyes, big and alert. A better behaved baby, no one ever saw. Little Rose ate and slept and bawled only when she was hungry or in need of having her diaper changed. "Wait until you see her, just wait until you see her," she ended her litany of praises.

The day after her sister-in-law left, Maureen was alone in the house for the first time in a week. Only she and the baby. Al was off to work. Maureen quickly settled into a routine of caring for husband and home as before, and the new addition to her chores, taking care of little Rose. She cooked and cleaned as she used to, but now she spent less time at that, in order to feed and rock the baby to sleep by the stove.

It was Friday of the week now, and Maureen had just settled in her accustomed place in the rocking chair by the stove with the baby cradled in her arms. As she began to hum softly, there was a knock on the kitchen door. The door opened, and Mike walked in. He stood there for a moment, on the threshold, shaking off powdery snow from his coat, for it had started snowing again.

"Oh, Michael. I thought perhaps, it would be you. Do come in." Her welcome was warm and sincere. "Come, see your niece."

"That is just why I have come." He grinned. I'm getting to be a real pest."

"Never," Maureen replied'.

This was the third time during the week that he had stopped by, just to gaze in fascination at the baby. He walked up to the stove where he warmed his hands together over the heat. "May I hold her, Maureen?" he asked. Gently she placed the baby in his arms. With his finger, Mike tickled the baby's chin. He laughed as the baby puckered up her lips and began making sucking motions. He laughed again. "No milk from me, sweetheart." Then a dreamy look came into his eyes.

Maureen could well imagine what was going through his mind. Across the ocean there had been a baby of his own, as tiny as little Rose, his baby that he had never held in his arms, never had tickled, never had kissed. Her eyes misted over for a moment at the sadness of it. Suddenly the spell was broken for both of them. "Oops!" Mike laughed out loud. "My hand is all wet. I think Rosie peed." Before he handed the baby back to her mother, he kissed the little one's forehead. "Thanks, Maureen. See you again."

"Stay and have a cup of coffee, Michael."

"No thanks, Maureen. See you again. He walked to the door and left, still chuckling to himself.

When Al came home that night, he was glad to hear that Mike had come by and that she had had a little company. Al had begun to have doubts about not having had Gilda stay a little longer. But Maureen seemed to be able to manage by herself. The house was tidy, supper was on the stove, and Rosie was warm and snug in her bassinette. Nothing to worry about. Maureen was doing fine, for all that she wasn't Italian.

The weekend came. A Saturday, and for Maureen the day was proceeding along as had all the others of the week. She was sitting at the table, peeling potatoes. It was already four-thirty, and she was expecting her husband home at six, the usual hour of his return.

She hadn't heard the front door open, and when she did hear footsteps coming into the kitchen from the front room, she looked up, a little startled. Even more so, when she saw Al standing in the doorway. "Alfred, what are you doing home this early?" But before he had a chance to answer, she spied the figure behind him, and her hand flew to her chest, her mouth opened wide in surprise. She gasped, "My God, Helen! Oh, Helen." The two sisters raced towards each other.

Anticipating her sister's question, Helen answered as she removed her coat: "Alfred picked me up at the finish of school. Now, before another minute passes, I should like to see my niece." As the two made their way to the bedroom, Al called out, "I will leave you two to yourselves. I'm sure you have a lot of catching up to do, and I've really got to get back to work. A lot of catching up for me to do, too. See you at six or so."

Before Maureen could answer him, Al was out the door. Maureen took her sister's hand and led her into the bedroom and to the bassinette. There, Helen looked down in evident happiness at the face of the sleeping child. The room was bathed in a warm half-light from the fading winter sun coming through the windows.

The glint of the copper-colored hair framing the baby's face glowed like a halo. A blush of pink against the whiteness of the skin formed an exquisite contrast. Taking Maureen's hand in hers, Helen whispered sweetly, "She has the face of a cherub, Maureen. She is adorable. I've never seen any baby so beautiful." Only after a full five minutes, did Helen start to tear herself away from the sleeping baby.

"Stay," Maureen told her sister quietly. "I am going to put the kettle on for some tea." She left her sister standing by the bassinette and went to busy herself at her task. Minutes later, Helen came into the kitchen. For an hour and a half, the two conversed over tea. Maureen spoke mainly about the baby, the birth, her own well-being and the baby's. In turn, Helen spoke about the state of conditions at home on Dwight Street. There, she explained, things continued along in an atmosphere of icy calm. Father said little to either her or to Mother. "And that is no hardship to bear, I tell you," Helen said with emphasis.

Mother was well. She carried on, as she always had, going about the house and her tasks in her own quiet, unobtrusive manner. How delighted she was sure to be to hear about little Rose, her granddaughter. "It will be the one thing to bring a gleam of hope, a ray of joy, to her hurting heart and her dreary existence," Helen foretold.

"And Father?" Maureen almost hesitated to ask. "Does he ever speak of me?" Helen took a short moment before responding. She would not wound her sister's feelings by relating the occasional instances when he would ask sarcastically, "And have you met again with your sister and her wop husband?"

Instead Helen lied, "No, darling." She uttered the words quietly, but raised her voice significantly when she went on: "He rails and fulminates now against the government, the president, and the congress. He's preoccupied, you see, with this Prohibition Amendment. He's much worried about the saloon and his livelihood. The very idea of the government telling a man what to drink and what not to drink, puts him into an apoplectic fit. He deems it a dastardly impudence on the part of the authorities to say a man cannot indulge himself with a wee drop of good, Irish whiskey after a hard day's work." She laughed. "A wee drop, indeed!" She was still laughing. "A tumbler full, and another, is his definition of the wee drop. He believes they are all fools and scoundrels in Washington."

She had no sooner ended her chuckling, when Al popped in the door. No amount of insisting would entice Helen to stay for supper. She wanted to hurry home and tell Mother about her visit, all about little Rose. At the doorway the sisters said goodbye. As she was leaving, Helen turned and faced Maureen. "I wish I had had the courage to have done what you did." Then she started towards the car with Al following behind her.

Chapter Seventy

Two weeks later, on the twenty-second of February, Nora gave birth to her baby, also a little girl. Another Rose. Since Giovanni's mother was also Rose by name, and keeping true to the old custom in Italian families, whereby sons named their firstborn son or daughter after their own parents, this child, too received the name of Rose.

Again Gilda was called upon, this time to be with her own sister to do what she had done for her sister-in-law. But it was much easier going now for Gilda. Nora was just upstairs in the same house, and Gilda slept in her own bed, in her own house. And then, Nora, work-horse that she was, only needed Gilda's attention for two days. On the third day, Nora even made her way down the stairs and into Mama's kitchen. In her arms, she held a tiny bundle wrapped in pink.

"Look what I've brought you," she said, and placed the baby in her mother's arms. Mama was ecstatic to be holding a baby, her own granddaughter. The sunlight shining through the windows, paled in comparison to the glow that lit up the old lady's face. While in her arms, the baby opened wide her eyes and seemed to follow the sound of her grandmother's voice that was cooing and clucking at her. Rosa began rocking her body backwards and forwards in the wheel chair. As she did so, she began singing softly the *ninna nanna*, the lullaby that lulled to sleep every Italian baby ever born. The refrain worked its charm again, and soon this little Rose was fast asleep, pressed close to her grandmother's heart. And for Rosa, it was so good to be *nonna*.

The first Sunday in March arrived unseasonably warm and bright, a good day for a baptism. Al and Giovanni carried their infants in their arms to the church just across from Mama's house. Aptly, the church was under the patronage of Saint Rose of Lima. There, at the font in the vestibule of the church, the priest poured water on the two little heads, placed salt on their tongues, and asked them to abjure Satan and all his works. Speaking for the infants, the godparents vowed that they would. Thereupon, the two little Roses had been made children of God.

The ceremony had been brief, and it took but minutes to cross the street to Mama's. They all trooped into the kitchen. Al took the baby from Maureen's arms. "Here, *nonna*," Al said. He proudly placed his daughter in the cradle of her grandmother's arm. "Nora," he fairly shouted, "put your Rosie in Mama's other arm. I've got to take a picture of this." He fumbled around a few moments with the new box camera he had bought. He focused, and when Mama's ecstatic smile was just right, he snapped away.

"There," he said. "The three most beautiful Roses in the world!"

Chapter Seventy-one

That evening after all the festivities were over, Mike returned to the flat he had rented some time ago in the two-storey house a few blocks from his brickyard. A cot and a hot plate in a small, dark room on the worksite had not seemed to him to constitute much of a home. He hadn't been able to stand the silence and the loneliness after all the workers left the yard at the end of the day. When the chatter and the clatter of the workday was over, he had been left alone, like a watchman in a graveyard. The tiny, two-by-four room in the back of the office reminded him of a hermit's cell. So a few months after Al's marriage, Mike found a rent and moved out of the monk's cell. He wasn't sorry a bit that he had given Al and Maureen the bungalow. True, he had acted on impulse when he told his brother to come back from his honeymoon and live there with his new wife, but he had no regrets over doing it.

Now he was in a house again, just down the street from the yard. He welcomed the sounds he heard in his new place. The slamming of the back door downstairs when the kids ran in and out, and their noisy squabbles didn't bother him in the least. Nor the mother's strident voice when she was scolding her offspring or berating her husband. And it was kind of nice, too, when Mrs. Clancy sent up one of the kids now and then with a slice of freshly baked pie or cake, for the "nice" gentleman upstairs, that nice Mr. Lang, who always paid his rent on time.

The night that Mike arrived home after the baptism, he climbed the back stairs to the flat as usual. He never used the front entrance because at the end of the front hall, a door led into the Clancy kitchen, and it was usually open. The stale reek of cabbage had left its indelible mark over the years, and the whole hallway smelled like shit. After a few sallies through the front, Mike avoided using it. The back staircase was exposed to the open air, and even in winter time, Mike preferred to go up to his flat by that way.

That was the staircase he used tonight. At the top of the stairs, he walked across the rickety, railed porch and went into his kitchen. He took off his jacket and his tie and flung them on the back of a chair. He found himself smiling to himself, thinking: "Here I am, not only uncle, but god-father to both Rosies, Rosie One and Rosie Two." That's how he designated Al's little Rose, and Nora's. Soon the whole family had begun calling the babies in the same way. "They're as cute as a button," he said to himself, "and Mama is the happiest I've ever seen her in a long time. Before you know it, they'll be running after her, calling her *nonna*. Will she love that!"

He made his way into the bedroom and went over to a chest of drawers. He removed his cuff links and tie pin and dropped them into a little tray without looking at what he was doing. Instead, he fixed an intent gaze on an old, sepia photograph framed in gold. Smiling back at him was the figure of a beautiful girl forever young in his mind and heart, exactly the way he last saw her when he departed Italy those long fifteen years ago. He picked up the picture and held it close to his face. He scrutinized the photo, as he had done so often through the many years. He studied the gleam in Adelina's eyes, the little smile on her lips, the contours of her breasts showing above the tight bodice around her waist. In a whisper full of sadness he said to himself, "Adelina, Adelina mia." Then his thoughts turned black. "No, she's not mine. She can never be Adelina mia. " Adelina was lost to him forever. The dreams of his youth, their love for one another, the hopes, the promises they had made to each other then, were beyond fulfillment.

He placed the picture back on the bureau. He slipped off his pants, turned off the light, and got into bed. But his mind was in turmoil. He couldn't sleep. He lay there, restless and agitated. He lay in bed thinking a thousand thoughts. He had come to America a young man with promises to keep, dreams to fulfill, all for her. Instead, whatever he had managed to accomplish here gave him no joy. There, was no purpose to it. The one person it was all to have been done for, was only a phantom, never to know, never to smile over what successes he had achieved in America.

His life in America for the most part, had been spent in a vacuum. Mike realized more than once, that he was living vicariously through the lives of Mama and Papa, Al and Maureen, Nora and Giovanni. "I'm forty years old," he said to himself aloud. "The best years of my life are over. Yeah, I've got a few bucks, things I never would have had if I hadn't come here." He paused. Almost in a shout, he blurted: "I wish to Christ that I had never come here, never heard of America."

Like a bolt, he shot up out of bed. "I'm going back! Dammit! I'm going back. I've got a kid of my own over there. My own flesh and blood, and I've never seen that kid. I don't even know if it's a son or a daughter. But the kid is mine. I've got a right to that kid. Oh, Adelina, Adelina." And he started to cry.

All night long he walked the floor, thinking. Then, when all the details fell into place and he formulated his plans in his mind, only then was he able to return to bed. His heart no longer raced, his head no longer throbbed. He was at peace with himself for the first time in years.

The following Saturday, Al was working on the account books in the quiet of Mike's little office at the brickyard. His brother paid Al well, and the extra money was a boon, especially now with the baby. With this money, his salary at the newspaper office, and the occasional interpreting jobs, put all together, Al was making a comfortable living.

Al glanced at the clock. It was almost five-thirty. A few more columns of figures to balance off, and he would call it quits for the day. So intent was he at his computations, he had not heard his brother open the door and walk in. But he did smell the cigarette Mike was smoking, so he looked up to see Mike coming towards him. With a smile on his face, Mike pulled the pencil from Al's hand. "Enough for tonight," he said.

Al stretched his arms up and above his head, then rubbed the back of his neck. "Yeah. I'm just about done, anyway. Not much to tally up or down, not with the winter slow-down." Then he started to rise from his chair.

"Don't go yet, Al. I want to talk to you for a minute. Got some booze here. Have a drink with me." Mike walked over to the file cabinet, pulled open a drawer and took out a bottle and two glasses. He set them down on the desk. "Frankie's stuff," he murmured, adding, "*buonanima*," the old Italian expression of respect whenever the name of a dead loved one was mentioned.

"Eh," he sighed, and then poured the whiskey. "That's a beautiful kid you got there, brother. And Nora's, too. Two beautiful girls. Mama's as happy as I've ever seen her, over those two kids." Then abruptly he changed the subject. He pointed to the books. "Not much figuring to do there, eh, Al? Things are pretty slow for us during the winter months."

For a moment Al flushed with the panicked thought: "Jesus, he's going to cut me off, tell me to take a hike." He heard Mike's voice go on. "That's why it's a good time for me to go. I want you to handle the place for me while I'm away. I know you can do it, and I'll take care of you, don't worry, for the extra time you put in. By the time things start up again, I'll be back, end of April, beginning of May, I figure. Depends."

A puzzled look crossed Al's face. "Where the hell are you going, for so long a time, Mike?"

For a moment Mike said nothing. He poured another drink in his brother's glass, and then in his own. He swallowed the drink in one gulp. A dreamy look came into his eyes. "I'm going back to the old country." Again he paused. He raised his eyes and looked straight into Al's. "The best part of me is over there, my kid. A kid I've never seen. A son? A daughter? I don't even know that. But my kid. I want to see, touch, put my arms around and kiss that kid of mine. I want to hear it say just once, 'Papa.' Just once more I want to look at Adelina's face, if only to tell her how sorry I am. I want to ask her forgiveness for ruining her life." Then, so quietly that Al barely heard him, he added, "And my own."

His voice picked up. "I didn't have the guts to tell Papa that you guys should leave without me, that I had to stay with Adelina and marry her after what I did. You know, that day in the fields. Instead, I left her to face the music alone. I could have told Papa that I wanted to stay, had to stay with Adelina. Papa and Mama would have understood that. We could have married and no one would have been the wiser. The first time, Al. The only time, and she got pregnant. I should have stayed. I should have stayed with her. I didn't use my head, about anything."

His voice cracked. He shook his head as if to hurl out of it all the remorse, all the guilt he felt. Al went up to Mike and put his arm around his brother's shoulder. He pulled him close.

Al spit out the old cliche: "What's done is done. Besides, I know that you would have gone back to her if there had been something to go back to, if her old man hadn't married her off. You would have done the right thing."

Al removed his arm from around his brother's shoulder. He ran his hand through his own hair. "But Mike, are you doing the right thing now by going back? Can you barge in on their lives if you find them, after fifteen years, and say, 'Hi, I'm your father, kid.' And to Adelina, 'How are you, Adelina?' And what about her; can you walk in on her just like that, after all the time that has gone by? She's got a home, a husband, maybe other kids. Maybe she's happy the way things are. Maybe she's put you and everything that has happened behind her. Maybe, Mike, it's too late to go back, for your sake and everybody else's."

Al saw his brother ball up his fists, and a wild look come into his eyes. It was at that moment that Al realized what torment, what suffering, what regrets his brother had been living with all these past years. He could have bitten his tongue for saying what he had just said to Mike. His eyes clouded over.

Al fairly spit out his next words. "Go ahead, Mike, go. Forget what I just said. In fact, it's the only thing you've got to do, or you'll spend the rest of your life never living in the present, only in the past, thinking of a future that might have been. I see it now. Who knows? Maybe you can change the future for yourself, for Adelina, for the child. Maybe you can change things for the better after all." Al put on his coat. "Good night, Mike. *La Madonna t 'accompagna.*" He headed towards the door to leave. Suddenly, stopping short, he turned to Mike and asked as an after-thought, "What are you going to tell Mama and Papa?"

It only took Mike a second to answer. "That I am going to the old country to contract a bunch of paesani to work in the brickyard." His face broke out in a sheepish smile.

"Sounds good," Al answered quietly. Then he opened the door and walked out into the night. He had a wife and baby to go home to.

On the Saturday evening before his departure for Europe, the next day, Mike stopped by Mama's to say his goodbyes. He had told the family earlier in the week that he was going, and now they were all at Mama's to see him off. Emotions were at a fever pitch in Mama's kitchen. Memories, people, places from the past were being relived again. They talked, they laughed, they remembered together.

Before he finally said his last goodbye, Mike found himself charged with messages to relate, photographs, and little gifts from everyone in America to deliver to his sisters in Italy. And not to forget, when in Scafati, to look up Papa's good friends, Cosimo and Anna Perrelli, from whom he had purchased this very house. Mike's head was filled with the names of people to look up, places to visit, and items to bring back. Mike assented, assuring everyone that he would try his best to do everything they had asked him to do.

Rising from the table around which they were all seated, he said, "I must leave now. Got an early start tomorrow, and I have a few more things to pack yet. One by one, he hugged them all. Lastly he bent over Mama sitting in her wheel chair. He kissed her on the forehead. She took his face in her hands. There was a smile on her lips, but tears in her eyes. She whispered only one word. "*Finalmente!*"

"She knows why I am really going." The thought raced across Mike's mind in a flash. "You can't fool Mama."

Chapter Seventy-two

Ignoring the cold, icy air whistling about his ears, Mike leaned over the ship's rail. He watched intently as the waves below him swelled and fell. Each wave that passed meant that he was that much closer to the land of his birth, to the fate that lay in wait for him there. In cadence with the rolling of the ship over the waves, the lines of a poem repeated themselves over and over in his head:

Bell' Italia, amate sponde,
Pur vi torno a ri veder.
Trema in petto e si confonde
L'alma oppressa dal piacer.

Book-loving Al had come across the lines in a book of Italian poetry in those days when he used to haunt the library. He loved the poem so much, that he copied it over onto a piece of parchment in an exquisite script. Then he framed it and hung it in the office. Underneath, he had translated it into English:

Beautiful Italy, beloved shores,
Yet will I return, thee to behold.
My soul a-tremble within my breast
Confounded is, by joy o'erwhelmed.

The icy March winds off the waters of the Atlantic caused Mike to shiver. Even the heavy, woolen jacket he was wearing was no defense against their bite. Mike returned to his second-class cabin below. How different this crossing was from the first. This time he was on a ship of the White Star Line, with all its amenities. He lay on the bunk, quiet and alone. In his mind's eye, all the images of those awful days he spent in steerage with the other immigrants, those fifteen years ago, flashed across his consciousness. The noise, the babble, the stink of the hold became real again. The stale air, the stench from hundreds of unwashed bodies, from babies' shit-filled diapers, vomit, smelly cheeses, rancid wines, and moldy salamis assailed his nose as if they were now with him in his very cabin.

The call of the steward in the corridor announcing lunch in the second-class dining room jolted him back to the present. As he found his way to his table, he wondered what was on the menu. Chops, stew, potatoes au gratin, chicken? Back in 1906, he had never to wonder about a menu. It was always the same. Mushy macaroni in a watery sauce, or beans.

Ten days after embarcation in New York, Mike stood by the railings of the deck, along with the excited, almost hysterical throngs massed on every deck of the ship which was coming into the Bay of Naples. Off across the waters of the bay, loomed Vesuvius. Majestic against a blue sky, the mountain was as when he left. Somewhere, at its foot lay the fulfillment of his quest.

The ship docked alongside the quay in the Santa Lucia section of the harbor, the very same stretch of shoreline from which he had departed Italy with Papa and his brothers fifteen years ago. Passengers in their eagerness to get off the ship, pushed and shoved one another. He pushed and shoved, too. He was as anxious as the rest of them to get through customs. He followed the mob in line from one station to the next. At last, the formalities at the port of entry were done with.

Out into the open air, the sounds of the city burst upon his ears. On the streets the Neapolitans were in a frenzy of movement. Mike was impatient to be in the midst of it all. Everything about the scene playing before his eyes, was familiar; and, as Odysseus was lured by the song of the Sirens to Italy's enchanting shore, so too, was he. The magic of the Sirens' song was again taking hold. The shouts and curses of the dock workers and the melodious intonations of the street vendors hawking their wares, were music to Mike's ears. All around him, children darted among the horses, carts and cars filing through the streets like columns of ants. With the agility and skill that defied the laws of chance, the urchins weaved in and out among vehicles and animals. When the drivers cursed at them, they thumbed their noses or grabbed at their crotches in gestures of defiance and laughed as they scurried away.

Above all the din, Mike discerned the strains of mandolins and the tinkling of tambourines, and the thumping of drums. Across the way, in the haven of a little *piazzetta*, a band of strolling musicians, the *giullari*, had found an appreciative audience. Mike made his way through the crowds and paused to listen. The performers were dressed as jesters and clowns, and the girl singing, clacked her castanets in time with the rhythm. The song she was singing was an old one that Mike hadn't heard in years. But he recalled it. "Let's hold each other tight," went the refrain. "Let's kiss. Youth passes away quickly." The words stung him like a barb. When the singer finished, he dropped a coin in a tambourine on the ground and walked away with the words of the song repeating themselves in his head.

The growling in his stomach told him he was hungry. Along the Via Caracciolo, at a small *trattoria*, he satisfied his need for nourishment with a dish of pasta and peas, a frittata of squash and eggs, bread, and tomato salad with basil and mozzarella, and a glass of wine to top off the meal. He left a tip amounting to ten cents, American.

A little later, standing on the platform in Garibaldi Station, he looked at his watch. Half-past two. Fifteen miles to the south from where he stood, were his two sisters. He had not seen them in fifteen years. His blood began racing in anticipation of seeing them again. Of course, they would recognize him, he thought. Just as he would recognize them. Enough photographs had been exchanged through the years across the ocean that separated them. Even Carolina in her habit of the Daughters of Charity, had sent a picture of herself at Christmas, in the center of a group of the orphans to whom she had dedicated her life.

The train lumbered on slowly. Mike gazed out the window as the cars passed the little towns and villages dotting the countryside. The vineyards, the olive groves, the orchards of orange and lemon trees, the palm trees, flooded him with a sense of nostalgia. When he alighted at the little whistle-stop station at Scafati, the pungent smell of the earth of the fields on the other side of the tracks caused him to halt his steps. He paused to watch the farmers and their animals in the fields across the way for some minutes. And in his mind he saw himself again and Papa and his brothers as they were in the days of his boyhood.

At length, he turned away and followed his way past the massive stone houses that lined the side streets, alleys, rather that brought him to the piazza. The mother church of the town dominated the square. Across the square was the *Pasticceria Vincenzo*, his brother-in-law's pastry shop. He headed towards it in a quick pace.

Chapter Seventy-three

The reception Mike received at the home of his sister was like a scene straight out of a melodrama. There were cries of surprise, tears, embraces and kisses; and then he was regaled with food and drink, fussed over and attended to as if he were visiting royalty. Time and again, just to reassure herself that he was not a figment of her imagination, his sister Filumena touched his face lovingly, or his arm, or his hair. To her children, he was Zio Michele, their very own uncle from far-away America. Mike remained in his sister's house in Scafati for a week, a time for brother and sister to find each other, to relive the days of their youth, when they were together. But more interesting, more important than recollections of the past, was the filling in of the vacuum created by fifteen years of separation. The days of the week they spent with each other were as minutes.

Often in the late evenings after Filumena's three sons, Mike's nephews, whom he came to know and love in that one week, and when even Vincenzo, her husband had gone to their beds, brother and sister talked late into the night. The recent tragic events of the loss of Mama's leg and Frankie's death were still fresh enough to cause Filumena to shed an abundance of tears, so that Mike refused to speak anymore about them whenever his sister made mention of them. But Filumena insisted he tell her every detail of the lives of the family in America, time and time again.

And on Mike's part, he listened as Filumena narrated in minutest detail what she told him more than once, about the destruction of Bosco in 1906; how Mama and the girls had turned the old blacksmith shed into their living quarters; how, often they had had to make a meal out of the bitter greens and wild onions they were able to gather from the fields and the roadsides; how Mama had made bread out of cow corn; how Mama had made skirts for the girls out of old shawls.

"If it hadn't been for the money Papa began sending, who knows! Eh!" And to accent the misery the women had undergone in those days, she twirled her extended thumb and index finger in a semi-circle in front of her face.

But not all the days of the week Mike spent with his sister were spent just in talk. On the very next morning after his arrival in Scafati, Filumena brought him to the convent of the Daughters of Charity where his other sister, Carolina, now Suor Maria Giuseppe, was a nun. The convent was located in Pompei, the next town over, and after a half-hour's walk, they were there asking to speak to their sister; Filumena explained the purpose of their visit, and a nun escorted them into the waiting room of the convent.

Mike sat nervously in the reception parlor of the convent. Not a sound was to be heard, except the ticking of a clock hanging on otherwise bare walls. A table sat in the middle of the room, and around it, a half-dozen chairs, straight-backed and made of hard wood. They seemed uncomfortable, and they were, as Mike found out when he took his seat in one of them. A solitary crucifix hung above a doorway through which he and Filumena had entered. At the far end of the room, there was another doorway.

"She will be here soon," whispered Filumena to Mike. "I know. It is always the same. I have been here other times before."

Even as she finished her words, Mike heard the opening of a door, to see a nun enter. He stood up respectfully. At first he did not recognize this nun. Her face was framed by the coif and wimple, and her form was shapeless in the dark habit that reached down to her toes. She walked noiselessly and unhurriedly across the room towards them; Mike's eyes lit up in recognition as the nun continued her decorous pace, halting a few feet away from him.

There was a moment of awkward silence. Mike was uncomfortably embarrassed. Does one dare to kiss a nun, even if she is his own sister? He bowed reverently and kissed her hand. The nun suddenly burst into laughter. "What! Am I a bishop, that you kiss my hand? Am I not your sister, dear brother mine?" She reached up, took his hand in hers, then leaned over to kiss him on both cheeks. "Michele, Michele, dear brother. Oh, how good to see you, how good to see you again." There were tears in her eyes, in Mike's eyes, in Filumena's eyes.

She took both her brother and her sister each by a hand and led them into the convent garden. There, in the privacy of the quiet retreat, the three of them passed the morning hours in warm reunion. They talked, they reminisced, they laughed. How different the two sisters were. Mike could not but note how unlike they were. Carolina spoke calmly, without gestures; her movements were slow and dignified. She listened politely to what Michele said, never interrupted his words nor asked him to repeat. There was an aura of peace about her that seemed to flow from her to him, and Mike felt himself transported to an unreal world where there was no pain, no sorrow. Even as he told her about Mama's sufferings and Frankie's death, Carolina gave no outburst of grief, no gesture of dismay. Just a fleeting moment when she closed her eyes, did she seem to be thinking deeply; and a slight fall of the shoulders was all that Mike noticed of any reaction.

When Mike stopped talking, she turned to Filumena. "And how are the boys?" In a rush of words, Filumena went into raptures about her sons. Mike took the opportunity to study his sister. In spite of her nun's habit, she was Carolina, the same sister he knew when they were children together. Carolina, who was always ready to put herself last for the comfort of her brothers and sisters. The same Carolina, even-tempered, always with a ready smile. She was the sister who always gave her pennies to the ragged gypsy children begging in the piazza on feast days. He looked at her, and remembered how he and his brothers used to tease her for giving away her pennies instead of buying torrone or gelato for herself, as they did. "Never mind," she would say. "The gypsy children are God's poor, and more in need of bread than I am of torrone."

The sound of a bell that summoned the nuns to the recitation of prayer jarred him back from his reflections of those days. It also brought an end to the visit. The three of them began their walk along the garden path, and once more they entered the reception parlor. Mike promised that he would return once more before he left for America. Then he took his sister's hand and into it he placed an envelope bulging with lire. "Buy some torrone for your little orphans." He smiled and walked away. "And some bread for the gypsy children, too!" he called across the room.

Chapter Seventy-four

Mike and Filumena began their leisure walk back to Scafati. All along the way home they talked about the visit they had had at the convent with Carolina. They hadn't gone too far when Mike suddenly stopped. "Tell me. Truly, she is happy in that life, is she not?" Mike asked. Filumena shook her head, her lips pulled down. "For me, such a life I could not live. My man and my boys, they are my life. Carolina, she has found her man in the good Jesus, and the orphans are her children. Each of us has a different path to walk. Carolina has found her path, and she walks it. She is content with her lot in life, as I am with mine." The two walked on a little further in silence, and then Mike spoke again. "You know, I have never seen the old Pompeii. The ruins, I mean. Let me take the boys tomorrow to see them. I want to get to know my nephews. Three brothers, just like me and Alfredo and Francesco."

The next day's excursion to the ruins with his nephews would prove to be the happiest, the best day that Mike spent in Scafati. It was a relief for Mike to be in the carefree company of kids, where there was not a serious talk about sad events or memories dredged up out of the past. He and the boys were on a lark, and Mike felt like a kid himself. The boys ran and scampered here and there among broken columns of the town's forum, chased each other up and down the seats of the amphitheater and hid from each other in the House of the Vetii. Mike had occasion more than once to smile to himself at catching twelve year-old Vincenzo, the oldest, study in fascination the mosaics and paintings of the nude, buxom matrons and goddesses adorning the walls of the houses of the rich. Once he nudged his nephew with his elbow, and with a mischievous wink of his eye, he said, "Nice, eh?" The boy gave a sheepish grin and started to turn red. Mike laughed out loud.

On their walk through the ruins, Mike chuckled. "I could fix this place up in no time with my blocks. Did you fellows know that your uncle is a *capomastro* in the art of building?" The boys listened in awe to hear him tell of his early days working with the mason, Angelo, and then about his blocks. Mario, the middle son, spoke up excitedly, "Zio, will you take me someday to America? I do not wish to be a pastry cook like my brother Vincenzo. You will teach me how to make the blocks and I will work with you, I will help you." Mike rumpled the boy's hair and answered, "Gladly, if that's what you want, and if your mama will let you come." The boy was all smiles at his uncle's answer.

The morning went by fast, and their uncle said, "Are you boys hungry? It is noon and my stomach says, 'Hey, Michele, are you not going to feed this belly?' Enough of this. Let us go to the *trattoria* on the piazza for a dish of pasta, then afterwards a nice gelato to cool us off." The boys needed no persuasion, and they all made their way out of the past and into the present, back to town, a meal, and home. It was a day Mike would recount to Mama with pleasure.

For the next two days, the boys' father hauled Michael around to visit every relative of his in Scafati. His relatives, Mike's brother-in-law explained, would feel slighted not to have been introduced to his wife Filumena's brother from far off America. "Such an oversight, they would never forgive," Vincenzo said, and so Michael went with Vincenzo, who dragged him from one house to another. Not to have gone with Vincenzo would have been considered an unpardonable breech of etiquette and custom, and without doubt, Mike would have been tagged as a *screanzato*, a person of ill-breeding. Mike understood the obligations of the guest in the house of a host, and so he accompanied Vincenzo willingly.

In each house that he visited with his brother-in-law, he was treated warmly, as a member of the family. He drank endless cups of espresso, endless glasses of wine, and ate with seeming pleasure, whatever delicacy was placed before him. To have refused the profuse offerings of the host, would have been a blatant example of *mala figura*. And so, with a smile on his face, Mike ate and drank, and in turn regaled his hosts with the account of his experiences, his life in America. They hung on to his every word, as if Michael were an oracle.

In every house he went, it was the same. One host had a cousin in Boston, another host, a great nephew in Philadelphia, another, an uncle in Hoboken. They all charged Mike with messages to relay to them upon his return. No matter how much Mike tried to explain that these places were not just around the corner from each other, his protestations were met with disbelief. Surely in America, everything is easy to do, a land where people travel about from place to place with speed and ease. Michael smiled, listened attentively, and promised he would try. That satisfied them, and when he left they showered him with their blessings for a safe voyage and a reminder to look up this cousin, that uncle, and when he was gone, they said among themselves that Vincenzo was certainly fortunate to have a brother-in-law of such *bella figura*.

By Thursday, Mike was worn out. He woke up late. The house was quiet, and when he came into the kitchen, he saw Filumena at the table snapping green string beans. Her husband was in the shop; the children were at school. As soon as she caught sight of her brother, she dropped the beans in her hands and rose from the table. "Ah, Michele, a good sleep you had for yourself. Good! That Vincenzo, pulling you here and pulling you there! Go wash yourself now, and I will have your breakfast on the table by the time it takes you to clean yourself."

True to her word, when Mike returned, he found a steaming cup of coffee, slices of bread and a plate of fruit at his place at the table. "Eat, eat," she ordered, and went on snapping the beans. He had taken a few sips of coffee and a few bites of the bread, then laid down the cup, and began talking.

"Tomorrow," he said, "I must go to Bosco. All the aunts and uncles and the cousins, I must see them all." Filumena nodded in assent. "Ah, si, of course. You must see them all."

He went on to ask first about this aunt, and then that aunt, this uncle, and then that uncle. He asked about friends and neighbors of the old days in Bosco. He hesitated. He looked at his sister and began, "And of, eh, and of..."

"Adelina? It is of Adelina you wish to know, is it not true? I was wondering how long it would be before you mentioned her name." Filumena let out a long sigh. With her head lowered, she wiped her aproned lap as if brushing away crumbs. She raised her eyes to his, those eyes of his pleading for her to speak. His sister reached across the table and took his hand in hers, and began stroking it.

"Only this can I tell you, dear brother mine. In the years after you left her, I saw her but once. In 1910, or perhaps it was 1911, her father died. And it was at his funeral that I last spoke to her. I shed tears on that day, not for the father, but for the daughter. And her tears—they were not the tears for the father, but for you. Perhaps others thought that her tears were the dutiful weeping of a daughter for a father, but I knew better. In seeing me, she saw you; and when she embraced me, she was embracing you."

Mike tried to quell the tears beginning to blur his vision. Filumena dabbed her own eyes beginning to fill, with the corner of her apron.

Almost in a whisper, she told him: "I promised her I would never tell you what I am about to say. She made me promise on the grave of her father that I should never tell. It was your child, of course, she gave birth to, but she had no regrets. Instead, she said that she felt only happiness because in this child, she had a part of you. Because of that, her father's fury and the scorn of the others towards her, meant little to her. This child of love was all there was that now gave meaning to her life. Michele, she sacrificed herself for your sake. You had your fortune to pursue, hopes to realize in America, and she would not stand in your way, so she said nothing. The rest, you know. Her father rushed her into marriage, and away from Bosco."

Filumena picked up the bowl of beans and rose from the table. She threw the beans into a pot of boiling water. Mike remained silent in his chair. Then he heard his sister's voice say from where she stood, "The child is a girl, Michele. Her name is Rosa."

Mike flew up from his seat. He rushed to his sister's side. He grabbed her arms. "Where are they? Where is Adelina now, and my daughter? Tell me, tell me, Filumena. You know the place. Now tell me, please, for the love of God. It is for this reason that I have come back, to see Adelina and the child, if only from afar. Filumena, Filumena." His head fell to her shoulder, and it began to shake from side to side, buried in the crook of her neck. His sister lifted his head and looked at his face intently through the tears that were beginning to form in her eyes.

"Should you do this thing, go to them, after all the years? Would it not be better to let things stay as they are?" Filumena hesitated for a moment. "She is mother to that man's child also, so she told me at the time we talked together. There perhaps now may even be others. Should you really want to go to San Sebastiano, now?" Her face went white, and she clapped her hand to her mouth. She had let the cat out of the bag. Now, her brother knew where to find Adelina and Rosa. She regained her composure and put her hand to Michele's cheek.

"Well, then. Yes, that is where you will find them, Adelina and your daughter, in San Sebastiano." Filumena's tears were rolling down her face. Mike pulled out a handkerchief from his pocket and wiped away her tears. Quietly he asked, "And what is the man's name, the name of Adelina's husband, Filumena?" His voice quavered at the word "husband." I must know, if I am to find Adelina and Rosa. Sister mine, for the love you bear me, tell me."

As if she were afraid to say, Filumena said in a whisper, "Pandolfi, Eugenio Pandolfi. At that time when I spoke to Adelina, she told me that her husband owned vineyards in San Sebastiano, and made his living by transporting his wines and his grapes to Naples. That is all I know, that is all I know." Mike patted her cheek and left the house.

Chapter Seventy-five

Mike sat looking out the window as the train made its way to Bosco from Scafati. It was a short ride, but he had enough time to go over in is mind all that his sister had told him. He looked out at the farms and vineyards he passed, but didn't see them. Over and over in his mind were his sister's words and the names "Adelina, Rosa, Adelina, Rosa." The wheels seemed to be saying them too. "San Sebastiano, Eugenio Pandolfi, Eugenio Pandolfi." And again, "Rosa, Rosa." The girl had to be thirteen or fourteen years old by now. What did she look like? Was she pretty? Did she resemble him or did she look like Adelina? He remembered Adelina's face when he first saw her, a pretty girl of fourteen.

His Rosa must look like that. He couldn't imagine a girl looking like him. Then Filumena's words flashed across his mind. She had said the same things Al had said, should he do this? Should he dare set his eyes on Adelina and this daughter whom he had never seen? As Al had said, he thought, "Should I dare intrude on their lives now? I haven't been a part of their lives since the day I left Adelina, nor since the day the child was born." He closed his eyes for a minute, then flew them open. "Yes," he said to himself, "I've got to see them. To see them together, happy and well. Then I will be able to go back to America, content with myself for the rest of my days. That's all I want, to see them with my own eyes."

He got off the train at Bosco. He was calm, resolute in his decision to carry through with his determination to see Adelina again, and his daughter.

The two days Mike spent in Bosco in the homes of his aunts and uncles, who were the sisters and brothers of Mama and Papa, went by in a whirlwind of floods of tears, embraces, kisses, food and drink. It was not the ordeal it had been with Vincenzo; these were family, and the stories they told and retold brought back a flood of memories to him. They all laughed and cried together in the recounting of events of those days long ago when he was a child in their midst.

Finally, on the second day, his last day in Bosco, Luciano, a cousin his own age, and with whom he had shared many a boyhood adventure, took Mike to all the sites and haunts that remained of the old Bosco they had known together as boys. Much was changed in Bosco after the catastrophe of 1906, and many of the old landmarks were gone. Lastly, Luciano took hold of Mike and said, "Come, I will take you to the old homestead, where it used to be." It was the one place that Mike's heart ached to see.

On the way, Luciano said to him: "Michele, you will not know the place. Everything of those days is gone. But you will see for yourself."

Luciano brought Mike to a site Mike did not recognize. When they alit from the car, Luciano said, "This is it." Mike looked around him in bewilderment. There was nothing he could recognize of the place where he had been born. Not a vestige remained of the old massive stone house or the forge. The well from which he used to draw water was gone; there was no longer the lemon orchard, or Papa's vineyards. Even the fields where he and Papa and his brothers used to toil under the hot sun to grow the crops that fed them, had disappeared. Where once the green of fields, the purple of grape clusters on the vine, the brown of the rich earth had scented the air in a blend of fragrances, now Mike saw rows of houses and shops. The houses were ugly—square pillboxes of cement and mortar. They were all of the same styling, as if they had been poured from a mold. A study in monotony. The facade of each of the houses was the same, with the front entry in the same place, the same number of windows facing the street, two balconies ringed in wrought iron, jutting out over the street below. Houses all painted white, where the only distinct touch of individuality was to be seen in the differing colors of the shutters and doors. Some in blue, some in green, some in yellow.

For a minute, Mike closed his eyes to block out what he was seeing, and he tried to recreate in his mind, the beauty that once was. He and Al and Frankie crossing the fields at the end of the day, washing and sporting around the well, Mama calling them to hurry, the roses by the door of the house. He opened his eyes and the images faded, as he looked on the stark reality before him.

That night Michael left Bosco to return to his sister in Scafati. Along the way, he was overwhelmed by a deep feeling of sadness. His mind was crowded with a thousand images from the past and the present. A hodge-podge of people and places. He felt emotionally drained, and more so, when his thoughts turned to Adelina and what he might find in San Sebastiano. The events of his life, past and present, unrolled before his eyes, as if coming off a movie reel. He wavered between feelings of elation and despair. By the time he arrived in Scafati, his mind was in a state of utter confusion.

But the boisterous welcome by his nephews and the warmth of Filumena's smile and words, drove away the dark clouds from his weary brain. In no time at all, he was telling the family about his stay in Bosco. He ate Filumena's good supper, drank a few glasses of good wine, and was ready for bed.

After a good night's sleep, refreshed and self-confident again, he said his goodbyes to his sister in the morning. He insisted on going alone to the station to board the train for San Sebastiano. His parting words to his sister were short: "I don't know how long I will be away. But do not worry. When I have found what I went to find, I shall return." He swung around and started to walk away. A little way off, he turned to them, waved and shouted, "Don't worry. See you when I get back." The family waved back, and Filumena murmured, "Go with God, brother mine. Please God, you will find what you are seeking." She and the others went back into the house.

San Sebastiano was situated on the mountain's northern base, directly opposite Bosco, straight as the crow flies. The train which Michael boarded began chugging on its circuitous route that followed an arc swinging east and north. Looking out the window of the train, Mike read the signs of the stations of the towns through which the train passed. First Bosco, then Terzigno, and beyond that, San Giuseppe Vesuviano. Then Ottaviano, Somma Vesuviana, Santa Anastasia, and last, San Sebastiano.

The train came to a stop at San Sebastiano's little station-house. Mike descended from the car onto the little, deserted platform, and his heart began to pound. His fate lay here, in this old, insignificant, unimportant little village. He had crossed three thousand miles of ocean to come to this place.

As he began his walk off the platform and into the streets of the village, old doubts started running through his mind. Had he come to a world in which he had no place, no right to be? He cast aside those thoughts, and said aloud to himself, "I am here now. Adelina is here somewhere. My daughter is here. I must go through with it. I won't turn my back on them again. I did that once. I can't, I won't do it again." He felt better with himself. "No more, no more vacillating, Mike!"

He arrived at the town piazza, and when he spotted the church, his blood rushed through his veins. It was there, where he had to first begin his search for Adelina and the child. He turned his gaze away from the church, and scanned the rest of the piazza. A few old *palazzi*,—the homes of the town's well-to-do; a *trattoria* and some shops. Across the square he spied The Three Fountains Pensione, to which he directed his steps.

He opened the door to the modest, little boarding house, and as he did, a little bell above the door began to tinkle. Out came the proprietor. Spotting the valise in Mike's hand, the man's eyes lit up at the prospect of a customer. "Ah, *buon giorno, signore, buon giorno.*" By the cut of Mike's clothes, the proprietor guessed that the traveler was a foreigner. An American perhaps? Or maybe English. Quite a few of these foreigners came to the towns at the base of Vesuvius to marvel at the sight of it and walk up the paths to its crater in order to snap countless photographs. What fools they must be, these crazy foreigners, to "ooh" and "aah" over a mountain. Do they not have mountains in their own countries?

Keeping such thoughts to himself, the man fairly tripped over his feet in the rush to accommodate the guest. A nice room overlooking the square for the signore? A comfortable, bed-bug free bed; the toilet just down the hall; and of course, The Three Fountains, it goes without saying, is noted throughout the region for its cleanliness. All the way up to the second floor and to the room, the fellow went on singing the praises of his establishment. Once in the room itself, he led Mike immediately to the window to admire the view of the square, the church, and the mountain. "*Bella vista, no, signore*? Look, look with your own eyes!" Then he went to the bed, pulled back the coverlet so that Michael could see how clean the sheets were. He took Mike's hand and pressed it against the mattress to test its firmness.

Mike asked the price of the room for a week's stay, and the man's, eyes lit up. Ah! a week. Nice. But before Mike got to know the price, he had to listen to the man's sad tale of woe—how hard life was in this little town; how hard it was to make a living; how the government crushed the little people with taxes, taxes and more taxes. Why, did the signore know that the government even taxed a house for every window it had!

Finally he said: "Since you are staying the week, signore, five thousand lire. I get eight hundred lire for the day, but since you are staying for a week, a little discount for you, eh?" Mike didn't argue the point; he let the fellow have his little victory. He didn't care about the three or four hundred lire he was being gouged. Besides, Mike knew that half of what the old soul said about the difficulty of life here was true enough. He took the room without protest, and the happy landlord was elated and more convinced than ever, in his belief that all foreigners were gullible. He left the room, and Mike began his unpacking.

The room was small. It held just a bed, a nightstand and a small chest of drawers. Mike emptied his valise and put away his things. Then he went to the window and looked out. The square was empty of people. It was the siesta hour, and both houses and shops were shuttered tight. He hadn't eaten all day, except for a cup of coffee and some slices of bread that morning. And he knew there was no chance of getting something to eat now. No matter. He was too keyed up to eat, anyway. He removed his jacket, opened his shirt collar, and without taking off his shoes, he lay down on the bed. He closed his eyes and before long, fell into a fitful sleep.

Chapter Seventy-six

Noises coming from below, woke up Michael. He opened his eyes with a start to find himself in a strange room. It took him a moment to realize where he was. He walked to the window and looked down on the square. It was alive with people strolling, talking, gesticulating. A few donkey carts were clip-clopping from one end of the piazza to the other. The shutters of the shops were open. At the *trattoria* there were people sitting at tables in the open air, dining and drinking. At the "Bar Vesuvio," where, in spite of its name, no alcoholic beverages were served—only coffee, soft drinks and sandwiches—knots of young men stood lounging outside. With cigarettes hanging out of their mouths, they were busy ogling the pretty girls walking in the company of their mothers or aunts as chaperones. The sotto-voce comments they exchanged now and then, among themselves, left no doubts as to what was on their minds.

Mike smiled to himself. The scene brought back memories of those days when he and the other young bucks of his time used to do the same ogling and wise-cracking. He and his pals used to go to the piazza of Bosco to eye the girls passing by, to give a furtive wink, to blow a furtive kiss. The female response, then as now, was either a sly smile and maidenly lowering of the eyes, or a sneer of disdain. But it was the same game neither boy nor girl ever tire playing.

The rumbling in the pit of Mike's stomach broke into his thoughts. His hunger was keen now, and his stomach would not be put off. So he put on his jacket, descended the stairs of the pensione, and was in the piazza in minutes. He ambled across to the *trattoria*, all the while being eyed by the curious locals who spotted him for the stranger in their midst that he was. Mike, however, was oblivious to their stares. He wanted only to satisfy his gnawing hunger and then think out what he must do. The few salutations he received as he headed to the eatery, he ignored. He walked straight to the restaurant and sat down at one of the outdoor tables. When he had ordered and was served, he ate the dish of pasta set before him and the wine, barely tasting the food. Deep in thought, he looked steadily at the church; it was there, he knew, that he would find out where he must start his search for Adelina and his daughter.

He counted the months from April on his fingers. Give or take a few weeks one way or the other, the birth of his daughter had to have taken place either in December, or if late, in January. The baby would no doubt have been baptized within a month of the birth, that being the usual practice. Once he found Rosa's name in the baptismal registry in that church across from where he was sitting, all he needed to know to find her, should be there.

The sun was beginning to set. It was too late in the day to begin looking through records; besides, priests don't like to be disturbed at supper time. Tomorrow he would attend the daily Mass in the morning, and afterwards go to the sacristy located in the rear of the church and talk to the priest.

From the proprietor of the pensione, Mike learned that the last Mass of the morning was at eight o'clock. He awoke at seven the next day, and by a quarter to eight, he was making his way to the church. It was a glorious morning, and the ringing of the church bells from the campanile, was a song of joy to his ears. In America, the sound of church bells was a rarity.

Inside the church, a few old women, a couple of ancient men getting on the good side of the eternity they were close to entering, made up the congregation. The Mass was a low one, and as Mike listened to the familiar Latin ritual of his younger days, his soul was flooded with an aura of peace that he had not sensed in a long time.

The priest turned to the worshippers. Making the sign of the cross, he murmured the final blessing: *"Benedicat vos in nomine Patris et Filii et Spiritus sancti."*

The church emptied, but Mike remained to recite a fervent prayer to Saint Anthony, the saint of miracles. Then he left the pew and walked up the nave of the church. He genuflected before the tabernacle and made his way to the sacristy. He knocked gently at the door and entered.

"Buon giorno," he said on entering. An old priest, his face covered in white stubble, turned to Mike, and continued to divest himself of his vestments. He croaked back in acknowledgment of Mike's salutation, *"Si?"* With a pleasant smile on his face, Mike introduced himself to the priest as an Italo-American by name of Michele Porto. He hated to lie to the holy man, but he thought it prudent not to take the chance that someone might have heard of the name Alanga in relation to either Adelina or the child.

Would it be possible, he inquired, to look through the baptismal records of the parish? He was here in San Sebastiano, on a tour of Italy and would soon be returning to America. But he had thought it would be interesting to come to this place where his family had originated generations ago, and perhaps gain some knowledge of the family's genealogy. If it would not be an inconvenience, could he not satisfy his curiosity by looking through the church's records?

Just as he finished his made-up story, Mike took out his wallet and made a show of extracting two notes of one hundred lire each. "Of course, padre," he said as he smiled broadly, "I would not ask you to spend your valuable time going through the pages, since I am not sure of dates. But it is a nice morning, and I have nothing better to do. If I could find some information to bring back to the family, it would make them happy to know something more of our origins."

"True, true," the priest answered joyfully, glad that he was relieved of the boring, time-consuming task of scanning page after page; besides, his eyesight was poor. And the old man's mind was already filled with visions of the bountiful feast the two hundred lire would provide. He smacked his lips and pocketed the notes. More sprightly now in his movements, the priest went over to a ponderous cabinet from which he removed two large leather-bound tomes. Michael went over to assist him.

"Thank you, thank you, my son. You will find the baptisms, marriages and deaths recorded for the past one hundred years in the books. Before that time, we no longer have records. They were destroyed, the older volumes, in the disaster of 1906. But now I leave you to your search, and I hope you find what you are seeking. When you have finished, be so kind as to replace them." He shuffled to the door and left Michael alone by himself. Only the ticking of an old clock disturbed the silence in the room.

The first volume Mike picked up bore the dates 1800-1875, and he pushed it aside. He flipped hurriedly through the pages of the second volume, 1875-1920. He thumbed through the pages rapidly until he came to the year 1906. He studied every entry for the month of December of that year. Nothing. January, 1907, nothing. Then at last, there it was, what he was looking for.

In a near, precise, beautiful script, he found the words that made his heart skip a beat:

Scarpa, Rosa, baptized February 14, 1907
Date of Birth: January 15, 1907, San Sebastiano, Provincia
di Napoli.
Mother: Scarpa, Adelina
Father: _____
Place of residence: Via delle Vigne, Numero 10

Mike read the entry over and over again. So, Pandolfi had not given the child his name. In one way Mike was relieved that he hadn't. But then, again, those old feelings of remorse, guilt and sadness began to overtake him. By not giving the child a name, she was then branded as illegitimate. Mike shuddered to think of the shame that both Adelina and Rosa must have had to have suffered as the targets of gossip and derision in this little village where everybody knew everyone else's affairs.

His eyes closed, and the image of Adelina appeared before him, as she was on that day so long ago, as they lay together in the field. They had united themselves in the act of love, ecstatically overcome by passion, and that act of ultimate union had become for them, the act of ultimate disunion.

Mike closed the registry. He carried both tomes to the cabinet where he placed them on a shelf. Quietly he left the sacristy. Once outside, he walked pensively along the path that led from the church to the deserted piazza. The scent of flowers beginning to bloom along the path's borders, filled the warm May air. Roses. The beautiful roses Mama loved so much, lined the way to the gate. He thought of his mother, her courage, her strength through all the adversities she had undergone in her life. The thought of her gave him a renewal of courage. Filled with reawakening hope, he cast off his somber mood and hastened his steps across the piazza, back to his room in the pensione.

Chapter Seventy-seven

When he entered his room, Mike went straight to the little night table beside the bed. On it lay a little street map of San Sebastiano that he had purchased at the tobacco shop the previous day. He opened the folded map and spread it out on the bed, his eyes hungry to find the Via delle Vigne. And then, there it was, on the edge of town, a thin ribbon of black ink on the map. With his finger, he traced the route from the pensione all the way along the Corso. At the end of the Corso, Via delle Vigne lay to the left. At most, it was but a walk of a mile or so.

Mike folded the map, put it back on the table and picked up an envelope. He put it in his shirt pocket, close to his breast and patted it lovingly. On his way out of the pensione, he stopped to pass the time of day with the owner of the establishment, whom by now, he was calling by the man's first name. *"Buon giorno, Carlo.* Beautiful day for a walk, eh?"

"Ah, si, certo, certo."

Before the old man could say more, Mike was out the door.

It was Saturday; the piazza was filled with women, mostly, who were haggling with vendors who had set up their carts along the periphery of the square. Mike stopped for a moment to watch a group of kids playing *morra.* The sight made him recall the days when he and his brothers, and Papa, too, sometimes, amused themselves in the same way. The object of the game was to call out a number as each of the two players thrust out so many fingers of one hand. The winner was the one who had called out the correct number of fingers. Sometime, they played for a little pot of a few *centesimi.*

When a squabble broke out between the boys he was watching, Mike turned away smiling to himself. He could still hear the accusations of cheating the boys were hurling at one another as he started down the Corso. The further he traveled along the avenue, the more rural the area became. He was coming into the countryside. Finally, the Corso came to an end, meeting the Via delle Vigne. Turning left, Mike began the gradual ascent of the via, as it snaked up the slopes of the mountain. As he traveled along its length, he understood that the road had been aptly named. This was good wine country; acres and acres of vineyards covered the slopes. Old stone farmhouses were set back off the road, each one at a distance from the other. The higher he climbed up the foothill, the lower the numbers on the gates became. Then his eye caught sight of the number 10, over a trellised gateway. Michael's heart began to thump rapidly.

"Good Jesus, good Jesus," he murmured to himself. Like a thief in the night, he crossed the road and sidled along the low brambles that grew on either side of the gate. Off in the distance on the slopes beyond the house, he spied the figures of a man and a boy working among the vines. He walked up to the gateway and stood by a post of the trellis. The climbing ivy that canopied the trellis provided a perfect place of concealment.

Spying through the leaves, he saw the door of the house suddenly open. A little dog darted out, followed by a boy about five or six years old.

"Come here, Gigi, come back and play with me. Don't run away. Come back." But the puppy sped forward straight down the path to the half-opened gate. Just as he sprang beyond the gate, Michael scooped up the little mongrel in his arms. The breathless little boy stopped short when he came upon Michael holding his puppy.

Mike was smiling as he handed the animal back to the boy. "He's a cute little thing. What is his name?" Before the child could answer, he added "It's a good thing that I came along and caught him. He runs faster than you do." And they both, the boy and the man began to laugh.

Then the tyke spoke. "Bad doggie. I only want to play with you." He looked up at Mike. "His name is Gigi."

"So. His name is Gigi. That's a nice name. But maybe you shouldn't play too rough with him, and he won't run away. And tell me, little fellow, what is your name?"

"Bruno, Bruno Pandolfi." Then, with his pudgy finger he pointed to the slope and said, "And that's my papa and my brother Eugenio. I have a big sister, too, but Papa always has to slap her." Mike's face lost all its color; a lump as big as a chestnut formed in his throat. For an instant, he lost his breath. Regaining his composure, he reached into his pants pocket and withdrew a couple of coins. With his other hand he pulled out an envelope from his shirt pocket.

"Is your mama inside the house?" The boy nodded "yes." Mike handed the coins to the boy. "These are for you," he said. "Will you be a good boy, and give this to Mama?" He gave the envelope to Bruno. In a minute, with the coins and the envelope in one hand, and his puppy safe in the crook of his arm, Bruno skipped away up the path to the house. Mike saw him disappear into the house; then for what seemed like an eternity to him, he kept his gaze glued to the doorway.

Suddenly, through the foliage, Mike saw a woman come to the door. Close to her breast, she was clutching the photograph of herself as a young girl, taken those many years ago when her eyes and smile were full of love for the man she had given it to. Mike stepped away from the shadow of the vines and into the open archway of the trellis. When she saw him, the woman began racing towards him down the path. As Mike saw her coming ever closer, his vision became blurred by the tears beginning to well up in his eyes. A few feet away from him, the woman stopped short, threw up her arms over her head, then covered her face with her hands. Tears bled through her fingers, as she sobbed his name over and over again, muffled though the words were. "Michele, Michele, Michele."

"Adelina, cara Adelina, Adelina mia." Mike's voice was choked with emotion as he uttered her name. He went up to her and gently removed her hands from her face. The moment he touched her, the agony and heartache of fifteen years of separation both vanished and renewed itself at the same time. Through their tears, the two of them studied each other's face. When his vision cleared, Mike saw that the woman standing before him was not the same Adelina whose face had been etched in his memory all these past years.

The woman who now stood before him was an Adelina he could scarcely recognize. Those once big, beautiful, brown eyes had narrowed and the sparkle was gone out of them. The face, once glowing with smoothness and freshness of the young girl he remembered, was now gaunt and care worn. The hair was streaked with wide bands of gray. The hardness of the life she must have endured during the past fifteen years was plain to see in the lines etched across her brow and around her eyes. And the skin of her face was leathery, while her hands were callused and rough.

But then she smiled, and became transformed before Michael's eyes into the beautiful Adelina of the past, and Michael, with a yearning to hold her in his arms and wipe away her tears, and kiss her, and stroke her hair, moved towards her. She backed away with a look of wild alarm on her face, as if being accosted by a stranger. It was then that Mike realized that the expanse of time and ocean could never be bridged. The feeling of despair that he felt at that moment when she drew away from him was like a stab to the heart. Adelina was Adelina Pandolfi now, the mother of that man's two sons. In that circle he had no place. She could never be his again; he could never be hers. The only common bond between them at this moment in time, was their daughter, Rosa.

His heart dropped to his feet. All he could manage to say, with a sadness in his voice that mirrored heartache, was, "How has it been with you, Adelina?" A look of unmistakable anguish crossed her face, and it mirrored all the pain, all the heartbreak and suffering of the past fifteen years. The look on her face was answer enough for Michael. She turned her face to the side in order to avoid his gaze. Suddenly her whole body began to shudder uncontrollably, and she burst into a torrent of tears. Again Michael tried to approach her, but again, she drew back. In between sobs, Michael heard her moan his name over and over again. Finally, picking up her head, she said, "You must go now, Michele." She whispered, and it was as if she could not bring herself to say the words: "My husband and my son will be coming down from the mountain for their meal. I must go now."

"Adelina, I have so much to say to you. I must see you again. I must see Rosa. Tomorrow is Sunday. To what Mass do you go? I will be there."

She merely looked at Michael and said quietly, "I do not go to the church anymore. But I go there, and she pointed to the end of the road. In the distance, in the direction to which she was pointing, Mike's eyes rested on a covered shrine to the Madonna, another of the typical makeshift oratories that dotted the Italian countryside everywhere. "I talk to the Madonna there, just she and I together.

The thought came to Mike: "Away from the stares and the whisperings of the old crones who delight in the misfortunes of others."

"You will find me in the shrine at seven in the morning, while *he* and the children are asleep." She said that, turned, and quickly walked back to the house. Before she entered, Adelina glanced back toward the road. Mike was in view. He waved, and she disappeared into the house.

Chapter Seventy-eight

Mike had been waiting for at least half an hour in the little chapel-like shrine. The small, roofed enclosure looked like a mausoleum. A statue of Our Lady of Sorrows, her heart pierced by swords, stood on a pedestal. Flowers and the stubs of candles lay at the foot of the statue. A stone slab bench sat before the figure of Our Lady. In the tomb-like silence, Michael sat on the bench, his head bowed, one hand holding up his forehead. Quietly he spoke to the Madonna, laying at her feet all the pain of his broken heart, begging her help. Then he heard a slight rustling. He turned to see Adelina. Her head was covered in a lace mantilia of black. She was standing at the entrance, and in her hands she was holding a bouquet of flowers. Mike rose immediately and called out her name. "Adelina, oh Adelina." He gave her a smile and walked to her.

With a note of sadness in her voice that was inescapable of discernment, she said softly, "Michele, oh, how I dreamed of the day that I would behold you again. But you come too late, too late." Then she began to sob quietly into her hands. Mike, no longer able to hold himself back from her, took her in his arms; she laid her head against his chest. Mike laid his head against the softness of her hair.

"All these fifteen years, I have never stopped thinking of you, never stopped loving you, Adelina. I have never married. It is only you I love; there is no other woman I could ever love." The tenderness of his words brought a fresh stream of tears to Adelina's eyes, and to Mike's too. He caught his breath and went on: "I have you in my heart always. No one can take you away from me there."

When he finished, they remained for a moment locked in embrace, weeping silently together. Then Adelina pulled away. She walked to the statue and placed the flowers on the pedestal. Then she raised her head and gazed devotedly upon the face of the Madonna. After a minute or two, she went to the bench and sat. Mike sat beside her and took her hand in his. "The child, tell me about the child."

Adelina's head began to sway from side to side. She took a deep breath. She began to speak, emotionless, about her flight to San

Sebastiano with the man her father had forced her to marry, her treatment at Pandolfi's hands. "He is a harsh man," she said matter-of-factly. Then her face lit up as she told Mike about Rosa's birth, and the happiness of holding her daughter close to her breast, knowing that she was holding a part of him in her arms. Then her face clouded over. "He has hated the child from the moment she was born." She sobbed as she recounted Pandolfi's cruelty towards her child, the beatings, the curses, the mental torture he had inflicted on little Rosa; and then, of the countless times Adelina herself had absorbed the blows meant for the child. Her sad narration went on: he would not permit Rosa to receive any schooling, and he worked her like a slave, digging, hoeing, manuring the fields and pruning the vines, almost from the moment the child was able to walk.

"It is only within the past year, that I managed to have our older son, Eugenio, take her place in the fields. 'Rosa must stay with me in the house,' I said. 'She must help me with the cleaning, cooking and the washing. Eugenio is a big, strong boy, and can do his own work in the fields as well as hers. He should be with his father more to learn the ways of tending the vines.'"

All the while during this recitation of brutality and violence, Michael's blood was boiling, and he had to clench his teeth and ball his fists in order to control the rage that had begun to surge in his throat.

Then Adelina shuddered and began to weep. She closed her eyes as if to shut out the horror of it all. "But now," —her voice hesitated to go on. "But now, I, I am even more frightened for the child. He ogles her with eyes full of lust, the eyes of a man full of evil intent. I smashed his hand with the skillet when once Rosa ran to me from the fields and told me that he had caressed her breast. Since then, I have not let her out of my sight, and I keep her in the house with me."

It was at these words, that Mike's anger erupted with all the fury of a man bereft of reason. "I will kill him! I will kill him! By the Madonna standing here, I will kill him!" He jumped up from the bench and made a lunge towards the doorway of the chapel. If Pandolfi had been there, without a doubt, Mike would have carried out his threat on the spot.

With both her hands, Adelina took hold of Mike's arm and restrained him in a vise-like grip. Her eyes never left his. "No, Michele, instead, instead," and then for a moment she could not go on for the tremor in her throat that had begun to choke her words. "You," and she was breathing hard now, "You must take the child away with you, away to America, so that she can live without fear, and be happy with a father that loves her." Intently, Adelina searched deeply into Michael's eyes.

She sank to the bench. The echoes of her heart-rending sobs reverberated like thunder in the confines of the little chapel. Her whole body was heaving as she sat hunched over, holding her head in her hands. Lowering himself to her side on the bench, Michael gently enfolded her in his arms. Filled with emotion, he kissed her hair. "I have never seen her, and I love her, my Rosa. Rosa is mine and yours. Come away with us, Adelina, and I promise you with all my heart that nothing will ever hurt her, or you, again. We, all three of us, will have a new beginning, a new life together. Once long ago I promised you a new life. Now let me at last keep my promise."

She pulled away from him. "For me, that promise can never come true. But it can for our daughter, if you take her with you to America. I have two sons here, whom I also love. My place is with them—and their father."

With a scowl on his face, Mike shouted: "You would stay with that man!" Then he lowered his voice. "You would, you will give up Rosa, let her leave you?"

"I am not giving up Rosa. I am giving her to her father, a father she loves, because I have told her so many wonderful things about him. I am giving her the chance to have a happy life with people who will love her—her father, and Mama Rosa, and *nonno* Giuseppe, and the aunts and uncles that she has not here." Adelina stopped and looked intently at Mike. She was waiting for his answer.

At one and the same time, Mike felt the deepest joy at the thought of taking Rosa away with him, and the deepest sorrow for the sacrifice the girl's mother was willing to make, and for the harshness of what Adelina's life had been during all these years. "Oh, how you have suffered, my Adelina, all because of me." Mike smashed his fist to his knee. "It was all my fault, my fault. What did I do to you?"

Adelina raised her head and put her hand across his mouth. "You loved me, Michele, that is what you did. There is no blame in that. Whenever I looked upon little Rosa, I saw your face, and thus I always had you with me." She smiled for a brief moment. "Your daughter is so beautiful. And now your answer?"

"I will make her the happiest, the most loved creature on the face of this earth. This is the promise that nothing will prevent me from keeping." When he had finished, Adelina reached over and took his face in both her hands. For a minute, Michael's blood rushed to his head as her face drew closer to his, so close that he wanted to put his mouth to hers in a kiss. But she jerked back. "You have made me very happy," she said, and turned away.

Mike's head drooped, and he bit his tongue. Suddenly he flung out his hands. "But you have left the child alone! With him!" A look of frantic desperation flashed over his face. It seemed for a moment that he was getting ready to rush madly down the road to the house. Again, Adelina took hold of his arm. She smiled, and put a finger to his lips. Removing the mantilia from her head, she walked to the doorway and waved it above her head. Off in the distance, suddenly Mike saw the figure of a girl, her head covered in a white lace mantilia, emerge, like an apparition from a grove of olive trees.

Chapter Seventy-nine

The girl came closer and closer, and with every step she took, Mike's heart pounded louder and louder. A few feet away from her mother, Rosa hesitated as Michael came clearly into view, from where he had been standing behind Adelina. As soon as he saw the girl close up, Michael's eyes misted over, and for a moment he lost his breath. This was his daughter, and to his eyes, she was the most beautiful girl he had ever seen. There could never be any doubt that this was the daughter of Michael Alanga. The face was his—shape of the face, the eyes, the mouth, the nose—all his, but more delicately cast in the same mold. The auburn hair, the petiteness of her form were from her mother.

Michael's whole being was flooded with such joy, that he had to restrain himself from rushing to her. When he heard her voice call out softly, "Mama?" it sounded to Michael as if an angel from heaven had spoken. Adelina went the few steps to the girl's side. Putting her arm around Rosa's shoulder, she pressed her daughter close. "This is your father, Rosa. He has come as I said he would someday." Then she pressed the girl even more tightly against her body and began to weep. Through her tears, she sought Michael's hand and pulled it to her. "Come to your daughter," she said. She placed his arm across the child's shoulder, and placed his other arm around her own waist. For Michael, that moment was the ecstatic fulfillment of his dream over the past empty fifteen years. In his arms he held the two persons he loved most. In this one embrace all the emptiness of existence for fifteen years disappeared. He felt whole again.

Then Rosa began to cry a little and pulled away. But Adelina took her daughter's hand and led her once more to Michael. "Go to your father," she said, and the three of them made their way into the chapel. Adelina sat Rosa on the bench next to Michael, and he began gently to stroke the child's hair. He lifted her head and wiped away her tears with his handkerchief. "I love you, my child, I love you very much." He kissed her on the forehead, and Rosa raised her eyes to her father and smiled. Then in a soft voice, she whispered, "Papa, Papa."

Her mother came to her and lifted her to her feet, "We must return to the house now. They will be rising and we must be there to prepare their food." She threw her mantilia over her head. Rosa put on hers. Adelina turned to Mike and said, "Behind the chapel there is a winding path. Follow it and it will take you to the Corso. Rosa and I will be here tomorrow after he has gone to the slopes, and Eugenio and Bruno to school. At nine, let us say, Rosa and I will be here."

"Until tomorrow then," Mike assented. He was overjoyed at the thought of seeing them again. He stood at the doorway of the chapel, his eyes following the two's every step, until they disappeared from sight below a rise in the road.

The very next day, and all the following days of that week, and the next week, the three of them, mother, father and daughter came together at the chapel. Not a day went by during that time, that Michael did not come with his hands full of good things for them. Sometimes is was delicious sweets which they all consumed as they sat on the bench. He brought torrone, sugared almonds, or pastries and cookies. At other times his gifts were pieces of exquisite jewelry. He brought matching gold crosses for each of them, earrings, coral necklaces, and mosaic cameos. He gave them presents of delicately embroidered shawls and fine lace mantillas. All these, Adelina surreptitiously put under lock and key in the little chest in the cubicle that she and her daughter shared, for she now no longer slept with Pandolfi.

The hour that the three of them spent in each other's company there in the quiet chapel, was an hour spent in paradise for all three. Michael regaled them with the wonders of life in America, where there were radios, telephones, autos, trolleys, and mechanical contrivances of all kinds to make life easier. Adelina and Rosa shook their heads in incredulous astonishment to hear tell of the wonders Mike described to them during those magic hours. The child's eyes opened wide in amazement to hear about schools where children learned to read and write and do numbers, and of the libraries where books were to be had for the taking. Enthralled, she and her mother listened as if they were in the presence of a *cantastorie* recounting the glorious deeds of Charlemagne and his brave knights who battled against the evil Saracens, and the thrilling tales of fair ladies snatched from the grasp of dragons and evil sorcerers.

They wept when Mike told them of Mama Rosa's sufferings, and Uncle Francesco's death. But they laughed in joy to hear him tell of the two little Roses that were the girl's cousins. They came to know each other during the span of two weeks as they had never had the opportunity to do for fifteen years. In the space of those two weeks, Michael had found a daughter, and Rosa a father in the haven of the chapel at the end of the Via delle Vigne.

The days spent in the refuge of the chapel was a time of peace and contentment for all three, mother, father and daughter. But Michael and Adelina knew that this was but a brief interlude. It could not go on forever. A few days before the end of the second week, Michael gently asked Rosa to leave him and her mother alone for a little while. The girl left, as her father had asked. At the doorway the parents watched Rosa make her way to the meadow a little way off and begin to gather wild flowers. Neither of them spoke for a few minutes; they stood in wrapt attention as they watched Rosa among the flowers.

Mike put his arm through Adelina's and led her into the chapel. "These weeks have been the happiest of my life, Adelina." She looked up to his eyes. "And now you wish to say that this must end, that you must go. Is it not so, Michele?" she asked.

Mike nodded. He couldn't bring himself to say the words.

"I am glad that you must leave. I want you to leave."

Michael blanched. Her words hurt him. But Adelina lifted her hand and caressed his face. "For, you will take the child with you, and I will find peace at last. You will give her the love of a father. She will be able to live without fear and grow up in a family that I know will give her love and care. All the Alangas will. I know them all, and they are good. All her life Rosa has had only me, me alone, to kiss her and embrace her. But now, when you take her to Mama Rosa, our Rosa will be one of a loving family. Ah! how I loved to be with you all in those days when I, myself was a little girl. Those happy days."

"You remember, then, Adelina?" Both their minds wandered back in time for a moment to recapture the feel of those bygone days of laughter and joy.

"Our Rosa will know such times, Adelina," Mike said smiling. "She will be happy with me and Mama." His face glowed, as the picture of his Rosa at table for Sunday dinner at his mother's house with all the family around, came to mind. In another moment, his face became serious, and the smile left his face. "Adelina, will Rosa want to come with me, to America? Will she leave you?"

Without hesitation, Adelina answered, "She has always loved you, Michele. I have seen to that. When she was sad and hurting and confused, I wiped away her tears and brought her hope and peace by telling her about you. About her real father. She has always pictured you someone wonderful, who would one day come and take her to a place where there were no beatings, no curses, no angry words. Ever since she could understand my words, she has kept that image of you in her heart. And now that she has seen you in the flesh, even for just this short time, she has not been disappointed.

"Each night as we have lain in bed together, these past weeks, I have been preparing her for the time that she and I must part. She knows her salvation and the chance for a happy life can only come by leaving this place." She stopped speaking for a moment, then she said: "She will go with you."

"And you, Adelina, you can part with her?" Mike could barely bring himself to ask the question.

"When she goes from this house, all the pain I have suffered in seeing her suffer, all the tears I have shed in wiping away hers, all the times I have stood between her and his hand and foot will be forgotten. Instead, I will have her image in my mind as I see her smiling and laughing in a place where there will no longer be harsh commands and curses for her to hear. No, Michele, the sorrow I have borne these fifteen years will vanish like a bad dream, because I know that her father and Mama Rosa will make up for all the misery the child has had to bear at his hands." Adelina paused again, and said softly, "She will be safe in her father's hands."

Mike looked into her eyes. "I promise you this, Adelina cara. The whole of the rest of my life will have only one purpose. I will devote all my days in bringing her happiness." Then in a whisper, he added, "Someday, somehow, we will all be together."

Chapter Eighty

Michael, Adelina, and Rosa met at the chapel for the last time on Saturday. Mike had decided that that Sunday, the day of Our Lord, was to be the fateful day to bring all this to a close. The day would be the day of his own rebirth, Adelina's and especially Rosa's.

Mike told Adelina that he would be at the house Sunday to fetch Rosa. Adelina answered in alarm, "No, no, Michele, I will bring the child here to the chapel, tomorrow, and you must leave quietly, secretly. I will say to him that she has run away," Adelina pleaded. She wrung her hands nervously together.

"No, Adelina, no. I will not do it the way you say, as if I were a thief in the night, stealing something that is not mine. Rosa is my daughter. He has no right to her; I have every right. She is mine, not his. Had he loved her, had he treated her as "*una figlia della Madonna*," I would come and kiss his hand. I would bless him, and then I would go, happy only to have seen her, satisfied in my heart. No, Adelina, I will be the man in this matter." Mike clenched his fists, and through clenched teeth he spat out: "I want to see with these eyes, this beast that calls himself a man. And when I leave with my daughter, he will know that I will come from the ends of the earth to kill him if he lays but a hand on you. This will I make known to him."

Mike reached into his pocket and withdrew a three-by-five card on which he had neatly printed his address in America. And also the address of Alfredo, Nora, and Papa. At the very last line, the address of Filumena in Scafati. "Take this card and keep it. From America I shall write to you now and again and you must let me know how it goes here with you. In this way we will not be separated again."

His words, so determined, so confident, gave her confidence. She became quiet and took the card and carefully tucked it away.

"When will you come, then?" she asked with resignation.

"I will be at the house at ten o'clock."

"At ten, then."

Mike touched her face, then Rosa's. "There is much that I must do.

A domani," and he turned away from them and made his way to the path behind the chapel.

Back in his room in the pensione, Mike packed his valise. He carefully folded the copy of Rosa's birth certificate which he had obtained from the town hall on the piazza, and stuck it in his wallet. He planned to apply for the child's passport in Naples, and began to fret at the thought of the delay that obtaining the passport might entail. He smoked cigarette after cigarette and paced back and forth across the floor of his room. He kept staring out the window, in hopes of seeing the sun go down. He was anxious for night to fall. And when night finally did come, he lay on the bed. In a long while he finally fell into a restless sleep, tossing and turning. It was well into the wee hours when at last, exhausted both physically and mentally, he was able to fall asleep.

When the first rays of sunlight began to stream into the room, Mike awoke. His eyes focused on the calendar on the wall. May 12, 1921. Above the dates of the month, his gaze alighted upon the face of a Madonna. Her eyes seemed soft and kind; she seemed to be smiling encouragement. He went up to the print, touched his hand to his lips, and then to hers. Silently he murmured, "Madonna mia, grant me the grace of success in what I must do this day."

In spite of a sleepless night, he was full of energy. He washed, shaved and dressed with alacrity. Then he raced to the kitchen downstairs where he and Carlo breakfasted together on coffee and bread.

"A beautiful day today," exclaimed Carlo, wiping away crumbs from his mouth.

"A most beautiful day, a wonderful day. The most beautiful day of my life," rejoined Mike.

"Aha! And you have found yourself a woman in San Sebastiano, eh?" And Carlo broke out in hearty laughter.

"Indeed I have," Mike answered, and he joined in the laughter "By the way, Carlo, I leave today. Here." Mike took out a wad of lire notes and thrust them into the man's hands. Carlo's practiced eye saw at once the generous overpayment. He jumped up and started pumping Mike's hand in gratitude.

"Come again, come again. Whenever you are in San Sebastiano you will always be welcome in Carlo's house." Mike permitted one last handshake before he broke away and departed the kitchen. In the square, the bells from the church's campanile began to toll, summoning the worshippers to the eight o'clock Mass. He joined the throng entering the church. Once inside, a sense of calm filled his soul. The soft murmuring of the priest and the cadenced responses of the alcolyte quieted his excitement. Mike prayed as he did when he was a little boy, full of innocence and confidence in the goodness of God.

Mike had taken a seat in the last pew. He arose unobserved and silently left the church just as the priest began to intone the ending prayers of the Mass at the foot of the altar. He had just enough time to reach the house on the Via delle Vigne by ten o'clock. As he walked along the Corso, his excitement began to return. He felt choked by his tie, so he loosened it. But he kept his jacket tightly buttoned.

The Corso came to an end. He started to climb up the incline of the via. With every step he took that brought him closer to Number 10, he began nervously to clench and unclench his fists. Either from the exertion of the climb, or from the heat, beads of sweat formed on his forehead. At last he reached the trellised gateway of the farmhouse that was his destination. He stopped, wiped his brow with the sleeve of his jacket, and looked toward the house. The day was very warm. The huge portone, the heavy, wooden door that well could have served to barricade a fortress, was open to the air. As he stood there, at the end of the path, once or twice he could see a figure move in view, then disappear.

Compressing his lips tightly together, and with slow, measured steps, Mike began his walk to the house. He stepped up to the doorway and stood motionless on the threshold. He peered into the room, and was able to take in the scene before him at a glance. His eyes found their way first to Adelina and his daughter. They were standing with their backs to him, over the stove in the rear of the kitchen area. Sharply, he turned away from them to fix his gaze at the table in the center of the room. Mike riveted his eyes on the figure of the man hunched over a bowl into which he was dunking a piece of hard bread. On either end of the table the two boys, little Bruno and his brother, Eugenio, were intent on the food set before them. No one was aware of Mike's silent presence in the doorway. It was only when he took a step forward into the house and his shadow fell across the table, that those at the table raised their heads.

The man jerked up his head; his brow was knitted in puzzlement at the sight of Mike standing in the room. Mike stared hard at the face of this man, a man he had never before seen, but a man he hated and despised. Even though, from the corner of his eye, Mike could see Adelina and the girl suddenly turn, his gaze never left the man's face. As Pandolfi rose from his chair, Mike continued to study him, taking in every feature. It was a hard face, carved out of granite. A square jaw, a sharp nose, high cheekbones covered by leathery skin deeply creased and tanned by exposure to sun and wind off the slopes of the mountain. There was no trace of any softness, any refinement, either in the eyes or the gaunt, wiry frame of the man before him. A full head of uncombed, gray hair that never saw the use of a comb, covered the long, angular head. The long, thin lips were set hard in a mouth that never smiled. Mike recognized the type of man Pandolfi was, a peasant of the lowest type, more animal than human. The fellow was only slightly younger than Mike's own father, and this was the *cafone*, the stupid, brutal man into whose hands , the father of beautiful, gentle Adelina, had given her. To himself, Mike cursed old Scarpa, her father, dead and buried as he was. This, in spite of all Mike had been taught to reverence the dead.

"And who the hell are you, that you come into my house without so much as a knock?" Pandolfi barked out at Mike. The voice was rough and gravelly, surprisingly deep coming from such a spare, bony man. Mike did not answer him, but rather took a step further, and as he neared the table, it was then that Pandolfi's eyes began to take on a look of alarm. He had never laid eyes on Mike, but he knew instinctively who this man standing before him was. He turned his head sharply to Rosa, and then back to Mike. There was no mistaking the resemblance in the two faces.

"Yes, I am the girl's father." And Mike stepped to the very edge of the table. Pandolfi moved back, knocking over his chair. The look of hatred, of menace on Mike's face needed no interpretation. Even the boys began to sense the atmosphere of danger and fear in the room. Little Bruno ran to his mother, and the older boy sat staring first at his father and then at the stranger.

The sound of Mike's voice, sharp and dry, crackled again through the room, like glass shattering. "Adelina, leave the house. Take the children with you. Pandolfi and I have things to discuss. Now, go." Adelina took hold of little Bruno by one hand and Rosa by the other. As she neared Mike, her eyes met his. They were pleading for him to exercise forbearance. Her eyes were so full of sadness, that for a moment Michael almost lost his resolve for vendetta against the man that was the father of Adelina's sons. But the spell was broken when he heard Adelina's voice call across the room to Eugenio. The boy came running, and with all three around her, she left the house. Michael closed the door and turned to face Pandolfi. The brief interlude had given the old man enough time to regain his composure. With as much bravado as he was able to muster, Pandolfi shouted across the table, "I command in this house. You are not welcome. Get the hell out!" His face was purple with rage, and he made a move to come around the table. Mike never blinked an eye. First, he unbuttoned one button of his jacket, then a second, and threw back the flaps. The sight of the long blade of a stiletto thrust into Mike's belt, caused Pandolfi to stop dead in his tracks.

"Sit!" The one word shot out of Mike's mouth like a knife thrust. Pandolfi, his eyes wide with fear, collapsed onto a chair. Even the tan of his weather-beaten face could not mask the white that began to suffuse through the skin. Pulling the blade slowly from his belt, Mike laid it on the edge of the table in front of himself. He leaned over with both hands flat on the table's surface, until he was only inches from Pandolfi's face, who pushed back in his chair as Mike's words blasted into his face. "You stinking piece of carrion! Show me your hands! Put them on the table in front of you." Pandolfi hesitated, but as Mike made a motion to lunge, with a look of unmistakable rage on his face, the old man thrust his hands obediently in front of himself, close to the edge of the table. Before he could even think of pulling them back, Mike's fists, clenched into balls of iron, came crashing down on them with all his force. Pandolfi leaped up from his chair, howling in pain and holding his mangled hands before his face. Several fingers on both hands hung grotesquely out of joint.

"That, for all the times those hands were raised against my defenseless daughter," Michael spat out in anger. "You bastard." Then with the speed of lightning, and the stiletto in his hand, Mike rushed toward Pandolfi who recoiled in terror. As he did so, he tripped over the chair and fell to the floor. He tried to break his fall, but as his hands hit the stone floor, the old man let out a yelp of pain.

Michael yanked Pandolfi up by the scruff of his collar, as one would a puppy or a kitten. He pressed the needle-like point of the blade into the man's neck hard enough to break the skin. Sure that his last hour on earth had come, he whispered weakly, "Gesu! Maria! Don't kill me, don't kill me. Gesu Cristo!" The man's invocation of those holy names caught Mike off guard. Had he cursed, had he shouted words of defiance in Mike's face, the knife would have gone in a little deeper. The mention of Mary's name, the mother of the Christ Child, brought the image of Adelina's sad, pleading look to his mind, and he lowered the knife.

Mike stooped and picked up the overturned chair. He placed Pandolfi's limp body on it. As he stood over the bruised, old man slumped onto the table and breathing in pain with every breath he drew, Mike's rage ebbed. He walked away to a chair and sat opposite Pandolfi. For moments, the only sound in the room was the labored breathing from the figure slumped over the table.

"Look at me, Pandolfi."

The man lifted his head, and as he did, Mike flung the knife across the room. It hit the far wall and fell to the floor with a clang. "I leave you your miserable life, you piece of carrion. And I am leaving this house, and I am taking my daughter with me. I am going to give her back the life you have stolen from her. I am going to give her the innocence of a childhood she has never known in this house.

"The day will come, old man, that when you lie rotting in your grave, I will return for Adelina. And may that day come soon!" Mike rose from the chair, buttoned his jacket and brushed his hands through his hair. He pointed his finger as if it were the barrel of a pistol into Pandolfi's face. His last words were: "Until that day comes, Adelina remains in your filthy hands. I did not kill you now, but I swear on the grave of my dead brother I will come back and cut off your hands at the wrists, if I learn that just once, you laid those hands of yours on her."

Mike went to the door, opened it, and stepped into the fresh air. Off across the yard, he saw Adelina sitting under the grape arbor. In her lap, she was cuddling little Bruno. Rosa was sitting beside them, tickling her half-brother under the chin. The older boy ran off the instant he caught sight of Michael approaching. His mother called him back, spoke to him, and he ran off in the direction of the house.

Mike was smiling as he came up to the group sitting in the shade of the arbor. And as he bent over to tousle little Bruno's hair, Adelina's face brightened. Michael was safe. And her husband? "He will live," was Mike's terse answer to her question. "You can tend to his hands when you go in."

There, under the bower, they made their last, tearful goodbyes. For a full ten, fifteen minutes, Mike, Adelina, Rosa wept, and embraced one another and gave vent to their emotions. It was when Eugenio came running from the house, carrying a small valise in his hands that the moment came for the final goodbye. In the valise, on the night before, Adelina had packed the few possessions dear to Rosa—the jewelry, the mantilia, the pretty combs her father had given her, and some clothes.

At the last word of farewell, Mike slipped his hand into that of his daughter. "Come, Rosa. We are going home." The two of them started walking down the path, the path that was taking them from the old world and leading them to a new world, and a new life for both of them, father and daughter.

Mike held tightly onto Rosa's hand. The two turned back once more and waved to Adelina. Then they began their way down the Via delle Vigne. Mike was smiling to himself as he thought: "I'm coming home, Mama. and I am bringing you another rose, my Rose."

The End